Assassin Prince

P.G. BADZEY

DEDICATION

For my brothers (Paul, Frank, Tom, Rob) and my sister (Veronica).
See? This is what all those games of Dungeons and Dragons gets you!

Novels by P.G. Badzey

The Grey Rider Series

Whitehorse Peak
Eye of Truth
Helm of Shadows

CONTENTS

ACKNOWLEDGMENTS

The author would like to acknowledge the following individuals for their most excellent contributions:
Eugene and Dora Badzey for their editing prowess,
Veronica Badzey for typesetting,
the people at Bookfuel for the wonderful cover art and my friends in the Orange County Writers Guild Critique Group, whose invaluable insights and expertise made this a far better manuscript than he could have done on his own.

"For whoever desires to save his life will lose it, but whoever loses his life for My sake will find it." – Matthew 16:25

MAPS

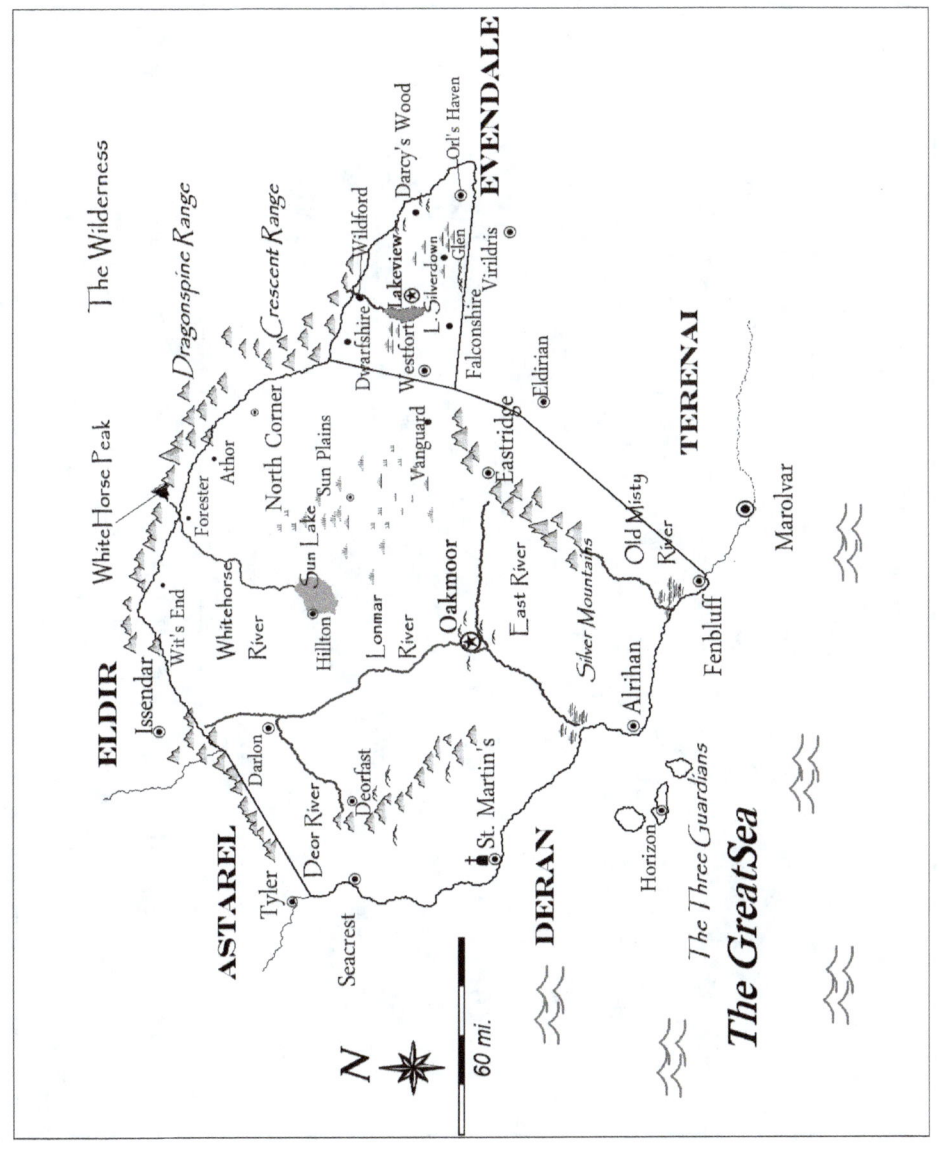

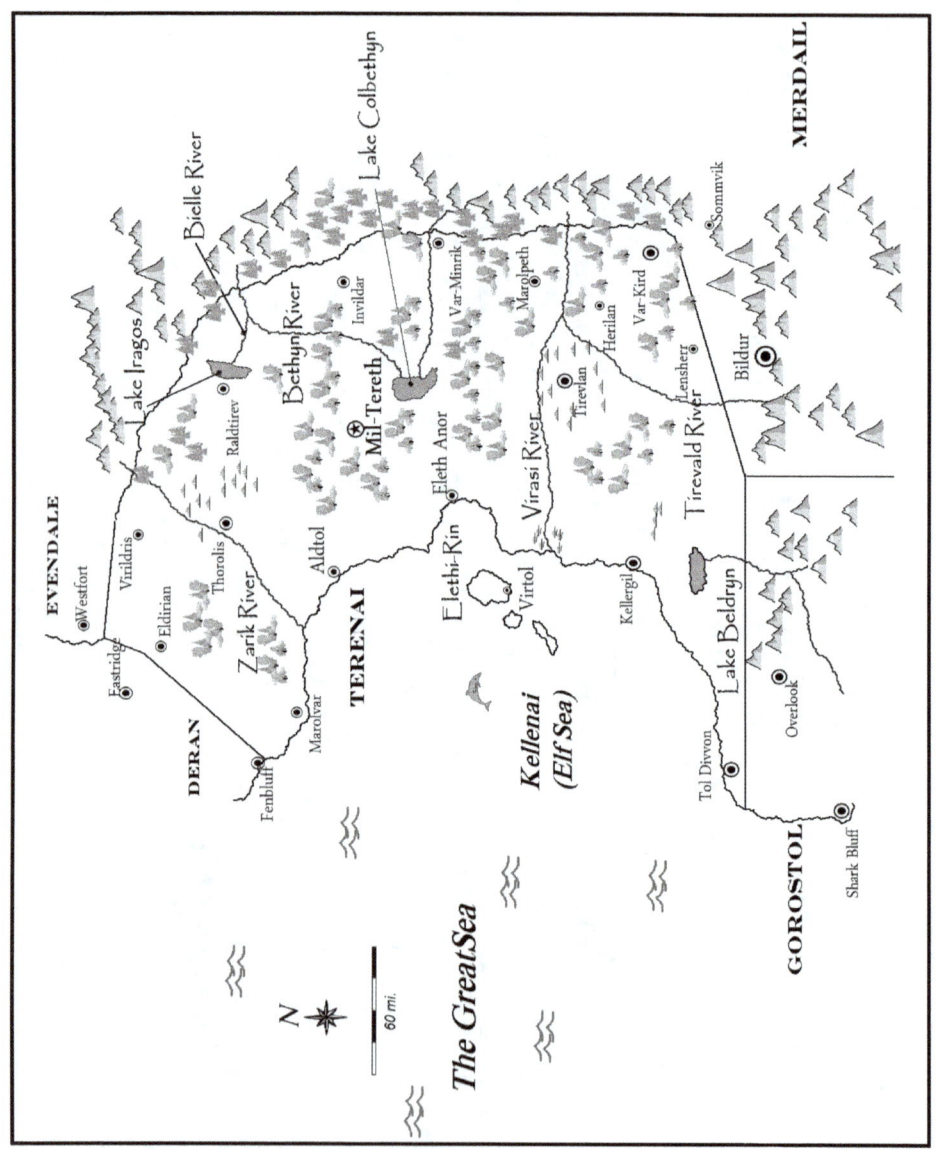

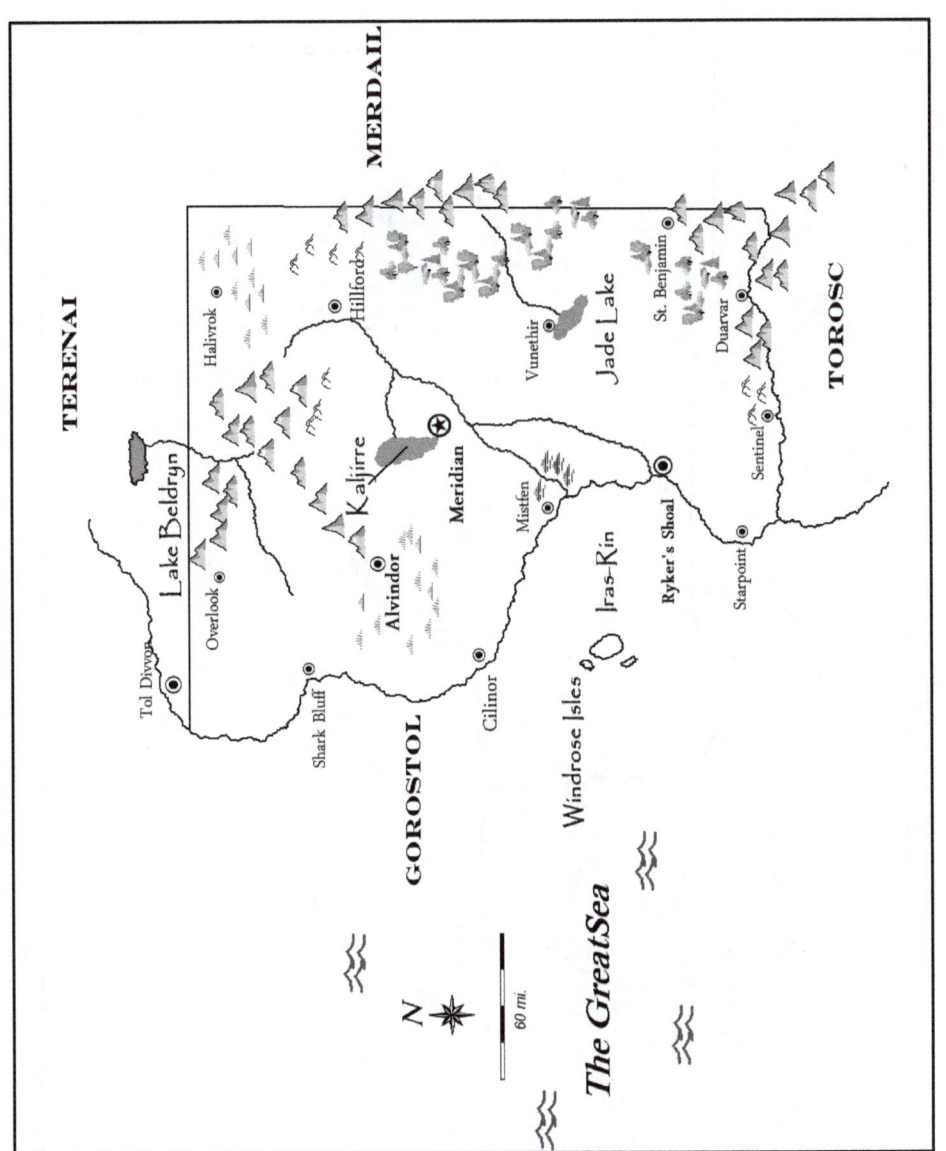

TERENAI

MERDAIL

TOROSC

GOROSTOL

Lake Beldryn

Tol Divwyn

Overlook

Shark Bluff

Halivrok

Kaljirre

Alvindor

Meridian

Hillford

Vunethir

Jade Lake

St. Benjamin

Duarvar

Sentinel

Mistfen

Cilinor

Iras-Rin

Ryker's Shoal

Starpoint

Windrose Isles

The GreatSea

N

60 mi.

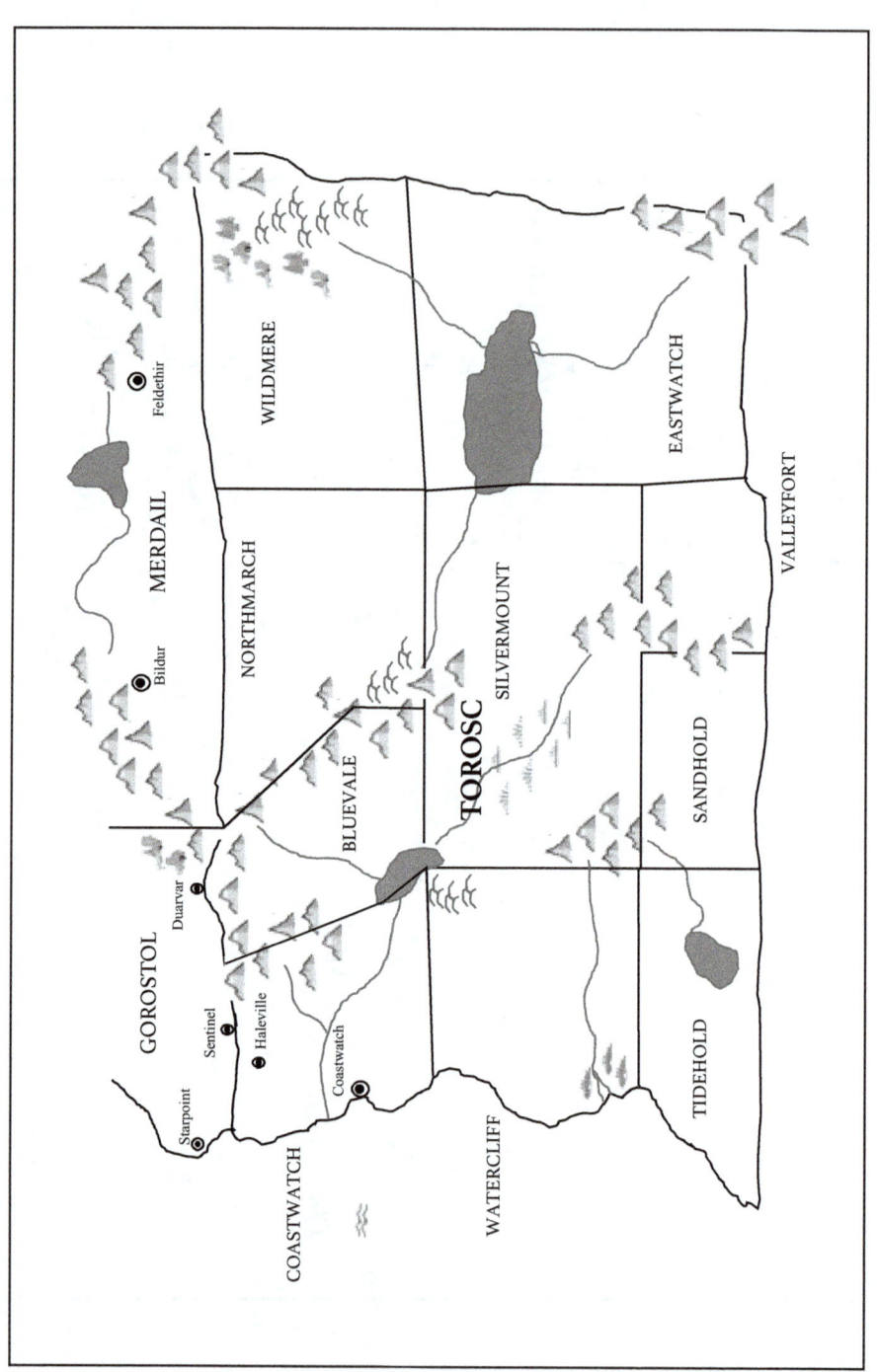

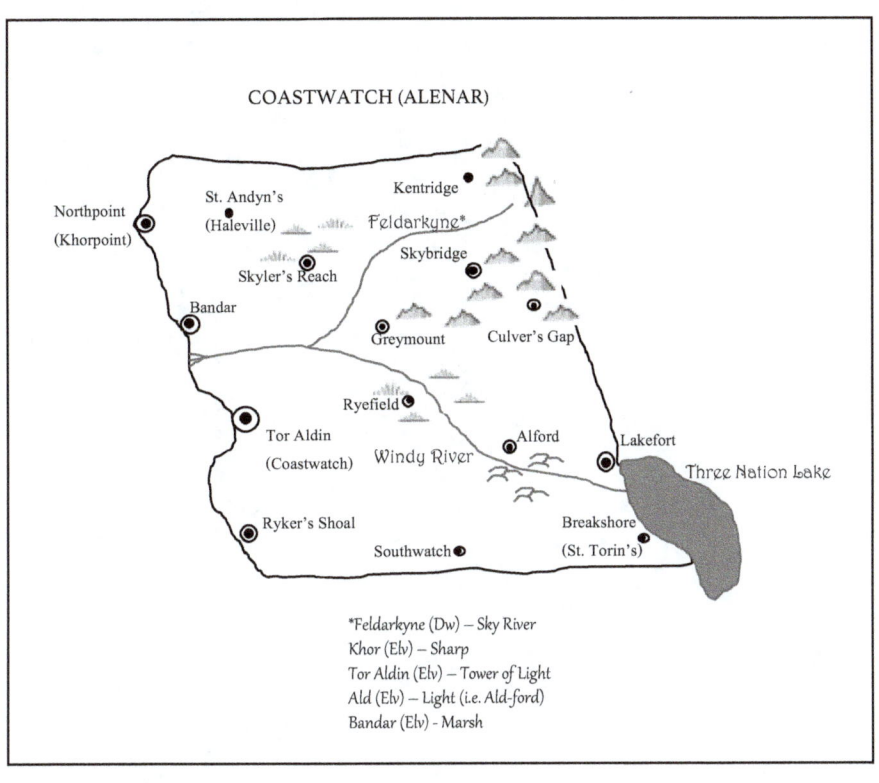

COASTWATCH (ALENAR)

Northpoint (Khorpoint)

St. Andyn's (Haleville)

Kentridge

Feldarkyne*

Skyler's Reach

Skybridge

Bandar

Greymount

Culver's Gap

Ryefield

Tor Aldin (Coastwatch)

Windy River

Alford

Lakefort

Three Nation Lake

Ryker's Shoal

Southwatch

Breakshore (St. Torin's)

*Feldarkyne (Dw) – Sky River
Khor (Elv) – Sharp
Tor Aldin (Elv) – Tower of Light
Ald (Elv) – Light (i.e. Ald-ford)
Bandar (Elv) - Marsh

Chapter One - The Long Hunt

If this goes badly, I'm going to need a pine box...

Connor Lomin wrapped his cloak around himself and turned aside as a gust of ocean wind whirled snow in a cloud of white flakes. He felt thankful for both his doublet — and the combat leathers hidden underneath the doublet. The comforting weight of his sword, Tiuz, rested at his hip under his cloak.

After waiting for the snow to settle, he resumed his watch of the battered-looking inn across the street. The cold pale light of a winter's afternoon did little to illuminate either the thoroughfare or the snow-dusted buildings. When dark fell, the lamplighters would bring the streets alive with brightness but, even so, Connor didn't really want to be in this part of town after dark.

The leaden skies seemed to weigh on him. He waited, watching the scene. A slight movement on the roof of the inn drew his eye and he saw a pair of tall figures, so tall that Connor's head would only reach their midsections. The larger of the two on the roof touched a hand to his head and the pair moved towards the left side of the roof, stopping near the edge.

Connor made a face under his hood. *We put the humans, the tallest and heaviest of our group, on the roof. Why? I have no idea. This is the last time I let Dar Cabot buy me a dwarven brandy before planning the assault.*

"Humans," he said under his breath, feeling the word roll off his tongue.

The name of every race on Damora means something in the languages of Elves or Dwarves, but not "human". Where did they come from? No mention of them before the Skyfire, thousands of years ago, but now, humans appear everywhere.

"What would the world be like without you?" he whispered. He frowned, refocusing his thoughts on their mission. Connor scanned the street, looking for his other allies.

Only a few other figures moved about in the wintry air. Two, in particular, stood under the awning in front of a potter's shop. A slim man with short-cropped blond hair, slightly pointed ears and violet eyes leaned back against a post. He put an arm around his fair companion, a young woman with long blonde hair of her own and amber eyes. Two amethyst earrings flashed in the dim light.

He smirked. *Well, there would be no children with human and Elf parents, for one.* The woman glanced up at the man and kissed him on the cheek.

Connor acknowledged the signal by pulling his hood over his head. Knowing what awaited him at the inn, he let out a deep breath, then headed across the street and inside. As he closed the door behind him, warmth surrounded him immediately. He stamped his boots on the grate at the entrance.

A human woman of middle years ambled through a door on the left side of the entryway, carrying a knapsack. As she opened a door on the opposite side, Connor caught a glimpse of a bar, a roaring fire, shadowy figures and the glint of steel mugs. Tantalizing aromas of meat, bread, ale and vegetables wafted in as the door closed behind the woman.

Similar to its exterior, the interior of the Hawk's Perch Inn had seen better days. A wooden counter with faded blue paint stood across from him and a couple of oil lanterns burned merrily in tarnished cases on either side. Like many establishments in this town, the inn catered to folk of all sizes, so the counter had a high level for dealing with elves and humans and a lower section for halflings and dwarves. Connor stepped up to the lower counter, hand reaching for a tarnished brass bell.

"No need for the bell," said a man's voice. Footsteps on wooden boards sounded behind the counter. A halfling man like Connor, all three and a half feet of him, stumped up with a ledger in his hands and wary eyes. With some degree of satisfaction, Connor saw that he was taller than the clerk.

"What'll it be?" asked the clerk in a clipped tone. His clothes, though clean, looked frayed and patched and his black hair showed streaks of grey.

"I'm told that a man named Patian is in one of your suites," Connor said, placing a gold piece on the counter. "I am expected."

The coin disappeared almost as soon as it hit wood. "Your name?" asked the clerk.

"Neville Pennyhand."

The clerk's eyes narrowed and his lips formed a thin line as he consulted the ledger. With a nod, he disappeared behind the taller counter for a few heartbeats before reappearing.

"Room eleven," he said, jerking a thumb at a set of stairs to the left of the counters. "Second floor and third door on the left."

Without further fanfare, Connor walked up the stairs and to Room Eleven. He fiddled with his cloak, undoing the clasp but surreptitiously examining the area in front of the door. He swirled the cloak to settle it on his arm and, as he did so, his wrist flicked out twice, making small marks in the doorframe with a knife hidden in his sleeve. He drew himself up to his full height of three feet, eight (and a half!) inches and replaced the wrist knife.

He knocked.

The door eased open and two dwarven males blocked his path. They looked every bit the bodyguards: burly, strong and alert, openly wearing brigandine, with swords and hand axes in their belts. Bearded like many of their race, their dark eyes showed no emotion as they looked down at him.

Connor smiled. Even though his head only came up to their chins, he took the measure of them and knew he could take them easily. "I am here to see Richard Patian."

"Your name?" one of them rumbled.

"Neville Pennyhand."

"Let him in," said a male voice from inside the room.

Patian apparently liked to live in style. Based on the couch, desk, table, rugs and light fixtures, this was the best room in the Inn (which still wasn't saying much, in Connor's estimation). The ceiling towered over Connor. The tall windows let what remained of the day's sunlight and provided a view of a warehouse across the street. A fire burned merrily in a fireplace and the soft glow of magical lights twinkled from glass balls in metal holders on the walls.

Connor bowed. "Mister Patian."

A tall, spare human male with dark hair, piercing blue eyes and a velvet indigo cloak nodded to him. Connor noted Patian's saber and dirk and dark leathers, as well as a gold ring on each hand. Two humans stood to either side of Patian, dull chainmail visible under their cloaks. A man and a woman, both carried swords and daggers. A halfling woman in a black skirt and blouse sat atop a table, booted feet swinging in the air. She looked at him with blue eyes and smiled, twining a finger in her curly brown hair.

Yes. Hired muscle, in human and dwarven flavors, with an innocent-looking halfling lass thrown in to boot.

"Mister Pennyhand. The note, if you don't mind."

Connor kept his smile and carefully pulled a note from under his doublet. He held it out to Patian but the female guard took it instead. She read it and handed it him.

Patian ran a finger alongside his narrow nose and sniffed as he perused the note. The guards eyed Connor, hands near their weapons. The halfling woman gave him a coquettish wink. Connor might have been interested, except that she probably earned her living by means of seduction and murder.

Patian pursed his lip and slipped the note into belt purse. "George Walters recommended you? I'm surprised he's still alive."

"It could be a forgery," remarked one of the dwarves.

And a very good one at that, thought Connor.

"I haven't heard from Mister Walters in quite a while," said Patian, leaning back against the edge of the desk. "When and where did you last see him?"

He indicated a chair and Connor sat.

"Two weeks ago, in Seacrest," he answered, "but I got the impression he had to keep moving."

"Naturally," Patian replied with a lazy smile of his own. "Given his line of work."

Connor grinned. "Naturally."

"This doesn't feel right," said the human woman. "It could all be faked."

"Yes, it could," said Patian.

Connor Lomin made as if to stand from his seat. "Well then," he said, "I could just take my business elsewhere. I'm sure the Whiteclaw or the Shrikes would be happy to receive my coin in exchange for their services. They aren't nearly so picky who hires them to kill."

Patian waved a hand. "No, no, don't be offended. We just want to make sure you're not a Deranese agent. You must realize we get plenty of those, what with the "sort of person" sitting on the throne nowadays."

"Of course," said Connor, relaxing and settling back in his seat. His right hand itched to go to the special brooch pinned under his doublet but he waited, biding his time.

"That's a nice sword you have there," noted the human man standing next to Patian.

Connor nodded. "Thank you. A gift from my aunt. Charming old lady but didn't even know what it was when she bought it at an estate sale. Magic sword, too."

The dwarves exchanged impressed glances.

Patian drew back his cloak, a casual gesture that nonetheless freed his saber and dirk for quick access. Connor noted his hand position. "So, what do you offer to settle our nerves and assure us you're not a filthy royal spy, Mister Pennyhand. You must know that we have to be cautious."

Connor listened with one ear for the sound of his companions but heard nothing. *Okay Dar Cabot… now would be a good time to come charging in…*

"Naturally," he replied. "Well, I'm only one person, armed with one sword and there are six of you. I came here on your terms. I believe the advantages are all in your favor. I would have to be a bold spy indeed to walk into the teeth of the wolf, as it were, all by myself."

"And exactly why are you here?" asked the halfling girl.

Connor flicked a bit of dirt from his trousers. "Because my dear old aunt may be a little daft, but my cousins are not, and they suspect something. If they're dead, I get the inheritance, and they know it. They also know my somewhat unconventional past. It was no easy task to lose the agents they had tailing me."

"That's interesting," the leader agreed. "However, I think we need more. Your bona fides, now — where did you say your aunt resides?"

Connor lounged in his seat. "In Dwarfshire, Evendale. Her name is Elisa Fortuna. She lives on Handmaiden Way."

Patian considered this. "Tahni, does that ring a bell?" he asked the halfling.

Tahni kept her innocent blue eyes on Connor. "It sure does. I've been up and down Handmaiden Way a whole bunch of times."

Connor nodded, relaxing.

"However," she continued, "It's an industrial section with blacksmiths shops and foundries. Lots of dwarves too. But no houses."

Crap…

Patian drew his saber and his companions straightened. "So, your halfling aunt is a blacksmith then?" he asked, eyes now hard as flint.

"Not her, but she inherited four shops from my uncle's side of the family," Connor lied. "Where did you think she got all the money from, selling flowers on street corners?"

"Sure. And I'm a Royal Guard," spat one of the dwarves, drawing a sword that glimmered red.

A faint thud sounded from the window. Reflexively, everyone turned.

Two armored figures clung to ropes just outside the glass. The figures kicked away from the building and then swung forward to crash through the windows. Behind Connor, a blast of magic fire blew open the door: Andyn and Eric had joined him.

Connor whispered a word and touched the magic pin under his doublet. A shimmering, ghostly sword sprang up in mid-air. Tahni and the dwarf with the red-glowing blade stumbled to a halt as the ethereal weapon bobbed in front of them.

"What in Vardu's crotch is that?" growled the dwarf.

Tahni gasped. "Spectral Sword — a high honor given to heroes of Evendale."

The room rang with the clashing of steel, shouts and curses but Connor kept his eyes fixed on the two before him.

The halfling girl stalked left.

Connor drew Tiuz, calling its blade to fiery life. He smiled, seeing the alarm in their eyes. "See? You're outmanned, so to speak. Just lay your weapons down. There's no shame in giving up."

In answer, they charged. Connor's spectral sword attacked Tahni, driving her back in a flurry of cuts and thrusts. Unsure of what to do, she dodged, parrying the ghostly blade.

For his part, the dwarf lunged at Connor. Connor sidestepped and cut at the assassin's legs. The dwarf leaped over the arc of his flaming sword and Connor spun, slashing out. The dwarf parried and Connor let his blade bounce back a little, twisting his wrist to stab at the dwarf's stomach. The dwarf hammered the strike downwards, so Connor turned his wrist again, curving his blade up at the dwarf's neck. A red flash of light told him he hit enchanted armor and the dwarf weaved back, eyes wide.

Connor didn't miss a beat. He whipped Tiuz around again to knock aside a thrust, then reversed, punctured the dwarf's brigandine and buried the fiery blade in his side. The assassin shrieked a curse at him, slashing Connor in the arm and kicking him away. Connor almost lost his grip on Tiuz but managed to pull it free, stumbling back and bouncing off a table. His arm stung and he felt warm blood dripping down his left bicep. The dwarf grimaced in pain, his side covered in blood and flames. He lurched forward, sword upheld and eyes wild.

Connor dodged the overhand blow and ran him through.

A stinging pain hit him in the low back and he cried out, feeling a sickening poison spread in his body. Dizzy and nauseous, he stumbled over the corpse of the dwarf. He turned. Tahni drew back twin daggers for another strike. The spectral sword intervened, slashing, and she stepped back. Connor snatched a vial of pink liquid from a belt loop and downed it, tasting a bizarre combination of onions, cinnamon and bacon. The sickening feeling faded and the sting of his injuries diminished. Tahni tried to get to him but the spectral sword danced and darted and she was forced to bang aside attack after attack.

Connor lunged to disarm Tahni. Instead, she turned full on him, slashing. Her clothes turned ghostly and spectral, like his sword. He parried and dodged, then thrust, only to find she wasn't there any more.

Connor's ghostly weapon lashed at her from behind, cutting through her phantom armor. The misty sheen faded and she cursed, then dodged, right into Connor's thrust. She staggered and tried to spin away. The spectral sword stabbed her and she fell. Prone, she still slashed Connor in the calf and he lurched, catching himself against a table with a grimace, expecting more poison. She raised a dagger to throw it and the dancing sword stabbed her in the chest. She screamed, flopping back on the floor.

Connor called his Spectral Sword as the sounds of battle subsided around him. The blade vanished in a cloud of glowing, pale mist as he pointed Tiuz at Tahni.

"It's over," he said, the flickering light of his magic blade casting weird shadows on Tahni's pale face. "Drop your weapons. I promise I won't hurt you if you surrender."

She grimaced and crawled back to prop herself up against the couch. "Well," she breathed in gasps. "You're right that it's over. It's too bad, though. A tumble with you would have been great fun. But the Crossed Swords never surrender."

She pulled a tiny knife from her bodice and, before he could move, slashed her own wrist. A pale green gas puffed up and her eyes rolled back in her head.

"Andyn!" cried Connor.

A golden-haired half-elven woman with amethyst earrings knelt next to him. Silvery chainmail seemed to glow under her grey cloak.

"It's poison," he said.

Andyn Eleandir nodded, removing her helmet and gloves. "Understood."

She closed her amber eyes and murmured under her breath. A faint blue light glowed in her palm and she placed her hand over the halfling woman's wrist.

Connor stood, favoring his injured leg as his companions joined them.

He looked up at a slim, muscular human with dark hair.

"Any prisoners, Dar?" Connor asked.

Dar Cabot shook his head, sheathing a black bastard sword. The blade glittered with stars. "They attack too hard to use stunning techniques, almost as if they have a death wish."

"They do," said Eric Indidarc as he stepped up next to Dar. In one hand he held a spear of light grey wood with a shining golden head. A white hauberk emblazoned with the gold angel wings and sword of Saint Michael's Order lay over his white-enameled chain mail.

"Fidelis," he said, holding out the spear. The haft shrank down until the weapon was the size of a dagger. He placed it in a sheath in his belt.

Eric Indidarc looked down at Andyn and Tahni. "One of the Hylar family gods is Torvu. One of his domains is death, so it makes sense that they'd devote themselves to killing, even if it's themselves."

Connor made a face, then shook his head. "Eric, this is going to be tough. Your family has quite a hold on its slaves and lackeys if they would rather die than give up any information."

"Any luck, Andyn?" Dar asked, rubbing at a blood stain on his dark green tunic. A medallion of Saint Kira's Order lay against his chest.

Andyn stood up with a sigh. "No good. The poison was too fast-acting and I think it was magically augmented. I'd have to be a high matriarch of Verian or one of your Christian bishops, Dar, in order to counteract that kind of venom."

Connor regarded Andyn and his friends and the dead halfling girl, suddenly struck by the dichotomy — a priestess of Verian and followers of the New Faith, trying to save someone who moments ago had tried to kill him.

A sandy-haired human with banded armor under his cloak strode over to them. He held a round metal shield on one arm and a golden-hilted longsword of dwarven design in his hand. He towered over most of the party, standing a full three or four inches taller than Dar. A metal arm curved around the front of his helmet, ending in a round setting before his left eye that contained a sparkling diamond.

"Well, I've finished a scan," said Buckminster Bydecy, sheathing his weapon and rotating the metal arm so that the jewel pointed at the ceiling. "There aren't any illusions or hidden items in here and we already know those guys were evil, so there's not much more that the Eye of Truth can tell us."

"Did you search them?" asked Andyn.

Buck nodded. "Coins, gems, armor, weapons, all worth a pretty penny, though a few of the weapons are cursed so I doubt if we could sell them. Nothing else, though."

He handed a roll of parchment to Eric. "I think it's in Elven. Connor's contact in the black velvet doublet had it."

Eric nodded, unrolling the document.

Connor sighed. "We're zero for six now." He winced at the remnants of pain in his back and arm and flopped down on the couch.

Andyn fixed him with a critical eye. "Let's have a look at you."

He removed his doublet and unstrapped the battle leathers underneath, then took off his slashed boot without complaint, relaxing as her gentle hands touched his injuries.

"You have Verian's own hand on you, Connor Lomin," she murmured as she examined his back. "A few inches up and she would have hit your kidney instead of your hip, and that would have been very bad."

She whispered words of comfort and peace. Connor felt a pleasant warmth spread from his back to his arm and then his leg as she touched each injury. He could almost see his muscles and skin and blood vessels knitting back together under the influence of the healing energy Andyn directed into them. He looked down.

Only a faint pink scar remained on his calf. Judging by the amount of blood on the floor and on his boot, it had been a substantial wound.

"The shoemaker will be able to take his wife out to a nice dinner tonight," he muttered, holding up his slashed boot.

Andyn helped him get his doublet and armor back on. "Stop your griping, you big baby," she said with a grin, slapping him on the shoulder. "You'll be fine. And we're going to get plenty of cash from this loot."

Dar put a booted foot up on a chair. "Well, now what? Any ideas?"

Buck shrugged. "Eric's the lead on this mission."

Connor finished with his armor and looked at Eric. "Well?"

Eric Hylar Indidarc, son and heir of Harkin Hylar, Master of the Crossed Swords Assassins Guild, nodded as he re-rolled the parchment.

"This scroll is important. It's in Elven all right, but it's also in code. I'll take a stab at deciphering it back at the base. My father took a lot of care to re-locate all his operations after I ran away and I'm sure he changed ciphers."

Dar clapped him on the shoulder. "Don't worry. We'll get him. The time of the Guild of Crossed Swords will be ended, and we'll make sure of it."

Eric smiled wryly. "It's not my father I'm worried about. My mother is the really nasty one."

"Well," said Connor, stretching. "Let's clear out and notify the Command. I think I need a bath and an ale."

***

Dar Cabot removed his cloak as he entered the antechamber, stomping the last of the snow from his boots. An orderly in the blue and white livery of the Duke of Alrihan took the cloak. Three guards in scale mail with maces and swords stood next to a pair of double doors at the end of the chamber.

"His Lordship is here already, Sir Dar. Shall I inform him of your arrival?" the orderly asked.

"Yes, Fielding. And thank you."

Fielding bowed and left. Dar joined his companions, already striding towards the doors.

The Crown located this outpost well, he had to admit. From the outside, it looked like an old warehouse in the waterfront district of the mighty Deranese port city of Alrihan. Once inside, a short trip led through a storage area into an old meat locker. There, they opened a secret door in the floor and climbed down a ladder into this antechamber.

Dar sighed as the double doors opened. He didn't like formalities or procedures, preferring to get right into action. However, he had learned the benefit of planning, coordination, and analysis through experience, though he still had to fight the urge to fidget.

No longer just a free-lance sell-sword, Dar Cabot, he told himself. *Knights of Saint Kira don't get to just wander off when they feel like it, even if they have flying horses to ride.*

Buck, Connor, Eric and Andyn preceded him into the meeting hall. Dark wood paneling reached from floor to ceiling, broken by immense cork boards with a myriad of charts, diagrams and lists arranged in neat rows. Oil lamps burned in cressets, casting a warm light around them. Across a long table, a dusky-skinned, angular man with a mustache and beard talked with a thin, middle-aged woman. A pile of papers and maps lay scattered on the table. A stocky dwarf next to the man and woman peered through a magnifying glass at one of the maps, his fingers tracing a line on the paper.

Dar stopped at the table. "Grey Riders, reporting as ordered," he said with a bow.

The dark-skinned man straightened. "Ah, yes, Sir Cabot. I've been expecting you. I understand you had another run-in with the Crossed Swords."

He motioned to the dwarf and woman, who bowed and left.

Andyn nodded. "Yes, Lord Gerardo. At the Hawk's Perch Inn. Unfortunately, just like our last encounter, they preferred to die rather than be captured."

Colonel Lord Gerardo Benitez of the Royal Deran Intelligence Service came around the table to greet them. His narrow face and dark eyes gave him a sly appearance and formed the basis for his nickname: The Fox.

"Do not be discouraged, Lady Andyn," he said. "After many years of fighting against the Crossed Swords, I have only a handful of captives to boast about." He bowed to kiss her hand.

Dar kept the smile off his face. The manners and etiquette of knights and lords felt new to him and his friends — only recently elevated to noble rank due to their role in the defeat of the lich-princess Zhinia Margoth. Even now, months after Margoth's destruction at the Battle of Hillton, it seemed as if they had been knighted yesterday.

He knew Andyn was both flattered and unnerved at the courtesies paid to her with her new honors, the highest of any of the Riders. She not only carried the hereditary title of Lady of the Order of Mindra of the Elven Empire of Terenai, but also the name of Lichslayer and Light of Justice. This last honor marked her as unique among nobles and royalty of the lands of Damora - protocol demanded that even kings show her special respect. Not a dozen Lichslayers lived in Deran among its million and a half souls and maybe three score lived in total among the nations of the Northern Alliance. She even out-ranked Buck, who held a hereditary knighthood.

"Be that as it may, My Lord Colonel," she said with a shy smile, "we feel we are making no progress against the Guild of Crossed Swords."

Gerardo shrugged. "In finding the chapter house of the Guild, perhaps, but not in rooting out those evildoers. You slew six today, correct? Six fewer to terrorize, enslave and murder the people of Deran."

Dar shot a glance at Eric Indidarc, who held his peace. He knew his friend's burning desire to bring his family to justice, both for their role in crimes in Deran and its allied nations, but also for the murder of Andyn Eleandir's husband, years ago.

Lord Gerardo continued. "You have been on the trail of the Crossed Swords now for how long? Three months, correct, since the last week of

Setamber? Mostly you've been in Oakmoor but also here in Alrihan from what I understand. And all this after you fought at the Battle of Hillton. That's a lot to ask anyone, Grey Riders or not."

The colonel picked up a map on the table and looked at it, pursing his lip. "Six safe houses of the Crossed Swords broken up in that time. I'm not sure how you do it, but your source of information, whoever it is, provides good intelligence."

He raised an eyebrow at Dar, who smiled. "Our source must remain confidential, my lord. I'm sure you understand. Rest assured that it is very reputable and reliable."

It helped that Eric knew the strategies and tactics of the Crossed Swords intimately, permitting a series of lightning raids in rapid succession to try to keep the enemy off balance. But Dar would never betray Eric's confidence. There were few in the Kingdom who knew his real identity.

"Yet with all your recent success you are still, I think, a bit weary?" answered the Colonel.

Dar said nothing but looked at his companions and shrugged.

Lord Gerardo nodded. "I did not get these grey hairs yesterday. You all need a rest. May I make a suggestion, as your "concerned superior officer"? Since it is the Christian season of Advent and Christmas is only a few days away, you should all return to Oakmoor and recuperate. After the holiday and some time to think, you can consider your next move."

"The scroll that Sir Indidarc deciphered does indeed have a few clues," the Colonel continued, "One points to Harlinsville, a suburb of Oakmoor, and mentions the Sign of the Serpent, though I'm not sure exactly what that means. If you return to Oakmoor for the Christmas season, you can pick up your search in Harlinsville thereafter."

Dar met Eric's eyes. His friend let out a breath and nodded.

"I think I can speak for all of us," Dar offered, "We will take your suggestion to heart, my lord. We have had little rest during these last few weeks and perhaps we need some time to gain perspective."

"Excellent," replied Lord Gerardo. "I didn't want to have to make it an order."

"Besides," Andyn said with a raised eyebrow at Dar and Eric. "I've heard that Christmas parties are quite festive. Perhaps Sir Cabot and Sir Indidarc will escort me and Sir Buck and Master Lomin."

Dar had an unnerving vision of Buck and Connor on the loose at a Christmas party but smiled back at her anyway.

"It would be my honor, O Light of Justice."

Chapter Two - Comfort and Joy

Must be getting old, thought Sir Buckminster Horatio Bydecy, Knight of the Kingdom of Astarel. *Winter didn't used to bother me so much.*

He continued meditating, seated on the carved log, eyes closed. He listened to the soft hiss of snowfall through the trees and tried to concentrate. He felt the intricate patterns etched into the log beneath him, knowing that the magical symbols warded evil things away from the grove. His thoughts turned to the Earth Mother and her gifts to all peoples, both those who believed in her and those who didn't.

The knife's-edge chill of morning even cut through his thick cloak. Fingers of iciness reached their way through his tunic and between seams in his armor. He pulled the cloak tighter around himself. The scent of pine, earth, and lichens wafted to him.

Part of him wondered why he was sitting out here in the snow, trying to meditate. In the past, he would have counted it an honor to visit a druid's grove on his own. Now, though?

Maybe I've been hanging around Mrs. Andyn Creature-Comforts too much, he continued with a wry sense of humor. *I swear she's part halfling.*

He sensed, rather than heard, a person moving through the grove behind him and tried to focus his thoughts. He sat motionless, using his other senses to attempt to discern direction, weight, pace, and relative agility. He felt no danger, only a presence that watched and gauged him.

Light footsteps stopped next to his log.

"Druid Anthan?" Buck guessed.

An amused alto voice answered. "No. Druidess Carine."

Buck opened his eyes and looked up at a dark-haired woman in heavy black robes. Her green eyes twinkled at him from a delicate face with a small nose and graceful eyebrows.

"You're getting better though." She leaned her brown staff against a nearby tree and sat next to him on the log.

He shrugged. "I hope so. I haven't been to a grove in a long time."

"How long?"

Buck searched his memory. "Last Februar, before I met Eric in Wit's End. It was near Darlon."

"Ah. Druid Heraz cares for the grove there."

"Yes."

The druidess looked out beyond the snowy field towards the glittering city of Oakmoor. The metropolis covered three hills, split by the two large rivers, the East and Lonmar. It looked like some elegant sculpture in the early morning light, the winter sun shining off grey walls and towers dusted with snow. Even now, traffic moved out along the road: caravans getting an early start, wagons full of goods, individual riders on errands, even a column of cavalry leaving from the south gate of Tallemar, the westernmost suburb. River traffic glided on the frigid waters, mostly barges and merchant craft joined by an occasional Port Authority patrol boat. Boatmen pushed clots of ice away from their craft as they went.

"Tell me," Carine said, resting her hands on the log and leaning back, "Do you feel any different now that you have seen the bones of the earth as well as the trees and hills and lakes and rivers of the surface world? Does your time in the underground give you a new perspective on nature? What do you perceive of the natural world that lives in darkness?"

He considered that for a while, then nodded at the city of Oakmoor. "I'd have to say it makes me appreciate this setting all the more, though we haven't been in a truly large city until just recently. I was in Tyler last winter, but I'm not sure that counts. Even with a hundred thousand people, I think it's still less than half the size of Oakmoor."

Carine nodded but remained silent. Buck watched the metropolis of Oakmoor for a while. A pair of hippogriffs launched from a tower on the east side of the easternmost hill. Half eagle and half horse, their odd shapes made them conspicuous as they winged away to the north. He saw the gleam of metal in the pale sunlight, probably from metal horse armor, modified to the unique anatomy of the hippogriffs.

Probably military if they have barding…

"How was your experience traveling with the other Grey Riders?" Carine asked, tossing her head so her raven hair fell back over her shoulders. "Journeying with Christians and a Verian priestess can be educational, but also a bit challenging. After all, your companions don't follow the Earth Mother, except your halfling friend, Connor."

Buck looked at her, brow furrowed. "We usually don't discuss religion unless it has a bearing on our mission," he replied.

"And the Christians don't try to convert you?" Carine asked.

He shook his head. "No. They accept me as I am and don't make an issue of it."

Carine watched him for a few heartbeats, then turned to look at the city again. "This is good. Some followers of the Druidic path still find Christians difficult to comprehend. Recall that Christians arrived with all the other humans during the Skyfire, eons ago, yet we know few details about what happened."

Buck frowned. "Well, I guess we've all had our differences, especially at first, but I don't feel like I can't discuss things with Dar and Eric. And Andyn is from the Church of Verian, who have been allies of the Druids for hundreds of years. We all get along well."

She nodded and appeared lost in thought, then gave him an amused look. "Listen to the two of us. Isn't it odd that we are both human but still don't know how our race arrived on Damora?"

Buck grinned. "Four thousand years is a long time and wars burn a lot of documents."

"Just so." Carine nodded and said no more for a while.

He said no more, content for the time in quiet and stillness, enjoying the peace and the presence of a pretty woman at his side. He wondered: would he ever want to stop his restless exploration in the wide world and settle down, have a home of his own?

If someone like Carine were with me, I might be able to do that…

"That is a remarkable city, isn't it?" Carine remarked finally.

"Yes."

She stood, taking up her staff again. "Its Christian rulers are careful to manage the growth of the city so that it does not become destructive or polluting. Still, it is a city, and they cannot help affecting the environment. They have their challenges."

Buck stood with her.

"It is a reflection of their philosophy and outlook," she continued, eyes still on Oakmoor, "based on their belief that the world is to be subdued. Philosophy and outlook, Buck, define behavior. Though the Christians are relatively benign, I don't need to remind you that there are others of differing philosophies who are not quite as benevolent."

He felt a certain unease now. "I have seen that already, Druidess Carine. The Ja'al are destructive and evil."

The druidess turned to face him. "Yes. They exploit without caring about the cost and do not think beyond their own greed and desires. However, I am not speaking of them. Though the Druids do not take sides in the wars of Good and Evil, we can be affected by them, and there are some in our faith with very pointed opinions about associations with nonbelievers, whether Christian or Ja'al. Their philosophy and outlook may not be as forgiving. You may be pressed into a choice of sides. Choose wisely."

Buck dropped his gaze to the snowy ground. "It will not be easy, Druidess."

She nodded. "Then you echo my thoughts. I am also troubled by more than mere philosophical differences. There is a shadow growing in the land, and the Earth Mother is uneasy. Something stirs, something unwholesome, something twisted and unnatural."

Carine held out her hand. He took it and looked up, eyes narrowing.

"Why are you telling me this?" he asked.

Her eyes held an intensity, a flame of spiritual quality that bored into his soul. "You have achieved standing in the world and have allies of great ability. You can do much to preserve the Earth Mother from harm and protect all the living. We depend on you to aid all Nature as a sword-knight of Astarel."

Her voice took on an urgent tone. "Always have the preservation of the world and of nature in your mind, no matter what. Do not fear: I think you will find that your goal aligns with that of your Christian friends and the Verian priestess. But be vigilant. There are those, even among the Old Faith, who hold enough of a grudge for past hurts to be tempted by silken words and honeyed lies. I fear all religions will discover they have a similar problem in their ranks."

Unable to tear his gaze away, he could only nod.

The fire in Carine's eyes faded and she smiled, embracing him. "Return to your path, Buckminster. You are welcome here any time."

Buck took both her hands and bowed over them, kissing each. "Thank you, Carine."

Her cheeks were a little flushed as placed a hand on his head in blessing. Then she swept away and her form shimmered and warped. Buck blinked. A gorgeous black doe with piercing green eyes regarded him for a second, then bounded away.

He shook himself, unable to break a chill that had nothing to do with the winter temperature.

I've met known other druids, but she's not like them. And those eyes...

Buck watched the doe until she disappeared among the dark trees.

I wonder if she feels anything towards me.

He picked up his bow and turned back towards Oakmoor. Choosing an arrow whose head crackled with purple sparks, he walked away from the grove onto the snowy field, aimed straight up and loosed. The shiny missile soared upwards, then flared in a burst of faerie lights.

Away over the forest, he saw a winged horse rise up and soar towards him over the trees.

I think the others might be interested in what Druidess Carine had to say.

***

"Buck is late, as usual," Dar said, shrugging his cloak over his tunic and chainmail. He patted the side of his pegasus, Virasi, with a gloved hand.

Eric laughed from his saddle, turning Niveral before he could nip Virasi. "Ease off, Dar. He said he was going to the grove. Besides, my sister said to come any time we're ready."

Connor Lomin shrugged. "I'm ready now. It's been a while since breakfast."

Phantom tossed her head and Connor lifted his hands.

"See? Phantom agrees with me."

Dar snorted. "We just ate breakfast. I think Phantom is taking on halfling traits."

Connor smiled. "And well she should. She's an uncommonly intelligent pegasus. Aren't you, Phantom?"

The winged horse tossed her head again and nickered.

Andyn Eleandir shook her head, patting Medianox on the neck. "Now I've seen everything."

The four of them sat their mounts in the massive market square of the suburb of Tallemar, near a snow-covered fountain of four angels. Townsfolk swirled around them, visiting stalls, shops, and street vendors. Smoke wafted from chimneys and braziers alike, sending up exotic smells of meats, vegetables, spices and baked goods. Pale light from the cloudy sky glowed on glass windows and metal cook-pots, silken cloaks and homespun robes, wrinkled elderly faces and sleeping babies. Despite the press of humans, elves, dwarves and halflings, everyone gave the four Riders plenty of space.

Dar and his friends scarcely took notice any more of the stares, whispers and furtive glances they and their unusual mounts attracted. Each flying horse stood out immediately, armored in studded leather barding and sporting a grey caparison. The Riders themselves also drew attention in their livery of grey and black, the badge of their group on the left breast stitched in white.

Dar sniffed the cooking food and secretly agreed with Connor. Oakmoor's cosmopolitan nature guaranteed the bounty of many nations flowed into its suburban marketplaces. Tallemar was no exception. Some of the dishes smelled positively heavenly.

He watched as a small boy and girl walked away from a street vendor with their mother, carrying paper bowls steaming in the morning air. Their clothing looked well-made yet simple — probably an artisan's family. The boy met his gaze and tried to hide behind his mother, his eyes shy and excited all at once. The mother coaxed him to a seat by the fountain. The little family noticed Dar.

He nodded gravely at the children and winked. The mother curtseyed. He smiled back as the little ones attempted to mimic their mother, then settled down to their meal.

"You are Sir Dar Cabot of Saint Kira's Order," noted Eric with a jaunty grin, "yet you gain admirers wherever you go, despite your reputation and obvious lack of style."

"Not so, Sir Eric Indidarc of Saint Michael's," Dar responded haughtily. "They know quality when they see it."

"Then they would be looking at me, thou ignorant lout."

Dar opened his mouth for a retort but Andyn interrupted him.

"He's here," she said.

Dar looked up into the sky. A pegasus with a single rider floated down at them, adjusting his course to avoid the crowd.

Connor spurred Phantom forward to clear a path. He didn't need to. The townsfolk hurried to provide space for Buck and Shadowbane, eager to watch a Grey Rider landing his steed.

Shadowbane landed lightly and clattered over to Dar.

"Sorry I'm late," Buck said, brushing a bit of snow from his sandy hair. "Druidess Carine had some information for me."

Andyn raised an eyebrow. "I can't wait to hear it."

To Dar's surprise, Buck didn't respond with his characteristic bravado and merely nodded. "I'll tell you later. Where's Puup?"

As if in answer, a white pigeon fluttered down, landed on his shoulder and preened its feathers.

"Well then," said Eric with a smile, "Now that our most important member is here, we are ready. Follow me."

Buck pointedly ignored him and urged Shadowbane into a canter. Dar followed Buck, eyes scanning storefronts, windows, rooftops and alleyways more by habit than a feeling of danger. The past months of conflict with the cult of the Ja'al and pursuit of the Crossed Swords had cultivated in him a healthy dose of vigilance.

Their path led from commercial districts to neighborhoods with tall apartment buildings and then to larger homes with gardens and yards. The street climbed the side of Oakmoor's westernmost hill to a wide boulevard lined with large, ornate homes and bare, snow-sprinkled trees. A line of fluted columns led down the middle of the street to a tall iron gate between two towers of worn white stone. An imposing wall encircled a dark grey manor house with a slate roof and two more glowering towers. Dar saw a large garden in the courtyard, robed in winter's white mantle.

Guards in burgundy and grey hauberks and banded armor snapped to attention at Eric's approach, raising their spears in salute. Another soldier with the insignia of a sword and star on his collar opened the gate.

"Welcome to the Manor, Sir Indidarc," he announced, placing his fist over his heart. "Lady Saren awaits you and Lord Terenil is on his way."

"Thank you, Sergeant," Eric replied. "We'll stable the pegasi first."

The soldier motioned to other troops near a barracks. "We will take care of them for you, sir, if you'd prefer."

Dar raised a hand. "I'm sure you are well-versed in taking care of horses, but pegasi can be particular. We'd prefer to do it ourselves, though you can come along if you want to learn."

The sergeant bowed. "Of course, Sir Cabot."

The Riders dismounted. Dar held one side of the bridle as a soldier held the other side. Virasi rolled his eyes at the trooper, but Dar placed a hand on his neck.

"Calsha," he whispered in soothing tones, "Calsha, Eynem."

The pegasus became less agitated and the soldier looked impressed. "What did you say, Sir?"

"It's Elven," Dar answered, patting his mount. "It means 'Be calm, my favorite'. My, er, someone taught it to me months ago."

Once in the stables, Dar showed a young blond corporal how to remove the pilot's saddle and blanket, then inspected Virasi's wings and cleaned them with a special brush.

"You can curry his hide while I do this," Dar instructed, "and comb out his mane and tail. It takes a lot of practice to maintain the wings unless you have experience in falconry."

The soldier looked a bit apprehensive. "Of course, Sir. What shall I feed him?"

"Oats, alfalfa, and strips of meat."

"Meat?" The corporal turned a shade paler.

"He is part bird, you know. Raptor characteristics. But don't worry. They're quite dainty about it and don't bite except in defense if that's what you're thinking. They only have a few pointed teeth."

The corporal scratched his head. "I'll see what I can do. But, Sir Cabot, this is a stallion. Is it wise to have him close to the other stallions? They may compete for the mares." He indicated Andyn's Medianox and Connor's Phantom.

Dar shook his head. "In that respect, you have nothing to fear. Pegasi won't mate while in captivity or in service. The males have nothing to compete for."

The corporal looked thoughtful. "So how do we actually capture any of them? I mean, even an armored pegasus is supposed to be very fast, and it must be impossible to catch one in the wild."

"Only nearly impossible. You can't trap them because the entire herd descends on the trapped one and defends it. The purpose is to capture one and tame it, not fight the herd."

"So how —?"

"Very patiently. A handler sets up camp near their herd lands and the pegasi grow accustomed to him or her. After the foaling, the handler can select one mare or stallion to cultivate and the herd won't cause much of a fuss. Some handlers are even good enough to get two. But no more than that. It's no wonder they are so expensive, agreed?"

The corporal nodded and Dar went to join his companions. The soldier departed and Dar waited with Eric for the others.

"Terenil and Saren don't have their own riders, do they?" he asked.

Eric shook his head. "Too expensive. Only a duke or marquis of a large city like Darlon or Alrihan could have the means to maintain their own squadron. As it is, most of the time the air force is part of a national military because of the cost."

"We're lucky we've been given training in their care and some extra money from our incidents with Zhinia Margoth and the Crossed Swords," noted Connor.

"We do have an advantage," said Eric, leading them across the courtyard towards the double doors of the manor house. "I'm not sure I could keep Niveral when I retire though. I'd need a serious income to afford him."

"I won't have a problem with that," said Buck, adjusting his sword belt. "I'm going to be independently wealthy. You'll see."

Andyn rolled her eyes. "Let's get inside before Buck goes off and claims a small country. Saren's probably waiting for us."

Connor tapped Eric on the shoulder. "Why did you rename your pegasus? He was Falcon for the longest time."

Eric made a face at Dar and Buck. "Those two kept after me because I picked a 'mundane' name. Buck, in particular — he insisted he hadn't seen any coal-black falcons. So I named him Niveral. I think Niveral likes it better too."

"And Niveral means?"

"Snow-bright," Eric answered with a grin. "Just to tweak Buck."

Dar waggled his eyebrows at Connor, who smirked in response.

The doors of the manor swung open and a beaming woman in a white dress and matching boots held out her hands to them. Tiny ivory horns peeked out from her forehead under silky raven hair. Her face looked positively angelic, delicate and refined, with a small nose and high cheekbones and shining black eyes. From her upper back, two ivory bat wings lay furled against her shoulders.

She reminded Dar of the Elohir warrior, Melissa from Celestia, who had given the Riders their special weapons months ago to help defeat Margoth. Where Melissa was the definition of beauty and grace and womanly physical charms, Saren looked like her dark shadow, embodying femininity with a more sinister appearance.

Saren's smile held warmth and affection as she took Eric's hands in her own and drew him close in a warm embrace.

"Finally you come to visit us, you rogue!" she teased, closing her eyes as she held her adopted half-brother in a long hug. "How long has it been?"

Eric hugged her back, then held her at arm's length. "Too long for me, probably not long enough for your security officer."

She wrinkled her nose at him. "Captain Resal is just a worrier. But that's why we have him around."

She turned to the other Riders. Connor started to bow to her and she shook a finger at him.

"Connor, what did I say about that last time?" She knelt to hug him.

Connor grinned sheepishly. "I'm sorry, Lady Sa — I mean, Saren. We've been meeting so many lords and high officers lately it's a reflex by now."

Saren nodded gravely. "I know what you mean. I have to deal with that every day. That's why I don't want to have any of that from you."

She gave each of them affectionate hugs. By now, Dar had become accustomed to her appearance and didn't even give it a second thought, comforted by her warmth and kindliness and humor instead.

He wondered, though, at Buck's perpetual uneasiness around her. It was as if he still couldn't come to terms with who she was: Eric's half-sister, an orphan child adopted by Melinor Indidarc, a half-daemon, a Christian, a countess, a wife of a Lord of Deran, and a fierce defender of the Light.

If she noted Buck's lack of enthusiasm, she either decided to let him work through it or resolved not to let it alter her behavior towards him. She still treated him like family.

Dar found this to be most endearing aspect about Saren DeMey, Countess of Tallemar. Her acceptance of others and gentle sweetness of character contrasted so sharply with a form associated with cruelty, lust and savagery.

Maybe it's the fact that her wings and horns aren't blood red or deep purple, he mused.

"Come in out of the cold," she offered, sweeping back into the entrance hall with them. A pair of servants arrived to take their cloaks.

Eric gave her a questioning look, one hand on Fidelis at his belt.

She shrugged. "I don't mind if you're armed, but you have little to worry about here, and I think some of the heavier items will be a burden on you. Maybe you can bring them into the library. I'll have tea brought in."

Dar agreed. "Thank you, Saren. It's just that our current mission…" he trailed off.

She smiled again, showing perfect white teeth and fangs. "I understand, Dar. Don't worry. I'm not offended either way. We'll take care of you."

Her eyes flashed for a split second. Dar remembered a day of fire and blood on the battlefield at Hillton, when Saren defended the Grey Riders with all the deadly ferocity of her daemonic bloodline.

Here, even unarmed and clad in a dress, Saren would provide a nasty surprise for any assassins.

They followed her down the great hall, their boots echoing on white marble floors. Paintings hung on the walls, each depicting a previous Earl or Countess of Tallemar. In a nod to the upcoming holiday, poinsettias and holly branches decorated the hall, along with a finely-carved Nativity scene on a side table near the vast, arching staircase.

Dar took a closer look at the creche as he went by. A magical light hovered over the stable where the Child lay, a symbol of the Star that guided the Magi. The small donkey and cow and sheep seemed almost alive — indeed, tiny puffs of fog curled from their mouths in imitation of their breath in chilly air.

Melinor's handiwork, he thought with amusement. *He sure does dote on his children, even after they've grown up.*

Saren led them through a side door into a library with tall windows, bookshelves and display cases of warm wood. Dar took in light-colored curtains, elegant vases with curving elven designs in gold filigree, and comfortable padded furniture in the Tallemar house colors of burgundy and grey.

A maid and a butler brought a cart with tea and two platters of colorful little cakes no bigger than Dar's thumb, along with a bowl of apples, oranges and persimmons. The servants began to slice the fruit and arrange plates for each of them.

"Please, sit," Saren offered, resting in a tall chair next to a small burnished table holding the crystal figure of a pegasus. "Terenil will be home any minute. Ministry meeting."

Dar found himself relaxing even as he rested his sword against a table and sat back on the couch next to Buck. He accepted a hot cup of tea and a plate with two cakes and slices of fruit. He particularly enjoyed the cakes: one of cinnamon and chocolate, the other with raspberry and lemon. He let his eyes roam around the library as he sipped his tea. A large desk sat under one of the windows. Fading sunlight shone on the padded window-benches, the impressive array of books, the paintings on the walls, and a prominent silver crucifix behind the desk.

Elegant, but this is home to them.

An air of warmth and comfort enfolded him that had little to do with the merry blaze in the fireplace. Saren's calm happiness affected him as surely as a magic spell. She even held out her hand with some crumbs for Puup, smiling as Buck's pigeon ate from her hand.

Love lives here, Dar mused, sipping his tea. His eyes and his mind wandered.

When will I have my own home? When will I stop wandering around on dangerous missions, settle down and have a place of my own? It doesn't have to be a manor. A little sea-side cottage would be fine with me… and Megan. If God wills it.

Andyn and Eric sat next to Saren, who soon engaged them in animated conversation about their recent activities — at least, the part that they were permitted to tell her. A veteran of government security arrangements, Saren knew enough when to pry and when not to.

"How is your family?" Saren asked, turning to Dar.

He swallowed a bite of persimmon. "They are well. Lord DeGrance has made sure that they are attended and guarded daily."

"I am glad to hear it. It must be a rude shock for them to be brought so suddenly into the world of free-lance blank-shields, monsters, war and danger — though I suppose you are hardly blank-shields any longer, now that you are knighted."

Dar grinned. "Yes. Actually, I think my parents find it rather exciting, though my brother less so with a wife and children. His profession seems so mundane by comparison, but he likes it that way, though I think he's secretly glad for the people watching over him."

Another voice came to them from the door to the grand hall. "And what's wrong with a little excitement, Sir Cabot?"

Dar stood with the other Riders as a trim man with dark hair and grey eyes strode into the library, removing gloves from his hands. He wore a silver tabard over black trousers and matching woolen shirt, shiny black boots on his feet. A golden circlet wound around his head, the pointed tips of his ears just visible next to the shiny metal. Saren glided over to him, her smile luminous.

"How did you get away from the meeting so early? Did you have to use The Spell of Forty Winks on the councilors or just turn invisible?" Saren asked as she unbuckled his sword belt and planted a firm kiss on his lips.

"I bribed some and got the others drunk," he replied, hugging her tightly. She laughed.

Dar grinned as Terenil, Earl of Tallemar winked at him. He always found Terenil's wry sense of humor and thinly veiled irreverence for rank to be positively refreshing, compared to some of the haughtier nobles Dar had run into before. Considering that Terenil was a confidant of King Phillip and Queen Ahlana and one of the higher-ranked noblemen in the kingdom, it seemed odd. Then again, he had started his career as a simple officer in the

Deranese intelligence service. Then he had met Saren.

"The Riders Grey are looking warm and well-fed," he said, releasing Saren but keeping his arm over her shoulders. "This is scandalous. What's to be done?"

"You could bring us some mulled wine, I suppose," offered Connor brightly with an innocent smile. "And some cold chicken and pickles."

Andyn gave Saren a martyred look.

"We'll have something more than that for lunch," Saren replied, kissing Terenil's cheek. "We knew Connor was coming so we prepared."

Eric embraced his brother-in-law. Terenil greeted each of the Riders in turn, accepted a kiss from Andyn and plopped down in another chair, looping his sword belt over the arm.

"So, will you fly off on another mission of derring-do or are you really going to take some time to rest?" he asked, taking a cup of tea.

"We received a pointed suggestion that we recuperate for a while," Eric answered. "I think we were getting a little frayed around the edges and the Command took note. It's my fault, really. I've been pushing too hard."

Dar shook his head. "Not just you. We pushed ourselves just as hard and we didn't try to slow you down."

Terenil inquired about their progress, omitting any reference to specifics in much the same way as Saren. Dar could see from his expression that his mind filled in the missing information which couldn't be voiced in the presence of servants, some of whom might certainly gossip with other servants and then, who knew? The assassin's guilds of Damora were famous for their ability to pry information from those with weak minds and strong greed or strong libidos.

Dar found himself marveling at the scene before his eyes: he, the son of a county clerk, taking tea and cakes in the library of the Earl and Countess of Tallemar. His eyes drifted to his companions: Buck, a former refugee from the law and the son of a shopkeeper, Andyn, an army brat and widow, Eric, adopted son of a famous wizard and prince of an assassin's guild, and Connor, a widower and the son of a high cleric of the Church of Irial.

He smiled. *What an odd bunch…*

His thoughts brought other memories to mind and his mood turned more somber. He could almost see Alenar sisters, half-elves like Eric. He heard their voices in his mind, saw their lovely figures as they walked alongside the other Riders near Whitehorse Peak so many months ago: Brandawyn — serious and virtuous and brave, a warrior and combat medic, the love of Eric Indidarc, and Megan, the woman Dar loved — vivacious, brilliant, wise, a wizard of amazing ability for one so young.

Dar saw in his mind's eye the small figure of Hlerv the gnome, a half-breed himself, part dwarf and part halfling. He had left the Riders after the defeat of Zhinia Margoth, escaping with the lich's cursed magic helmet that allowed its wearer to teleport. Dar still remembered the look on Hlerv's face, a look of resolution and, he thought, regret, as the gnome vanished from their company on some mysterious errand.

We will find you, Hlerv, and help you out of whatever trouble you're in. And we'll see you again, Megan and Brandi. I promise.

He shook himself from his mood as Terenil addressed Buck Bydecy.

"I hear that you met with one of the druids this morning," the earl said. "What did he or she have to say?"

Buck nodded and took a deep breath. "This is unnerving for some reason. Carine senses something, and I don't think she's the only druid who does so."

Dar listened with a nagging feeling of unease as Buck described his meeting. He exchanged a look with Andyn, who raised her eyebrows.

Terenil digested Buck's information. "This suggests that there may be subversives within each of the churches. Well, the druids have their finger on the pulse of the world in ways that we do not. We will have to be vigilant. I'm glad you told us, Buck. I will pass this along to the cardinal archbishop and the patriarchs of Verian, Kurental and Irial in the city — and to the King."

Everyone remained silent, digesting Buck's account of Carine's warning.

Saren finally rose. "I'll have Adalbert and Minnie show you to your rooms. Then you can rest until lunch. Relax. You need do nothing here that you do not want to. And remember: you will be our guests at the Christmas Party tomorrow night, so you will not be bored."

Connor glanced at Buck. "We're counting on it," he said brightly.

Saren's eyes twinkled and she arched an elegant eyebrow. "Just remember to behave, please."

"Yes ma'am," Connor said, but his eyes matched the twinkle in Saren's.

The butler, Adalbert, guided Dar to a large upstairs room with a window overlooking the city. Dar figured he really shouldn't be surprised at the spacious and comfortable rooms afforded to each of them. Rather than a reflection of profligate spending on the part of the DeMeys, they indicated the role that Saren and Terenil played as hosts for visiting dignitaries as part of the Foreign Ministry of Deran.

Deran was a meritocracy, with noble title handed on through particular families only insofar as their members showed the requisite amount of skill and dedication. Upon the death or abdication of a noble, the King and Senate had to approve of every change in title. If no one from a particular family line showed the right inclination and ability, the Crown would replace them with someone else. Simply being a member of an aristocratic family wasn't enough.

Saren and Terenil were a case in point. Terenil had gained the rulership of Tallemar after the previous Earl had been deposed for treason.

Dar lay back on the large bed. He stared up at the white-painted ceiling and filigreed crown molding, finally allowing himself to relax. Though he felt a desire to press on and find Eric's evil parents, he knew that they couldn't work themselves to exhaustion. The Crossed Swords would eventually get to them if they did.

Besides, a Christmas Party at the Paladin's Rest Inn? Who could complain about that?

His thoughts drifted to the events of the past few months: their acquisition of the pegasi, the conflict against the Ja'al, the savage Battle of Hillton, and his romance with Megan Alenar.

She and her sister Brandawyn, refugees from the oppressive southern regime of Torosc, aided Dar and his friends in finding the pegasi in the Wilderness near Whitehorse Peak. Dar and Megan had formed a strong attachment, as had Eric and Brandawyn. However, the sisters had been whisked away by their aunt and uncle on a secret mission for the Christian Church in unknown lands. Dar only received occasional letters from Megan and knew that Eric received the same from Brandi. The fact that Megan's notes referenced events he had written in his own love letters meant that his correspondence found its way to her.

He sighed, remembering her amber eyes and red-gold hair, yet feeling annoyed that he had difficulty remembering her face, even though he could pick her out of a crowd immediately.

God, will I ever see her again? Is it time to move on, maybe? When is it time to face facts and give up?

That thought depressed him immensely. He yawned, feeling the fatigue from weeks of pursuing assassins taking its toll. To his surprise, he drifted off. Moreover, Heaven seemed to answer his unspoken prayer and he dreamed of Megan, her beautiful features remembered just as if he had parted with her yesterday.

A light, silvery bell awoke him not long after.

"Lunch is served, Sir Cabot," announced Adalbert from the door to his room.

"Coming…" Dar bounded out of the bed to jar himself to wakefulness, then headed down to lunch, rubbing the sleep from his eyes.

Chapter Three - An Uneasy Time

He watched the old man stride briskly down the street, his white staff tapping the cobblestones with every step. The elderly chap clasped his grey cloak about him against the drifting snow and stiff breeze, looking neither right nor left. The fading afternoon sunlight shone on the man's face, illuminating a neatly trimmed grey beard and grey eyes.

Got you, Melinor Indidarc...

Kili Mikman, halfling spy of the Ja'al High Command, huddled in the doorway. He followed the man's progress out of the corner of his eye. Even when Melinor passed, Kili didn't move, instead settling deeper within his cloak. As the tapping of the staff faded into the distance behind him, Kili stretched, then headed down the street in the opposite direction. When he came to an alleyway, he nonchalantly turned into it.

The instant he was out of view of the street, he swept back his cloak and downed a glittering silver potion from a vial in his hand. His pulse rate increased and he felt more alert and agile. Moving twice as fast as normal, he pulled special gloves out of a shoulder bag: gloves with metal claws on the fingers. With a quick look up and down the alley, he gripped the stone wall of the building and pulled himself up. Tapping his boots against the wall, he released metal spikes from the toe of each and, thus equipped, swarmed up the wall with the speed of a giant spider.

Reaching the roof, he kept low and scampered across, going in the direction Melinor had taken. When he reached a gap between two buildings, he simply backed up, then charged forward at inhuman speed. His heart threatened to burst from his chest from the magical energy of the potion. At the edge of the roof, he leaped, clearing the gap easily and hurrying onward. At the next gap, he waited, listening for the tapping of the staff. Satisfied he was on the right track, he continued on in the same manner, leaping over other alleyways until he arrived at an intersection.

The old man had turned right and now headed towards the door of a tavern with the sign of a red griffon. Kili noted a lamplighter walking down the street towards him, his long staff in his hands as he lifted the leather covers from the glass street lamps and brought them down to the ground, rolling them up and placing them in a small hand cart at his side. Magical light flared to life and illuminated the snowy streets with each globe he uncovered.

Kili scuttled down the side of the building as soon as the lamplighter bent to put a cover into the cart. He pressed the points of his climbing spikes into the wall to stow them in his boot soles. Confident the worker had not seen him, he wrapped his cloak around himself and hurried down the avenue, putting on his best imitation of a laborer eager to get to a nice warm room with a mug of stout.

Melinor entered the tavern. Kili went past it to the store next to it, then turned to look into the window, using the reflection to see behind him. The road remained empty except for him and the lamplighter, who slowly advanced on his patient task, a string of street lights glowing behind him.

Kili removed his special gloves, stuffed them into a pocket in his cloak, then slipped into the Red Griffon Inn. He stepped to the side, eyes darting around. His gaze drifted over the dark wooden walls of the tavern, decorated with paintings of flying creatures that were half lion and half eagle. In a glass case behind the bar, he saw two crossed feathers, each over a foot long and brown, tipped with red. Many customers sat at tables, men and women alike, dwarf, human, elf and halfling alike. They laid cloaks on the backs of chairs and spooned up dinners from steaming trenchers or wooden bowls, with mugs of ale or hot tea at hand.

Now where... Ah! Gariil's own luck!

He spied a grey-cloaked old man with a white staff speaking to a blonde barmaid in a blue dress. Melinor nodded and left through a door that led into the back courtyard. Kili received a mug of ale from another barmaid and paid her with silver coins and a tip, then sauntered across the room the way the old man had gone.

It took all his control not to give in to the surge of adrenaline from the potion and dart through the room like a hunting hawk, but he got to the back door without incident. He left the common room and closed the door behind him, eyes scanning the courtyard for the old man.

Kili ground his teeth in frustration. The yard stood empty. Designed to handle at least three coaches or carts and their occupants or cargo, only a dusting of snow lay on the dirt yard or stone pathways. On the far side, a wooden fence bordered another street. To Kili's left and right, closed doors and glowing lights of guest rooms showed no sign of the old man.

By all the daemons in Hades! He couldn't have gotten away that fast.

Furious, Kili pulled a small wand from his sleeve. With a glance around to make sure he wasn't seen, he waved it in an S-pattern in front of him, the tip of the wand glowing purple.

Nothing! No magical traces.

He stood indecisive in the yard, tapping the wand in his hand.

He's not invisible and didn't use an illusion, that's for sure. So where did he go?

Shaking his head in vexation, Kili slipped back into the shadows, feeling the effects of the acceleration potion start to wear off. His muscles began to ache and he felt the familiar weariness kick in.

He finished his cup of ale and placed the empty container on a nearby barrel, trying to think. Had the wizard slipped into a room before he could have come out of the tavern? Kill estimated it had only been three or four seconds between Melinor's exit and his own, not enough time to get to a guest room or across to the other street. He inspected the pathway, his apprehension growing.

No footprints showed in the snow.

With a vile oath, Kili pulled his hood over his head and re-entered the tavern. His mind raced over various scenarios, trying to figure out where the wizard had gone. Not coming up with anything, he scanned the crowd, looking for the blonde wench with the blue dress.

Every barmaid in the room had brown or black hair. He muttered a curse and headed back out to the street.

Only the glow of street lamps and gently drifting snow greeted him.

He stood unmoving for long seconds, a gnawing anxiety growing in his stomach. He tried to figure out a convenient excuse to tell his commander as to why he couldn't follow an old man through the wintry streets of Oakmoor. He could just decide not to report in, but then discarded that idea. He needed the money and was unlikely to get another job any time soon.

Of course, he could point out that it wasn't just any old man he followed, but Melinor Indidarc. He could claim he was the victim of a spell that Melinor fired from ambush.

And I could also claim I got kidnapped by a sultry trio of lonely halfling heiresses, he thought sourly.

On inspiration, Kili stepped over to the corner of the tavern wall and with a quick look around, banged his forehead into the stone. Gritting his teeth against the pain, he felt his head, drawing back fingers tinged with blood.

Yes, some street ruffians hit me with a rock just as I was turning the corner and I lost him. That's it.

It might work this time, but it wouldn't do for the future. He was going to have to figure out another way to keep tabs on the wizard from now on.

Kili slipped off into the shadows, heading back to his masters.

***

"Were you followed?" asked Lady Sidara Faldanor. Magical light glimmered from flame-shaped lamps set in the walls. Clad in a dark grey dress with a golden Star of Bethlehem above her left breast, she wore a silver belt around her slender waist and a similar circlet around her honey-blonde tresses.

"Of course," he replied.

Melinor Indidarc, Wizard of the North and King's Councilor of Deran, smiled at her. He removed his grey cloak with a flourish. A matching Star on Melinor's tunic winked in the light as he turned to give the cloak and his white staff to a waiting guard in black livery trimmed with white and gold. The soldier bowed and accepted both, turning to go.

Melinor regarded the young human as he left the entrance chamber. "Hmm… new guards?"

"Yes, Knights of the Kestrel."

"Kestrel?"

"Yes. Kestrel Knights, Servants of Mary. Special Operations Group from the Order of the Falcon."

"Hmm. Someone is worried?"

"Let's just say cautious. How did you slip away from your shadow?"

"First, a Shadow Sculpt spell," Melinor replied.

"Ah, to make yourself blurry to the eye. Good move. Then what?"

"I made an illusion of me and a barmaid talking near the back door. Then I used a telekinesis spell on the door."

"*Mense Motus*, I'm guessing? And then you made your illusion exit." Sidara nodded. "Simple but effective."

"Just enough." Melinor said with a satisfied look. "A halfling or gnome followed not four seconds later, then returned less than ten seconds later, looking agitated. He left without even looking in my direction."

Lady Sidara shook her head. "You have to give them credit for trying."

"Yes. But I doubt they would ever find the way in here, even if they could see me get in."

After waiting for the halfling to leave, Melinor had walked over to the bar, spoken to the bartender, then slipped through a small door to the right of the bar, entering a closet. After placing his hand on a hidden metal plate in the floor, he opened a trapdoor and climbed down an iron ladder into a narrow passage under the tavern. As he walked down the passage, lights of mild blue, green and yellow flashed, magic surging around him as he was scanned to make sure he was authorized to enter. Then, a password, magic key and palm-plate later, he walked into this entrance room to be greeted by Lady Sidara.

Sidara smiled at him. "But you know they'll figure it out some day." Her violet eyes seemed to tease him.

He smiled back. "And we'll close down this area and head off to one of the backup safe houses when that day comes."

"A bit cavalier, Melinor."

He shrugged. "Life is full of risks and opportunities, is it not?"

She gave him a look. "Quoting from Tolan the First Prophet of Verian instead of the Bible tonight?"

He laughed. "Whatever suits. Are the others here?"

She swept him a mock bow with all the lithe grace of her elven heritage.

"Of course. You are usually the last to arrive these days."

He offered his arm in response. "How is your family?"

"Andareth is doing well, and so are the children. It seems like only yester-day when little Carawyn was born, but now she's ten." She sighed as she accompanied him. "You humans have all the advantages. I only have two children to show for one hundred eighty years of life and fifty years of mar-riage and you have twice that number and you're not even half my age."

"Half of my children are adopted, my dear. Not all humans are as fertile as elves hope."

She gave his arm a squeeze. "I'm sorry. It was only in jest. I know you and Anne had some trouble conceiving, so, believe me, I am not trying to cause you pain. Your children have turned out quite well, I'd say. Even the adopted ones."

"Agreed, and thank you."

They approached a double door. Two more black-clad Kestrel Knights saluted and opened it at their arrival.

The round, domed chamber held a circular table with chairs and five other occupants. All except one wore the same livery as Melinor: dark grey tunic with the Star of Bethlehem prominently displayed over lighter grey shirt or blouse and either dark grey pants or skirt. Each wore a silver circlet like Sidara's. Melinor nodded to them.

A blonde woman of middle years with a round face and plump figure glided over to him. "Melinor! I'm so glad you're late. It makes me look good."

He took both her hands and gave them a squeeze. "I thought it would be good for someone else to take over from you, Lady Jordan, so you could have some rest."

She pursed her lip, blue eyes twinkling. "I don't think that amount of chivalry is in your makeup, Lord Melinor, but I will take what I can get."

A blond human male with blue eyes and a scar along his jaw grinned and took Melinor's hand. "I, for one, am glad for a change now and again."

"So am I, Lord Finbar. So am I."

A dark-haired, dark-skinned and slender man joined them. "Pay no atten-tion to Finbar or Jordan, Melinor. None of us arrived early."

"Except you, Simrit," retorted Jordan, elbowing him lightly with a slight giggle.

"I wasn't early. I was late. For me, anyway."

An elderly human male attired in a black cassock with a white tab collar joined them, moving with an energy that belied his years. He wore a dark purple skullcap trimmed with white.

He placed a friendly hand on Melinor's shoulder. "How was your trip here, Melinor?"

Melinor bowed over the hand of Edward Simpson, Papal Nuncio to Damora, and kissed his signet ring. "I had an admirer to avoid, but he was dissuaded from following me any farther than the Red Griffon."

"Forcefully?"

"No, Eminence, with illusion."

Edward Simpson's mouth quirked in a smile. "Excellent."

"All right, the lot of you," announced a loud and gruff voice as the last member of their group stumped forwards. A dwarf with piercing grey eyes, a dark complexion and greying black hair pushed his way into the crowd around Melinor. "Clear out and let Lord Indidarc have a seat so we can get this meeting started. I just rode in from Darlon and it's late."

Instead of being put off by the dwarf's demeanor, Father Edward chuckled. "Quite so, Lord Konadar. Let us begin."

The assembly took their seats at the circular table, Edward taking his place near the middle of the arc formed by their group.

"The other members of the Order are on field assignment," stated the Nuncio. "We will discuss their reports after prayer."

The group bowed their heads as Father Edward said a short prayer asking for the Holy Spirit to bestow wisdom and courage on them all, then they recited the Our Father together.

"Lady Jordan?"

Jordan, the secretary of the group for the year, nodded, opening a leather mapcase at her side. "Field reports from Lord Evan and Lady Tamara are available. The other three reports are not due for another two weeks so we will have to review them at our post-Christmas meeting."

She distributed copies of the reports to each of them.

They all read silently. Melinor's eyes darted along the neat lines of script, digesting every word. A vague sense of unease grew in him. He removed a pencil from his belt purse and underlined specific passages here and circled other ones there, paying particular attention to a finely drawn map at the bottom of the third page. He tapped his pencil on the table, feeling frustrated, as if an important clue lay before him and he didn't have the wit to read it.

He finished after everyone else, looking up at them. Their expressions confirmed he was not alone.

Father Edward sat back in his chair, fingers steepled in front of his mouth. His eyes darted to Melinor.

"You are seeing what I'm seeing." Edward made it a statement, not a question.

Melinor nodded, irritated at his apprehension and still more at at his inability to put his finger on some nagging clue he felt he should recognize.

Simrit sighed. "If it was just one land where councilors and aldermen are proposing legislation like this, I wouldn't be so nervous. It's all over the place."

Konadar snorted. "Legalizing prostitution and dangerous drugs, reducing penalties for slavery, legalizing polygamy, lowering the legal marriage age from eighteen to fourteen and removing parental consent requirements, even a request to de-criminalize the worship of Vardu. You'd think everyone had lost their senses."

"If it was just that, I wouldn't be concerned," added Finbar, running a hand through his hair. "We occasionally see tomfoolery like this in various precincts. It's the fact that these proposals were actually passed by town councils or regional assemblies. If it wasn't for the local lords vetoing the bills, some of this would be permitted."

Sidara looked viciously angry, a countenance shocking in someone so beautiful. "And it's not just Deran. Astarel, Rokon, Eldir and even Imperial Terenai are reporting similar incidents."

Edward leaned his head back. "Well, need we be concerned, after all? Lord Finbar is correct: things like these have been floated in past years, only to meet with a similar fate."

He's being devil's advocate again…

"Yes, we should!" retorted Jordan. "In previous incidents, the proposals were just that. None were even voted on by legislators. These bills had to be vetoed."

Melinor nodded. "Even more, some magistrates and judges appear to be supporting the proposals in tacit form, at least, handing down greatly reduced sentences for offenders in these particular areas. It's almost as if they're encouraging it."

Simrit stacked his papers in front of him, rotated them and stacked them again. "That's not all. A lot of journals guilds and handbill publishers appear to be portraying these things in a positive light, even going so far as to print articles critical of the lords who vetoed the bills."

Melinor frowned. A tiny idea teased him just outside of his mental acuity.

Sidara shook her head. "We should get this news to the Orders of Mindra and Saint Thomas as soon as possible. They were helpful in counteracting similar things that Margoth's agents were trying to push months ago."

"That's it!" Melinor said, slapping the table.

"Oh, sorry," he said at the startled expressions of his friends.

Jordan laughed. "Well, come out with it already, Mel, now that you've made all of us jump."

A bit sheepishly, he avoided Father Edward's amused look and addressed the others. "Zhinia Margoth, the Lich Princess. She had a propaganda machine spouting the same kind of libertine philosophy before the Grey Riders took her out at the Battle of Hillton. Not the same scope or the same geographical reach as this time, but similar. And we know full well who she was working for."

The Councilors exchanged looks.

"The Ja'al," hissed Sidara, eyes flashing.

"Yes," said Father Edward. "The Ja'al. The Manipulator Church, the religion of misdirection, lies and falsehood. Masters of long-laid plans. If they are the originators, then the scope of this points to something major."

Simrit looked unconvinced. "But some of the proposals seem to promote Vardu. The Ja'al and the Vardish aren't exactly friends. Remember that the Ja'al god Torvu claims lordship over the undead, which the Vardish also consider to be the rightful sphere of their god. Why would the Ja'al promote a rival?"

Father Edward considered this for a long moment. "I wouldn't be surprised," he said slowly, "if that were just a smoke screen to distract us."

Melinor looked at the reports. The sheer extent of the incidents over the last four months and the geographical areas involved: nations all over the

Northern Alliance, Terenai, and even across the Sea in Kortos and Melen. He felt his uneasiness grow.

"They're prepping the battlefield."

The Councilors all stared at Konadar. He fixed them all with a flinty gaze. "Well, why not? If you're going to attack, one of the things that gets you a lot of benefit is to prepare the battlefield by sowing confusion, dissension and chaos in the ranks of your enemy, isn't it? What military commander doesn't have a fifth column of special forces or spies behind enemy lines to cause as much havoc as possible? Why doesn't that apply to things like the law and politics as well?"

Melinor's unease transformed into a gnawing sensation in his stomach. "But what could they hope to gain?" he asked, trying as much to reason with Konadar as to quell his nerves. "No Ja'al organization is strong enough to assail a single nation of the Alliance, even if we weren't bound together by treaty to support one another. They would need to recruit a massive force to conquer Evendale, the smallest of the Alliance countries, and the Armies of Terenai and Deran would be there in weeks to crush the invasion."

"But if they had daemons to help them," Jordan said with a worried look at Father Edward. "With what the Alenars sent to us, if those structures really are interstellar gates to Hades…"

"That would make it harder to counter them," the Nuncio admitted, "but recall also that if daemons openly gate in to assist in military action, the Elohir will teleport agents from their hidden gates and counter them. It would be a zero-sum game. No, I don't think that is a wise tactic on their part and what-ever else we think of the Ja'al, they are judicious. Besides, the amount of power needed to open an interstellar gate is massive, and there are few in the world who possess the knowledge of how to garner that much energy. Four of them are in this room."

They all sat in silence.

Finally, Father Edward gathered his papers and placed them into his leather case. "While I share Lord Melinor's assessment, the sense of what Lord Konadar says is inescapable. Coupled with the avowed goal of the Ja'al to subjugate the entire world to their twisted faith, there is the very real pos-sibility that they are involved in a major plot. To what end and in what time-line, I cannot say. The fact that all of this is happening in these days, after the defeat of Zhinia Margoth, is, I believe, not a coincidence."

He folded his hands and laid them on the table. "I would propose several things. First, each Councilor should commission a free-lance team to investigate the source of the recently proposed legislation, making sure that they are very discreet and with the aim of uncovering the ultimate entity responsible for both forwarding the ideas and providing material assistance in promoting them. Second, I will speak to Their Majesties and suggest that Alliance intelligence services be similarly employed. Last, I will contact the Patriarch of Verian and suggest that the Orders of Mindra and Saint Thomas join forces to publicize the reasons why each of the proposed laws were struck down. The public has to be alerted to the danger of the siren's song brought about by these things."

"I would ask each of you," he continued, rising from his chair, "to use your contacts, knowledge, resources and considerable skills in formulating a possible motive and line of action of how the Ja'al would implement a plan of international significance."

Melinor looked at him sharply.

"Yes," said the Nuncio. "International significance. In addition to the intelligence provided by the Alenars, the Grey Riders have also provided information that leads me to believe that the Ja'al, or the Vardish, any of their allies or a combination thereof are planning something horrible. All of this may be linked or it may not. We cannot risk a catastrophe, such as those we avoided in the past."

"Like the Firefall Conspiracy," breathed Finbar with a significant look at Melinor. "Something that hasn't been seen since - "

" - the time of my parents," finished Melinor with a grim expression. "Thanks be to God that was thwarted before a disaster befell us."

Even now, the mention of the Firefall Conspiracy gave him a chill, just as it had years ago when his father and mother, Telric and Cara, took him aside as a young man and explained the whole incident and its implications. The very idea made him shudder.

"Just so," said the Nuncio with a nod. "We have our work cut out for us. Let us pray we are successful."

The other Councilors of the Order of the Three Magi joined him as he offered up a prayer for wisdom, discernment and protection for all of them.

Melinor stared at the papers in his hand as the others stood and began filing out of the room. His mind whirred in a dozen directions, speculating. He shook his head. Without firsthand knowledge, he was blind. Sure, freelance mercenaries might provide information, but he felt a pressing need to see for himself.

I need to get a sense of the enemy, to hear their philosophies for myself, to experience people's reactions. Maybe I will perform my own investigation when the need and opportunity arise.

He looked up to see Konadar staring at him.

"I think I need a drink," said the dwarf. His eyes looked nervous and that struck Melinor — Konadar was seldom nervous.

Then he remembered that Konadar had known Telric and Cara Indidarc.

"In that case, I'm buying," replied Melinor.

Chapter Four- Pursuit

Rongit Devrin took a long sip from the goblet, savoring the flavor of whiskey. The last time he drank the good stuff, his purse had been full and his clothes more befitting his station. The warmth from the liquor would keep the chill at bay for a little while, until he could get home to his sparse room above a barn at the stables. Then, who knew? Maybe he could work enough odd jobs to make it through the winter.

"Sure you don't want some?" he asked the tall human next to him at the bar.

The man chuckled and shook his head. "I learned a long time ago to leave the dwarven whiskey to the dwarves. Gives me fewer headaches."

Rongit shrugged. "In that case, thank you for the drink. I haven't had this in ages, since - well, in a long time."

The human exchanged a glance with the woman at his side. Rongit eyed them over the rim of his cup. They had the same red-gold hair, the same attractive features, and the same green eyes: obviously related, probably brother and sister from the looks of it, or Rongit was a goblin's paramour.

The usual tumult of a late evening racketed around the tavern, raucous calls of customers mingling with the music of lute and fife and the gentler rumble of normal conversation. He looked past the pair to where two more hooded figures sat in a booth, shadowed from the rest of the busy tavern. He caught a glimpse of red-gold hair from under one of the hoods.

More relatives? Bodyguards?

"Are you a miner?" the man asked.

Rongit nodded and took another swig of liquor. "Yes, but only recently. I used to be, er, do something different."

The man looked interested. "What was that?"

"An expert in ancient histories and archeology, no less, employed by the Duke of Bildur himself," he lifted his goblet in salute. "And thanks for bringing up unpleasant memories."

The man inclined his head in a gesture of respectful apology. "Sorry. I didn't realize."

Rongit looked into his drink. Gonosz's face still hovered in his memory, triumphant and gloating at having ousted Rongit from his professorship. Rongit thought he was helping out when instead he fell right into the trap. The university could forgive many things, but plagiarism wasn't one of them, and Gonosz had made sure that all evidence to clear Rongit had been destroyed. What made the betrayal sting even more was that he was the one who had given Gonosz a second chance all those years ago — and then found out the bastard's true nature too late.

Should have killed him when I had the chance.

"You didn't cause pain," he said with a sigh. "Someone else did that, long ago."

The woman's voice sounded melodious and gentle. "I am sorry. We have all experienced that, in some fashion. But good things attained by underhanded means tend to tarnish with time."

Rongit shrugged. "We will see, I guess. I still have my knowledge, and no one can take that from me."

The woman leaned on the bar, chin in her hand. "An excellent point. And knowledge is valuable, no matter what your occupation or title. Might you know information about the lands south of here, such the lands of Torosc? Perhaps in the time before the overthrow of the ancient kingdoms?"

He eyed her. Would they be willing to pay for his time and expertise?

"Maybe," he replied, "But my memory isn't as good as it used to be."

Five gold coins appeared on the bar and disappeared into Rongit's belt purse before anyone could blink.

"It's been a long time," Rongit said, fingering his long beard, trying to hide a smile.

A platinum coin slipped onto the counter and he made that one disappear as well.

"I might know something. You have a name?"

The man hesitated for a second. "Stephen. This is Daphne."

"That's better," said Rongit, tasting his whiskey again. "I need to know who I'm working for."

Daphne's eyes looked amused. "We understand that there were certain family names associated with the royal houses. Some of those family names might still be in use."

Rongit nodded. "If they were in use by descendants of the royal families, it might. I doubt you'll find that, though. Torosc is an oppressive place, and the authorities would have incentive to wipe out those families. Naturally, I wouldn't know if they were successful or not. Bear in mind that simply having the last name doesn't necessarily mean the bearer is royalty. It would have to be a unique spelling or form, and if any royals still exist, I'm sure they'd keep their identities secret."

"Can you give us an example?" asked Stephen.

Rongit pursed his lip. "Well, let's see. Take the old kingdom of Tielo, for instance. Telor and Telorman are fairly common names in Gorostol or even southern Terenai. The same goes for people from the former realm of Turis Rhi. You'll meet a lot of people with the surname of Turin, Rhion, or Turil nowadays."

"But what if the name were Rhivan?" Daphne persisted.

Rongit nodded. "That would be one. Of course, these days, it would be most unwise to use that name openly."

Stephen nodded. "Perhaps there would be some knowledge of how the names changed to protect the old families."

Rongit let his eyes scan the teeming crowd for a second, then keeping his voice low, he leaned as if he were taking another drink.

"Quite so. And there might be a place with the proper records, for those bold enough to go looking."

Daphne and Stephen exchanged surprised looks.

"Records?" asked Daphne.

Rongit licked his lips. "Yes. Dwarven archivists were quite the commodity in the old days. After all, we have kept accurate records of our own people for centuries, and we developed many techniques to keep the records inviolate even with the passage of time."

The man motioned for him to continue. "Where might these records be located?"

Rongit stretched, then relaxed, draining the last of his whiskey. "You might want to look near Saint Benjamin or Vunethir, somewhere in the hills, probably in rocky, wild places where no one lives. Those places are far enough removed from Torosc to keep sensitive things from unworthy eyes, yet close enough at hand if needed. The caches were placed in desolate areas deliberately. Look for old stonework, regular lines in the landscape where nature wouldn't have made a straight line. Find the the sign of a sextant, but be careful. Fell and dangerous things lurk in the wilds after all this time. The archivists would have had powerful free-lance sell-swords available to accompany them in case they needed access, so they were well-protected, but for anyone else…?"

Stephen nodded. He clasped Rongit's hand firmly. The dwarf felt several coins in the human's palm.

"Thank you for your help, Master Devrin." Stephen started to get up.

Rongit slipped his hand inside his tunic and placed the extra coins into an inside pocket. "One other thing," he said.

The pair stopped.

"Don't act as if you noticed or anything, but there's some rather unsavory dwarven and human types that just came into the tavern. They're not regulars, you know. I'd be a bit careful about letting people see money in your hand. And take yourselves and your friends out by the back door, near the stables. Double back to the main road right away and head east, then curl around to the Silver Axe Inn. There's a little road out of town that cuts behind it."

Daphne reached over and gave his hand a squeeze. "Thank you. You are most kind. May God bless you."

He nodded and turned back to the bar. He sat for a while, debating whether to order another whiskey, and decided against it. The coin from the travelers might help him turn his life around, if he used it wisely. He stood to go.

He saw no sign of Daphne, Stephen or the hooded figures, but three dwarves lurked nearby, eyes scanning the crowd. Rongit took in their polished scale mail, broadswords, and axes. They weren't city guard.

With a final look around, Rongit slipped out a side door behind a group of miners coming in, then stepped to the side of the door and waited, eyes scanning the dark alley for telltale heat outlines that might indicate hidden adversaries.

He saw none. Whistling an airy tune, he walked towards the main street and turned the corner.

"Excuse me," said a man from an alleyway.

His skin crawled but he turned, trying to look nonchalant. "Who's asking?"

Any further remarks died on his lips. A tall blond human male in dark purple clothes stood in the alley. A gorgeous young human brunette accompanied him, clad in a ridiculously skimpy chainmail outfit that seemed to glow with a faint purple light - or was it the reflection of the light of the moons? At their side, a two-headed wolf strained at the leash, fiery yellow eyes glowing as it sniffed the ground.

Something about them made his heart beat faster and his palms grow sweaty. Rongit stepped back, reaching for the short sword at his belt. He opened his mouth to call for the guard.

The man held up a hand. His eyes flared bright pink and Rongit's mind grew foggy.

"Well, you know," said the man, "I was looking for our friends, but they seem to have left before we got here."

"Yes," said Rongit, "They did." Part of his brain seemed to be nagging him, as if it were trying to tell him not to do something — like talking to this friendly man and his beautiful companion.

"Do you know where they went?" the man asked, pulling the wolf closer. It whined, but the woman put one hand on each head and aimed a lazy smile at Rongit.

"Um..." Rongit tried to remember. "Is it important?"

"Oh yes. We have something we need to give them. Our pet seems to have lost their scent somehow. Most curious."

"Ah, well," Rongit said, trying without success to remember why he shouldn't be talking to this man. "They went to the south, southeast I think.

Vunethir. They were interested in records about the ancient Torosc king-doms."

The woman frowned at the man, who shrugged. "They're staying in Gorostol," he said. "Nothing we can't handle."

To Rongit, he smiled again. "Thank you, sir. You have been most help-ful. When we leave, you will turn towards the tavern, count to twenty, and turn back. You did not see us or talk to us."

"Sure," said Rongit. This was easy.

He did as commanded, turning back after twenty. He stood, blinking and shook his head.

"Why the hell am I standing in the middle of the street?" Rongit mut-tered to himself. Any thugs looking for the two humans and their guards would see him for sure.

He lurched towards an alley, trying to act like he'd had a bit too much to drink - the dwarven whiskey made it a bit easier to fake. He stopped in an alleyway and surreptitiously scanned the nearby area. Nothing seemed amiss.

There, he congratulated himself as he walked home, feeling the comfort-ing weight of coin in his pockets. He felt satisfied that the thugs from the tavern searched for their quarry in vain.

Fooled the lurking wag-halters. The brother and sister and their guards will be well on their way by now, and no one the wiser for it.

***

Brandawyn Alenar wheeled her pegasus around in the cool night air, winging away from the outskirts of Hillford, Gorostol, and heading south. She looked to her left and right, seeing Megan riding Larinor and her Aunt Daphne and Uncle Stephen riding the giant owl, Paractus.

Next stop, Vunethir.

She cast a glance down at Hillford, looking for the tavern where they met Rongit. A cluster of torch lights and lanterns scurried around the region near the Silver Axe Inn, looking like fire beetles descending on a piece of carrion in a dungeon.

Master Rongit gave good advice then, she thought with a bit of satisfac-tion. *Whoever is tracking us doesn't know we can fly, not yet. Best to keep* them in the dark as long as possible.

She turned Amicus briskly, feeling the lift of the pegasus' wings and the air ruffling her hair under her helmet as they soared through the air. She smiled. No matter how many times she did this, she never lost the wonder of flying and felt gratitude to God for letting her have the opportunity. The freedom, the speed, the almost-spiritual euphoria — it made her forget her dangerous life and perilous mission.

Brandi kept pace with the others, pointing Amicus straight to the south, following over the King's East Road. Many miles stood between them and Vunethir, and the pegasi would need rest after a couple of hours of flying. Not to worry, though. Even staying away from populated areas, they had enough food for themselves and the pegasi for the two-day flight. The most efficient caravan from Hillford to Vunethir consumed more than five days and a fast courier took at least three, but those methods depended on roads that avoided rough terrain and obstacles. Brandi could simply fly over them.

At least we were able to get supplies in Hillford, especially the magical ones. Her hand went reflexively to the tiny potion vials in her belt and under her tabard.

Her thoughts drifted as Amicus soared through the winter air, the sliver of the nearer moon Diometrius and the smaller, more distant half-moon of Kaliri casting a pale light over the cloudy skies. She moved her hand to her chest, where a letter from Eric Indidarc lay next to her skin, the closest she could get to her love for the time being.

She smiled. His last letter gladdened her heart and filled her with happiness and pride. Knight of Saint Michael's Order indeed! She made a mental note to tease him about it when she saw him next, whenever that would be. The details of the final victory over Zhinia Margoth fascinated her, especially his tale of Andyn and the Crown of Saint Alyssa, the holy relic that made it possible to match the lich power for power. Eric included a description of the battle written by Terenil DeMey, his brother-in-law, since, as he had noted, Eric had been dead at the time Andyn hammered Margoth into the dust.

A familiar and odd mix of horror and anguish, joy and wonder came over her again at the thought of her love lying dead on a battlefield, struck down by the vile sorceries of Margoth, yet preserved in the first moment of death by the magic of the Crown and then raised to life again.

Raised by the power of God Almighty shown through the relic of his blessed servant Saint Alyssa of Tor Haldin.

The chill racing down her spine was from the cool air, she decided.

She shook herself. Wool-gathering in these areas could be dangerous. To refocus, she performed a flight protocol, looking up, down, behind, left and right. Daphne caught her eye from the back of her giant owl, waving and pointing east. Brandi cast a glance that way, seeing the hills give way to mountains, thickly carpeted with forests. She raised her hand in the air and dropped it, signifying she understood.

The three flying mounts turned away from the curve of the highway below and headed over unsettled territory. The lights of another town glimmered ahead and below, but she knew the drill: avoid populated areas until they reached their destination. If agents of the evil regime of Torosc pursued them, best to give them as few opportunities as possible. In a few minutes they passed over the wild areas and yet kept the highway in sight.

They flew ever southward, always keeping the road and its scattered villages to their right. Brandi stifled a yawn. They just needed to get far enough away from Hillford to foil any immediate pursuit, then they could make camp and rest for the night. With Daphne's woodland skills and Stephen's formidable magical abilities, they would easily find a decent campsite.

Amicus suddenly whinnied and banked to the right. With an oath, Brandi gripped the saddle horn, thankful for the extra straps keeping her in her seat. She looked to her left and her mouth dropped open in alarm. A great winged lizard, fifty feet long, swept up out of the darkness towards them, its armored hide flashing green. Baleful eyes of flaming orange-red seemed to bore into her with malice. It opened its jaws and shot a stream of glowing, sizzling green liquid at her. She turned Amicus even more and the stream missed, spattering them with droplets that burned like fire. Amicus whinnied again, in pain this time.

Gritting her teeth against the sting of the acid, Brandi rolled Amicus and then curved upwards, heart in her throat as she saw another creature of the same color and malevolent aspect join its mate.

Without even stopping to think, Brandi fired off a light spell in their direction and another in front of Daphne's owl. Megan, Daphne and Stephen turned to look, then pulled their mounts to the right, towards the road.

She looked over her shoulder at the creatures, now pursuing them. Despite their large size, she knew they were the smallest and swiftest of the dragon sub-races: Sarkany. Her mouth set in a grim line. As fast as the Sarkany flew, Brandi and Megan could easily outrun them. Pegasus airspeed defied description when they felt the need but the giant owl Paractus was not a pegasus, and the group could only go as fast as their slowest member.

She looked down at Daphne, who nodded and pointed left.

Brandi and Megan looped down towards the mountains, diving to gain speed. The wind whipped over her chainmail and helmet with crisp ferocity. She shot another glance over her shoulder. One of the dragons turned to follow them while the other pursued the giant owl.

Megan pointed at herself and Brandi raised her hand overhead and dropped it again. Brandi wheeled her mount to the left, climbing and curling around. A quick look showed the dragon chasing Megan.

Perfect.

Brandi pulled her bow from its case and slowed Amicus, drawing a glittering arrow from her quiver and following the flight of the Sarkany and her sister. Using her knees and a firm command, she stopped her pegasus in a hover.

Megan and Larinor flashed past with the Sarkany in hot pursuit, spraying acid. Brandi loosed two arrows in rapid succession. Both flew true, striking the dragon in the underbelly and unleashing a burst of tiny lightning bolts each time. The dragon screeched in anger and swept away.

Brandi urged Amicus to speed and raced after Megan.

She looked over her shoulder. The wounded Sarkany turned after her, murder in its fiery eyes.

Brandi slowed Amicus, matching the dragon's speed, knowing Megan would soon come to assist. Then she growled another oath as the dragon turned away and headed up, on a collision course with Megan.

Damn it.

Brandi spurred Amicus and reached for another arrow. The Sarkany charged in at Megan. It opened its maw and spat a blast of sparkling acid at her. The liquid struck an invisible shield, surrounding them with a flare of blue light for a moment before disappearing.

Megan barrel-rolled her pegasus and dove, hissing past in a blur of hooves and wings. The dragon beat its wings, trying to match Megan's maneuver and struggling to right its course. It lashed out with its tail, narrowly missed Larinor's neck.

Heart in her throat, Brandi suddenly found herself in its path. She jerked on the reins, nearly losing her arrow, bringing Amicus around. The Sarkany lashed out again with its tail as it passed, striking Brandi in the back. She felt the air leave her lungs in a rush and fought to regain her breath, her ribs and back aching. Wincing in pain, she urged Amicus to follow.

She saw Megan slow and then make Larinor back up in midair. The Sarkany let out a screech and raced at her, jaws agape. With a sharp command, Megan made her mount stop his wings and fall towards the earth, plummeting down with his back to the ground.

What is she doing? She can't control Larinor like that. They'll crash!

The dragon soared past, snapping its jaws on empty air as its prey plummeted down. Megan put forth her hands and a sun-bright bolt of lightning snapped out at the creature, striking it dead-center with a loud crack.

Well, Brandi thought with relief. *That's a new move we haven't seen before.*

The wounded dragon gave a half-moan, half-shriek and jerked backwards in midair. It started to fall, then fluttered and regained its wings again. With an anguished cry, it limped off towards the mountain, trailing a stream of blood. Brandi levered another arrow into its back for good measure, feeling rewarded when it shrieked again and fled faster.

Megan turned her mount into a controlled dive and then curved back upwards towards Brandi. She waved to her sister and they flew off, heading towards a flash of light and whirling winged figures in the distance. Brandi followed, pulling out another arrow, hoping to help her aunt and uncle. She and Megan drew close in a matter of seconds.

She needn't have worried. Even as she watched, a flaming arrow and a white-hot beam of light both struck the second Sarkany and it faltered in mid-air. Like its fellow, it now turned and quit the battlefield, but not before loosing a jet of acid as a parting shot.

Brandi had to wheel Amicus to avoid getting hit by the random blast. As it was, some of the acid hit her pegasus in the neck and Brandi on the back of her arms and hands. She hissed in pain and Amicus whinnied, but they hovered near Paractus.

Daphne pointed down and they dove towards the dark forest, following the owl. Daphne guided them to a dark meadow, full of tall grass and a few large boulders, but devoid of any life.

Megan conjured a mage-light over their heads. Brandi removed her helmet, the sting of the acid still smarting and feeling like she had been hit by a runaway wagon. She rolled out of the saddle, leaning on Larinor for a moment and pulling a tiny vial from a belt loop. She popped the cork, downing the liquid in a sip, sighing with relief as the soreness and sting faded.

Yech. Potions taste weird. Salt, lemon and oats. Blasted wizards.

"You'll be fine, Amicus," she said, taking off a glove and gently stroking the pegasus near his injuries. She let out a slow breath, concentrating on the wounds and closing her eyes. In her mind, she saw the surface of his hide, then formed a beam of energy that heated the remaining acid until it evaporated, then a gentler stream of healing to accelerate the drawing of platelets and red blood cells to the sites. She opened her eyes, seeing the fading golden glow of her spell, only a faint scar remaining.

"Use some of that on us, why don't you?" called Daphne, sounding peeved.

"Sorry." Brandi moved over to her relatives, feeling guilty.

Daphne spoke a short word and Paractus glowed, then shrank into the shape of a small medallion, which she stuffed into a pouch as she flopped down on a nearby rock.

Brandi knelt by her, focusing her healing powers on Daphne's sprained wrist and burns. Thankfully, they weren't serious and disappeared quickly.

"Why didn't you see them earlier?" Daphne asked.

"I…" Brandi's guilty feeling remained. "I don't know. I looked before and they weren't there, then…"

"You have to be attentive, Brandawyn," Daphne scolded in a weary voice, letting her head drop back. "There are so many areas to watch when airborne, more than on the ground, and your senses are dulled."

"I know," she said. "I'm sorry."

Stephen chuckled. "Don't mind your aunt. She gets feisty when she's tired. Or burned by acid."

"Speak for yourself, brother."

Brandi used her healing magic on slash wounds on Stephen's leg and arm. Megan led her mount over to join them, craning her neck to look at her uncle's injuries.

"Claw?" she asked.

Stephen nodded. "We got too close. Could have been worse."

Daphne shook her head. "Speaking of worse, that was just the worst possible combination: two Sarkany and us riding Paractus."

Megan came to join them. "But we can keep going now, right?"

Daphne shook her head with a look at Megan. "That light and magic display, not to mention all the noise, will certainly draw attention from the outlying hamlets, especially at that altitude. Anyone following after us will have no trouble loosening tongues to talk about the battle in the sky."

Megan looked chagrined. "I shouldn't have used a lightning spell - too flashy," she berated herself.

Daphne sighed and opened her mouth but her brother stopped her, putting an arm around Megan.

"Don't blame yourself. That was well-done and drove off the dragon. Lightning Dagger or no, the Sarkany would have awoken anyone with their screeching."

Megan looked at her uncle, her pretty face less grim. "Yes, you're right. I'm worrying too much."

"What now?" asked Brandi. "Do we go on to find a campsite?"

Daphne gave the meadow a once-over. "Actually, this is pretty good. Let's just move back into the trees a bit and we should be fine."

Suddenly bone-weary, Brandi was only too glad to make a cold camp among the trees, taking third watch. She settled down into her blankets after removing her chainmail.

God, please take care of Eric and the others, she prayed, yawning and surprised that hard ground and random sticks didn't seem to bother her in her state of exhaustion. *Please let them have an easier time of it than we...*

Chapter Five- Handor of the House of Lervion

He drew back into the corner of the booth, watching the other patrons from under his hooded cloak. Pipe smoke curled up lazily from various tables where dice and card games maintained a constant hum of chatter, with coin, insults and laughter flying from one side to another. He smelled the odor of stale beer, sweat, cheap perfume and pipe leaf. The hard, wooden seat felt as if it were made of stone instead of planks from a formerly living tree, but he remained motionless. Dwarves, halflings and gnomes entered and exited the tavern. Their forms turned from shadow to person and back to shadow again as they passed through the cones of light cast by lamps hung overhead.

Handor — scion and heir of the House of Lervion (owners of the Lervion Shipping Line, Ltd), former Grey Rider, and known to others simply as Hlerv — sipped ale from his mug. Two fancily-dressed halfling girls sauntered up to a pair of gnomes and a halfling at the bar. He listened to the verbal inter-play between them, sizing up the girls' figures with his eyes.

The two gnomes looked a lot like Handor: a little over four feet tall, dark-haired and dark-eyed, with round faces, beards and sturdy builds, a mix of dwarven and halfling parentage. He took in the plain workmen's clothes, drab yet clean and new. Both of them wore shiny boots and had daggers at their belts.

The girls, on the other hand, wore dresses designed to show off their best assets. Unlike the gnomes, their faces were more narrow and refined, their eyes green or blue, and they stood only a few inches above three feet. One blonde and the other brunette, they laughed and flirted with the men at the table. Handor wondered what drove them to their current profession. Both looked pretty enough to be able to attract men without having to sell themselves. With an uncomfortable twinge, he realized they were about the same age as his sister.

After a lot of jostling between them, ribald jokes and flirtatious sashaying about, the gnomes left with the girls, leaving the halfling behind. The halfling cast a baleful look in their direction, hefted his coin purse and seemed to sag in his seat, nursing a mug.

Handor picked up his drink and joined the halfling at the bar. He sat without speaking, looking at the collection of paintings and etchings of dubious quality on the wall behind the bar.

The halfling next to him stared down at his almost-empty mug. He shot a look at Hlerv.

Hlerv kept his eyes on a painting of a naked witch dancing in a moonlit grove.

"They weren't worth the coin," he said.

The halfling's eye narrowed. "So says you. You have coin."

Handor shrugged. "But I wouldn't use it for them. I'm sure there are other places in Meridian where the company is more refined."

"Ha! Refined! Too haughty for me."

Handor nodded. "Maybe so. I just thought they looked a little, well, ratty."

The halfling next to him snorted. "Probably." He rubbed the stubble on his chin.

Handor turned to him. "Name's Hlerv."

The other halfling hesitated, then gave him a curt nod. "Jervan."

Handor dropped a few silver coins on the bar and motioned to the barkeep. "Next one's on me, in celebration of avoiding ratty ladies of the evening."

Jervan guffawed. "I like your style, Hlerv."

They knocked their wooden mugs together and drank.

"I'd like to get better accommodations but I don't really know where to go. Know of any?" Handor asked.

Jervan belched. "Oh aye. Some parts of town are really fine. Take Silvervale now. Very nice parts there, and pretty girls too. You're a gnome, so even the dwarven lasses might be tempted, though they won't spend time with the likes of me."

Handor frowned. "Too haughty, eh?"

"Aye. But the homes they come from? Whew!"

"Do you know the area well?"

Jervan measured him with his eyes. "I might."

Handor finished his ale. "I could use some directions, or a guide. And information."

Jervan shrugged. "I'm sure you could find someone."

Handor put a gold piece on the countertop. Jervan froze. Handor ignored him. The gold piece disappeared.

"What do you need to know?" Jervan asked.

"Well, where are the wealthiest parts of this Silvervale area?"

"You a thief?"

Handor smirked. "Even if I was, would I tell you?"

"Probably not. Well, there are a few. The best houses are on Bright Street. The Algidor home, the Tenpenny estate, the Lervion manor…"

"Anything interesting about them?"

Jervan shook his head. "Just mansions, really. The people in them don't mingle with us folks — leastways, not unless they need something done in the shadows."

"Ever done that kind of work?"

Jervan gave him a sidelong look. "Maybe. Maybe not."

"Well, maybe not so interesting then. Thanks anyway." Handor stood as if to leave.

"But the Lervions now," Jervan added hastily. "Come to think of it, dark doings were rumored there more than a year ago, but nothing came of it."

Handor sat back down. "Really?"

Jervan nodded. "Yeah, the two parents, gnome and halfling, passed away within a month of each other. A sudden heart attack with the husband and a rare virus fever with the wife. Then…"

"Yes?"

Jervan squirmed in his seat. "The Lervions had two children, a son and daughter, one a gnome and the other a halfling, respectively. The son disappeared soon after the funerals. There were rumors that he somehow had a hand in the deaths but most folks didn't believe it. I always thought the Lervions a bit of a standoffish lot, except for the daughter, Hannah. She's a right pretty lass, to be sure, and smart too. Helped out poor folks a lot. People don't see much of her these days though. I hear that she's spending much of her time helping her uncle Beol run the Lervion Shipping Line."

It took all of Handor's control not to snarl at the mention of his uncle's name. He covered his desire to spit by taking another swallow of the mediocre ale.

"Do they get many visitors?" he asked.

Jervan shrugged. "Sometimes. Dwarves mostly but humans too, which might seem odd, but the Lervion Line runs from Gorostol all the way up to Rokon, so I guess that makes sense."

"Any word of the brother who left?"

"No. Folks say he went off north somewhere and died plying his trade as a sell-sword mage. Others say he joined the Shrikes Assassins Guild or went to the Erleth Isles. No one's seen him for a long time. Nobody mentions him any more. His name was Handor, I think."

He shot Handor a look. "You thinking of taking on the House of Lervion? If you are, I'd advise against it. They have some pretty tough guards now, new fellows with curt attitudes. I hear there were a few attempted burglaries but the burglars never made it to trial, if you get my meaning."

Handor shook his head. "If I was the thieving kind, I'd look elsewhere. I would like to go look at the area though, if you don't mind."

"We can leave any time you like," Jervan said, setting down his mug with a thump.

Without another word, Handor stood and left the tavern, standing outside the front door and watching the traffic on the street. He looked up at the tavern sign.

"Witches Brew" indeed...

Jervan joined him. "I'll take you down Agate Street to Beryl Way if you want to see the Lervion place."

Handor shook his head. "Sounds like a place to avoid. Show me the other parts."

He followed Jervan as the halfling led him out and to a carriage stand where Handor paid for a ride to Silvervale. Once there, he listened with half an ear as Jervan told him the merits of various establishments and features of the mansions and their occupants. He paid close attention only when he mentioned the Lervion house and its business prospects, information on Beol, or rumors about what was really going on in the manor. After a suitable amount of time, he thanked Jervan, paid him with a few more gold coins, and entered the lobby of the Nine Cats Inn, waiting until Jervan had left before heading back out.

Handor Lervion knew the neighborhood like his own bedroom. He wanted Jervan to pass along knowledge of the level of vigilance in his family estate and any recent news. Now that he had that, he could set the rest of his plan into motion.

He strolled down to a cafe and lingered over an early dinner, waiting for evening before departing, heading towards the Lervion estate. There, he slipped between two buildings, watching his former home, observing the pairs of dwarven guards, watching as one of them opened the front gate to admit an ornate carriage, noting how a pattern of magical light raced around the gate at opening and closing.

He nodded. He had observed this before upon his initial arrival in Meridian. Coupled with Jervan's news, it looked consistent to him. Now he just had to figure out when to move. Still, he waited as evening came and night fell. When he saw the lamplighters moving down the street a distance away, he made his decision.

Now is as good a time as any…

Casting a furtive glance around him, he reached under the armor beneath his doublet and pulled out a small bag, no bigger than his two hands put together. He reached in and drew out an object that looked far too large to have fit into the bag, a helmet of dark purple metal that seemed to swirl and shift.

He gazed at it, remembering anew the dark day of battle near the city of Hillton, far to the north in Deran. There, the lich princess Zhinia Margoth, an undead sorceress with some unknown dark plan, invaded the kingdom from the Wilderness. She was the one who had made the object of great power in his hands, the relic that he and the other Grey Riders had wrested from its hiding place in a ruined fortress. The only problem was that the Riders wanted to destroy it, and Handor knew its ability to teleport was his only way to get back into his family home unseen. So, he simply took it when the found it. There, Handor's plan encountered its first bump in the road. Anyone who claimed the Helm teleported to Margoth's vicinity immediately, along with people nearby.

His mind strayed again, to the battlefield and the skeletal visage of the lich as she unleashed a spell that stopped his heart. His memory thereafter became a confused jumble of his past life, a quiet light that beckoned, a dark, seductive voice that whispered of power, and a tug on his heart as he saw Hannah's face. Then, impossibly, he had heard Andyn Eleandir's voice calling him back, and he had came back from death, summoned by another relic of great power: the Crown of Saint Alyssa.

He had returned to a scene that still amazed him: Zhinia Margoth reduced to a pile of ashes, a maelstrom of battle, and Andyn using the Crown to resurrect Dar Cabot. Then, fighting off grogginess, he joined his friends in defending against attacking goblin soldiers. He had used his magic skills and enchanted sword until the Riders and defenders from Hillton vanquished their foes. Then, the battle ended, he had claimed the Helm for real, taking it for his own and leaving.

He felt a pang of regret and he shook his head.

No. They don't understand. They will never understand. The Guide said they wouldn't, and he was right. I have to do this on my own.

Tired of fighting against his remorse at leaving the other Riders and impatient to get on with his plan, he slipped the Helm onto his head. He gritted his teeth against the tingling sensation as the Helm of Shadows attempted to take control of him. Using the knowledge gained months ago from the Guide, he formed an image in his mind of a complex series of symbols and equations. With an effort, he released the magic, took control of the Helm and let out a deep breath.

If he didn't know better, he thought it was getting harder to tamp down the will of Margoth's relic of dark magic. No matter. He had the skills and mental acuity to stay in command.

That stupid lich is a pile of ashes now and I'm the boss of this thing.

He looked up at the mansion, envisioned his old room in his mind, and spoke a whispering, vaguely harsh phrase. The universe warped around him and he suddenly stood in the darkness of his room.

He crouched in silence, teeth bared, hand on the hilt of Shriek, his enchanted sword. Nothing moved. His vision, augmented by the Helm to see in the infrared and ultraviolet spectra, showed him cloths still covering his furniture. It looked like no one had bothered anything for at least a year.

Now, unless they moved her to another room...

He debated whether to keep the Helm on, then decided to remove it and rely on his magical skills to remain hidden. He put his hands to the Helm and pulled it off his head slowly, suddenly feeling tired. With a muttered curse, he shoved it back into his magic bag and let out his breath slowly.

His hands shook and he fought to still them.

I'm okay. I still control that thing. Just a little edgy at being home again, that's all.

He cast a spell of invisibility on himself, stepping towards the door to the hallway and listening. With a short motion of his hand, he concentrated and used his magic to search for people in the hall. Finding none, he eased the door open and slipped out.

Listening carefully, he took a path so familiar he could have followed it blindfolded, through hallways glowing from the light of oil lamps in etched glass balls in wall sconces. Looking around the corner, he saw what he had feared, yet expected.

A dwarven guard in black chainmail lounged against the wall, his crossbow next to him.

Handor nodded to himself. It confirmed his decision to enter via his own room first to reconnoiter. If he had decided to materialize inside his sister's room and find it turned into a guard chamber or conference room, then the game would have been up. Now, he knew the guard posted at the door meant Hannah still lived and was being held prisoner.

Now he could use the Helm to get in without worrying. He quickly jammed the Helm on his head, again battling the surge of magical power. He focused on her room, attempting to materialize inside her wardrobe.

He instead ended up on top of a clothing chest. Fortunately for him, he happened to land on a flat-topped hope chest instead of a container with a rounded top. He froze in place, the dark energies of the Helm swirling around him as the magic faded.

Only the filtered light of the two moons illuminated the room through the gossamer fabric of the curtains, casting pale shadows on her bed and dresser. He saw her still form under the covers and let out a deep breath. The familiar scent of lavender made him relax.

Mother and Hannah always had the same taste in perfumes.

He removed the Helm again and returned it to the magic bag. Looking around for a moment, he identified possible locations for trapping spells and alarms, then settled into a trance and cast a detection spell, feeling his eyes become sensitive and sharp.

Two symbols glowed on the tall windows and one on the lock of her door. Still he waited. Stronger magic often took longer to discern, as many spells of that type often had obscuring and misdirection algorithms laid on them to fool the unwary.

One more symbol glowed on the floor in front of her door, on a rug.

Handor slipped off the chest, careful not to get in range of the magical sentries. First, he applied a silencing screen between her and the door, ensuring that the guard would hear nothing. Another spell placed a band of darkness around the door to screen out light. Then, putting forth his hand and extending two fingers, he cast a very simple ventriloquism spell.

"Hannah," he whispered.

The form under the covers stirred. Handor cancelled his invisibility with the wave of his hand and he flickered back into sight again.

"Hannah," he said again. "It's me, Handor. Wake up but be very quiet. I have a silencing spell on the door, but there's a guard outside."

The figure sat up.

After all this time, Handor really hadn't known how he would react when he saw his sister again. Seeing her wide blue eyes, tousled brown hair and pretty features reminded him of his mother. He felt anew a jolt of pain, remembering the day he had learned of her death and his pell-mell race to return home from the university.

Something within him awoke, a fierce love, loyalty and protectiveness. Hannah was the only family he had left, and he now knew that he would sacrifice himself to make sure she escaped her prison and went on to lead a normal life.

Partly shadowed, she drew back on the bed.

"Who's there?" she whispered, following instructions, her hand straying to the hilt of a short sword hung from a bedpost on its baldric.

She always was the more sensible of us.

"Shhh…" he held up his hand. "I've used a silencing spell near the door and put a light shunt there, but I don't want to tempt Fate. It's me, Handor."

"Handor?" she slid out of the bed, clad in her blue nightgown, the one he had seen her wear countless times.

He stepped into the moonlight.

She gasped and her hands flew to her mouth. Wordlessly, she shook her head, tears springing to her eyes as she bounded forward and threw herself into his arms.

In all his dealings with the Grey Riders, he regretted now that he had never let much affection grow between them, for he remembered what it felt like to hold a dear family member and know that he was loved. And the Riders had tried to break past his shell — but no, Hannah came first.

"Handor! Oh Handor! I thought you were dead!"

"Not yet," he replied in a gruff voice, feeling tears sting his eyes. "Not yet, Hannah. But I'm back."

She hugged him tightly for long seconds, then he pulled back. She held him at arm's length.

"Where have you been?"

"North."

"And? Doing what? Why didn't you write?"

He hesitated. "I thought about it many times, but I knew Beol might intercept my letters and use them to try to trick you into signing over the inheritance."

She shook her head, mouth set in a firm line. "I would never have believed him. And he knows what will happen if anything happens to me - our safety net, remember?"

Handor shifted uncomfortably. "Yes but I was still poor and not very powerful, and his connections - "

" - have gotten worse," she finished for him, drawing him to the bed. "Time for that later. Let's have a look at you."

She drew the heavy curtains across the window and lit a candle with a wave of her hand, a simple spell he had taught her years ago when they were both children.

He gave a wry smile.

Her eyes narrowed as she looked him over. "You look different. What's happened to you?"

"Of course I'm different. I'm a year and two months older."

"No…" she said slowly. "Come look in the mirror."

He did so, standing next to her in front of her dressing mirror. At three feet nine, he still stood three inches taller than she, but then he saw his own face and it took all his control not to jump.

Yes, he still had a dark beard and dark eyes and the build of a gnome, a half-breed between his dwarven father and halfling mother, but his face - it seemed to have taken on almost a skeletal aspect and a pale sheen.

By the gods, what's going on with my eyes?

He stared at his image. His pupils seemed to be misty black, with a swirl of deep purple. He shivered involuntarily.

It's nothing! Probably the aftereffects of using the Helm so often in a short period of time.

"I've had, er, experiences," he replied slowly. "Things I've seen, things that have happened to me. They leave an aftereffect."

"What kinds of things?" she asked softly. "Dear Handor, you look like Death grabbed you by the soul and squeezed the life out of you."

Something tickled at his mind and he became impatient. What did she know? She always had talents in the martial areas anyway. She studied history and ancient battles and strategy, like her grandfather, General Lervion, the one who started the company that now bore his name. She had no magical inclination other than what he taught her.

Something next to his chest thrummed, something in an enchanted bag under his armor. Thoughts sprang unbidden into his head.

Simple little fool! How can she appreciate the secret mysteries and ancient power it takes to control the Helm of Shadows? She's just a meddlesome female.

With an effort, he forced himself to ignore the voice of the Guide, echoing in his memory from long ago, in the Chamber of Decision.

"It's an aftereffect of the magic I used to get in here," he said in a clipped voice, part of him amazed at how brusque he sounded. "It's a wizard thing. Don't worry about it. It will pass."

She led him back to the bed. "It makes you look…"

"Stop, Hannah. I know what I'm doing."

He didn't meet her gaze but felt her eyes on him.

"Of course, big brother. I trust you. But now, look at me."

He did so.

She took his hands in hers. "What do you hope to accomplish? If you have magic powerful enough to bring you here, can you use it to take me out?"

Why did she ask so many questions? Something nagged his mind again, suggesting that he just leave her here, since she obviously knew nothing about true power or how it was wielded.

He shook himself. *What's the matter with me?*

He sighed. "No, actually, I can't. I have a magic item. It allows me to teleport in and out of places, and my other skills ensure I can't be easily detected, but it only works for me. I'm going to get you out, but I have to figure out another way. If I can get a good idea of what's changed since I left - "

She nodded. "Is it this magic item that makes you look so exhausted? Worn out?"

He felt a vibration from the Helm inside its magic bag and the Guide's voice whispered inside his head.

This stupid woman is meddling in things she doesn't understand! To the Nine Hells with her!

He stood up quickly, trying to master his sudden belligerence, feeling a growing unease. He tried to remember how much she meant to him, how she was his only family left, how much he cared for her. Suddenly tired of the mental wrestling match against the Helm, he pulled the bag out from under his armor and cast it on the pillows.

The irritating tingle in his head faded, the whispering voices ceased and he turned to her with a sigh, feeling more in control again. "No. Well, yes. The item in that bag has effects on me. I just have to be careful about how many times I use it. But, no, Hannah, I'm in control."

Her eyes strayed to the bag, but she made no move towards it. The concern on her face meant she knew something was awry.

"Of course. But I don't know how this thing is going to help me escape."

He took a deep breath, then sat. "I don't either, but now I'm inside and I can try to figure something out. Tell me everything you know."

"Of course," Hannah said, sitting back against the headboard. "After father's funeral, mother was sad, of course, but then seemed to be finding a way to cope. We leaned on each other a lot, as you know. She consulted with Beol often on company matters and he went with her to meetings and on inspections. I don't think she really liked it, because Beol was only father's half-brother anyway and she never cared for his attitude and habits, but she put up with it. Then when she got sick…" her voice trailed off.

"I never should have gone back to the university after father died," he muttered, a bitter taste in his mouth.

She put a hand on his. "We all needed to get back to something normal, and you going off to study was what you needed. I was all set to return to the military academy when mother became ill, so I had to stop to take care of her."

"Was the illness really that sudden?"

"Yes. Very sudden. No matter what the healers and doctors did, she would get better for a day, then worse. The end was very fast."

He met her eyes. "You know I suspected Beol."

"Yes. So did I. Not that we can do anything about it."

"We'll see about that. Have you learned anything more?"

She shrugged. "Beol has the ear of the town council, and as my guardian per the will, I have to follow his direction. I can't strike out on my own until next year, at any rate. However, he knows we have information against him, and is afraid to do anything to me in case we left instructions to publicize everything if anything happened to us. Which we did, of course."

"He won't ever let you out alive, Hannah. He thinks I'm dead and now you're in the way of the inheritance."

She hit her fists into a pillow in frustration. "I know you suspect him, but there's nothing that can prove a connection - "

" - there is, Hannah. I found more evidence, but he had his goons go into my room just before I ran away. They took everything. Then they tried to have me killed."

"That's when you left!" She dropped her hands in her lap. "Now it all makes sense. I didn't know why you suddenly disappeared. Beol said you had left to go seek your fortune, but I never dreamed it was true."

They sat in silence for a while. Despite the situation, despite the tension of their common fate, despite the circumstances, he felt a warm, comforting feeling in her presence. It was a premonition of a brighter day, as if they had a future outside of their family and all its dark machinations.

"You said it was worse?" he asked.

She nodded, looking grim. "Yes. Uncle Beol keeps the standard routes and deliveries and customers, of course - it would look like something was wrong if he suddenly dropped them. But I've seen…"

Her voice dropped to an even lighter whisper. "The Shrikes. He meets with them on occasion and sends them off on tasks. He doesn't think I know, but I've seen them."

He felt a chill. "Shrike assassins," he breathed.

Her eyes looked haunted, frightened. "And worse. There are others who visit. Humans and elves. I think they're Ja'al cultists. They have Cerberus hounds."

Handor's chill travelled down his spine and settled in his stomach, where it became a gnawing fear. Cerberus creatures could detect almost anything, as they had two or more heads and superior senses of smell and sight. Rumors even said they could track invisible creatures to a certain extent and were almost impossible to surprise.

"How many?"

"There are at least four, I think, in the cellars. Handor, Beol has had workers going down into the cellars for more than three months now. He's building something, or extending the area for some vile purpose. I don't know what's going on, but it scares me. Assassins, Ja'al, Cerberus hounds…"

Despite her competent demeanor and determination, she looked scared and he hugged her, more resolved than ever to protect her and get her away from their now-accursed home. He fought against the feeling of helplessness, trying not to give in to despair, aching for what she had gone through this last year, held against her will by someone she suspected of murder with no way to escape.

I'll change that. If I have to die trying, I'll change it.

"Don't worry, Hannah. I'll find a way out. I promise."

Chapter Six - Trail of the Serpent

"I could get to like this," said Andyn Eleandir, relaxing in her seat.

Buck Bydecy raised his glass of wine in salute. "Here's to Christian celebrations!"

She gave him a brilliant smile and raised her own glass in response and the two drank. Buck took a small meat pastry from the platter on the table and munched on it, enjoying the savory beef and mushroom filling.

Buck's eyes roamed over the scene before him. The domed transparent roof of the Paladin's Rest Inn soared overhead to a height of thirty feet at its crest, enchanted with a resistive heating spell that melted snow as soon as it touched the glass. Another enchantment shunted the melted snow aside and left ribbons of water running down the dome, illuminated by the lights below so that they looked like shiny snakes. Dar had told him that the massive dome was removed in sections in the spring, using airborne mounts and levitation, a spectacle that drew onlookers from all over the city.

A gorgeous elven maiden in a silver and white gown floated past Buck's table. Hairpins in the shape of silver snowflakes glittered against her honey blonde.

And I could get used to the scenery. Yes, nice scenery indeed, he thought, watching her movements as she slid into the crowd.

The rooftop atrium looked like a well-tended garden. In fact, as Dar had told him, it served as a greenhouse in winter for the Inn, providing fresh herbs and vegetables for the kitchen. In addition to planters with produce, other pots held decorative trees and shrubs.

Buck had to admit he appreciated the arrangement. He remembered Druidess Carine's words about how the city tried to avoid destroying nature. Such a verdant place protected by magic in winter spoke well of the owner's intent to follow that philosophy and even do it one better.

He wondered if Carine would have felt comfortable at the party among the greenery and the people and imagined her in an evening dress (an enticing picture, to say the least).

She probably would, he decided.

"Where's Eric?" he asked Andyn.

Andyn peered out at the crowded atrium, eyes searching. The diameter of the rooftop level of the inn measured more than a hundred feet and with this many people, it was easy to lose someone. Couples, groups and families swirled around the pathways, gathered around the three open bars, or sat conversing at tables among the plants and trees. The soft music of a band of minstrels floated in the air above the hum of conversation. Everyone wore their best finery, typically in colors of silver, white, red or green. Buck guessed there were at least two hundred people in attendance.

The Count of Harlinsville is a wealthy man, he surmised. *Even though there are multiple parties going on at once, it must cost a pretty penny to have a celebration here.*

"There," said Andyn, sitting back in her chair and pointing. "With Terenil and Saren, of course."

Buck eyed Eric's untouched goblet. "A pity to waste this, then," he added, appropriating his friend's wine.

Andyn frowned at him. "Now you owe him another."

"Plenty to go around," he replied, indicating a servant nearby with another platter of dainties.

Andyn tossed her head, her blonde hair held back by her golden lady's circlet. Amethysts flashing in the lamplight. "Well I, for one, am going to take a little stroll and see what they're up to."

The servant stopped, proffering the tray, and Buck inspected the arrangement of treats. He waved a hand at Andyn. "I'll keep an eye on our table. You go ahead."

Andyn stood, smoothing her emerald, one-shoulder gown. "Suit yourself. Just don't spoil your appetite. I hear they have roast boar and turkey for the main course."

Buck nodded, popping another pastry into his mouth, this one filled with vegetables and cheese.

He watched her glide into the crowd. Many other people watched her as well. Though Buck would always think of her as a comrade-in-arms, even he had to admit the dress showed off her lithe curves to maximum advantage. Barring that, the glittering pin of the Lichslayer and knightly circlet of the Order of Mindra served to attract attention.

He smiled to himself. On his own part, he had already made several promising contacts with some of the young ladies present. Of course, half of them were Christian and a few were slightly inebriated, but he shrugged off these facts. He wasn't going to let that stop him. It promised to be an entertaining evening.

He watched Andyn join Eric, Saren and Terenil. Though Eric and Terenil looked resplendent in clothes of dark blue and silver or forest green and white, respectively, Saren dazzled every time he looked at her. A stunning black dress with white and gold thread graced her beautiful body and brought her white horns and bat wings into sharp contrast. Her gold coronet sparkled brilliantly from atop ebony tresses, sapphires and emeralds casting liquid fire at every nod of her head. The dress had an open back that allowed her wings free movement. A jeweled dagger hung at her side, mute testimony to the fact that Tallemar's lady was still hunted by enemies.

He watched as she looked behind her to make sure she had room, then unfurled her wings to their full six-foot span and furled them again. No one in the atrium seemed to take notice.

Saren greeted Andyn warmly and introduced her to an elderly man and his wife next to Terenil.

I'll never get over Saren's eyes...

He always found he had trouble meeting them: Dark, black as midnight, with a hint of swirling rainbow colors in the pupils that mesmerized the unwary. It was as if her half-daemon heritage and her allegiance to the Christ-God reminded him that those who appeared evil could always turn to good.

If she wasn't so damn sweet all the time, I might actually dislike her.

"Ah!"

He saw what he wanted: a floating beer pitcher that signaled an air golem standing at the ready. He motioned to it and the force-field drifted over to him, then delivered the ale right into his goblet. Buck waved his hand and the air golem returned to its post.

He turned to pick up another pastry from the platter and found it empty. Connor Lomin smiled at him from across the table, wiping his mouth with a napkin.

He raised an eyebrow. As usual, Connor's natural stealth and small size ensured he could filch the pastries from under Buck's nose without even trying hard.

"I don't know much about these Christian celebrations," Connor said around a mouthful of raspberry tart, "but I sure like them. I especially like that they have the parties at least a week prior to the actual festival. Too bad this one is only once a year."

Buck gave a significant look at the platter, which had held three other snacks not moments ago. "I don't know how you manage to put it away so fast," he said.

Connor shrugged. "Two kinds of people in my house growing up: the quick and the hungry."

Buck snorted in derision, then quaffed his ale, enjoying the heart, nutty flavor. He looked at his empty goblet with appreciation.

Even better than the ale in Forester.

He saw Eric, Saren and Terenil turn and head towards them, followed by Andyn and the elderly couple. From the look in Eric's eyes, he knew this was not a social call.

Damn. I don't want to talk shop tonight.

He stood. "I'll be back in a minute," he said to Connor. "I have to see a young lady about something."

"Really? Who is it this time?" asked a voice from behind him.

Buck turned, exasperated, to see a smiling Dar Cabot walk up their table, clad in dark green finery of his own.

"Have you been taking lessons from Connor?" he asked with deep suspicion.

Dar's smile brightened. "Maybe."

Buck turned to go but Dar stopped him. "I think you better hear this."

"Oh, come on. We're supposed to be involved in revelry, not hatching plots."

Dar's eyes remained steady. "I know. And letting Eric do something in a small way tonight will make him feel like he's accomplishing something. Then we can get back to the party and he won't be so edgy."

Buck sighed. "Oh, all right. It's better than watching him fidget."

Eric arrived at their table. Buck, Dar and Connor bowed to the DeMeys. "Your Excellencies," Buck said.

In this public setting, formality reigned. Saren and Terenil accepted the courtesies due their rank and inclined their heads in response.

Andyn brought up the rear with the older couple in tow. "This is Count Dunston and Countess Arlene of Harlinsville. They have a most unusual tale to tell."

Visions of a pleasurable evening in the company of tipsy, beautiful young women vanished from Buck's brain and he stopped himself from sighing again.

"Your Excellencies," he said, bowing once more.

Count Dunston, a slim gentleman with an impeccable white goatee and mustache, nodded to him and sat. He looked to be at least seventy, if not more. His wife, a motherly-looking middle-aged woman with brown hair and shrewd green eyes, smiled as she slipped into a seat next to him.

Everyone took a seat. Buck waited, noting the age difference between the Count and Countess: at least a dozen years if not more.

"Count Dunston has some interesting information for us, Grey Riders," said Terenil with a look at the old man.

"Yes," Dunston said in a remarkably strong voice. "When I heard that the Grey Riders were at the party, I simply had to bring the matter to Lord Terenil's attention. We've had a distressing run of assassinations in Harlinsville."

Buck sat up straighter. "Assassinations?"

Connor shot him a look. "Tell us, Excellency. What do you know?"

The count shrugged. "Not much. My intelligence service has not been able to find anything of substance. Just a puddle of blood in the street somewhere in one of our neighborhoods, sometimes a scrap of clothing — and the tracks of a large hound or wolf. No one hears or sees anything. The body is simply found elsewhere the next morning."

"How many killings?" asked Dar.

"Six in the last four weeks," said Countess Arlene in a mellow, almost husky voice, "We have a map of the locations we can provide. Our urban trackers can follow for a while but they lose the trail on the rooftops."

Buck watched his comrades, seeing them lost in thought. The scroll they had captured in Alrihan mentioned Harlinsville and the Sign of the Serpent. With assassinations in that city, Buck knew there was a connection.

"Time of death?" asked Connor, sipping his wine.

"Different times in the early morning or at night." The Countess answered, looking at Buck over the rim of her glass. He felt an unnerving feeling that she weighed and measured him.

"Who were the victims?" asked Andyn.

"People of means," said the Count. "Investigation showed each of them to be involved with, shall we say, unsavory elements in society. Some were in debt, others had a hidden addiction, at least two were cheating spouses."

Eric sat back in his seat. "Crossed Swords targets if ever I heard of them."

"I suspect magic," noted Terenil.

Saren nodded. "The fact that no one hears a sound is very unusual. I think a mage is involved somehow. And a large dog? It could be a fell hound, but those are hard to hide, which only makes it that much more likely that it's a mage with a guard animal, or maybe a lycanthrope."

The Count fixed Dar with bright blue eyes. "The question is, are the Grey Riders available to help? With your ability to patrol from the sky, you have an advantage."

Connor placed his goblet back on the table. "Why not ask the Royal Air Service? They have more mounts than we and know your city better."

Count Dunston pursed his lip. "There are other matters occupying the Air Force these days. This needs to be done discreetly, without official involvement, if you catch my meaning. There are certain allies who want to make sure the iron hand of justice is felt by those responsible without publicizing anything. Due to circumstances, the situation is delicate. I'm sure you understand."

Buck looked at Eric. He knew his friend had to relax, to lay off his relentless quest to bring his parents to justice. Despite his friendly and optimistic demeanor, Eric's obsessive streak now drove him — that and a personal sense of responsibility for the people who had caused so much devastation to Andyn and her family.

Andyn's had told him that he needn't push himself so hard. Buck could tell Eric had a hard time holding to her advice.

"We are on a different mission for the Crown here in Oakmoor, so we will have to discuss it among ourselves," Andyn said after a long pause. "However, since your problem also involves investigation in Oakmoor, I see no reason not to help you."

Count Dunston beamed. "Excellent. I had hoped so. Countess Arlene will handle the details for you. It is her charge to be the liaison with our security service. In the name of the people of Harlinsville, I thank you."

He rose and the Riders rose with him, bowing as he and the Countess left with the DeMeys to join others in the swirl of the party.

Buck and his friends stood silently for a while.

Dar spoke casually, as if he were mentioning the weather. "Seems like we might need a little assistance in dark places."

Eric readjusted his cloak. "If the Papal Nuncio can spare him. I don't want to go to the well too often."

Connor shrugged. "He's usually enthusiastic in helping us. I don't think it will be a problem."

Andyn nodded, hiding a smile. "I think our dear Gorlak considers this a privilege, compared to his previous life. I'm sure he'll jump at the chance."

***

"Your Eminence."

"Yes, Detlef?"

Edward Simpson turned from contemplating the gardens outside the rectory. Detlef Richards bowed as he entered the study.

"Your, er, Gorlak is here."

Edward smiled. "Ah yes. Show him in."

He turned as a short, bandy-legged figure entered and bowed low.

"Eminence," the figure said in a low, guttural voice.

Edward nodded as Gorlak straightened. "Good to see you again, Gorlak."

He met the goblin's dark eyes steadily. Gorlak looked for all the world like any other of his race: a little taller than a halfling, with a burly physique and short, dark-brown fur, two small horns on his forehead, monkey-like features and sharp little teeth. Yet Gorlak differed from his kin in two important points. First, he wore the livery of Edward's personal retinue (dark blue and gold). Second, instead of peering at the world with suspicion and furtive greed, he looked at Father Edward with a mixture of friendliness and curiosity. This by itself marked him as someone unique, for goblins spent most of their short lives in pursuit of food, slaves and treasure at the expense of others and often allied themselves with evil cults or rulers.

So different from the time Eric Indidarc brought him here those months ago after the Battle of Hillton. I thought he would bolt at the first opportunity, or maybe steal something, or perhaps die of fright. But no: he stayed and learned and grew.

"What news, Gorlak?" Father Edward said, motioning to a nearby chair as he sat.

Gorlak vaulted into the seat and settled himself. "Grey Riders ask me to find evil plots in Harslin…Harlasin… Harlinsville."

Edward suppressed another smile. The common tongue of Humana came to Gorlak with difficulty. Sometimes his pronunciations made Edward want to chuckle, but he wouldn't dream of hurting the goblin's feelings because he tried so hard. Gorlak even told him he wanted to learn Elven, a remarkable statement considering that goblins and elves hated each other with a passion.

"Did you find anything?"

Gorlak nodded, smiling and showing his fangs. "Many things, Eminence. People of Darkness speak secrets to simple goblin in the night. They see I wear symbol of Ja'al and carry letter from Commander Zavalin of Fourth Battalion, a forgery you give me. It is most excellent forgery. Then they tell what I asks. Using gold to buy them beer and liquor helps."

Edward nodded again. "You are sure they suspect nothing?"

Gorlak nodded, his grin wider. "Yes. People don't consider one goblin. Think me stupid. Too hard on brains to think of goblin working for High Priest of Christ-God."

Now Edward did chuckle. "An excellent way to put it. What did they say?"

Gorlak turned more somber. "They tell of a dark agent in Harlins…ville. One with shape change, but also magic. Some of the dark ones afraid of it. This agent prized by assassins of Crossed Sword. Agent cost much gold."

"Do you think this agent is that highly placed? Maybe working for Harkin

Hylar himself?"

Gorlak considered this. "Maybe. Agent only do special tasks. Not hear of other agents like this before. Probably only get orders from high bosses."

A shape-changing wizard? Or priest of some evil cult? Edward frowned.

"This sort of enemy will be difficult to bring down," he mused.

Gorlak nodded. "They say this agent change into savage thing, not human."

Edward mulled over this for a while, nodding slowly as his mind turned over the information. Regarding his helper at last, he said, "This is all good information and I will pass it along. Speaking of shape-change, do you need your illusion ring recharged?"

"Oh, yes, please. I almost forget. It not seem as bright any more."

"Not a problem. Ask Detlef to have one of the mages see to it."

Inexplicably (or perhaps not), Edward felt more protective of his little goblin spy than of any of his other agents. His small size and the fact that he could be killed outright by unknowing city guards made the Cardinal reluctant to expose him to danger. Thus, he equipped him with an illusion ring that covered Gorlak with the form of a young halfling man. As long as he didn't speak, it worked well enough to allow him to travel around most Deranese cities unhindered. Not one to leave things to chance, Edward also gave Gorlak a special medallion that he could use in case he was accosted by overzealous police. The medallion glowed with magic on command and projected an image of Edward pronouncing that the bearer served him and the Church.

On a rational basis, he probably didn't need to worry. In his life prior to capture by the Grey Riders, Gorlak showed a remarkable talent for survival. He had served as a scout, sergeant, and captain for various evil leaders, including the late Halkith, a Ja'al commander, and the unlamented King Vorquul of the Whiteskull goblin tribe, an erstwhile ally of the equally unlamented Zhinia Margoth, lich sorceress. Both Vorquul and Margoth perished on the field at Hillton more than three months ago. Gorlak's resume' showed resiliency and capability with all manner of skills.

"What is your assessment, then?" Edward asked, leaning back in his chair and crossing his arms. "Given the fact that the Grey Riders, among others, have tried to draw out the Crossed Swords by posing as customers, would that be a possible method to find this shape-changer?"

Gorlak looked pleased, as he always did when Edward treated him like a trusted advisor. The Cardinal thought it probably came from a lifetime of being treated like a tool or trained animal as opposed to a thinking creature.

"I thinks Cross-swords may take bait. I hear things when searching, whispers in taverns and alleys. Grey Riders causing problems for Cross-swords assassins. They unsure of who is really customer and who is agent now, but need to do death-work to earn money. Ja'al not pay if assassins not cause trouble in cities by killings."

Edward considered this. "Cause trouble? So you're still sure that all the recent mayhem is a distraction?"

Gorlak nodded vigorously. "I sure. I hear things in all missions for Eminence. Think on them. Only thing that make sense. No other purpose because..." he appeared to search for the right word.

"Random?"

"Yes! Not focused. No missions to take over city or country or to gain wealth or slaves. Just cause trouble."

"I see." Edward sat in silence for a while. Like Gorlak's evil former employers, he recognized the little goblin's superior intelligence, instincts and insight, particularly honed now that he was in a benign environment where he didn't have to struggle to survive all the time. Gorlak showed himself to be an eager student in everything Edward and his staff tried to teach him.

"Well, this is good work, Gorlak," he said and stood, noting with pleasure that Gorlak smiled and sat up straighter at the words of praise. "If you would provide the list of addresses and your notes to Detlef, he will make sure to get them to the Riders for their next move."

Gorlak hopped off the chair and bowed again, his hand on the silver dagger in his belt. "Yes, Eminence."

"Is there anything I can do for you, my friend? I know you had showed interest in one of Detlef's magic items — the cloak of flying, was it?"

Gorlak hesitated. "Yes, but not sure want to try without practice. I not like falling."

Edward laughed. "Gorlak, you are a breath of fresh air! I like your blunt way of addressing things: very goblin-like."

Gorlak looked at him quizzically. "No goblins where you come from?"

Edward regarded Gorlak for a second, then his gaze shifted to the gardens. "No, Gorlak," he replied after a while, "Where I come from there are no goblins, no elves, no dwarves, not even a halfling."

His thoughts wandered momentarily to a white shore and a setting sun with one moon in the sky, then he stopped himself. Gorlak waited expectantly. Edward shook himself from his reverie.

"Forgive an old man, Gorlak. With respect to the cloak, of course I'll ask Detlef to teach you how to use it."

"Thank you!" Gorlak looked immensely pleased as he turned to go and then hesitated. "Eminence?"

"Yes?"

The goblin fidgeted. "Do the Lord and Lady of Tallemar need anything? Spy work maybe?"

Edward paused before answering. "Well, you've completed four assignments recently without a break. I think you need a little time off for Christmas. What do you say I contact Lady Saren and see if you can stay with them for a while?"

Gorlak's eyes shone and he actually looked shy. "Yes, Eminence. I think that great idea. Thank you."

"Consider it done then."

With another bow, Gorlak left.

Edward felt a wave of fatigue come over him and he sat back down again, feeling the pain in his abdomen just under his rib. Despite the medications, despite the magical healers at his disposal, he could feel his illness growing, not diminishing. In this world, he aged differently and he had certain advantages, but he also knew his time grew short and his journey to meet the Lord would happen — not today, but soon.

The feeling passed and he sighed, then chuckled at Gorlak's eagerness to go to Tallemar. Of all the people in the world, the goblin latched onto Lady Saren as his favorite. Edward couldn't figure it out. By all rights, Gorlak should have been petrified at the sight of Saren, half human and half daemon. Indeed, to hear Dar Cabot tell it, Gorlak's first encounter with Saren had made the goblin quake in terror, yet she won him over with charm and kindness. Now the goblin's devotion to the Countess of Tallemar verged on the fanatical. Maybe he felt an affinity with her because they were similar — they served the Light but looked more like creatures of Darkness. Or maybe he found in her a mother-figure he had never had growing up in the uncaring and vicious society of goblin-kind.

Gorlak also treated Terenil with a healthy respect as Saren's mate, a deference that Terenil rewarded with training in just about any martial skill Gorlak requested.

An odd little fellowship, certainly... but heartwarming in its way. God's mysterious ways are even more incomprehensible in this world of Damora.

He stood. "Detlef? After you send Gorlak's notes to the Riders, I'd like you to deliver a message to Lady Saren for me."

Chapter Seven - The Hound of Harlinsville

Terrell Hylar hid his disdain behind an expression of disinterest.

"Impatient?" he asked.

The auburn-haired woman sitting across the table from him let out an exasperated sigh, the feather on her mauve hat bobbing with every move of her head.

"I'm used to more prompt service, I will tell you," she replied. She toyed with the crystal wine goblet on the polished wood table. "Why must they be so secretive about this?"

Terrell suppressed a smirk. "They are assassins, Mistress Jandren. They have to be secretive."

She rolled her eyes. "My maidservants are on the spot when I call. Why can't these Sword-crossers show up on time anyway?"

"Crossed Swords, ma'am."

"Whatever," she said with a bored wave of her hand. Her voice slurred just a bit. "I just want this stupid business taken care of."

After two glasses of wine? A lightweight indeed.

Terrell leaned back in his seat, crossing his arms over his chest and playing the part of neutral broker of dark deeds. The late afternoon sunlight shone through the carved glass windows and made a rainbow of blue, red, green and orange on the tabletop. High overhead, the ceiling arched up to a skylight of frosted glass, now dusted with snow.

Tall potted plants and woven screens sectioned off the dining room for

81

privacy. Not that Terrell had to worry: most of the staff in the place were bought and paid for and wouldn't tell anyone of his latest potential customer. He regarded the woman for a moment.

She acts like a spoiled brat. Probably close to the truth, if she's not a royal spy.

"I'm sure they will provide what you need, ma'am," he replied after a moment. "The bonus you have offered is certainly generous."

She waved a hand as she downed more of her wine, then wiped her mouth with a napkin. "Money is no object. After all, I need special helpers in order to get Victor out of the way. He can fight, you know, and has magical items. Your assassin friends can't just try to plug him with crossbow bolts out of the dark."

Terrell nodded and considered the background information they had on Victor Jameson. Unfortunately for the Guild, the heat applied by the Grey Riders and Royal Intelligence these days cut down on the amount of independent information out there. What they had indicated that Jameson preferred trying out women of all kinds, including the delicacy across the table. However, Terrell, as one of his father's picked commanders, knew the possibility that this woman was actually a spy increased with the amount of attacks the Crossed Swords sustained.

Damned Grey Riders.

He sorely wished his father had decided to keep the three hippogriffs they stole a decade ago, instead of selling them for their ridiculously high asking price to the Church of Vardu, of all people.

Too much trouble to train riders and maintain the mounts, his father had said. Well, that would come back to haunt them now, just as Terrell had warned him. The Guild had no airborne capability to counter the Riders. Instead, they resorted to doubling guards, using magical sentries and being extra careful about any new contracts in order to protect themselves.

"You know the going price for the Serpent, don't you?" he asked.

She frowned. "Yes. And I've offered 1200 gold as a bonus. But I want Victor dead, do you hear? He's slept with his last trollop. I won't be made a fool of."

Neither will the Guild.

He pushed his chair back. "If you will excuse me for a minute, ma'am. I believe I saw our signal. I will meet with the agent of the Crossed Swords now."

She looked even more exasperated, if that were possible. He bowed and headed back towards the bar, then slipped around a screen leading to the more secluded portions of the restaurant. Terrell knew he took a risk meeting anyone here at the Silver Griffon, but it actually was less risky than some of the dingier parts of Oakmoor. It didn't play to type for the Crossed Swords to take contracts in the wide-open dining room of an upscale tavern in Harlinsville. Of course, it helped that they were here during a weekday more than an hour before the evening rush.

He looked back through the screen at Mistress Jandren. A plump woman in a dark purple dress stepped up next to him.

"Well?" the woman asked, turning her round, friendly face to look at him.

"I'm not sure."

She fluffed her greying dark hair. "Whether to take the job or whether she's a spy?"

"Both."

She sniffed. "She's certainly a handsome little harlot, I'll give her that. What's the price?"

"Four thousand, and a bonus of twelve hundred if it's done tonight."

"Jilted lover?"

"Lover who doesn't know to appreciate what he has. Too adventurous, if you get my meaning."

"Well," Juliette Tennyson said, turning away with a swish of fabric. "The price is certainly good. I think she's a spy, so take the money, then kill her and whoever poses as the lover."

"We can't kill off our clients, Jules. Bad for business."

Her soft voice floated back at him. "She's not a client. My contacts say Lord Dunston hired freelancers to take out the Serpent and I think she's one of them. Get it done, Terrell. Your father will approve."

Terrell turned back to watch the woman at the table. He bit his lip. Making money by murder was difficult enough without getting a reputation for instability, and if the Crossed Swords had obtained anything in their long history, it was the mark of an organization known for discretion, honored contracts, and completed jobs. If Juliette was wrong…

He straightened his doublet and strode around the screen again, approaching the table with a smile.

"Good news," he said with a short bow. "I think we can accommodate you, Mistress Jandren. If you will give us the time and place for the job, we will get it done tonight."

***

"There she goes," said Eric Indidarc, watching Andyn flounce out of the Silver Griffon Inn and wait at a covered bench in front of the building, looking for a carriage. "She is such a good actress. She should go to work for a spy agency."

"Though it did take her a long time to dye her hair," noted Connor Lomin, crouched on the rooftop next to him. "Think she got something?"

Andyn tossed her head and flipped her braid over her left shoulder, smoothing her purple velvet dress.

Eric nodded. "That's the signal. Is Dar in place?"

"Yes. So is Buck."

Eric reached into his belt pouch and drew out a ball of silver that fit neatly into his palm. He hefted it.

Connor gave him a look. "Are you sure about that thing?"

"Melinor made it. Believe me, it will work."

Eric inspected the ball. Smooth as glass, its surface was made entirely of silver. Below the shiny shell, a volatile substance that Melinor called "thermite" surrounded a smaller ball at the center of the sphere. Both the thermite and the inner ball contained small purple crystals, sensitive to magical energy. Eric had to be careful with spells around it. The inner ball contained something Melinor called "nitric glycerine" and he had warned Eric about its explosive power.

Connor didn't sound too confident. "That thing will kill a lycanthrope?"

Eric shook his head. "Not kill, wound. We just want to hurt it and make it run away, so we can follow it to its lair."

Connor slapped his shoulder. "Look now."

A carriage drawn by two brown horses pulled up. At the same time, one man, then another, casually walked out of the tavern, approaching a hitching post where steeds waited. Andyn waved to the carriage driver and climbed in with an imperious order. The carriage headed off to the west.

"Time to go," said Eric. He slipped back and walked to a level spot on the roof, where Niveral and Phantom waited. A few flakes of snow floated by them, white crystals of ice in the twilight.

He put a hand on a brooch pinned to his cloak and whispered a command word, then held out his arm. A silvery glittering field sprang up above his wrist and quickly formed into a brown hawk with black-tipped feathers that regarded him with beady eyes.

"Go Stealth," he whispered. The hawk took wing and soared off, following the path of Andyn's carriage.

Eric shifted his vision and now saw everything through Stealth's eyes. The hawk soared lazily over the suburb of Harlinsville, over winding paths, straight boulevards, snow-covered parks and many white rooftops. He clearly picked out Andyn's coach as well as the three horsemen who followed her. One street away to the south, another pair of horsemen matched her progress.

"Three following the coach, two others to the south," he reported to Connor.

The halfling nodded, swinging into the saddle. "Are they far enough now?"

"Yes. We can go."

Eric mounted Niveral and both pegasi lifted off from the roof, speeding away from Andyn's path. Eric devoted himself only to following Connor - he knew they had to maintain distance to avoid tipping off the assassins trailing Andyn, yet still make it to the rendezvous before she got there. Maintaining the link with Stealth was tricky while flying and he had to concentrate completely. By the time they reached the empty market square on Phillip Street, his forehead was drenched with perspiration and he felt as if he had run two miles in full armor.

"Steady," Connor said, vaulting from the saddle and helping him down.

Eric let out a deep breath and leaned on the saddle as Buck Bydecy loped towards them. Connor sent the pegasi away with a hand signal.

"Ready?"

Buck nodded, flipping down the Eye of Truth on his helmet. "Andyn and Dar are in the stable yard. I made sure the livery staff went off to get a beer, courtesy of the Grey Riders. Do you see Andyn?"

Eric concentrated again, using Stealth's eyes. He saw the assassins spread out, approaching the yard from connecting alleyways and rooftops. Two of them reached into their jackets, swallowed something, and vanished.

"Two just turned invisible on the south side near the hardware store. The other three are on the east side by the saddler's shop."

Buck nodded. "I'll be there with the Eye of Truth. They won't get past me. Besides, Puup is on the roof, and he doesn't like strangers."

Connor drew his sword and put up the hood of his cloak. "I'm on the other three. Anything else?"

Eric waited for a few seconds, using Stealth's vision. He saw a flicker of movement in the jumble of containers near a garbage collection station and he froze. A cloud of shadow grew in that dark place, an even darker patch in the evening gloom. He swooped lower with Stealth and saw two glowing red eyes in the darkness.

"We have our target, near the garbage station." Eric recalled Stealth and returned to his normal vision. "You two stay on your assignments and I'll help Andyn and Dar with the mage. Watch yourselves and be prepared for anything."

Buck hefted his shield and took off towards the right side of the snowy yard, using stalls and covered feed boxes for cover. Connor slipped away to the left, disappearing among the dark places between buildings and containers. Stealth swooped in from the cloudy sky, landing on Eric's forearm. With another word, the hawk glittered out of existence and became a brooch again.

Eric took a deep breath. Andyn played the part of the haughty, wealthy woman, waiting impatiently for her "lover". He saw Dar stride imperiously into the yard and approach her. He didn't hear any words, but the pair obviously threw themselves into their roles, based on the body language he saw.

Despite the tension, he had to grin. *Actually, both of them have second careers in theater waiting for them.*

Eric knew his assignment: find the shape-changer and deliver Melinor's volatile globe on target. After that, survive long enough to follow it back to its lair, if none of the others got into serious trouble, if the assassins didn't have reinforcements, if the lycanthrope didn't decide to fight to the death: if, if, if...

The attack came with alarming suddenness and he now remembered why the Crossed Swords were so feared.

Crossbow bolts zipped in from two different directions, aimed not at Dar and Andyn, but in front of them. The missiles struck the snowy earth and detonated, casting up blinding lights and earth and snow. Dar and Andyn drew back, blinking.

The trio of assassins charged, one of them tossing a glittering object to the ground. It broke and a sizzling net of energy hissed out at Dar and Andyn, wrapping their arms and legs in a tight embrace.

Eric concentrated, firing off a counter-spell. One section of the magical netting flickered and faded, freeing Andyn's arms. She reached behind her neck, pulling forth her mace, Eleison, and using her other hand to cast a spell at the remaining magical net. It also flickered and vanished.

One of the three attackers suddenly lurched and fell. Eric saw a small figure with a fiery sword flit out from behind the other two assassins, who whirled to attack. They found themselves faced by a leaping, tumbling halfling with a flaming blade and a ghostly sword hovering and dancing in midair.

By now, Dar had drawn Rhindara Starblade and stood at the ready, but he recoiled from a cloud of roiling fog that issued from the area of the refuse containers. A seven-foot tall wolf-man emerged, red eyes glowing and intent. He flexed arms corded with muscle and his black fur bristled as he drew back his lips to expose gleaming fangs.

With a flurry of white wings, a pigeon fluttered up from a nearby roof. Buck charged from the shadows and swung. A body flickered into sight, falling to the ground, blood staining the snow. Another assassin became visible and slashed at Buck, who blocked with his shield and stepped back.

The werewolf howled, a sound that froze Eric's blood and made his knees wobble. It had the same effect on his companions, making them falter.

No!

He pulled Fidelis from its scabbard and engaged it to full size with a word, then hurled it at the lycanthrope. The glittering golden spear flew unerringly towards the creature, but the werewolf raised a hand with a flicking gesture. The spear shunted to the side, burying itself into a barrel. There, it vanished in a cloud of glittering sparkles and re-appeared in Eric's hand. He stepped forward, Melinor's silver globe in one hand and the spear in the other.

Buck and an assassin exchanged blows as the werewolf snarled and charged. Dar stood to meet it and Andyn cast a trio of glowing firedarts. The magic missiles detonated with sharp cracks but the monster didn't even break stride. Dar swung and it leaped over his blade, then dodged to the side as Dar swung twice more without connecting.

Buck ran his opponent through and jumped to help. The werewolf changed direction, jumped over Dar and slammed into Buck with the force of a cavalry horse, hurling him backwards into a water trough, shattering it.

Andyn planted a ball of light on the werewolf's eyes. The lycanthrope dodged back. This turned out to be a good move, as it avoided getting Eleison planted in its forehead. With a snarled word and a motion, the werewolf made the ball of light disappear and slashed at Andyn with wicked claws. Andyn whirled away and staggered, her dress and bodice torn, revealing the chain armor underneath. She drew her other mace from a hook at her belt.

The werewolf's eyes narrowed.

Eric saw the remaining assassins dueling with Connor and realized the halfling couldn't join the fight. He let fly with Fidelis again. The werewolf actually caught the spear this time and reversed it to throw it at Eric. With a grin, he recalled the magic spear to his hand. The spear materialized in his fist and the werewolf stepped back, snarling.

Buck limped to join them as Dar waded in, aiming a complicated set of thrusts and cuts at the werewolf, which gave ground as Andyn joined him. It thrust its paws forward. A bright hemisphere of fire shot out at the pair, striking them and hurling them backwards. They rolled on the snowy ground, clothes in flames, trying to beat out the small fires as Buck stood guard over them, shield upraised.

To his left, he saw Connor finally drop the last assassin with a sword stroke as his spectral defender blade ran through the other criminal.

Now!

Eric tossed Melinor's silver ball up into the air, above the werewolf, who reflexively turned to watch it.

He shouted the magic word. Suspended within the thermite, the first tiny crystal flared to life, setting off the thermite while also sending a signal to the crystal in the inner sphere. The thermite activated, raising the temperature under the silver shell to a thousand degrees in an instant. The silver shell turned liquid and a few microseconds later, the inner crystal activated. The nitro glycerine detonated in a fiery bloom, spraying molten silver down on the werewolf.

The results, while ear-shattering, were gratifying. The werewolf shrieked in pain and fury, beating at its smoking fur, flesh beginning to boil under the effects of the deadly metal. With a howl of rage, it retreated, then made a sweeping, circular motion with its claws. A boiling black fog instantly surrounded the Riders.

"I have this," said Andyn. She whispered an arcane syllable and a gentle wind filled the area, blowing the smoke away.

Connor ran to join them, his spectral sword fading into a silvery mist that whisked back under his armor. "I saw where he went," he said, pointing down an alleyway.

"Eric?" asked Andyn.

"On it." He called forth Stealth and sent it up, heading the way Connor indicated. Andyn took stock of their injuries, kneeling with medicines in her hand, applying magic with a skilled touch.

"Dolmide's Beard," Connor said, sizing up Dar and Buck. "You guys sure got the worst of it."

"Blow it out your ear," groaned Buck. "I think I have a plank of wood stuck in my skull."

"That might actually improve your mental abilities," suggested Dar, dodging a backhand.

Eric only half-heard the exchange, focusing instead on his augmented vision via the magical hawk. His sight cut through the dying twilight and he picked out the werewolf, fur still smoking from the effects of the liquid silver, leaping across rooftops and racing through dark streets. It headed about two miles south of their current position and stopped at an abandoned house in a particularly decrepit neighborhood. He saw it go onto a front porch and lost sight of it.

"Got him," he said, altering his vision and leaving Stealth to loiter over the location.

Andyn finished her healing spells, the golden light fading from her hand as she repaired one of Buck's injuries. She replaced Eleison and her other mace on belt hooks.

"Just a minute," she said, turning her attention to Dar's face, singed and bloodied.

"Good thing you had that little toy from Melinor," Dar commented, with a wince as Andyn attended him. "I don't even think I got close to that beast and that last spell really caused us trouble."

Eric waited impatiently. Finally, Andyn nodded.

"Ready," she said, casting aside the remnants of her dress, leaving her clad in chainmail armor and boots.

Eric led them through the streets towards the building he had seen. They moved in almost total darkness now, staying away from lanterns. In this part of town, there were none of the typical magical street lights that marked much of Oakmoor. Eric found that odd, knowing that the Count wasn't poor and street lights weren't that expensive.

He stopped his companions, holding them in silence about a hundred feet away from the dilapidated structure into which the werewolf had escaped.

"That's it." Eric recalled Stealth and turned the hawk back into a brooch again.

Connor nodded, lifting up his hood. His breath made a small fog cloud in the frosty evening air.

"Wait here."

He slid forward into the shadows and soon Eric completely lost sight of him. He tried tracking him by shifting his sight into the infrared spectrum but all he got were warm footprints in the snow.

"I'm glad he's on our side," said Andyn. "I still don't know how he can disappear like that."

They waited.

Eric thought he saw a flicker of motion on the porch, like a shadow under another shadow. A few heartbeats later, he saw the flare of a tiny light that vanished almost as soon as it flared.

After a few nervous moments, he detected Connor returning.

"Well, they certainly make it hard for a fellow," the halfling said, taking his hood down.

"What did you find?" asked Buck.

"The doors and windows are all boarded up. I checked for secret doors and special latches. Nothing. There's no way anyone got into that house."

Eric's felt his frustration rising. To come this close and now be stymied...

"But," added Connor with a smile, "I got suspicious, as you might expect. This shape-changer is a powerful mage, but not as strong as Melinor and Melinor is one of the few wizards I know of who can perform a personal teleport spell. I looked at the boards of the porch. Three guesses as to what I found."

"A trap door," Buck offered with an impressed look.

"With a pretty little carving," Connor continued, with a glance at Eric, "of a snake."

"Sign of the Serpent," Dar breathed.

A wave of conflicting emotions surged through Eric: relief, excitement, pain, regret, loathing and triumph. Now, at long last, maybe they were getting closer to his parents and their hiding place. Maybe justice would finally be served, if they played it smart. This shape changer assassin was the key.

"Let's go hunt a snake," he said, lifting Fidelis and slipping ahead towards the abandoned house.

Chapter Eight- A Little Geometry

At least I'm out in the open air this time.

Brandawyn Alenar paced behind the ruined wall, eyeing the boulder-strewn hilltop, dotted with scrub growth, boulders and short willow trees. She held her bow in one hand, arrow nocked, and tried to focus, gazing out at the quiet landscape under cloudy afternoon skies. She smelled the scents of moist earth and plants.

The air felt cool but not cold. Winter in the south-lands…

Satisfied that nothing lurked out there, she looked back at the jumble of stones behind her, overgrown with creepers and bushes. Somewhere below, her sister, aunt and uncle searched an underground cellar, hopeful of finding a secret door.

Brandi stepped back past the rubble and vegetation and peered down into the cellar, dimly lit by her sister's magefire and Uncle Stephen's own magical light.

Too much to hope for that this search ends better than the last one. All we have to show for that are the bruises from fighting that Earth Terror. Good thing Daphne knew what to look for or we might be a lot worse off. All we felt was a rumble underfoot before it attacked.

She resisted the urge to sigh and sent a prayer heavenward for patience instead. She vaulted over a large block of stone entwined by a small raspberry bush and leaned on the ruined wall, looking downslope to where a more tangled forest loomed darkly some two hundred yards away.

Not seeing anything dangerous, she returned to her previous watch post, casting a hopeful glance down into the cellar on the way. Only her relatives' low tones reached her, unintelligible at this distance.

She lifted a boot on top of a stone, looking out over the desolate landscape towards a magnificent city far in the distance. Though the metropolis of Saint Benjamin stood more than seventy miles away, it took them only a couple of hours of flying to reach the ruin.

Recalling the comfortable Dwarf Knight Inn, she smiled, wishing she were relaxing in an easy chair with a cup of tea instead of tramping about in the wilds.

I think Andyn had an effect on me.

The thought of her distant friend's fondness for comfortable accommodations sobered her and she wistfully remembered their time together as Grey Riders.

One day, Andyn, we can have a girl's night out with Megan and you can tell us how you blasted Zhinia Margoth into ash - and brought my love back to life again.

Now, instead, the Alenars roamed the wild lands near Saint Benjamin, searching for the elusive dwarf-libraries, hidden among the hills and cliffs.

Something moved in the bushes about a hundred feet away and she straightened, putting her foot down and pressing next to a tall stone to make a smaller target. Her eyes narrowed.

Another motion drew her gaze and she saw several creatures in the brush and rocks. She waited, undecided, not sure whether to summon the others or not.

A short antelope stepped out of the brush, not more than four feet tall, with small sharp horns. It lowered its nose to the ground and sniffed. Two others joined it.

Brandi relaxed. Dark brown with black spots, they actually looked kind of cute. She smiled.

More of them came out of the brush. The lead creature's eyes flared red. Brandi froze. The animal turned sideways to look at its companions, who now numbered about a dozen. Instead of a fluffy white ball for a tail, it had a shiny brown scorpion's stinger. Brandi felt a chill of fear and a knot in her stomach.

She held up her free hand and cast a mild spell to detect evil. The creatures' auras glowed with a sickening purple miasma.

Creatures of the Dark, that's for sure.

Heart in her throat, she slipped backwards towards the cellar door, keeping her eyes on the creatures.

"Megan!" she whispered sharply. "Daphne! Stephen! Come out here, quick! Trouble…"

The low voices from the cellar ceased and she heard Megan's quiet voice from the entrance.

"Big trouble?"

"About a dozen of them and they don't look friendly."

Brandi sneaked back towards the wall, hearing the light steps of her relatives emerging from the cellar. Just as she reached the ruined wall, the lead creature sniffed the air and its head snapped up to look right at her. The creature actually leered at her with an unnerving, human-like expression and opened its mouth, showing sharp fangs. It let out a low howl. The other creatures answered with howls of their own and they charged out of the scrub growth.

Her skin crawled and she sighted an arrow at the lead monster.

Saint Michael and all angels!

She let fly, then took another arrow from her case and loosed it, not waiting to see if it hit, then followed with another. Two of her shafts hit the lead creature and it jerked to the side, emitting a high-pitched screech.

Megan stood at her elbow in an instant.

"Oh my God! Scorplings!"

"Great," Brandi replied, nocking another arrow and letting fly.

Another bow sang next to her and she saw her aunt loosing her own shafts. Their arrows struck true, felling the leader and one other.

Stephen and Megan began magic spells. The scorplings surged forward now, bounding from rock to rock, dodging between bushes and avoiding arrows.

Megan released a spell. Two whirling pinwheels of rainbow colors hissed out at the scorplings, striking two of them. The monsters stumbled and went down, then rose again and began to wander aimlessly.

Stephen's defense was more direct. He pointed a finger at them, sword held in his other hand. A sizzling, forked bolt of lightning lanced out. Three of the creatures dodged but another pair lurched backwards to fall in flailing heaps among the rocks and brush, their fur ablaze.

Not enough!

At an astonishing distance of twenty feet, the scorplings leaped into the air, covering the gap with appalling speed. Brandi barely had time to drop her bow and draw her swords before they cleared the walls of the ruin and landed among them.

Her right hand blade glowed with blue fire and the one in her left hand sparked electricity along its razor edge. Two scorplings hurled themselves at her, nightmare tails lashing and horns thrusting. She parried their attacks methodically with her blades, losing her fear of them in her concentration.

She struck back but they merely dodged out of the way, using their horns and tails to parry her attacks in turn. They split apart, trying to get one on each side of her, but a ray of intense white light from Megan's hand struck one of them and it lurched to the side. Another took its place before Brandi could step in and finish it off. Three scorplings now crouched, then leaped, bounding over Brandi's head, straight at Megan.

Megan backpedaled, drawing two daggers from her belt. Brandi whirled around, attacking the creatures as they landed, drawing them away from her sister. The wounded scorpling lurched forward, trying to impale Megan, but she set her jaw and knocked the creature's horns aside, then parried the tail strike. She stabbed down, burying one blade into the thing's neck, then followed with a thrust into its side. It gave a hissing screech and collapsed.

The other two turned on Brandi, but she sidestepped, banging aside their attacks, narrowly missing a venomous tail stinger in her side. She thrust at the eyes of one of them, then whirled and slashed it in the back as it recoiled. She immediately followed that with another slash at its legs and a thrust. It stumbled and fell.

The last one leaped at her and she tripped on a rock. A cruel horn pierced her chain armor in her side under her left breast and she felt a searing pain. She gasped and turned away from the blow, blocking the inevitable tail strike, then cut the scorpling on the shoulder and stabbed it in the neck. A trio of fiery darts hummed in, striking it in the head, and it dropped.

Brandi staggered to her feet, grimacing in pain, as the last wounded scorpling leaped at her. She sidestepped, slashing with both blades as it shot past her. Her swords cut deeply and it skidded, slamming into a block of stone. Another trio of fire-darts exploded on its chest and it slid to the earth with a faint gurgle.

Brandi looked past her sister. Daphne and Stephen stood over the forms of three other scorplings, one of them missing a head.

"Bran! Are you okay?" Megan darted to her side, her face showing her concern.

Brandi's side ached with fire and she nodded, keeping pressure on her injury, feeling warm blood leaking between her fingers. "I'll be fine. Just need a little medicine…"

She let Megan lower her to the ground and pulled a tiny vial from a belt loop, uncorking it and sipping the blue liquid.

The flavor of chili, peaches and sage assaulted her tongue and she almost choked, but instantly a warm, pleasant feeling covered her wound. She lifted her bloody hand from her side and looked. Through the chain mail and leather, she saw only healthy skin with a faint scar.

Megan sighed. "Better?"

Brandi smiled at her. "I've had worse."

"I know. I've seen it."

Daphne and Stephen joined them. Both had slight cuts on their arms and faces, but otherwise looked unharmed. They sheathed their swords.

"Good work, Bran," Daphne said, lifting her up. "Scorplings are dangerous in numbers if they can get among you but you helped take out almost half of them before they got to us. The two that Megan hit with the confounding spell are still out there, wandering around."

Brandi felt the adrenaline rush begin to fade and she let out a deep breath to calm herself. "Where did they come from?"

Stephen shrugged. "They haunt the wilds in southern lands like Gorostol and Torosc, but usually in hills or plains away from forests or jungles."

"Evil mutations?" asked Megan.

"Yes, from the Esten Imperial era, according to legend."

Brandi remembered their eyes and human-like qualities and shuddered.

"I've never heard of them, but bizarre creatures are not part of standard military training, not even for battle medics. I leave that to you wizard people."

"Vile things," added Megan.

Daphne nodded. "No argument from me. Well, we found nothing in the cellar anyway. We should recall the pegasi and head back before more of them come."

Brandi looked at her. "You mean there will be others?"

Stephen nodded as Daphne took out her owl medallion and Megan readied her signal spell. "The two that wandered away will find the rest of the herd and they'll be back, seeking revenge."

Megan's recalling spell spiraled up into the air, a streak of purple and silver light that faded out to a glitter some two hundred feet overhead. Brandi looked to the south, gratified to see two winged horses soaring out towards them from the trees. With a flare of magic, Daphne's medallion transformed into a giant owl.

"How many in a herd?" Brandi replaced her swords and slung her bow over her shoulder.

"Only about forty or so," said Stephen with a sly wink. "Sure you don't want to stick around to see them?" He stepped up to Paractus as Daphne vaulted into the saddle.

Brandi made a face at him. "Only if I have a platoon at my back. Besides," she continued as Amicus circled overhead, looking for a clear landing spot, "you owe me for spotting them in the first place."

"Done," said her uncle, climbing into the seat. "First drink is on me."

Brandi patted her pegasus on the nose and kissed him, then lifted herself into the saddle. In a matter of seconds, the three creatures and their passengers lifted off, Daphne leading them.

Brandi looked down at the landscape - rough hills with trackless forest in the valleys and hollows between them. Without the maps Stephen had found in the city library in St. Benjamin, they would have had no chance whatsoever to find any of the ruins. As it was, they spent precious time circling and trying to find safe landing zones.

She contented herself with following her aunt's mount. Based on the amount of available light, they probably had one more chance before nightfall, and they definitely shouldn't be wandering around after dark no matter what their level of skill. All the guards and sages in the city emphatically warned them against moving at night.

So far their efforts for the day yielded them two ruins consisting only of low stones and bushes, two battles, and nothing else to show for it all.

Except for tiredness and battle damage, of course. And no sign of the sextant.

Brandi had suggested that they stock up on healing medicines and augmentation potions to bolster their resistances and endurance. She needed to know they would at least survive without her nearby: there was no guarantee that she would be able to get to them and use her healing magic in time. She also had stocked up on more mundane medicines for her healer's kit.

She kept her eyes on the giant owl. Paractus flew steadily for a while, then banked left. She followed, keeping Megan on her right as she followed. Daphne led them down and towards a hilltop with several large boulders. Even from here, Brandi could see the outline of a structure.

They landed one by one, Daphne and Stephen hitting the ground first, crouching and using detection magic prior to returning Paractus to medallion form and waving the sisters down. Brandi stepped down from her saddle and made a circular motion with her hand, then pointed up. Amicus whinnied and launched himself upwards, following Larinor as the other pegasus winged away to the east.

"Well?"

Stephen looked up from his map. "This might or might not be one. The dwarven runes were faded on the scroll, so I'm not completely sure. Let's have a look around."

"I'll set up camp," volunteered Megan. Brandi joined her aunt and uncle in pacing the area slowly, examining various stones and looking under bushes and plants. She brushed a gloved hand gently over a stone block the size of a small table, feeling the intricate yet faded angular patterns under her fingers.

So long ago... I wonder what happened.

The sky grew darker as she continued her search. Finally, she turned to their campsite, where Megan reclined against a stone, placing bread, cheese, dried meat and dried apples on round circles of leather on the thick grass.

Her sister looked up, handing her a water-skin. "Anything?"

Brandi shook her head, downing a few swallows. "Nothing. Definitely dwarven, from the carvings, but nothing I could find. A lot like the other places. They certainly don't look like they could be secret libraries."

"Same here," said Daphne, plopping down on the ground and appropriating one of the leather plates. "If I had to venture a guess, these look like watchtowers or little forts."

Stephen shook his head as he also sat. "Well, this makes six so far."

He laid his map out on the back of his map-case and carefully marked their location with a black pencil.

"No one said it would be easy," remarked Daphne, making a small sandwich. "But then again, it was supposed to be a safe house designed by dwarves for keeping secret records, so this is to be expected."

Brandi ate her own meal in silence, watching distractedly as Stephen made notes on his map. Her eyes wandered to the marked locations of the ruins they had found so far.

Eric, I wish you were here. You always inspired me to think differently, to consider alternatives. What am I missing?

Her eyes followed Stephen's pencil as he marked on the map. She lifted the water skin to her mouth and stopped, seeing the marks on the map with new eyes.

"Uncle Stephen?"

"Hmm?" He didn't look up.

"The ruins we've visited - they form an arc. An arc of watchtowers encircling something, like they're guarding it. "

Stephen blinked and sat upright. Daphne scooted to his side and Megan looked over their shoulders.

"Damn…" Stephen looked up at Brandi, impressed. "Now why didn't I see that?"

His sister smiled at her. "Brilliant, Brandawyn!"

She felt herself blushing and sat across from Stephen. "Well, one of you smart people would have figured it out eventually."

Daphne put her arm around her and gave her a hug. She smiled. "But we didn't! You did."

Brandi returned her smile, feeling again like a small child who had pleased her mother.

Stephen looked at Megan. "What do you think? Can you calculate it?"

"In an eyeblink. Do you have the measurements?"

Stephen handed over his notes and a pencil on top of the mapcase. Megan sat cross-legged and looped her hair over her ear, then wrote furiously.

"With the ruins forming an arc, based on the distance to a hypothetical center of radius, that places it just here."

She pointed on their map.

Daphne stood, looking in the direction indicated and reached for her backpack. She drew out a spyglass, then extended it and peered off into the distance.

"Brandawyn Alenar," she said in admiration, "you are a wonder. Look at this."

Brandi blushed again but looked through the glass. After moving it around a bit, she focused on a particularly overgrown section of a large hill crowned by tall trees. The section looked very regular.

"Ruins."

She handed the glass back to Daphne, who let out a satisfied sigh. "I think we have tomorrow morning's target."

***

"Hmm…Something is not right," said Daphne.

Brandawyn nodded. "Agreed."

She drew both swords and cast a look around the ruins. Large, moss-covered blocks of stone vied with overgrown creepers and bushes under the shade of towering trees. The pale morning light of winter shone even paler in the shadows.

Stephen drew his own blade and made a motion with his free hand. A trio of lights sprang up over his head and then darted forward. A set of stairs led down into darkness. He moved to the top step but no further, letting his fairy-lights precede him.

Megan joined Brandi. "Why do I feel like this is a mistake?" she asked, watching the ruins warily.

"Because it probably is." Brandi sniffed the air.

It smelled faintly of rot and dead things. Nothing moved and she heard no noises, not even of birds or insects.

She saw again in her mind's eye the words of Eric Indidarc in one of his letters, describing knowledge gained in his travels.

I've learned to be very careful when Creation holds its breath - one of old Sir Tanner Collins' lessons when I was training with him. Animals can sense the presence of evil, as they were created good by God and still retain some of their original nature. Anything that is not natural they can detect and avoid.

"Well," she murmured to herself, "Creation's definitely not breathing now."

Daphne crouched next to her brother. "What do you think?"

He pointed at the bottom of the steps, where they led down to a door-frame of carved stone, almost completely buried by rocks.

"See there? Scorch marks in the stones near the base, then more on the sides, and the rock-fall has similar marks."

Brandi looked up at the surrounding ruins. Taller stones surrounded an area that looked like it might have been a storeroom or laboratory, with a set of steps leading down to the stone doorway.

"Magical explosives?" she heard Daphne muse.

"Likely. But why? It's fairly recent. Certainly not centuries old."

Brandi joined Megan at her aunt's side. They stood silently by as Stephen entered a trance, then dismissed his fairy-lights and put out his hand, palm up. A translucent, faintly glowing orb popped up in his palm, looking rather like a soap bubble of light.

He opened his eyes and she watched, intrigued, as his pupils took on the same iridescent color as the bubble of light. He waved his hand and the bubble wafted forward, passing through the rockfall and doorway as if they were made of smoke.

She shook her head in amazement. Stephen's arsenal of magical tricks seemed bottomless.

Megan nodded. "Ethereal Eye. I hope I can learn that one from him some day."

They waited.

"Passage on the other side..." Stephen said in a sleepy voice. "...then a chamber... skeletons and... blue-colored undead with fangs and glowing eyes, like nimble zombies... maybe ghouls?.... broken door at the exit..."

He fell silent, then spoke again. "Another chamber... books strewn around. Other skeletons… not human or elf… probably goblin or hobgoblin… "

He shuddered. "The … desecration!… vile symbols on the walls… two stone boxes… six, no, seven feet long… evil signs on them…"

He began to perspire and tremble. Alarmed, Brandi stepped forward to help but he shook himself and the iridescent sheen disappeared from his eyes.

Daphne put a hand on his shoulder and he nodded. "I'm okay."

Stephen stood, swung his arms around in circles, stamping his feet as if trying to recover from extreme cold. In a few seconds, he looked like his cheerful, mischievous self.

"Well, we'd better get prepared. Brandi, your unique skills will be needed in there."

Brandi met her uncle's gaze. "Undead?"

He nodded.

She set her mouth in a grim line. Stephen and Megan cast protective spells on them all. Luminous sheets and nets of faint colored light covered their bodies for an instant before fading. Brandi added a couple of her own - one to protect their minds, and another against evil magic.

Stephen clapped a hand on Megan's shoulder. "Remember the *Mense Motus* spell?"

"Yes."

"Good. Together then."

Daphne drew her sword and whispered a word. Orange fire flickered along the edge. She pulled a dagger from her boot. It glittered briefly.

Brandi whispered a prayer to Saint Michael as Megan and Stephen concentrated. A glimmer, almost imperceptible, raced around the outlines of the boulders. They quivered and rose from their places, floating up above the edge of the floor, coming to rest about ten feet from her. The process repeated until all the stones lay neatly arranged in the old storehouse and the rectangular opening gaped at them.

"Follow me, and watch carefully." She took her crucifix from around her neck and held it in her left hand, alongside the handle of her sword.

"*Lux Aeterna*," she whispered, and a bright ball of light flared ahead of her. She focused on the luminous sphere and sent it into the blackness of the tunnel, her relatives following on her heels.

The passage opened into a large chamber. Eyes trying to see everywhere at once, she hesitated at the entrance, then suddenly leaped forwards and to the left.

Skeletons lay about on the floor, hopelessly jumbled up, bones mixing with skulls and ribcages and weapons and armor. Brandi's boot struck what she thought was a bowl only to find it was the top of a skull. Other shattered skulls lay nearby. She saw no moving creatures. What looked like the remnants of bunks, strongboxes, bureaus and racks stood against the walls or leaned into each other. The previous smell of rot was joined by something sickly sweet.

Stephen and Daphne and Megan moved in with her.

"*Malum reperio*," Brandi said and her vision shifted into another realm. She sensed golden light near her from her relatives, then a bright glow of purple from above. She looked up. Creatures crawled towards them from the ceiling, claws scrabbling into the stones, their nightmare heads pivoting around to regard her. Their faces looked like twisted caricatures of people, with hooked noses, jagged ears, protruding brows, swollen lips and sunken eyes that glowed with a baleful red light. Glowing spittle dripped from sharp fangs.

"Ghouls! Up above!" she called out as a dozen creatures swarmed at them, growling and slavering.

Megan cut loose with a beam of blinding light, blowing a hole through one of them. Stephen followed suit with a blast of orange-white flame, immolating another.

Brandi jammed her left-hand sword into a broken chair at her feet and held forth her crucifix. "*Deus, adiuva me!*"

A familiar jolt of cleansing, euphoric joy coursed through her body and she focused her mind on the figure of her Savior on the crucifix. The universe wheeled around her for a split second and a well of immense energy opened. Ghostly blue flame arced out from her hand and she released the power in a spherical explosion of light.

Four of the ghouls took shelter behind ruined furniture but the remainder caught the full force of the holy fire. They froze momentarily in the blinding light, then ruptured into flaming fragments of rotted flesh and bone chunks, some of the bones exploding as they struck the floor.

Brandi gasped at the release of power and knelt, taking up her sword despite a wave of dizziness.

The remaining ghouls howled in rage and leaped to the attack. Daphne met them head-on, decapitating one and slashing another. Stephen ran one through with a well-placed thrust. Megan felled a third with a hail of fire-darts and Brandi dispatched the last with a pair of slashes with her blades. The thing collapsed onto the pile of bones at her feet, snarling and spitting in rage as the red light faded from its eyes.

The four Alenars stood on guard for a few heartbeats, then relaxed.

"Nice work, Brandi."

She nodded, letting out a deep breath as she felt the last remnants of sacred power leave her.

"You okay?" asked Megan.

Brandi nodded with a smile. "I'm fine. I don't do it too often but it always seems to be more potent when I do it and it drains me more. I'm not sure why and neither were my mentors in the Academy."

Stephen gave her shoulder a squeeze. "I'm more worried about what's up ahead," he said, pointing at the broken door. "From what I saw with the Ethereal Eye, there's even worse things awaiting us."

Brandi looked down at the refuse at her feet. "Most of the bones look dwarven, but the ghouls were definitely the result of human corpse mutations. I wonder why."

Daphne shook her head. "I have no idea, Brandi. Almost anything could have happened in all those decades and centuries."

Megan's eyes narrowed and she shook her head. "But the entrance was sealed. How did they get in?"

Brandi sheathed her swords after cleaning them on some rags. "Undead don't need to eat and they don't age so they could have been here for a long time."

Megan pursed her lips, unconvinced. Daphne and Stephen moved ahead, picking their way over the flotsam and junk on the floor. Brandi moved her magic light up above them, her eyes scanning the refuse.

She knelt down, inspecting a whiter skeleton. It didn't have the signs of extreme age like the others. She wondered, gently touching the skull.

"Come on," Megan whispered. Brandi stood and followed. They passed beyond the broken door, careful not to disturb the hinges. Daphne gently pried a rotted slat away from the frame to make the opening wider and laid the wood on the floor. She stepped in and Brandi followed, making her mage-light hover in the center of the next chamber.

Chills raced up her spine as she looked around. A plethora of ruined books lay scattered around, most of the pages rotted or deteriorated into flimsy fragments. Shattered tubes of ceramic lay among them, their paper or vellum contents mouldering in the still air. Vile-looking runes marked the empty book shelves and walls, painted in lurid colors of blood-red, bone-white or sickly green.

Incongruously, four low stone coffins lay near the exit door on the other side of the room, marked with similar runes on their sides.

"Those don't look like original equipment," Megan noted in a soft voice.

"At least their covers are secure," Daphne said. "It will take someone strong to lift them."

Brandi looked all around, making sure to gaze up at the ceiling, unwilling to be surprised again by undead clinging in the corners. She saw nothing. Her boot struck something on the floor. A small skeleton clad in relatively shiny chain armor grinned up at her, one bony hand still clutching a mace. A larger skeleton lay next to it, wrapped in rotting strips of cloth. It had no head, with only a pile of small skull fragments above the shoulders.

A halfling and a human? Why are there strips of cloth? A sudden foreboding filled her and she drew her right-hand blade.

"The door is still closed on the other side," Stephen added, drawing his sword. "Let's see if there are any surprises."

He held his blade before him, murmuring arcane words. The weapon flared with yellow light that settled down to a mild glow.

"No traps on the door," he said in a speculative tone, then went rigid. "The coffins!"

Brandi lifted up her crucifix as the tops of the covers glittered and faded away. Four cloth-wrapped figures emerged from the coffins. Golden circlets with red gems glittered from their foreheads and they bore silver staves with the figures of scorpions entwining them. A miasma of rot rolled out from them in a wave.

This is not good.

Chapter Nine – Library of Lost Kings

Brandi gagged, trying to keep from retching. The mummies advanced towards the Alenars as her kin drew back, choking from the horrible cloud of corruption. The empty eye-sockets of the mummies held small balls of red light instead of eyes.

"*Adiuva me!*" Brandi gasped, holding up her crucifix. Again, the euphoric light and dizzying power filled her body. She cast it forth and a bright blue glow pulsed forth at the mummies and the horrid stench vanished. The mummies lurched backwards, slamming into the coffins or remnants of furniture, their rotted windings smoldering.

Again, the release of power made Brandi gasp and she shook her head to clear it.

The mummies righted themselves, then raised their staves as one and the red gems on their circlets flared. In shock, Brandi watched a veritable storm of fire-darts shoot at her. She barely had time to throw a magical shield in the way before they hit. Five detonated on her defenses but seven penetrated, hitting her in the chest, abdomen, legs and arms.

Searing pain burned through her and she stumbled backwards, tripping over a pile of ruined books and slamming into the wall. Her chest and stomach ached with a raw pain and she wondered if any of her armor remained.

She struggled to re-focus, pulling a healing phial from her belt-loop and jerking the stopper out with her teeth. She downed the potion, feeling warmth course through her body. She replaced her crucifix and drew her other sword, gritting her teeth against the remaining pain.

Daphne charged right at the mummies, sword and dagger flashing. Two of them swung staves at her, the scorpions on their staves coming to horrifying life, writhing and lashing at her with their stingers. She fell back, parrying their attacks.

Megan held out her hands and stepped next to Daphne. Her fingers glowed orange and a sheet of fire shot out, catching three of the mummies in its path. They burst into flame immediately and stumbled, ramming into each other and shrieking with hollow, echoing voices.

Stephen charged them, sword flashing, lightning flaring out with every hit on the now-blazing mummies. Daphne joined him, cutting deep into the monsters with her blades.

The fourth mummy raised its staff high and shouted a hoarse syllable. The flames died down to nothing. The undead regained their momentum, then moved their staves in concert. Their circlets glowed orange this time and small black spheres shot out, landing around Megan. They detonated with sharp cracks, spraying her with hot metal shards. Her magical screens and shields flared, casting aside some of the shrapnel, but the force hurled her backwards into a pile of ruined books. Her screens flickered and died.

Brandi raced to her side as a mummy slogged in. Out of the corner of her eye, she saw Stephen chant a spell and glowing cords shot out from his hand, wrapping around two of the mummies and setting them on fire again.

Megan stirred and tried to roll over. Brandi's heart skipped a beat. Her sister looked like a small army of sprites had attacked her with knives. What remained of her clothes rapidly turned dark under the effects of blood flowing from more than two dozen wounds.

"Stay down!" Brandi commanded, watching the mummy.

It raised its staff and she leaped in, striking at one of its arms with both swords. The enchanted blades sliced through, severing the arm. The staff fell to the floor and the undead staggered back. Brandi pressed her attack and the mummy shrieked, raising its other hand to swing at her. She ducked, then used both blades to chop through one of its legs.

The mummy toppled over. She charged in, both blades biting deep. One took off a hand while the other severed the head from the body.

It still moved. Horrified, Brandi watched in the flickering light as the head, arms and legs tried to reassemble themselves.

"Fire…"

She turned. Despite her injuries, Megan sat up, pointing her hand at the mummy. She grimaced, holding a hand to her side.

"Burn it," she hissed in pain, then released three fire darts. They detonated on the severed head, blowing it across the room.

Brandi shrugged off her backpack and reached inside for a flask of flame gel. Two blazing mummies struggled in the grip of Stephen's magical cords of fire, trying to untangle themselves. The room filled with dark smoke, dimming Brandi's mage-fire. She fought to keep from coughing.

Daphne and her brother battled the remaining mummy, slashing its limbs while it battered at them with its scorpion staff. As she watched, Brandi saw Stephen thrust his sword through the thing's head. Daphne hacked a leg off with her sword and took off a hand with her dagger. The mummy collapsed and the pair followed it down mercilessly, blades glowing as they hacked it to pieces.

Brandi stepped over to the pieces of the mummy she had cut up as they slithered towards each other. Unstoppering the flask, she poured the gel onto the monster, watching as the substance burst into a merry flame. The mummy parts writhed, but the gel did its work with gratifying speed, reducing it to a pile of burning scraps in seconds. The last thing she saw of it were its fading red eye-lights.

Brandi coughed in the cloud of smoke and looked to Daphne. Her aunt applied her own flask to a hacked pile of mummy as Stephen stood guard over the two he had ensnared with his Fire Cord. They burned, filling the room with more acrid smoke.

"We've got to get out of here. The smoke is too thick," Brandi choked out. She crouched next to Megan, who had laid back down.

"Agreed," said Stephen, racing over from the other side of the room. "How's Megan?"

Brandi shook her head, looking at her sister's injuries. "She's lost a lot of blood. Come help me get her to the surface. I can work on her there."

She took a healing phial from Megan's belt and held it to her lips, dripping the potion into her mouth. Megan coughed and regained consciousness, then moaned in agony.

"The fire…" she managed. "Everything burns."

Stephen arrived and together, he and Brandi carried Megan outside to the old ruins. Daphne joined them soon after.

Brandi bit her lip, assessing Megan's wounds. They looked more extensive than she had first thought.

Something else is at work here.

Brandi took a deep breath, forcing down her worries about Megan, and concentrated on her patient. She closed her eyes, praying to God and his angel Saint Raphael to guide her in her task of healing.

She crafted a diagnostic spell and triggered it. What she found amazed her. Not only had the explosive balls slashed her body with sharp, hot shards of metal, but also sprayed her with acid and an anti-coagulant to make her bleed more.

Brandi sent healing energy into her sister's body, sealing up the cuts, flushing the poison and acid, repairing muscle tissue, knitting skin together. She remained in a trance for what seemed like centuries, checking a second time to make sure she hadn't missed anything. She counted forty-seven separate injuries.

Satisfied she was done, Brandi let out another deep breath and came out of her trance.

Megan lay on the mossy stones, her travel dress shredded and bloodied, but resting peacefully.

A wave of fatigue hit Brandi and she sagged, hands on her knees. Every heartbeat felt like the thud of a bass drum.

"Well done," said Stephen, putting his arm around her shoulders. "Now it's your turn."

Brandi nodded, letting herself be led to a large stone to sit while Daphne tended Megan. Stephen gave her a phial of light green liquid that tasted like oranges and cheese and mint.

After long minutes, she felt like her old self again. She looked up at her uncle. His eyes changed from concerned to relieved.

"Good. You spent a lot of energy there."

She smiled, seeing Megan sitting up and talking to Daphne.

"For a good cause. Though she's still a flighty little brat sometimes…"

Stephen grinned. "Now I know you're back to normal."

"What was that spell? The one that they used to throw out those little explosive balls?"

Stephen's grin faded. "Mangle Bombs. It's not a very advanced spell, but fiendishly effective. Favorites of our friends in the Vardish church and the followers of Torvu in the Ja'al cult."

She looked at him quizzically.

"You may have noticed the effects of the spell. It's designed to bleed out the target so that the dead body can be used for... other purposes. Megan was wise in laying magical screens on herself. That many Mangle Bombs could have easily made her bleed to death before you could have helped her."

Brandi shuddered and felt nauseous. "So the Vardish have been here already."

"Most likely."

She stood and joined her sister and aunt. Daphne looked at Stephen.

"We're going to tend to Megan. Can you go down into the chambers and see if you can find any evidence of previous entry? And maybe warding magic?"

He nodded and left.

"Wanted to get him away while we help Megan get some decent clothes," Daphne said in a whisper. "Men can be so oblivious at times and I guess I could just ask him to turn around, but it's good to give him a job."

Megan giggled, now fully restored, then sighed and shook her head. "Why do my clothes always end up in tatters?"

Brandi rummaged around in her backpack, coming up with a spare tunic. "It's because you don't wear armor and you insist on mixing it up with the warriors, you ninny."

Megan snorted, stripping off the blood-stained remnants that used to be blouse, trousers, boots and shift. "As if I can do proper magic with all that metal. Besides, I'll bet that there's a monster out there that likes to eat metal and then you'd be standing there in your underwear, or less."

"Actually, there is," Daphne said as she tossed Megan's rags into a pile and handed her a clean shift.

Megan froze, the clothing in her hands. "There is?"

"Yes. It's called an Iron Leech or Ferrous Affinate. You wouldn't think so, but it's a danger to my armor and Stephen's because even Starsilver has some iron in it."

Megan shook her head and wiggled into the shift. "You better watch your-self, Brandi."

Brandi fingered the missing links in her chainmail, blown off by the fire-darts from the mummy wizards and pierced by the horns of the Scorplings. She wondered which was worse, getting her armor hacked or blown off or munched away by some iron-chewing creature.

Rummaging through spare clothes in their backpacks, they managed to come up with something resembling a travel outfit for Megan, though she had to tie the remnants of her boots to her feet.

"There is no way I'm going through that hell-pit barefoot," Megan growled. "Undead..." She shuddered.

Stephen arrived moments later, looking satisfied. "Well, I found out some interesting things. First, you were right, Brandi. There was apparently another group that came by, though it looks like it was some time ago. My guess is that they broke in, ran afoul of the undead and retreated, losing some of their number, then collapsed the entrance to keep the monsters from escaping. Some of the newer bones look to belong to halflings or gnomes and I found an elf skeleton in the mummy room. Second, I used the Ethereal Eye spell again to scout ahead. The door at the end of the last room leads to a short passage and another door which is heavily warded against evil. I don't think the mummies even got close to that one."

Brandi felt her pulse quicken. "Maybe this is it."

Stephen winked. "Only one way to find out."

He led them down into the mummy room, which by now only had a few wisps of smoke clinging to the ceiling. Brandi looked at the door on the op-posite side. It did not appear to have a handle or lock.

At her quizzical look, Stephen nodded and pointed two fingers at the door, closing his eyes. With a few murmured words, a blue light flared in the center of the door near the top and they heard a hissing noise, then a dull thump.

The door moved outward by a few inches, revealing darkness beyond.

"I could have done that," noted Megan with an injured look at her uncle.

"We need your skills for other things, dear," he said, joining Daphne at the portal. They pulled it open and Brandi conjured up another mage-light, sending it inside. True to Stephen's original statement, a short passage led to another, more ornate door.

"*Malum reperio*," Brandi said, then gasped as the ornate door glowed bright gold.

"Definitely nothing evil," she breathed, leading the way inside. A set of runes ran from left to right across the door and over the stone walls next to it, with a matching set running from the floor to the ceiling.

Stephen nodded. "My bet is that the runes run along the perimeter of whatever room is in there, in three dimensions, to prevent evil things from burrowing under the protections or going around them."

Daphne sheathed her sword and dagger, as did Stephen. Megan scooted forward and ran her hand along the runes.

"Can you read them?" Brandi asked.

She nodded. "Dwarven. It says "Ye of good mien and pure heart, give noble greeting here. An ye serve Holy Kurental, or the goodly allies of the Lord of Stone, entrance will be given ye." I'm not sure what "noble greeting" means."

Daphne pursed her lip. "This seems almost too simple." She stepped up to the door, holding her hand up in salute next to her face, then placed her palm on the stone surface. The outline of her hand flared golden, then several of the runes glowed white, so intense that Brandi had to squint. The light washed over Daphne, bright and warm, then snapped off. Other runes glowed blue and light shone on all of them, tracking over their bodies for a few seconds before fading.

Daphne hesitated, then took hold of the handle and pulled. With a hiss, the door opened. Heart pounding, Brandi followed her family inside and gasped.

Magical lamps came to brilliant life in tall, faceted crystals set into the floor. A set of finely wrought cases made entirely of glass stood in the room before them. True to Stephen's assessment, identical runes ran along all the walls as well as the ceiling and floor. Tiles of pure white, steel grey and darkest black made intricate patterns on the floor and ceiling, reminding Brandi of stained glass windows. She realized they formed a depiction of Kurental as the protector god of the dwarven people, a hood covering his features and one hand held up in benediction while the other wielded a hammer of silver.

She looked around the chamber. Along with the tall crystal lamps, more intricate tile-work surrounded them, forming images of dwarves in armor or robes, kneeling and praying.

"We may have found something here." Stephen stepped up to one of the cases, peering inside.

Brandi did likewise. It had four shelves and a glass door with a golden clasp for each. On the shelves, small stone objects sat in neat rows. Each object looked like a small dodecahedron, small enough to comfortably fit into her palm.

Her detection spell still active, Brandi nodded to Megan. "Nothing evil, certainly. I'm not sure how to make sure we don't set off something when we try to open the cases."

Megan considered that for a moment, then touched one of the cases and closed her eyes. After a few heartbeats, she looked up and shook her head.

"No safeguards I can see. I think they're okay to open."

Brandi reached out and lifted the clasp for the lowest shelf. The glass door swung open easily and she pulled out one of the objects.

It felt like stone, but so finely crafted that its surface was as polished as glass. Each face had tiny lines on it, arranged in rows. The rows ran in the same direction on a face, but not always the same direction on all sides.

"What do you think?" she asked Megan. Her sister came closer, running her fingers over the lines, then looked up with surprise.

"They're very tiny carvings."

Stephen and Daphne joined them. After pulling additional objects from the case, they examined them in detail.

"They all have the same tiny carvings," mused Stephen. He reached into his backpack and came up with a small flat box. He opened it and drew out a lens of glass.

"Megan is right," he said slowly, turning the dodecahedron in his fingers as he looked through the lens. "It's script, etched into the surface of the object, but on a very minute scale."

"What does it say?" asked Daphne.

He shook his head. "It's too small. This lens isn't strong enough, but the Nuncio has access to more powerful ones and he can magically augment them as well."

He looked at Megan. "Can you cast *True Vision?*"

She shook her head. "No. All I can do is detect any enchantments on them."

"Go ahead and give it a try."

She cupped her hand over the object, eyes closed. She opened her eyes, a look of awe on her face.

"Sweet Lord! Uncle Stephen, the script goes down into the stone in layers, many of them, and the facets are interconnected. It looks like a three-dimensional data repository or map." She shook her head with an expression of admiration. "I don't have the skill to read them or do any more."

Brandi thought of the level of magical and technological skill required to make such items and it made her dizzy. Dwarves continued to amaze her the more she learned about them.

"Fine then," Daphne said. "We have to transport these immediately."

She reached into her backpack and pulled out two of the special bags they used to teleport materials back to the Nuncio's offices in Saint Martin's. Collecting as many of the objects as they could they wrapped each one in cloth for protection and filled one bag. While Daphne readied the second one, Stephen took a medallion out of his belt purse and held it in his palm for a few heartbeats, murmuring words under his breath. The medallion glowed green and he touched it to the bag, then set it on the floor. The bag glittered like a jar full of a million captive fireflies, then vanished. He prepared the second bag in the same way and touched it with the medallion. That bag also vanished.

They gathered up all the objects from the cases. Megan used a note paper and pencil to keep track. With a glittering of tiny stars, the first bag re-appeared on the floor, empty. The Alenars used the procedure over and over until no objects remained in the cases.

Brandi looked at Megan's list after they finished. She had tallied up over a hundred of the little dodecahedrons.

Brandi let out a deep breath, feeling an immense relief. Now, finally, after all their searching, they had something to go on. They would have to trust in the Papal Nuncio and his advisors to figure out what it all meant.

"We can only do that a finite number of times," said Daphne as they waited for the bags to return. "We'll have to send a request for another set with our next delivery."

Lumpy shapes glittered into being on the floor and Stephen picked them up. He reached into one bag and his face broke into a grin. "I can tell you if there are letters in here, girls, but only for a price."

Brandi made a face at him. "Or I can steal Eric's letter in the middle of the night— or I can make you cook next time we camp."

"No need for be threatening," Daphne said with a wry smile as she appropriated two letters from Stephen's hands and gave one each to the sisters. Brandi's heart skipped a beat as she saw her name written in Eric's strong hand on the front.

"What now?" asked Megan, holding her own envelope to her breast and smiling happily.

Daphne nodded, looking thoughtful. "Now we head back to Saint Benjamin's, and hope and pray that someone can make sense of all this."

Chapter Ten - Choices and Consequences

The universe lurched and Handor's vision swam with distorted images of a garden, grey mist, a gazebo and trees. With a jolt, he felt wooden flooring under his hands and darkness all around him.

His stomach churned and he shook his head, fighting to quell the dizziness. Instead of his family gardens at the Lervion manor, he found himself on hands and knees in his room at the Twin Centaurs Inn, the curtains drawn. Scarcely able to believe it, he sat back against a nearby bureau with a groan.

I had him, right there, ripe for the skewering! What just happened?

The insidious buzzing from the Helm of Shadows continued, a swarm of angry hornets inside his head. He tried to focus his thoughts but it wouldn't give up. He put his hands on the sides of the Helm. It felt like a cap of lead and threatened to drag him down to the floor. Squeezing his eyes shut against the maddening sound, he forced out the releasing spell and ripped the Helm off his head. With a snort of disgust, he flung it onto the bed and put his head in his hands.

The buzzing faded and he felt a wave of relief. He rested his head against the bureau, waiting for the aftereffects to subside, trying to think. His head throbbed with every heartbeat and he ached all over, but slowly the pain receded, leaving only fatigue.

What happened? Why did the Helm transport me back here just when I was going to kill Beol?

He felt a headache growing, probably from the stress of getting the attack timing exactly right and from the fight. He reviewed all the steps leading up to his attempt on Beol's life. Everything seemed optimal: he'd timed it perfectly, using the Helm to teleport from a nearby rooftop to the gazebo in the garden just as Beol sat down to his morning meal, with his warriors at least fifty paces away.

Handor followed this up with a spell of obscuring fog to confound the guards. He still felt wicked satisfaction at the look of total shock on his uncle's face.

Without his guards around, Beol had been forced to fight, using a magical gemstone to nullify some of Handor's magic spells. The magic sword, Shriek, proved to be the ace in the hole. It slashed past Beol's hidden armor beneath his dressing robe, cutting him. Handor used it to punch a hole in a platter when the dwarf raised it as a shield in a vain attempt to ward off the assault. Then, just as Handor was about to strike the killing blow, the Helm teleported him away.

But why? He racked his brain, trying to find a flaw in his plan, something he could have missed. It almost seemed like the Helm had a mind of its own.

No, that can't be right! It's just a highly enchanted piece of armor. Besides, I have the key to the power. The Guide said so.

Finally, weary and aggravated, he stood and regarded the Helm sitting on the mattress. Its dark purple surface swirled imperceptibly and its empty eye-slits mocked him.

With a shudder, he slipped it back into his magic shrinking bag and laid it under his bed. Despite the early hour, he crawled under the covers. In moments he fell drifted off to sleep, exhausted.

***

That afternoon, Handor awakened and rubbed the sleep from his eyes, then grimly jammed the Helm of Shadows on his head. Despite the rest, his troubles with the Helm still weighed on him and he was in a vicious mood. He ran through the equations and algorithms in his mind and the world swirled and jolted and melted, then coalesced into the interior of Hannah's chamber. He crouched momentarily, eyes adjusting to the candle-lit room as he lifted the Helm off his head.

"Handor?"

Hannah moved around her bed to him, clad in a dark green dress, a dagger at her belt, brow creased with concern.

He stood to greet her, holding her momentarily. "I'm here. Guards at the door?"

"No," she said, hugging him back. "Beol reassigned them to himself to-night, something about an intruder out to get him. Just more delusions."

"It's not a delusion. I was the intruder."

She held him at arm's length, eyes wide in shock. She bit her lip and shook her head, tears starting in her eyes. "Oh Handor."

He took a deep breath and tried to smile. "I almost got him. But don't worry. I think I have his number now."

A tear ran down her cheek. "No, it's not that."

She gently turned him around so he could see his reflection in the mirror.

It took all his composure not to jump back. He looked like a shell of his former self, gaunt and pale. Though his beard and hair looked well-trimmed, they gave him a sinister aspect. And his eyes: dark black with a swirl of red in the pupils.

He looked down to avoid the image and saw his hands. His heart stopped.

They had a misty, insubstantial quality now, almost as if a purple fog em-anated from them. A stab of fear shot through his heart and he clenched his fists to keep his hands from shaking.

To divert her, he said, "It's an aftereffect of the item I've been using."

She choked back a sob. "It's killing you, Handor. I can see it. What thing is so valuable to you that you would let it do this to you? Is it that helmet?"

He heard the Guide's stubborn voice in his head, telling him to abandon her. He ignored it, then turned around, opened his eyes and nodded, holding up the Helm.

Her eyes narrowed as she inspected it. With her mouth set in a firm line, she shook her head.

"This thing is not good, Handor. I don't like it. I don't like what it's doing to you and it has an aura of evil."

"It was evil, Hannah. I took it from a destroyed lich."

Her eyes widened and she stepped back. "A lich? How did you manage? Certainly not by defeating it yourself. Very few people are powerful enough to defeat one single-handedly. I heard of a lich who was destroyed, up in

Deran. Is it from him?"

"Yes. And it was a her. Zhinia Margoth, former princess of a Paragon kingdom."

Hannah shook her head more vigorously now. "Get rid of it. If it came from a lich, no good will come of it."

The Guide's voice whispered in his mind. *What does that little wench know? Nothing! Abandon her to her fate! She isn't worthy of exalted knowledge and limitless power.*

With an effort, he ignored it again. "I know how to manage it, Hannah," he said with more calm than he felt. "I learned the control spells and I can make it do what I want."

"Who gave the control spells to you? Not the lich, certainly." She started to look agitated, almost angry.

Foolish little girl, the Guide whispered. *What does she know? Simpleton!*

Handor looked away, gritting his teeth until the voice faded. "I'd rather not say. Just know that it was someone who isn't a puppet to those insipid religions other people follow. He gave me the means to be the captain of my own destiny."

"Now I know I don't want you to have it!" she fairly hissed with intensity. "If you won't even tell me who gave you the spell-keys and it's doing this to you, I want nothing to do with it. Handor! I'm warning you! Get rid of that unholy thing!"

He looked at her. She lowered her head and clenched her fists, eyes glaring at the Helm in his hand as if she squared off against Margoth herself. He had seen her like this before and there was nothing for it. She looked so much like his mother just now.

Handor Lervion stood silently for a long moment, transfixed by her anger and fear. With a sudden shock, he realized his sister braced for battle — against him — to save him from what she saw as a mortal danger: his own pride.

The whisper started up in his head. *Selfish little bitch,* the Guide insisted.

Handor felt a hot rage build up. Hannah never did anything selfishly.

He spat an obscene insult at the Guide and shoved the Helm into the bag. Caution prevented him from hurling it into the corner, but he slammed the bag down on the mattress, then turned his back on it.

He heard Hannah slide the little bag into the corner, as far from them as possible. The accursed whisper in his mind faded to the sound of a faint breeze, then fell silent.

At that moment, something in him turned. He let go of his dreams of power and revenge, dreams of carving a mighty destiny by his own skills. He made a decision: nothing, not the Helm, not riches, not revenge, not magic, nothing was worth alienating his only family left in the world. He resolved to get his sister out of her prison, seek out the Grey Riders, and ask for their help and their forgiveness.

He sighed. "Okay. Hannah. As soon as I have you out of here, I'll get rid of it. I promise."

"No, Handor! Destroy it now!"

"I don't know if I can. But I can get it away from us. I'll do it, tonight. Just remember that I went to get Mom a cup of tea. You know where that is, right? I'll put a clue there."

She met his eyes, nodding in understanding. "You promise?"

"Double starlight promise."

A ghost of a smile graced her lips. "Double starlight promise it is then."

They sat on the edge of her bed. Quickly, he told her of his attempt to kill Beol. His description of the Helm taking control of the situation only confirmed her resolve to be rid of it.

"I thought I could catch him unawares," he finished.

She squeezed his hand. "That was foolish, knowing what that helmet is. Brilliant but foolish. Beol flew into a rage after you left. I saw him ordering the guards around and screaming at Lorferis, the Ja'al wizard, for his lack of protection."

He scoffed. "Fat lot of good that will do him. I know my way around here blindfolded and I can counteract any feeble spells the Ja'al can paste together."

"What are you going to do next?"

"Well," he said, "I want to see if the old passage in the cellars still leads out to the servants' gate. If they're building something nefarious down there, I can create a diversion. You stay out of it."

She made a face and raised an eyebrow. "I'm the one who went to a a military academy, big brother, remember? I can handle myself. The only problem is numbers. I know most of the guards are thugs and murderers, but there are at least twenty of them, not counting Lorferis and his acolytes."

"We won't have to take them all at once. And believe me, I've fought tougher than them when I was with the Grey Riders."

A look of wonder came over her face. "You were with the Grey Riders? Everyone has been talking about them! There are even songs in the taverns! Handor, I'm so proud of you! My brother, the Grey Rider!"

He smiled and ducked his head. "Well, thanks. They really weren't my kind of group — too many religious people — but they kind of grew on me."

"Why didn't you ask them to come help you?"

He waited a long time before answering, remembering Andyn's warmth, Connor's humor, Eric's easy friendliness, Dar's sense of honor, Buck's comradeship.

He dropped his hands in his lap. "Because I didn't trust them. We didn't meet under the best of circumstances and we patched things up, but I still didn't know if they would agree to come all the way down here. And there was a prophecy that guided them. You know how I am about metaphysical things. It didn't say anything about you or the Helm or anything like that."

She put a hand on his shoulder. "You should have told them about me."

He nodded. "I realize that now. Andyn, at least, or Connor, would have convinced them to come along. Connor Lomin would have understood. But I'm going to turn over a new leaf."

She smiled back, giving his shoulder a squeeze. "If everything I heard about them is true, they probably will be glad to do it. Did you know Andyn Eleandir is a Lady of the Empire of Terenai now? And the others were all knighted?"

"Really?" He considered it, then shrugged. "Well, I've never put much stock in such things. I'm glad for them, though."

He paused for a moment before continuing. "When you're free of this place, I'll take you up north to meet them. I'll apologize for my actions and we can ask them for help in regaining our home."

She hugged him. "That's the big brother I remember."

They sat in silence for a while.

"I wanted another chance at him," he finally mused.

"I'd rather you got us out of here," she said with feeling. "How do we do it?"

"Well, we have an escape route and I can get them distracted with a diversion but we'll have to coordinate and you'll need to move fast." He looked at her expectantly.

"Without guards at my door, it will be easier. I have some dark leather armor from the academy and there are a couple of windows that look out on the service entrance from the north wing of the servants' quarters."

He sat for a while, digesting this information. It was odd, but without the Helm on his person or even near him, his head seemed more clear, he had more energy, and he felt better than he had in weeks.

"I'll try it tomorrow evening. First, I'll get rid of the Helm, then I'll set up a mock attempt to sabotage their work. We'll set up the timing so that you're ready to go as soon as I come out near the gate."

"If you're sure you can do it safely."

He grinned at her. "No, not safely. But with a minimum of risk. I've learned a few tricks in my time with the Riders."

He patted his sword. "Besides, I have Shriek."

Her eyebrows rose. "Is that its name?"

"Yes. It's enchanted."

"A magic sword? Wonderful! Does it have special abilities? May I hold it?"

He pulled it from its sheath and gave it to her. "It has an electrical edge and strikes with particular power against the undead," he explained.

She held it in her hands, eyes shining, then took a few expert cuts and thrusts. He smiled. She always had a special talent for swordsmanship and athletics and for a moment it seemed like times past when she would demonstrate a new technique she had learned.

She regarded it with admiring eyes. "I like this one. It's light but the balance is excellent."

"It's pretty powerful. I'll be all right."

She smiled up at him and handed Shriek back, hilt-first. "All right then, if you have Shriek. And promise to be careful."

"Double starlight promise."

***

Handor put the finishing touches on his protective spells and downed his last potion. A warm wave of energy coursed through him.

He peeked out from around a huge planter, watching four guards in leather armor stroll across the gardens. The sky threatened rain, but enough sunshine peeked through the clouds for him to make out the servants' entrance near a fountain in the shape of a dryad.

Handor counted to ten after the guards passed, then sneaked up to the fountain. In another couple of seconds, he made it to the door, cast an unlocking spell and slipped inside.

Based on the timing, he knew he had only a few minutes, but he had rehearsed everything a dozen times in his mind, plotting out every step. Quickly moving to the huge pantry room, he entered and closed the door behind him.

In the glitter of a tiny mage-fire, he removed his magic bag and drew out the Helm. Almost as if it sensed his purpose, it appeared more powerful, more alluring, more wondrous. Glad that he would never hear the haunting whispers again, he moved aside a large container of oat flour and found his secret childhood place for hiding cookies: a loose floor tile with a nice, large space beneath. He unceremoniously dumped the Helm inside and replaced the tile.

"Fuck you, Margoth, you bitchy old hag," he muttered, feeling immense relief. For good measure, he made an obscene gesture at the Helm.

He slipped back out of the pantry. Before leaving the area, he took a piece of paper out of his pocket, scribbled on it and put it under his mother's favorite blue mug on a nearby shelf. Satisfied, he left the area.

Now that he roamed around inside the house, he didn't have the benefit of distance and shadows, so he cast a spell of invisibility on himself.

The patrols certainly made his next steps difficult. He almost mis-timed one of the cycles and got caught between two dwarves and a human in purple and red robes. He avoided that by stepping up onto a supply box that obstructed their passage and pressed himself up against the wall. When his heartbeat returned to normal, he let out a deep breath and continued on.

Handor turned a corner, passed through an open door and blinked in surprise. The old wine cellar now looked more like the staging area for some kind of engineering company. Two human men looked at a list tacked up on a wooden board, sorting metal parts and placing them into boxes. Other boxes sat in neat rows. Blueprints hung on the walls, depicting some kind of arched framework of bones. Two dwarven men conversed in low tones, looking through a book. One of them picked up a sack and dumped it out on the table.

Handor's skin crawled. He watched as the dwarves picked through an assortment of skulls, laying them into neat piles by size. Some looked human, others were maybe dwarven or halfling, and some were smaller, like children, or even tiny, like sprites or pixies. He shivered.

A sound to his right alerted him and he slunk back behind a pile of crates.

A tall human with grey hair and a beard stepped through a doorway on the opposite side of the cellar, a door that Handor knew hadn't been there when he had left home. The man wore riotously colored robes of red, purple and pink and carried a staff. The dwarves and humans looked up.

"Master Lorferis," said one of the humans with a bow.

"How goes it?" Lorferis asked in a mild tone.

"Well, my lord. We will have another assembly ready to go in tonight."

"Excellent. See that it is ready for the midnight pickup." Lorferis strolled around the area, casually watching the proceedings. All the workers in the room looked up at his approach, then ducked their heads to their work as he passed.

Now for the diversion.

He took his time, slipping through open spaces until he reached the new door, always staying clear of the most obvious pathways, Taking a deep breath, he put a hand on the knob, then turned towards the room and cast a very mild spell on the magical lanterns by the main entrance. The lights flickered, drawing everyone's eyes.

"What was that?" asked Lorferis, heading towards the lanterns.

Handor quickly cast another spell, smirking as three magical symbols puffed out of existence from the doorframe. He opened the door, darted through and eased it shut without a sound.

His senses prickled immediately as he smelled dogs, sulphur, and brimstone. Heartbeat accelerating, he waited, listening and watching. Not seeing any danger, he continued, watching for any movement. The passage led to another open area, stacked with barrels and crates.

Thankfully, he recognized the room from Hannah's descriptions. She had certainly played the part of the subdued heiress well: fading into the background, she had gathered information from overheard conversations and observed the movements of all of Beol's allies, guards and servants.

Handor detected and neutralized two more magical traps on the floor near the entrance. Satisfied that there were no other dangers, he searched around until he found two barrels of lamp oil. Taking two slim crystals from a pocket, he worked open the stoppers of the barrels and dropped a crystal into each, replacing the stopper.

He flitted to the other side of the room to another open doorway. There, he turned and focused his mind on the crystals in the barrels. He gathered magical energy, lancing it down into them, heating them rapidly.

Spell finished, he darted down the passage again, following Hannah's directions. Behind him, he heard a hissing noise, then loud pops as the stoppers shot out of the barrels. Two dull thuds sounded in the passageway and the darkness behind him came alive with flickering light as the oil burned.

He grinned. *Let them chew on that for a while.*

He found what he sought: a room with hand trucks and a sloping ramp leading up to a set of open double doors. He slipped out into the open just as he heard shouts and commotion from within the complex.

Freedom beckoned not fifty feet away: the service entrance. A wrought iron gate barred the exit, guarded by two dwarven women with chain armor and spears.

Now he could hear more shouts from the underground complex behind him. Moving to the side, he hid in a clump of bushes. Soon, smoke curled out from the open ramp way, followed by a human male, coughing.

"There's a fire in the main supply room! The lamp oil is burning!" he shouted to the women. "Look for an intruder!"

The guards looked at each other, then stalked away from the gate, spears up and eyes searching.

Then he saw something that made his blood run cold. Two human women emerged from the smoke-filled ramp way, holding cloths to their mouths and leading a pair of two-headed dogs with glowing red eyes. The tumult underground had turned into quite a racket. The hounds sniffed the air and whined, appearing confused. One of them sneezed.

Cerberus hounds... At least the smoke has fouled their sense of smell for a while. Where are you, Hannah?

The women immediately went to talk to the dwarven guards. After seconds of discussion, the dwarves raced down the ramp and the handlers uncovered their mouths. They began to lead the hounds around the area in a patient, slow search pattern.

Damn it!

A flicker of motion caught his eye. A small figure in an open window lower herself down. He slipped over to her, almost feeling the glowing eyes of the hounds as they sniffed the ground.

"Hannah," he whispered.

"Here," she replied, drawing a sword and dagger. Masked and clad in dark leather, she looked like a piece of the night. "Let's go."

"Cerberus hounds and handlers. We can't risk it."

She bit her lip, eying the servants' gate. "We're so close. We can take them and open the gate, Handor. Please, our opportunity is slipping away and after this I don't know when we'll have another."

His natural caution warred with an intense desire to escape. Fighting a sense of foreboding, he nodded, drawing Shriek.

"Okay, we'll go. You can't see me, but just head out the gate when it opens."

Hugging the wall of the manor, they approached the gate. Too close to the hounds for his comfort, he cast a spell of opening. The giant metal gates swung open.

"Now," Hannah hissed, charging forward.

Muttering under his breath about impetuous younger siblings, he followed her, taking a course that would take him behind the guards if they saw her.

They did. Both hounds let out an echoing double bark and pulled their handlers forward, the women drawing swords as they went.

"Halt!" they shouted

Hannah turned, on guard. Handor waited until they passed him, then plunged Shriek into the back of one of the dogs. Instantly, his invisibility screen vanished and he turned to face the amazed handler. He loosed five fire-darts at her, the small missiles detonating with loud cracks. She jerked backwards and fell, her armor smoking.

The second guard released her hound at Hannah and charged him. With satisfaction, Handor saw his sister dodge and weave, stab and slash. The hound had a hard time even getting close to her.

The guard laid into him but with his enhanced agility, he parried easily. A Cerberus hound snapped at Hannah. She dodged and lopped off on head with her sword, then plunged the dagger into the hound's body. It howled and fell. She raced towards the gate.

A dark blue ball of light leapt up from the gravel pathway as she approached and crackled with magical energy. Handor's heart went into his throat.

"Hannah!" he yelled as the blue ball exploded, hurling his sister backwards.

With a fury borne of desperation, he attacked with a flurry of cuts and thrusts, finally killing the guard with a blast of magic to the heart.

He slid to his knees next to Hannah, checking for a pulse. Dizzy with relief at finding her heartbeat, he stared at a smoking symbol in the gravel just in front of the gate.

Stunning spell! Why didn't I check for one?

Replacing Shriek, he lifted Hannah in his arms and headed towards the open gate, towards the alleyway and freedom.

Something struck him in the back of the leg and he gasped, stumbling. Another hit him in the lower back and he staggered against the open gate.

He turned, seeing two dwarves drawing a bead on him with crossbows from across the yard. He slid Hannah to the ground just outside the gate and turned, dodging two bolts as they sang past. He cast another spell.

Crackling, popping balls of light leaped up before the archers, making them stumble backwards. With a hiss of fury, he fired spears of lightning, burning through them and hurling them back to lie in flaming heaps.

Fiery pain burned into him from the bolts in his back. With a curse, he jerked them out, feeling warm blood run down his limbs. He heard shouts and saw lights and running figures heading towards him. His head began to ache from so many spells in a short time.

Get them away from Hannah!

He loped towards the window she had opened, thankful that his armor had taken the brunt of the crossbow bolts. He climbed through the window, gritting his teeth against the pain.

Taking out a small blue vial, he downed it, sighing as healing energy flowed through him. His wounds now felt merely sore instead of fiery.

He took a deep breath. With any luck, they would completely miss Hannah lying unconscious just on the other side of the gate and he could lead them on a merry chase until she awoke and escaped.

Then he would have to improvise.

Weary, trying to deal with a headache and desperately needing a rest, he sat for a while, controlling his breathing. Finally, when he heard more shouts and the barking of Cerberus hounds, he stood, cast a final invisibility spell on himself, and headed out towards his old room.

He never arrived. Near the main hall, he turned aside from a pair of hounds and handlers, then almost ran over a trio of human Ja'al acolytes striding through a passage, their eyes glowing pink with arcane magic as they searched for him.

The hounds behind him bayed and took up the chase.

How did they find me so fast?

He turned, seeing the hellish creatures burst through a doorway. Fiery eyes locked on him. They bared teeth, snarling as they charged forward. He turned to race away, heart in his throat, but rammed into a dwarven guard coming around a corner. They went down in a heap. Shriek found the guard's heart in a second. Handor leaped up, but the hounds hurled themselves at him, slavering.

He lopped off a head, blew off another and went down under gnashing teeth, lashing out with Shriek. Searing pain raged through his shoulder, arm, and chest. He slashed and stabbed and the hounds yelped in pain as they died. Staggering to his feet, blood running down his armor, he saw a pair of guards and a Ja'al acolyte pointing at him from the doorway. The mage raised his hand. Red lightning flickered in his palm, then lanced out at him.

The world went dark.

Chapter Eleven - The Head of the Snake

"Oh mighty hero, slay me not!"

"Gorlak, knock it off. Just give me the keys."

Gorlak grinned up at Andyn Eleandir. She held out her hand and tried to maintain a disapproving look.

"Yes, Lady Andyn," he said with a bow, but his eyes twinkled. He passed three small, flat hexagonal pieces of metal to her. She inspected them, then nodded, regarding him.

He maintained his impish grin.

She pursed her lip and shook her head. "It's not enough that I have to get teased by these oafs but now you have to join in. They don't need encouragement, you know."

He shrugged. "I not see Lady Andyn often. Have to take chances when they come up."

Now she chuckled. "Gorlak, you're impossible. Now scoot. Get to the rally point and tell the commander we're going in. He's to set a cordon so nothing gets in or out of the complex, but tell him to keep his eyes open. We may need help very quickly."

The goblin bowed, gathering around him a cloak of deepest, velvety black. "Yes, Lady Andyn."

She turned to go but his voice stopped her.

"Lady?"

He bit his lip and fidgeted with the clasp of his cloak. "Be careful, Lady.

I not have many friends. Please come back."

She felt a surge of protectiveness and affection for this little being who had risked so much to turn from evil to join her in the fight against the Dark. She smiled past the tears he couldn't see.

"I will, Gorlak. Stay safe."

The goblin spread the cloak out to his sides and it formed misty dark wings. He waved his arms, then soared up into the air and fluttered away like a giant bat.

The Papal Nuncio sure doesn't lack for toys.

Andyn strode down the short alleyway, then peeked around the corner. Her companions waited in the gloom near the abandoned house. She made out Buck easily enough. His tall, armored form looked like a statue in the light of the two moons, standing behind a dark lamp post. Shifting to thermal vision, she picked out the shapes of Eric and Dar, hidden among the bushes and junk near the house. Connor perched on top of the roof behind a dilapidated chimney, keeping watch.

She crouched down and slipped next to Eric, pressing a key into his hand.

He glanced at it, then passed it back. "How he gets these things out from under the noses of the worst thugs and killers in Deran, I'll never figure out. What would we do without Gorlak?"

"A lot worse."

Andyn took a measured breath and focused her magical senses on the faded wooden porch. Three symbols glowed in her sight, each a tiny hexagon. She tapped Eric on the shoulder and made a hand signal to Dar, who drew his night-black sword and followed her up to the porch.

She shot a glance at Buck. He nodded, indicating no danger nearby, then hefted his shield and drew golden Khelios. His dwarven blade flashed silvery bright for a moment in the moonlight before he slipped it under his cloak. With a flick of his wrist, he lowered the arm on his helmet which held the Eye of Truth.

Andyn waited as he scanned the area. Buck shook his head.

"No illusions or anything hidden by magic," he whispered. He whistled once and Puup fluttered down to land on his shoulder. With a low word to the pigeon, he set the bird on a nearby fence post. Puup flew up and landed on the top of the lamp, preening his feathers.

Andyn set the keys down on their matching symbols on the porch, watching as a tiny red gem in the center of each glittered for a second. For a long moment, she thought nothing would happen, but then an entire section of the floorboards grew a seam and Dar lifted up a hidden door. She looked down with thermal vision, seeing only a metal ladder set into the side of a shaft.

With a faint whisper of sound, Connor joined them.

Holding her voice to a low chant, Andyn prayed to Verian, laying protective spells on her friends, watchings as filmy nets of mild golden and green light drifted down on their bodies and vanished.

Connor drew Tiuz but did not ignite it.

"Remember," Dar murmured, "these are the Crossed Swords, sworn enemies of Deran. They will not hesitate to kill."

Andyn cast another spell on a silver coin and the area became deathly silent. She handed the coin to Connor, who slithered down the ladder into darkness.

They used no lanterns or magical spells for fear of giving themselves away. Instead, knowing that Dar and Buck would be blind without light, they waited for Connor to return or give them a sign. Now that Connor ranged below with the coin and silencing spell, she felt keenly aware of any sound. A nerve-wracking time followed, punctuated only by the rustle of a stray scrap of paper blown from a pile of refuse.

Then something glowed in the darkness below. Dar and Eric swarmed down the ladder. Andyn followed them, moving down as fast as she could, hearing Buck behind her. She dropped down into a circular chamber with an exit to an open door that led into another room.

Connor stood over the bodies of two men in dark leather armor, a glowing spectral sword suspended in midair nearby. As she entered, he touched the pin on his armor and the misty sword flowed back into the brooch like water down a drain.

She checked the bodies but both were dead. She handed belt purses to Buck, who put them into a shoulder bag.

She raised an eyebrow. Connor shrugged as if to say "I tried," then led the way to a door on the other side of the room.

Eric also checked the bodies, finally producing a small copper key from one of the guards.

Dar moved but Eric stopped him before he could touch anything. He motioned to Buck, who stepped up and cast his gaze around the portal. After a few seconds, he pointed at the lintel and doorposts, then held up three fingers.

Well, we expected this.

Andyn motioned for Connor then pointed at the entrance behind them. Since he carried the silent coin, she needed him to be away from their location if she were to use magic.

With short, sharp motions and whispered words, she dispelled three magical traps, the lurid red symbols in the wood flaring briefly before going dark. Now Eric moved up and opened the door as she motioned for Connor to rejoin them.

In this fashion they sneaked into the complex of the Crossed Swords. Part of Andyn's mind marveled that they were even in the place while another part held a constant and tense vigil, watching for any slight motion or sound.

Eric moved like a ghost. He pointed out dangerous places with traps or alarms, waiting patiently while Connor or Andyn removed them. Her respect for him grew with each one. How could he remember each type of safeguard and how to counteract it, after all these years? It was beyond her. Several times, the Eye of Truth saved them, as she found that the Crossed Swords layered their traps, using illusion to hide them.

Three times they came up on guards in groups of three or four. Each time, the assassins drew weapons and surged to attack. Each time, the weapons of the Grey Riders — Tiuz, Rindara, Khelios, Fidelis and Eleison — flashed in the magical lamplight. Each time, the Crossed Swords henchmen fell to lie in dark pools on the floor. All occurred in eerie silence from Andyn's spell on the simple coin borne by Connor.

At a crossroads, Eric halted, his face held still in concentration. He frowned as he considered first the left path, then the right. Finally, he motioned Buck forward and pointed at the wall. Buck peered at it through the Eye of Truth, then gave Eric a look of approval. At a motion from Eric, Connor slipped up and found a hidden lock in the wall, then opened a door that seemed to materialize out of nowhere.

A set of steps led down. A faint metallic odor and rotting stench reached

Andyn and her pulse quickened. Sending up a silent prayer to Verian and Andyn's patron, Mindra, she drew her maces with suddenly sweaty palms as Eric looked at his friends with a grim expression.

She saw his eyes, intense, hard and burning with righteous anger. All at once, she realized what this meant to him: justice for her slain husband, for his dead kin, for all the innocents slaughtered by the Hylar family.

How much is this costing his soul?

Eric led the way down the steps, the darkness broken by flickering, sickly green torchlight.

At the bottom, the area opened into a large, octagonal chamber. Andyn's breath caught in her throat. On the far side, a shrine to Neralia emanated a wave of pure evil. A tall statue of the Death's-Head goddess seemed ready to come to life. Beautiful yet depraved features regarded the room haughtily as it held forth the severed head of a sacrifice. Scanty armor made of bones covered its form and it held a bloody dirk in her other hand. Andyn felt her stomach lurch as she turned her eyes away from the belt of infant skulls around the statue's waist.

An altar dark with dried blood stood before the statue and a row of chairs sat to the right and left of the altar. Precious gems formed odd patterns on the walls. Strange, vile-looking symbols painted on the floor seemed to caper and dance in the green torchlight.

A door on the far side opened and a half-elven woman strode in, followed by a blond human who could only be Eric's father. Harkin Hylar's features held the same handsome lines as his son, without the humanizing compassion in Eric's face. He bore two swords in his belt and was attired completely in black brigandine. The pair conversed as they entered, not even looking up.

The woman… well, Andyn had to admit it was part female jealousy, but she hated her instantly. Taramis Hylar looked like a queen of evil: stunning, honey-blonde, with eyes of aquamarine and a lithe, supple figure. She had a handaxe and dagger at her belt and wore silvery chainmail. The screaming-demon medallion of the Ja'al rested at her throat on a choker.

"Really, Harkin," Taramis said as she moved towards the altar, "I think you're making too much of this. These 'Grey Riders' are not really all that much of a threat. Certainly, they have cut into our operations here in Oak-moor, but the other sectors are not in danger, and we continue to make good profit from Terenai."

"It's not the accounting that bothers me, my dear," replied Harkin, his brow furrowed. "It's the tactical aspects. Whoever is doing this has been able to circumvent our first layer of protection and seems to know how our networks are set up."

"We did sacrifice that royal spy to Neralia, didn't we? That should take care of it." Taramis snapped her fingers and two black candles blazed with crimson tongues of fire.

"Yes, but I'm not convinced he was the one," said Harkin with a frown, putting his hands on his sword hilts.

Eric motioned to Connor, who handed him the coin. Eric tossed it up the steps behind him.

"Hello Mother. Hello Father. Allow me to introduce my friends, the Grey Riders."

Andyn took a wicked satisfaction in seeing the looks of absolute astonishment on the faces of the Hylars. Eric's mother gaped at him. Her mouth closed into a thin, bitter line and her eyes flashed coldly. Harkin stared at him for a few heartbeats, then smirked.

"It's about time you showed up," he said. "We send you out to get supplies and look what happens."

Eric shrugged. "I didn't have much to come back to."

"You've done well for yourself, it seems," Harkin said, sliding to the left, fingering his weapons. "You must be the one they call Indidarc. Interesting. Didn't think old Melinor had room for any more after that half-daemon girl."

"You mean my sister? Melinor and Anne have love enough for twenty kids, unlike some I know."

"Love doesn't get you anywhere, Eric," said Taramis with a disdainful glance at his companions. "Power is what really matters."

She lounged against the altar, eyes mocking. "I presume you didn't bring this motley rout into our complex to just introduce them to us. And who's this? Your latest lover? My compliments - nice legs and tits. She looks like she might be a good fuck, but maybe not."

Andyn felt her seething anger turn to fury and took a step forward. Dar's hand on her shoulder stopped her.

Eric smiled. "She is the widow of one of the people you slaughtered. By the way, you probably know Liander Tolin is dead. We made sure he received justice for Andyn's husband."

"Ah. Well, good riddance to him." said Harkin, drawing his weapons. Purple lightning raced along the edge of one of his blades and red runes glowed on the other. "He was a blithering idiot, always pining away for some elven wench from his past life. So, I don't think I can convince you to return to your rightful place, with your true family, can I?"

Eric shook his head. "My rightful place is not here and you aren't my family. You haven't been since I was old enough to walk. I say openly that I do not know you."

Taramis hissed with anger. "Ungrateful whelp! You presume to disown us?"

In answer, Eric held up his spear in its shortened form. "Fidelis," he said. The spear lengthened and the tip glowed golden as he brought it to guard position.

Taramis actually started in surprise and her eyes narrowed as she drew her dagger and axe, both of which flickered with green light. "I see this will end badly."

"For you, bitch," said Dar, drawing Rindara.

Harkin made a face, looking at the Riders with distaste. "So you say. Well then, let's get started. Dinner is at seven and I don't want my soup to get cold."

Orange, gold, silver and blue weapon fire flashed in the light of the flickering torches.

Taramis clashed her weapons together and shouted a harsh word. The universe slowed to a crawl and Andyn struggled to bring her maces up in defense.

What's happening? Verian, aid me!

Taramis turned to the statue of Neralia and an arc of green light flew from her weapons. To Andyn's horror, the statue stepped down from its dais. Red light flared in its eyes and the severed head in its hand warped into a club topped with a fanged skull.

Andyn found her voice. "*Verian! Ald-adani!*"

With a wrenching heave and a flash of light, her lethargy vanished and she could move again at full speed. Taramis snarled and charged forward. Not seeing anything else but the woman whose men had slain her husband, Andyn met her with full force, lashing out with both her maces. Their weapons slammed into each other, casting up showers of sparks. She sensed Connor angling away from Taramis, trying to get to her blind side, but the statue swiped at him with its nightmare club and he dodged away.

Taramis swung at Andyn's legs. She leaped over attack. Without breaking her movements, Taramis whirled and swept her leg out in an arc as Andyn landed. Andyn tripped and tumbled backwards, rolling to ready position. The deadly axe and dagger swept down and Andyn parried both away, then thrust Eleison into Taramis' vision and and swiped at her leg with her other mace. Eric's mother banged aside both attacks and stepped back.

"I must compliment my son," Taramis said with an icy smile. "He chooses sluts who actually have some ability."

"Spoken like an expert on sluts, Taramis Hylar," Andyn spat.

That earned her a hiss of rage and a set of four complicated attack patterns, one after the other. Andyn gave ground, leaping onto chairs and dodging. Twice, the dagger hit her armor and twice blue sparks shot out. Andyn felt her magical shields buckle.

She spared a glance at the other parts of the battle. Connor and Buck hammered away at the animated statue, which tried repeatedly to pluck a skull from its belt but was constantly interrupted by hits from Khelios or Tiuz. Harkin dueled with Dar and Eric, their weapons clashing in bursts of silver, gold or red fire.

Taramis laid down her axe and made a circular motion with her hand, palm down. Andyn saw the floor stones of the chapel warp and boil, belching forth green fumes. The air filled with a horrid stench that reminded her of corpses and molten lead as the venomous cloud reached out towards Andyn and her companions.

Andyn leaped on top of a chair, looped a mace onto a belt hook and began a prayer to Verian. A disk of blue light grew from her open hand and she thrust it down at the vapors. With a shout, she released it and the cloud disappeared.

Taramis' mouth twisted into a snarl and she pointed a finger at Andyn, sending a grayish glob hurtling at her. Andyn tumbled down off the chair and popped up on one knee as the glob smacked into the wall, bursting into a fat gout of ill-smelling fog. Andyn held forth her hand and released four fire-darts into Taramis. The woman stepped back, trying to avoid the missiles, but they detonated on her armor with sharp reports, making her stumble.

Taramis sent a green ray from the palm of her hand at Andyn. The beam struck her in the abdomen and her protective screens wavered, flickering blue and yellow. She twisted to the side with a gasp, feeling the heat penetrate her armor and burn her skin.

Andyn followed that up with a ball of light on the bridge of her opponent's nose, but Taramis dispelled it with a word and a curt wave of her hand. Andyn swept up her mace. Taramis cast another spell and the very air seemed to constrict around Andyn.

Recalling her battle with Zhinia Margoth, Andyn centered her mind quickly, then released a bolt of lightning that hurled Taramis back against the altar. The woman reeled and righted herself, then shouted an obscenity and pointed a fist at the floor under Andyn. With a thunderous boom, the floor shattered, hurling Andyn through the air and into a heap in the corner, where stones pummeled her.

She shook her head, trying to stand, but her left knee buckled and she felt two ribs grate with shooting pain. She lurched to her feet and focused a spell on Taramis. Twin pinwheels of rainbow colors whirled out at the evil priestess and she was forced to dodge behind the altar. The pinwheels detonated, throwing up a mist of wild colors. Andyn quickly snatched a potion from a belt loop and downed it as Taramis tried to peer through the kaleidoscope. Warmth filled Andyn's body and the pain from her injuries receded.

Taramis came around the altar, panting, and placed a hand to her injuries. A warm orange glow covered her and she smiled. Sounds of battle rang in the chapel behind her.

"Two can play that game," she said, taking up her axe again. "This could go on for quite a while. Why don't we talk about this, just us girls? What is Eric promising you? Wealth? Fame? Sex? I know he can't deliver."

"None of the above, Taramis," Andyn snapped. "Those things I don't want from him. He's given me love and friendship, which you can never understand."

A loud, whining sound made them both look and they turned. Connor clung to the back of the statue, pulling its head back with one hand as he hacked at the neck with Tiuz. The golem staggered as Buck pounded away at it with Khelios, parrying the skull-club with his shield. Connor's spectral sword slashed at its legs, cutting fine cracks in the stone. Finally, the autom-aton managed to pluck a baby skull from its belt and hurl it to the floor. It exploded in a bloom of flame, bone chips and chunks of stone. Andyn crouched behind a chair as Buck hurtled into a wall with a loud, metallic thump. Connor finally jammed his blade into a seam in the golem's neck and twisted. The head flew off with a loud popping noise. Connor flew backwards and hit the wall with bruising force, landing in a heap on the floor. Buck struggled to rise. The golem staggered, then fell apart into crumbling chunks of stone.

"Sacrilege!" shrieked Taramis. She leaped towards Connor to finish him off but Andyn kicked a chair at her legs and followed it up with a swing with Eleison. With a loud crack, Andyn's mace broke a shinbone and Taramis stumbled with a scream. She leaned on the altar, face grey. Andyn waded in but Taramis whipped her axe around, slamming it into Andyn's side.

Blazing fire seared into Andyn as the axe blade shattered her screens, sliced through her chainmail and bit deep into her side. She went down on one knee, vision blurring. Taramis rose up for a killing blow but Buck's dag-ger thumped into her chest and she reeled.

Andyn looked up with misty eyes, seeing Buck on one knee. Behind him, Dar stood over a still form and Eric hefted Fidelis, the golden spear shining like the sun.

Taramis stared at the wreckage of the chapel, then turned pleading eyes to Eric.

"Darling," she gasped. "You wouldn't kill your own mother, would you? You're my flesh and blood."

He paused, uncertainty on his face. Taramis hissed a curse, hurling a now-glittering dagger at his heart. He threw his spear. Golden Fidelis shot through the air, impaling her. The dagger struck Eric in the shoulder and he lurched to the side.

"My mother's name was Anne," Eric said, grimacing. "Anne Indidarc."

Taramis Hylar stared at the holy spear through her heart.

"How...?" she made a slow turn and fell to the floor.

"Fidelis," Eric whispered, and the spear flickered back to his hand. He leaned against a wall and began to slide down towards the floor.

"Quick, Dar!" Andyn said, limping towards him. "Check Connor. Buck, come over here."

"I'll be okay. See to Eric," Buck said. He downed a potion, then another. A blue light glowed over him.

Andyn staggered to Eric's side. To her horror, his eyes became glassy and he slumped down. She dropped her maces and pulled out the dagger, quickly covering his bleeding wound.

Please, Verian, don't let him become another victim of his parents. Show me the way.

Deep within the wound, she detected a poison slowly sifting into Eric's bloodstream. Her heart went cold. She used a neutralizing spell but the poison kept up its deadly flow.

Magically augmented!

Thinking quickly, she slowed the spread of the poison by reducing Eric's heartbeat, then tried a combination of molecular keys. After using and discarding two of them, she recognized a pattern and whispered a counter-spell. In her mind's eye, she watched with relief as the vile substance unravelled and disintegrated, falling apart into harmless hydrocarbon chains.

"Is he...?" she heard Dar's voice.

"He'll be all right. I got it in time," she sighed, opening her eyes. She felt every breath as a stab and now held a hand to her bleeding side.

She concentrated, focusing healing power into her own wounds, then sighed with relief and slumped down next to Eric.

"The dagger was coated with a magically augmented poison," she explained, panting. "It's one of the ones I've seen before so I knew the key code, thank Verian's grace."

"What about Harkin?" asked Connor, limping over. "Looks like he's still breathing."

"For now," replied Buck with a shrug, "but I can solve that." He yanked his dagger from Taramis' chest and wiped it off in her hair.

"No," Eric said, sitting up and grimacing. "We won't be like them. She chose to fight to the death. We managed to knock him out. He'll live to see justice for all those he's murdered."

Buck shrugged and replaced the dagger, then walked over to join them. Despite their surroundings, they took the time to rest, Connor tying Harkin's hands securely.

"What's the quickest way out again?" Andyn asked Eric as she bandaged up his wounds.

"Back the way we came. We've cleared a path for now but I guarantee all this ruckus will bring someone," he said with a wince. "My mother always made it painfully clear that she wasn't to be disturbed when in the chapel, but eventually, someone will come. The silence spell on the coin served to muffle things a bit. Still, we have to get moving."

To Andyn's disappointment, Harkin awakened just as they were about to leave.

He blinked, looking around, then stared at Taramis' body lying against the altar. He nodded, his jaw working and eyes hard.

After a few heartbeats, he let out a deep breath. "Well, I knew it had to happen some day. Fine figure of a woman, but reckless and full of herself."

With a shrug, he looked up at his son. "At least I won't have to help her out with those damned ceremonies any more. Boring as hell and worthless, if you ask me."

"I didn't," said Eric, standing and returning Fidelis to its smaller size.

Buck hauled Harkin to his feet. "Don't worry," he said to the assassin prince in a cheerful voice, "You probably won't miss her, or your other mistresses, where you're going."

Connor tapped Harkin on the shoulder. The guild master looked down his nose at the halfling.

Connor smiled. "I'm sure you remember that I have a spectral sword. Now, it's just a magical tool, and it doesn't really care who it hurts if I'm in danger. Where my companions might look badly on me for hurting you, they can't punish a spectral sword. So play nice."

He touched his brooch and the ghostly sword glittered into being in front of him. Harkin Hylar eyed it warily.

Eric retrieved the silenced coin and, with Harkin at the center of their formation, they returned the way they had entered, moving quickly back towards the trap door.

Andyn felt about a hundred years old. Every movement brought creaking pain and her head throbbed. She tasted something bitter and sour in her mouth and she had to blink to clear her vision.

Just a little further. Verian, please let us get out of here.

With a feeling of great relief, they returned to the ladder at the entrance. Connor clambered up, carrying the coin. He opened the trap door and headed outside, then looked down and waved at them.

Prodded by Buck and watched closely by Dar, Harkin followed Eric up the ladder, assisted by both warriors since his hands were tied.

Andyn clambered up the ladder to the surface, then sighed and leaned against a nearby post, feeling the cold winter air. She didn't care that it nearly froze the sweat on her skin; they were out of that hellish place.

Connor tossed the silence coin into a nearby bush.

"Send up the signal," Dar said wearily, eyes watching the street. Nothing moved, but he and Eric kept watch on Harkin. Buck stood next to them, peering through the Eye of Truth.

Connor took out his bow and an arrow with a red head, aiming up at the dark sky. He loosed. At the apex of the arrow's path, it burst into a flickering crimson light.

"So," Harkin commented, sitting down on the porch. "You're one of the Grey Riders, eh?"

Eric didn't answer. Harkin looked up at him and chuckled.

"The silent treatment? You got that from your mother. Never mind. Servant of the idiot Christian Church or not, I have to admit you did a good one on Margoth. Heard about that in the underground, I did. Fine work. That boney witch was going to be trouble if she ever got any power, that's for certain. You did us all a favor."

Andyn looked at him. Harkin's eyes held cynical amusement but a measure of fatherly pride, something she did not expect.

"Well," he continued. "You have ability, there's no doubt. We can certainly use your talents, boy. I'm going to give you another chance."

Eric scoffed but otherwise remained silent.

Andyn stared at Harkin. "You have to be joking! Another chance at what? You're on your way to prison and probably the gallows!" she hissed.

Buck looked up at the lantern, then drew Khelios. "Where's Puup?"

With a shock, Andyn realized the pigeon had fled. That could only mean...

Harkin shrugged. "Have it your way, but you forgot to check me for my alarm medallion, Eric. As soon as you took me out of the complex, it caused a chime to sound in my room. You'll have about forty Crossed Swords to contend with in a minute."

Andyn's heart grew cold and she shot a look at Eric. Her friend stared at his father, then at her, looking stricken.

He didn't even know Harkin had it.

"A little trifle your mother cooked up to prevent me from leaving without her knowing it," Harkin continued, resting his bound hands on his knees. "Seems she didn't like me visiting the clandestine brothels in this city without her say-so. She had magical power on her side so it was useless trying to fight it, but I didn't mind too much as long as she or one of her assistant priestesses were willing to bend over. Now I think it's actually going to be useful."

"Get ready, guys," said Dar, hefting Rhindara.

Andyn readied her maces as dark figures emerged from the shadows along the street. Her weariness hit her like a wave, but she gritted her teeth, determined to go down fighting.

"You okay, boss?" came a voice from a hulking shadow across the street.

"Yeah," Harkin replied with a sniff, waving his bound hands. "These types won't kill me since I'm a prisoner. You can have at them any time you want. Double bounty. Kill the others, but keep my son and the elf bitch. She'll be worth something on the slave market after I try her out. Nice piece of ass."

Andyn prepared a Fire-Fan spell as the assassins surged forward. A swarm of crossbow bolts lanced out at her, but she burned them with her magic, the missiles fluttering at her feet in flaming scraps.

The assassins charged within reach. She could smell the rank breath on one of them, a leering fellow with a rakish mustache and twin sabers.

Then silver light burst all around and bows sang from the rooftops. Arrows hissed down at their targets, dropping assassins right and left. Figures charged down the streets, spears out, the symbol of Deran's Royal House emblazoned on hauberk and shield. The assassins whirled to meet them and the Grey Riders swung their weapons, beating off the attack and sending the Crossed Swords into disarray.

More arrows hummed in the night. Andyn tried to dodge and hit an assassin or two but took a few sword slashes on her armor. The chainmail held and flashed with white light, but the blows bruised her and she felt her weariness like a vest of lead. More dark figures stumbled or fell. The assassin force wheeled, their leaders casting down flash bombs that blinded Andyn and her allies. When she could see again, only a few remained, locked in combat with the guards. On the rooftops, Deranese rangers raced away, chasing after the dispersing assassins.

A burly dwarven officer loped up to her as she leaned against the lamp post, breathing heavily. The dwarf looked down at Harkin, who eyed a misty spectral sword hovering near his neck.

The dwarf bowed before her. "I am Captain Rugor, Lady Andyn of Terenai. May we render you assistance?"

She nodded. "This person here needs to be taken to prison. And we will all need healers."

An elven soldier caught her as she collapsed.

"As you command, O Light of Justice," said Captain Rugor as she closed her eyes. Before she passed out, she saw an image of Larad in her mind, smiling at her on a sunny day at their home in Eleth-Anor.

Chapter Twelve - Someone Old, Someone New

"Hey, at least leave me a few scraps, would you?" Dar Cabot shook his head as Connor Lomin held his hands out innocently.

"What? I think there's plenty left," Connor said around a mouthful of blueberry muffin. He waved a hand at the platters before him. "Of course, if you wait too long…"

Dar shook his head and eyed the selection of smoked meats, cubes of cheese, sliced fruit and pastries on the glass table. He took a plate and filled it, picking a muffin with a warning look at Connor, who smiled back. Despite the impressive array, he knew the halfling would put a dent in it soon enough.

Dar strolled over to the balcony of their suite. He gazed out the glass doors, watching snow float down on the city of Oakmoor. Somewhere above the grey sky, he knew the sun shone brightly, yet here, he saw a grey morning turning to white.

The Crown rewards well, he mused. *We were just here for the Christmas party. Now we have rooms, free of charge.*

Connor joined him. "I'm sure glad this is over."

Dar took a deep breath. "Yes, Eric has finally put his demons to rest — I hope. I can't imagine what this is costing him."

Connor sipped from his mug of tea. "Think of what you went through when you found out Margoth had turned your grandparents into undead, and what it felt like when you gave them release. That's probably pretty close."

Dar nodded. "We all have our share of sorrows, every one of us. Buck's childhood friend framed him for a crime he didn't commit, and it took the Eye of Truth to settle that issue in court."

He looked down at Connor. The halfling didn't reply, no doubt lost in memories of his wife and daughter, dead these long years, victims of a magical disease sent into his homeland by Margoth in her plot to find a magic key — the same key that the Riders used to find the holy Crown of Saint Alyssa.

That was the very same Crown that Andyn used to destroy Margoth once and for all…

His thoughts drifted. *So many lives spent or ruined — Andyn's husband, Connor's family, Buck's friend, my grandparents, and Megan and Brandi's parents killed in the Christian persecutions in Torosc. So much pain.*

He sighed. *God, we need peace.*

Connor and Dar watched the drifting snow, each lost in his own memories. The sound of a door opening behind them made them turn.

Buck stretched to his full height and yawned. "It's nice to not have to go charging off anywhere."

He poured himself some tea and filled a plate with fruit, sliced meat and pastries.

"What are you looking at?" he asked, joining them at the window.

Dar shrugged. "Nothing really. Thinking. Remembering. We've all been through a lot."

Buck made a face. "Me least of all."

Connor shook his head. "Your father was used as a hostage and almost got killed when we went after Liander Tolin, and now all our families have extra guards because of the Ja'al."

Dar felt a chill, unable to shake an ominous feeling.

A small brown bird alighted on the balustrade of the balcony outside, turning a curious eye to them as it hopped along, pecking at the snow.

"That little bird was here yesterday too," Connor noted.

"Andyn leaves crumbs on the balcony," Dar said.

"Where is she?" asked Buck.

"Probably still in bed, like Eric," Dar said. "You know her. Late riser if she can get away with it."

Buck and Connor exchanged a glance with raised eyebrows. Dar ignored them. He had tried to convince the two of them that Eric and Andyn didn't have that kind of relationship, that Eric's devotion to Brandawyn Alenar was complete, and that Andyn wouldn't dream of coming between them, but to no avail. They found it hard to believe that Eric wouldn't take advantage of Andyn's affection, beauty and proximity in Brandi's absence.

Some men would do that but not Eric, and, to be truthful, I doubt if Buck or Connor would do it either.

"The rooms are really nice," said Buck around a mouthful of spiced beef. "And this parlor lets us meet up if we want to. I don't think I could afford this on my own."

"With your reward money you will," Connor said with a smirk. "Have you heard?"

Buck shook his head.

"The Royal Council decided to give us all a bonus for extreme danger. Five thousand gold crowns."

Dar's eyes widened. "Seriously? That's ten times the average wages for a worker in Deran."

"That makes eight thousand each for this escapade with the initial fee," Connor said with satisfaction. "I think I will be able to buy my own ranch in Evendale soon at this rate."

Buck snorted. "Not me. My armor repair costs keep eating my commissions. It will be a long time for me."

"For all of us," said Dar.

"What will be a long time?" asked another voice from behind them.

Dar turned to see Andyn Eleandir, running a brush through her golden hair, clad in a simple, dark blue dress. She looked rested but her eyes held an introspective, haunted look.

"A long time until we'll get rich, Andyn," said Buck, saluting her with a slice of pear on his fork. "So have some breakfast and enjoy the treats before Connor gets them all."

She smiled, arching an eyebrow at the halfling, who gave her a deadpan look in return.

"He'd better be a gentleman if he knows what's good for him."

Appropriating a porcelain cup, she poured a dark brown liquid into it and then added a dollop of cream from a shallow bowl and a spoon of sugar. With another look at Connor, she picked up a small breakfast plate.

"Ah," she said, savoring a sip as she stepped next to Dar. "Gorostoli jekka. Hard to come by this far north. I'd almost forgotten what it tasted like."

Dar nodded, sipping from his own cup of bittersweet jekka.

They all stood without speaking, watching the snow fall.

This is the quietest we've ever been.

"I'm worried about him," Andyn said suddenly.

"Me too," said Dar. "Did you talk to him?"

She nodded, taking a bite of fruit. "Yes." Her voice trailed off.

Buck gestured. "And?"

She swallowed and sighed. "It's hard enough to have a horrible upbringing and break away from it at a young age, then try to leave the past behind. But to have to kill your own mother, no matter how evil — well, that leaves a scar. Frankly, it's a miracle he's not insane by now."

"I wish Brandi were here," Dar found himself saying. "Not that you don't help him, Andyn, no offense."

She waved a hand. "None taken. I miss her too. She is a wonderful woman, they share a common faith, and she loves him more than her own life."

Dar nodded. "By God's own hand, Eric has been saved from a terrible fate time and again, first by his own initiative, then by Melinor, then by Anne — who became the real mother he always wanted — then by Brandi. The problem is how he's going to move on from this."

"With faith and patience," Andyn said, taking another sip from her cup.

Dar gave her a look. "And you? Your Larad has finally been avenged."

She gave a bitter laugh. "I thought I had done that when we killed Liander Tolin, but it was an empty victory. Tolin was enslaved as surely as any of the thralls of the evil ones. And Eric? He didn't buy me any more peace by breaking up his family's gang. He tried to gain his own closure. I just hope he doesn't feel as empty as I did. If it wasn't for all of you, I probably would have gone insane myself."

They stood in silence again, watching the snow and the bird. A door opened and closed behind them.

Dar didn't turn to look, sensing instead of seeing Eric walk up behind them and pick up a cup of jekka for himself. He sipped absently.

"You okay?" asked Andyn, placing a hand on Eric's shoulder as he slipped next to her.

He looked down and nodded. "It's been two days."

Andyn gave him a sympathetic look. "It's been years for me, Eric."

He sighed. "I don't know if this is what you felt, Andyn, but in spite of the relief of finally finding closure and bringing them to justice for so many, I just feel…" He searched for the word.

"Empty?"

He nodded. "Yes. Why?"

Dar spoke. "Because we're not meant to revel in the downfall of evil people, but pity their fate. I felt kind of like that after Margoth. I owed her for what she did to my grandparents, but it wasn't my right to take vengeance. It's God's. He's the Emperor of the Universe. I haven't created any galaxies lately."

Andyn nodded. "There's a reason revenge is bitter. It's because it's not meant to be tasted."

Dar smiled. "A quote of Mindra?"

"Tolan the First Prophet."

"I'm beginning to like him," Dar said and sipped his jekka.

Andyn smiled brilliantly but turned her attention again to Eric.

"Your friends are here," she said softly, giving him a hug. "In time, the emptiness is filled with good things: love, life, peace."

He hugged her back. "It will take a while."

"Let it," said Connor, slipping up onto the arm of the couch. "Don't rush, but don't dwell either. Let us help you and let it go."

Eric nodded, wiping at his eyes, then let out a breath and took up his cup again to gaze out the window. Dar finished his breakfast and wondered what were his odds of getting anything more before Connor licked the crumbs off the platter.

"It's Christmas Eve," Eric finally said to Dar. "Hope you got me a good present."

"Lumps of coal," he replied.

"Good," said Eric, looking pleased. "I got you the same thing."

Dar nodded gravely, avoiding Eric's gaze.

Andyn looked at one of them, then the other, then shook her head. "I shouldn't have worried. You have a bit of the jester in you, Eric Indidarc."

"Seriously, though," Dar said, placing his cup down on the table. "Christmas is tomorrow. Eric and I will be hosting all of you tonight for dinner and then, well, just look for something special in the morning."

Andyn finished the last of her breakfast. "Charming custom. I mean, it's the birthday of your Jesus, yet you give presents to other people and alms for the poor."

Eric's voice became very quiet. "It's what God wants from us as a birthday present."

Dar wondered, then realized it had probably been a while since Eric had been home to Whitepine, Deran, the place where he had celebrated so many Christmases with the Indidarcs, before Anne's death.

"Then I salute your Jesus Christ," added Connor with an emphatic nod, hopping down. "Any religion that encourages gift-giving to one and sundry is all right in my book."

A knock sounded on the entrance door to the common area and Dar exchanged a look with Andyn.

"Yes?"

The door opened a crack and he saw the face of one of their guards. "Lord Melinor to see you, Sir Cabot."

"Well, if we must," he said with a sigh of mock exasperation.

Melinor swept into the room, attired in a dark grey mantle and cloak, smiling at all of them.

"Late risers I see? Good. You should rise as late as you want for a while."

He greeted the Riders in turn with a hug for Eric, a kiss for Andyn and firm handshakes for the others.

"It's a change, Father, after being on the go so hard for so long," Eric agreed.

Melinor reached for the now-empty platter, raised his eyebrows at Connor, then shrugged. "You deserve it. All Oakmoor is celebrating the demise of the Crossed Swords guild. Not even a dozen of those villains escaped."

Eric looked down and Melinor put an arm around his shoulders.

"I am always here, Eric," he said quietly. He put a hand on his son's hair and bent to touch his head to Eric's. Dar smiled at the old man, glad that Eric had a real father-figure at last.

Eric nodded but didn't speak. Melinor just stood with him for a while in silence, then patted him on the shoulder.

"Speaking of being here," Melinor said briskly, turning away, "I am here because I am to inform you of a few facts uncovered by our Intelligence analysts, using the captured records from the Crossed Swords headquarters."

He sat on another couch opposite Connor and motioned for the Riders to join him. Dar sat next to Connor across from Melinor as the others crowded around.

The wizard took a deep breath. "First of all, we learned the locations of all the other Crossed Sword guild houses in Deran, including alternate safe-houses and clandestine contacts and allies. There is now a nation-wide campaign to hunt them down. Second, the entire Northern Alliance is now involved, because some of the records indicate that the Crossed Swords were actually working for the Ja'al. Our military thought that the rapid pace of your attacks on the Guild would make them run for cover, but that did not happen, which led them to believe that there was another entity commanding them. We now know that it was the Manipulator Church, the Ja'al."

Dar sat back as Melinor continued. "Third, the Crossed Swords were not only on the Ja'al payroll, but they had instructions to cause as much havoc as possible. In addition to paid assassinations, they were involved in a clandestine war against the Intelligence Services of Deran, Astarel, Rokon, Eldir, Terenai and Evendale. They were to strike at anyone who dared interfere with the actions of the Ja'al with regard to a critical project."

"Which was?" Andyn asked before Dar could speak.

"Fact number four," Melinor said, appropriating Connor's cup and pouring jekka into it. "Apparently, the Ja'al have subverted the Lervion Shipping House for their own purpose, chief among which was the transport of special components for their critical project, something which I will describe to you in a more secure setting. You will doubtless remember that the Lervion House is one of many transnational shipping lines whose operations span all the nations north of Torosc."

Dar turned these facts over in his mind, then shot a glance at Melinor. The wizard met his gaze and Dar knew now that whatever critical project the Ja'al had in mind, it was enough to worry Melinor.

That thought sent a chill down Dar's spine. He felt a sudden urgent desire to know, but held it down, knowing that Melinor would meet with them in a secret facility to discuss it.

"The headquarters of Lervion House is in Meridian, Gorostol," Melinor concluded. "So, if you are of a mind to continue in the trail of the Crossed Swords and the Ja'al, that would be your next assignment."

To Dar's surprise, Eric spoke first. "I think we should go."

Andyn put a hand on his. "It's too soon, Eric."

He shook his head. "I need to be doing something, not lamenting my evil family. Besides, whatever the Ja'al are up to, we know it's a well-organized plan that likely has all manner of misdirection and long-range planning behind it."

Andyn looked at the others. They all nodded.

Melinor looked pleased. "Excellent. You can start when you're ready. Oh, and the Alliance has assigned a liaison officer to join you, someone from the Empire of Terenai with airborne riding training and military background. He should be joining us shortly."

"Who is it?" asked Buck.

"You will find out soon enough," said the wizard, then held up his hand when they heard a knock on the door.

"Yes?" asked Dar.

The door guard poked his head in again. "Major Demaris is here, Milord."

"What perfect timing!" said Melinor with a mysterious twinkle in his eye. "Send him in." He stood.

Dar joined him but stopped when he noticed Andyn's expression. Her mouth hung open, her eyes wide in amazement.

"You're going to swallow a fly, Andyn," said Connor, tapping her knee. "Come on."

"Major Khyron Demaris," announced Melinor, maintaining his conspiratorial look.

A blond half-elven man strode in carrying a helm under one arm, his other hand resting on the hilt of a longsword. A blue and white surcoat covered black leather armor with silver studs. He bowed, then turned a handsome face to the assembly, regarding them with sea-green eyes. A pale scar marked the left side of his jaw.

"My Lord. Sir Cabot, Sir Indidarc, Master Lomin. Sir Buckminster. Lady

Andyn."

"Khyron?"

The other riders turned to watch Andyn slowly walk towards the new-comer.

Khyron gave a small, affectionate smile and bowed again. "Light of Justice, it is an honor."

"Is it really you?" Andyn said, walking towards him as if in a dream and placing her hands on his forearms.

He straightened, his own eyes now mirroring the humor in Melinor's. "Last time I checked."

Andyn's lip trembled for a second, then she wrapped her arms around him. "For the love of Verian! I thought… I didn't know what happened to you. Some said you were dead! It's been so long…"

With a contented smile, Khyron returned her embrace.

Dar turned to the other Riders, who looked back at him in confusion. Eric shrugged.

"Andyn," Dar said finally, "I guess you know Major Demaris."

"I should say so," said Melinor with a smile. "Shall I tell them?"

Andyn spun on him. "You knew?"

"Of course I knew," Melinor said with a hurt expression. "We had to interview all the candidates. Once we found out who he was, we knew he would be a good match and well able to integrate into the team."

Andyn looked torn between fury, amazement and happiness, then stamped her foot. "Oh, you vile, sneaky old man, you! You should have at least warned me!"

"And miss this? Never, my dear," Melinor said, walking up to give her a kiss on the cheek. "I have to have my little instances of meddling and fun when I get them."

"Care to enlighten us, Andyn?" Connor asked.

Andyn looked at Khyron, who gave her an apologetic grin. She lifted her chin.

"Major Demaris and I grew up together in Eleth-Anor," she said. "Our families are close and so were we. There was some discussion as to whether we would marry, though we drifted apart in our adolescent years. After graduation from the academy, Khyron was assigned to the eastern borders for covert operations for a long time and we lost contact. Larad proposed to me a few months later."

"All true," said Khyron.

She rounded on him. "And you! I could punch you! You agreed to this? I almost had a heart attack!"

He held up a hand in defense. "I was outranked. Besides, my assignment is supposed to be kept under wraps until we leave on the next mission."

Andyn glared at him and Melinor in turn, then gave an explosive sigh. "Men!"

"Yes," said Eric, "You're surrounded by them. Lucky girl."

"Ha!" she retorted, but Dar saw the light in her eyes and knew she was pleased, though she wouldn't admit it.

"Have you been briefed?" Eric asked Khyron.

The officer nodded. "Yes, Lord Melinor gave me the details yesterday. My pegasus, Zasural, is stabled with your mounts, so we can leave whenever you are ready."

"Zasural?" Dar whispered to Eric.

"It means Windlight."

"Ah," he replied, trying to place that into his memory for later study. "I really have to brush up on my Elven before I see Megan again."

"You better," Eric replied, elbowing him.

Buck clapped a hand on Khyron's shoulder. "Welcome to the Grey Riders, Major Demaris."

"Kyron, please," the major responded, "I know you all have rank as brevet captains now but we're all one team here."

"Good," said Connor. "We're glad to have you with us."

"Though you may live to regret it," added Dar with a grin, watching Andyn roll her eyes.

Khyron's eyes flicked in her direction. "I just might…"

***

Well, this is grotesque, even for Ja'al.

Connor Lomin shook his head, looking over the drawings laid out on the

153

table. Though not engineer, he could still visualize what one of the monstrosities would look like once completed.

Dar Cabot tapped on one of the figures on the sheet, an odd-looking symbol resembling an octopus, but with thirteen arms and a skull in the center.

"Any idea what this means?" he asked. The bare walls and floors made his voice echo.

Melinor Indidarc made a face. "No," he replied, settling into one of the chairs at the long table. Above him, hovering magic lights cast a bright glow over them.

"We have cryptographers and wizards poring over it now," he continued, leaning back. "It doesn't match any of the other symbols we usually associate with the Ja'al, and there are a few other markings without any logical explanation. Even though the Alenars managed to get papers, we now know that they didn't get everything. We're missing a textbook, a kind of design manual. That likely has a correlation between those symbols and their function."

Connor stood on one of the chairs, leaning over the drawings, trying to puzzle out some kind of meaning.

Khyron shook his head. "My background is in engineering. I can tell you it would be no small feat to put all that together with the kind of precision specified in the other documents we have. Between the tolerances on the joints and junctions and the alignment of the various parts to each other, they would probably have to scrap the first few just due to assembly error."

Melinor shrugged. "Probably true, as our analysts have surmised. One has to assume that they have enough material to sustain several failures before getting one that worked."

"And you say this is some kind of gate," mused Andyn, fingers tracing one of the diagrams.

"But wouldn't that take a tremendous amount of power?" asked Eric, leaning back in his chair and tossing one of the schematics onto the table.

Melinor nodded.

"Where would they get that? How would they do it?" Dar asked.

Melinor steepled his fingers in front of his face. "Without getting too much into the technicalities of it, they would have to react matter itself with, well, non-matter. It's difficult to explain, but under certain conditions, wizards can draw out the "opposite of matter". In the presence of actual matter, the two react and emit a tremendous amount of energy. If they could channel that to their purpose, they could succeed."

Connor shook his head. He understood two words of that entire explanation. Maybe.

He turned his attention to the drawings again. Something bothered him about the whole concept of the gate.

He knelt down on the chair and leaned his elbows on the table. "But didn't you say that the Elohir would detect the use of the gate and open up their gates to bring in their own forces? That would defeat the purpose."

"Precisely," Melinor said, eyes looking up at the ceiling. "That's what really has us stumped. The Elohir and Daemons each have a finite number of existing gates here on Damora. We're not sure how many each side has, but adding one more to the mix on the side of Evil, no matter how capable the gate, wouldn't do very much."

Buck came to stand next to Connor. The halfling looked up at his human friend. Ever since coming to this top-secret meeting room in Oakmoor, hidden underneath layers of magical protections and guarded by dozens of elite troops and mages, Buck had not said much. Connor knew that things like magic and science really didn't interest him unless it had a direct bearing on him personally, so his silence didn't surprise any of them. The only magical items he carried were the Eye of Truth, the dwarven sword Khelios, his shield and his armor.

Buck's finger traced the strange symbol. "Thirteen arms, but like an octopus."

He suddenly straightened, giving Melinor a sharp look. "What if they aren't arms at all? What if they are pathways?"

Connor met Andyn's shocked gaze from across the table.

Melinor straightened, his face showing both amazement and alarm. "Pathways! And each pathway is a Skull Gate."

Dar shook his head. "Wait a minute. You mean there are going to make thirteen of these things?"

Melinor nodded slowly, looking grim. "Buckminster Horatio Bydecy, you are a genius. All this time we've been regarding that as a symbol for a power source, but it could be that it is in itself a schematic, which would be just like the Manipulator Church to hide their true meaning in something obscure."

"Melinor," Connor asked, dreading the answer, "what could the Ja'al do with that many Skull Gates?"

The wizard let out a deep breath. "One gate is easily countered. Four or five would be hard and there would be a short and vicious war, but each Elohir is equal to at least eight daemons. With this many gates, they could make it catastrophic. A horde of daemons…"

A chill raced down Connor's spine.

"Then all the assassinations, the social upheaval, the attacks on the borderlands — everything we've been doing up to now, including Zhinia Margoth — it's all just a diversion," Dar said, slapping a hand on the table. "Just a distraction to keep our eyes elsewhere while they start the wheels in motion."

Melinor stood. "And the Lervion House is the key to it all."

With a sudden realization, Connor saw it all clearly.

"If we find out where their distribution network leads," he started.

"We find out where the Skull Gates are," Eric finished. "Then we can send teams to take them out, or assault them outright with military force."

Connor looked at the faces of all his friends, seeing the same emotions he felt: shock, fear, desperation. No matter how few daemons these Skull Gates could disgorge in any span of time, the Ja'al would have fiendish and powerful allies for a time. Then it would be up to the people of Damora to hold them off until the Elohir could arrive.

"We have to get down to Meridian," said Melinor. "But this cannot be an overt action. If we don't do it right, the Ja'al will collect up their records and run for the nearest bolt-hole. Rest assured they have many. It has to be done carefully and with expert planning."

"And you want us to do this?" asked Dar.

"Well," Melinor replied with a wry smile. "The Northern Alliance does. I received a communique this morning from the Alliance Council authorizing me to assign whatever resources I needed to get to the bottom of the Skull Gate mystery and counteract the Ja'al's plans. You are the ones I need."

He reached under his robes and took out a small crystal bell from one of his pockets. He rang it and a tiny silvery ringing seemed to vibrate the very stones under Connor's feet.

"We will begin planning," Melinor said as the doors to the chamber opened and three nuns in dark grey robes entered. "But first we need to get you information on Gorostol, the capital city of Meridian, and the House of Lervion…"

Chapter Thirteen - What Hides Beneath

"Are you sure that was a wise idea?" Konadar groused, eyeing Simrit.

"No," Simrit responded, looking out the patterned glass window at the grounds of the Papal Nuncio's residence. Below, a crowd of schoolchildren followed their teacher, bundled against the cold. She led them along snow-covered pathways between barren trees and frozen fountains. A couple of kids stooped to make snowballs, but a sharp word from another teacher trailing the formation made them reluctantly drop their ice-cold missiles.

"And you didn't try to stop him?" Konadar said, stepping up next to his friend.

Simrit shrugged, watching the progress of the children. "I doubt if I could have succeeded. You know as well as I do how much the reports have disturbed him. He said he had to find out for himself."

Konadar chewed the end of his mustache, eyes distant.

"Don't worry, Konadar. He has some rather unique and well-qualified help. He'll come to no harm."

"It's not harm I'm worried about," Konadar replied. "I'm more concerned that someone will notice and then our enemies will know that they've drawn our attention."

Simrit gave a wry smile. "I think they already know that. No, I think the more immediate danger in that regard is that someone will set assassins on him."

Konadar snorted. "In that case, the difficult part will be cleaning up the remains of the assassins afterwards. No, our advantage lies in secrecy, in formulating ways to counteract their propaganda and make sure the truth gets out."

"Exactly," Simrit said, letting out a deep breath. "And that's why I think he went — to see it firsthand. Don't worry. It will work out just fine."

"It damned well better."

***

The old drunk stirred in the corner as the crowd of people grew louder and more vociferous. He lifted the edge of his hood to peer out at them with bleary eyes, then grunted and curled back up into the shadows of his resting place.

No one paid him any mind. Humans, dwarves, elves and halflings jostled together in the huge common room of The Freebooter, calling for ale as they waited. Many eyes flickered to the handbills on the walls and support posts. An empty podium stood before the massive stone fireplace.

In contrast to the icy cold outside the tavern, the interior now fairly throbbed with warmth, both from the fire and from the many people now swirling inside like fish in a lake. A young halfling man entered, casting his eyes at the old drunk. With a disgusted sneer, he strode over to one of the few empty stools next to a high table and vaulted up.

The hum of conversation increased in volume as beer and wine flowed, but the crowd waited patiently. Finally, a trio of bodyguards entered from a back door and took up positions near the podium. The crowd quieted.

A brown-haired young woman dressed in a smart traveling outfit of black and grey followed the guards and took up her position behind the podium. Her bright eyes swept over the crowd and she smiled from behind small round spectacles.

"Thank you all for coming to discuss some most important issues in the Kingdom of Deran," she began. "I am Councilor Aland. As a member of the Council, it is my privilege to represent your views to the Count of Deorfast and his Court."

Some of the listeners folded their arms while others whispered to each other, smiling.

"Our recent proposal was intended to provide a needed change to County laws," the speaker continued. "Currently, if two persons wish to marry and one of them is under the age of seventeen, parental permissions must be obtained. This has proven to be restrictive. A few fellow Councilors and I decided to enter a modification that would lower the age to fifteen and do away with the parental requirement. The Count chose to veto the law after the Council vote ended in a tie."

A murmur began in the assembly. The halfling man looked bored, following the design on the tabletop with his finger.

The councilor nodded. "For those who believe the Count to be misguided and ill-informed, I must say that I sympathize. We tried to explain to His Excellency the merits of the proposal, but he was unmoved and, I must say, a bit cold. However, do not be discouraged. Times are changing and our people are evolving in our understanding of the universe. Old ways are just that: old. Young people are much more sophisticated than their parents. The tide is changing in our favor and I am confident that future efforts will be successful."

A woman's voice rang out in the common room. "Why?"

The councilor's eyebrows rose. "Why? Why what?"

A dwarven woman stepped past a table, hands on her hips. "Why make such a proposal to begin with?"

Councilor Aland smiled. "As a representative, I have been approached by many people in recent days regarding the restrictions of the current law. I'm sure you will agree that young folk are more intelligent these days."

A bearded human nodded and joined the dwarf. "Intelligent? Yes. Wise? No. Wisdom comes with experience and age. People that young, no matter what their race, are not capable of knowing themselves well enough to make such a decision. They are susceptible to manipulation and deceit."

Aland shrugged. "You are stereotyping needlessly, sir. Such a rush to judgement is hasty. They can decide for themselves whom to love and when. When you couple this with the knowledge that some family situations are abusive and unhealthy places for our youth, it follows that it is to their benefit to be removed."

"And risk exploitation?" asked a grey-haired woman sitting at a table.

"Exploitation by whom?" asked a nearby human woman with a smirk.

"Their parents? Everyone knows that exploitation is not confined to those outside the family."

"Yes," said the dwarven woman, setting her mouth in a firm line. "But those situations are already addressed by existing laws and the local churches have good outreach programs to deal with them. The new law you proposed solves nothing. It inserts civil authorities into scenarios where they have no business."

A dwarven man in one of the booths waved a hand. "The churches?" he snorted, adjusting the collar of his purple cloak. "And what have they done lately? Lay down restrictions on everyone with their high and mighty moralizing, I say. We know they have opposed other laws that would increase freedom among our citizens. We aren't children. We can choose."

"Choose what?" asked the bearded man. "Drugs? Prostitution? How do those benefit our land?"

The murmuring in the crowd increased and some of the people stood, talking to others near them in agitated fashion. A trio of young human men laughed to each other, indicating the dwarven woman. The volume of sound increased and voices became more heated.

"Please," Councilor Aland intoned, raising her hands as her three bodyguards took a step towards her. "Let us remain calm and rational. As much as I agree with the gentleman in purple, we are here only to discuss the issue at hand. Now, everyone knows that many of the laws on the books were derived after the Interregnum, more than a thousand years ago. Times have changed and society has progressed beyond those parochial concerns."

The crowd quieted to a dull murmur and she smiled again. "We are a nation of many people with many different backgrounds and cultures and ideas. Such a nation requires an openness to progress. Progress cannot be achieved if one or another group or groups is allowed to impose their morality on everyone else. We must work together in a multi-faceted manner. It is in this spirit that the proposal was addressed."

"So what is a law then?" asked an elven woman in a hooded cloak.

The councilor blinked and the room went silent. "I beg your pardon?"

"What is a law, councilor?" the elf asked, her sea-grey eyes meeting the politician's gaze.

"Well, it is the decision of a people on how to govern themselves," Aland said, adjusting her spectacles with a frown. "It is a rule for managing the affairs of a nation, regulating the relationships of its citizens and the processes by which that nation moves forward and flourishes."

The elf shook her head. "That is not what a law is. A law is a decision by a community of what is right and what is wrong. It proscribes behavior and sets down penalties for violation of the law. By the establishment of right and wrong, it is morality defined. Therefore, to say that only particular groups impose morality on a society is incorrect: every law that has ever been made imposes some morality or other."

She looked at the dwarf in purple. "Or lack thereof."

He waved at her dismissively and the other people near him whispered to each other, laughing. Others shot her acid looks or rolled their eyes.

"And who gifted you with that knowledge?" jeered a voice from the crowd. "The great high god Verian? Please!"

The murmurs grew louder and Aland's bodyguards now stood right next to the podium. One of them rapped the wooden floor with the butt of a staff.

The councilor gave a forced smile, looking irritated. "That is a charming but irrelevant assessment, ma'am. The state decides what is a law and what is not. The people have recourse to obtain what their rights demand and if the state deems that certain folk give up privileges for the good of everyone, that is the way of it."

"I disagree," began the dwarven woman, but shouts from the back of the room interrupted her.

"You aren't allowed to disagree!"

"Prude!"

"Go back to your temple, spinster!"

That earned a chorus of laughter and the guard rapped the floor again.

Councilor Aland composed herself. "Now," she continued, "Rest assured that my fellow Councilors and I will address the issue at a later time. Those who oppose us are those on the wrong side of history, as it were, but they will not prevail. My office is, as always, open to receive any comments you wish to make."

She nodded to her guards and swept out of the back door. The tavern owner bowed his thanks to her and whispered something to his staff gathered nearby. The barkeeps and serving wenches dispersed.

The room exploded in heated discussion. The cloaked elven woman remained, speaking to those near her. After an intense, animated exchange with a trio of humans and elves, she shook her head and turned to leave. One of the humans, a young woman, eyes blazing and face screwed up in anger, made as if to follow her, but a gnome and a human man interposed themselves, holding her back. The cloaked elf left through the front door, past scowling patrons and others who smiled at her in encouragement. The halfling man hopped down off his seat and sauntered out of the front door without a word to anyone.

The crowd began to thin, pairs or trios departing into the early evening. Soon, the tavern held only half its former occupants.

Perhaps alerted by the change in sound volume, the drunk in the corner stirred and sat up, blinking uncertainly. He scratched his unkempt, scraggly beard and moved his mouth as if tasting something. He made a face and stood, leaning against the wall. A nearby pair of young human ladies looked at him in disgust and moved to another table. He immediately hunched over to a vacant booth, reaching for a couple of tankards. He slurped down the dregs from one of them and reached for the second.

"Oy! What are you about?" one of the barkeeps strode towards him. "Leave off there, I say. Begone! No freeloading here, you sot! Out!"

The drunk recoiled and stumbled towards the door. A halfling conveniently stuck out a foot and tripped him into the doorjamb, eliciting snickering from his fellows at the table. The drunk righted himself and looked around in confusion, then wrapped his cloak tighter around himself, settled his hood, and struck out into the snowy streets.

Looking up and down the thoroughfare, the drunk crossed the street after waiting for a wagon to pass by, then wavered his way past a closed tanner's shop and an empty stable yard. After reaching a corner, he leaned against a wall, catching his breath, then turned the corner.

He slipped between two buildings and crouched down behind a set of empty crates.

"Well?" asked a voice behind him.

The drunk turned and fixed a frowning goblin with a clear-eyed gaze. "Well what?"

Gorlak put his hands on his hips. "I can look like halfling man but my magic very mild. Yours is powerful, but you not use in there. Why?"

Melinor Indidarc stripped off his drunkard's garb, revealing serviceable leather armor. He dropped the rags into one of the crates, then reached down into another and pulled out a clean black cloak, wrapping it around himself.

"I have reason to believe that there were acolytes of the Ja'al in that crowd, primed to detect any wizard spells," he said. He removed his tattered boots and likewise dropped them in a crate, replacing them with cleaner ones.

"And you think they were waiting to unmask our agents?" asked a soprano voice. The elven woman from the tavern walked out of the alley shadows towards them.

"Maybe not as a prime directive, Sidara," Melinor continued, wrapping a belt around his waist and cinching it. "I think they are just on the lookout, as it were. However, I didn't want to risk derailing our surveillance. I say we did fine anyway."

He took a black ring out of a belt purse and slipped it on. "Here," he said, holding out his hands to Gorlak and Sidara.

They clasped hands with him and he spoke a sibilant, gentle word. Their forms glittered out of existence, leaving the alley empty except for a gust of wind swirling the snow over dirty pavement.

In a chamber beneath the Count's castle in Deorfast, their bodies sparkled and re-formed. Gorlak bent over, hands on his knees.

He squinted up at Melinor. "I not like that. How you stand it?"

Melinor smiled. "Practice. You get used to it."

Sidara smiled down at the goblin.

He made a disgusted face. "Make me feel like spewing. Blech."

Despite his obvious nausea, Gorlak followed Sidara and Melinor out of the tiny chamber. The trio tramped up stone steps, their breath making a fog before them in the chill air. After several flights, Melinor opened a door and held it for them.

They emerged in a warm, round room with wood paneling and a circular table with five chairs. A flat disk of what looked like solid amethyst hovered over the table. Sidara went to a shelf next to a door and rang a small bell.

Melinor took a seat and she palmed a disk of white metal from the underside of another shelf. This she inserted into a slit in the edge of the table before taking one of the other seats. The purple disk glowed and a translucent map of Deran shimmered into being above the disk.

The door opened and a smiling elven man entered, clad in green and silver livery with a golden circlet around his blond locks. His amber eyes shot to Sidara immediately. She rose and kissed him gently on the lips, smiling back. Gorlak watched them with attentive curiosity.

"Anything interesting?" Count Andareth Faldanor asked his wife.

"Lots," said Sidara, her smile fading. "And not much of it good."

The count shook hands with Melinor and accepted a bow from Gorlak. He took a seat next to his wife. "Do tell."

Melinor sat and waved a hand at the see-through map. The map rotated up on edge so that all of them could see it while seated. "What I had suspected is true. I have visited no less than five locations in disguises of various sorts and the phenomenon is similar. Someone is making concerted efforts to spread propaganda and false reports in Deorfast. All of them are disparaging of existing mores and laws and appeal to people's baser instincts."

He pointed to five spots and red dots appeared. "If it were merely people discussing issues and having differences of opinion, I would not worry. That has been part and parcel of Deranese society for a long time. Healthy discussion is good. In the light of day, the false withers and the true becomes evident. What worries me is that there appears to be an air of hostility and an attitude that whoever disagrees with the prevailing trend is either an idiot, selfish, cruel, or a troublemaker. No matter what they are called, any who oppose these new movements are shouted down, harangued, threatened and sometimes assaulted."

Count Faldanor's countenance darkened. "In my city? I'll soon teach them to be civil."

Sidara put a hand on his. "It is worse than that, my love. Some supporters of the new philosophies have been seen posting handbills around Deorfast, proclaiming that the old ways are dead and that those who retain them are to be rousted out of society. Several shopkeepers refused to allow handbills to be placed on the outer walls of their stores and have since come under attack both physically and legally. One man's shop was burned, a woman and her employee were beaten by masked figures on the way home, and three other store owners have been hauled into court and accused of racial discrimination. I doubt seriously if they are racist, since they all have admirers among the human, elven, dwarven and halfling communities."

Count Faldanor sat back in his chair, stroking his chin. "A coordinated campaign to mislead, discredit, distract, and harass. Hallmarks of the Ja'al."

Melinor nodded. "Indeed, we suspect as much, but we are having trouble tracking them down. We suspect some people of harboring or assisting them, particularly in the University District. Of course, we cannot prove anything."

The count glanced at Gorlak. "Have you found anything, Sergeant?"

Gorlak kept his eyes on the table and shook his head. "I try, Count. In large city like Oakmoor, is easier to hide and drift around to spy on suspects. Deorfast much smaller. People here less likely to tell what they know and harder to keep them from talking to each other. I not sure how much more use I be. Risk detection now, I think."

"But nothing yet?"

Gorlak looked resigned. "I find same things that Lord Melinor and Lady Sidara speak of. Nothing else for many days."

Melinor waved his hand and the map dispersed. "I think we should move Gorlak out of the city. While some of his targets were drunk when he questioned them, sooner or later, the denizens of the underbelly of Deorfast will add it up and start looking for an inquisitive goblin."

Gorlak's eyes flickered from Sidara to Melinor, dismayed. "No, please. I work harder, find agents — "

Melinor held up a hand. "We have done all we can in Deorfast, I think. There are other places you can use your unique skills, Gorlak."

The goblin still looked deflated until the Count leaned on the table to look him in the eye. "This is not a judgment on your work or your dedication. You have already given us intelligence we otherwise would never have been able to get. You are to be commended. But I agree with Lord Melinor. You are too valuable."

The goblin turned to Lady Sidara and she smiled. "I agree completely, Gorlak. We can't risk losing you. Lord Melinor is right. There are other places in Deran where you can find more information."

He nodded, resigned. Lord and Lady Faldanor rose.

Melinor put a hand on Gorlak's shoulder. "Your work here has been remarkable, Sergeant Gorlak, but you are needed elsewhere. We will travel back to Seacrest and the Nuncio, who will give you a new assignment."

The goblin bowed to the nobles, but Sidara took his hands. "Thank you for risking yourself. You did very well."

He smiled at her and kissed her hand, then bowed low to Lord Andareth.

Melinor also bowed. "We take our leave of you and advise that you remain vigilant for more mischief."

"Vigilant?" Count Faldanor asked, eyes glittering. "I'll be more than vigilant. I'll be positively annoying."

Sidara took his arm. Gorlak shifted shape into the form of a halfling using the Nuncio's ring.

Melinor and Gorlak left without speaking, their boots echoing in the halls of the manor. People nodded to them but hurried on about their business without comment.

The pair rode out of a rear gate, hooded and cloaked against the night. Near the Market Square, they slipped in the back door of an unremarkable warehouse. Inside, the manager's office door opened soundlessly for them and they found food, drink and two cots. The next morning they would leave the warehouse separately to join a caravan leaving for Seacrest.

Gorlak shape-changed back to his natural form before their meal and looked at Melinor for a long time.

"You troubled, Lord Melinor." It was not a question.

"Does it show that much?" Melinor chuckled, belying the tension evident around his eyes. "You are truly hard to fool, Gorlak. But yes, I am troubled. This latest trend is not like any other. There seems to be an undercurrent of viciousness and a general lack of civility. It is almost as if the adherents of this 'New Truth' feel that anyone who opposes them should be destroyed."

"Not see this before?"

Melinor's eyes grew distant as he took up a flagon of ale. "Not I. In my parents' time, there was a cult so fanatical that the only options for anyone were to join them, become a slave, or be killed."

Gorlak shuddered. "Sound like goblin kingdom. Or hobgoblin. Evil."

Melinor nodded. "My thoughts exactly."

Chapter Fourteen - A Homecoming of Sorts

"This seems familiar," Megan Alenar whispered to Brandi.

"Sadly, it does," her sister replied, adjusting the red veil in front of her face. "Just like Coastwatch back home."

Megan avoided looking at her for more than a few seconds. As Brandi's "employer", it wasn't considered proper for her to give her more than a passing glance in Torosc society.

It was just as well. Since Brandi wore the garb of a Red Veil mercenary, not many people would talk to her anyway. The Red Veils, comprised entirely of women, had a reputation for efficiency, honoring contracts, and savagery in protection of their masters. That alone kept many curious onlookers away.

More importantly, it made the county inspectors wary. Anyone who could afford a Red Veil had money and therefore, influence.

Megan turned to the wooden board in front of her and arranged the stacks of simple and fine cloth. She herself wore the simple blue skirt and white blouse of a merchant, as prescribed by local law. Behind her, Stephen and Daphne, attired in similar colors, haggled with one of the aforementioned inspectors. They showed him their writs of passage certifying that they were cloth merchants from Vunethir, Gorostol. The inspector, a hatchet-faced man with a thin mustache, sounded torn between starting a background check and leaving it be.

"Is there perhaps some local fee we forgot to pay?" Stephen asked. Megan suppressed a smile. She envisioned him scratching his head and looking dumb.

"No, brother," Daphne replied. "We paid enough fees at the border to last us a lifetime."

"Well, that might be the problem," said the inspector in a nasal, thin voice. "Sometimes the border officers forget to tell foreign merchants about local taxes."

A rotund, harried-looking woman approached and Megan nodded to her in greeting. Without meeting Megan's eyes, the woman nodded back.

"Ah," Megan heard Daphne say, "Eltor, didn't I tell you to ask the officer about all fees and special taxes?"

"I did, Zhinia," Stephen replied, sounding harried himself. "At least, I thought I did."

"Well, then, you see?" Daphne said with a sigh of exasperation. "How much is the local levy, then, inspector? Ten gold?"

Daphne and the inspector moved away from the stall and towards the wagon and Megan lost track of their conversation.

The rotund woman left and Megan's gaze drifted to the rest of the market square. Carts, tents and wagons with awnings crowded around the village square in Haleville, Shadowcliff Prefecture, Torosc. Most of the colors looked faded in the bright sunshine. Even the calls of gulls from the nearby harbor did little to lift the pall of gloom in the area. The central fountain, a carving of two warriors, looked new and well-tended, but the heroic poses of the figures didn't quite seem to match with the Skullhead and Greyfist symbols on their shields. Skullhead Legionnaires and Greyfist Guards were many things, most of them despicable and none heroic.

No one looked at the fountain, Megan noted, as if by refusing to look, the people could rebel silently against the lie represented by the statues.

Just like our home town: A veneer of prosperity, solidarity, and orderliness over a foundation of sadness, fear and quiet desperation.

She watched a trio of city guard stroll through the market in their black and red livery, casual hands on sword hilts, eyes watching everyone. Megan wasn't fooled. They were the visible oppressors, and few people would try outright thievery in broad daylight, not with Torosc's draconian laws. Strict edicts against defaming the government, its allies or the evil religions of the Ja'al, Vardish, or Cla'Agik made for an atmosphere of distrust and fear. No, the real peril lay in the network of spies and agents hidden in the population. Some were professionals, but others simply opportunistic citizens bribed with money, drugs, magic or sex.

A thin older woman came by and looked at some blue cotton cloth, then bought a few yards. Megan cut it carefully and wrapped it in brown paper, tying it with a string before pocketing the silver coins in payment. She resisted the natural urge to smile at her customer and instead gave a respectful nod.

She heard Daphne's voice behind her. "Are we settled then, inspector?"

"Yes, yes, all is quite in order," the inspector replied. "You should be just fine for your stay here. Two weeks only, and if you want an extension, you have to apply two days in advance."

"Excellent," Daphne smiled as she came up next to Megan's table. "Now if you would just stamp the writ."

The inspector looked at her sharply. "No one will question my word."

Daphne nodded. "I do not doubt that. I just want to make sure no one will question mine if you are not present."

The inspector frowned, then removed a seal stamp and an ink pad from a belt purse and stamped Daphne's writ of license.

"Thank you, sir." Daphne bowed.

With a snort of irritation, the man gave a curt nod and swept off into the crowded market square.

"Better you than me," Megan murmured as her aunt drew near.

"Penance for my many sins," Daphne replied in a low voice, reaching down to place a bolt of yellow fabric on the table. "How are sales?"

"Not too bad, considering. We've been here almost a week and people are finally starting to look us in the eye and buy something. No luck getting any conversation in the taverns though."

Daphne straightened, leaning back against the wagon, regarding the familiar scene of a market in Torosc. "We will have to be patient. We know someone will turn up. Speaking of taverns, be a good girl and go over to the Razor's Edge Inn and order lunch. I'll cover for you."

Megan handed her coin purse to her aunt, bowed like a good employee, and headed off to the aforementioned tavern. A few unshaven louts eyed her as she went in, but she ignored them. Again, in broad daylight, there was little danger, though at night...

The innkeeper took her order and money, the first with ill humor and the second with considerably more appreciation. She gave the interior a once-over before heading back out, but only a couple of patrons lingered. It was mid-morning and traffic would be light anyway.

She resisted the urge to sigh in frustration as she headed back out the door. From the information provided by Alliance agents in Gorostol, they knew that scions of the royal family of the old kingdom of Turis Rhi lived in Haleville — somewhere. The Papal Nuncio's scholars had managed to pull enough information out of one of the Heritage Stones and combine it with other data to give them a hint of a lead. Now it was up to the Alenars to find anyone who would admit to a connection with the ancient family name of Rhivan.

She stood for a moment next to the door. The louts had departed in search of darker surroundings and better prey. The hills stretched away to her right, beyond the old manor and garrison. Peppered with trees and homes, the heights held more expensive and luxurious domiciles for the privileged and connected.

Homes where the Torosc government officials live instead of the ancient families that used to own them, she thought sourly. *Homes stolen by soldiers stepping over the corpses of the former owners, no doubt.*

She heard a sound rather like a yelp to her right, followed by heated whispering and then a smack. She sauntered in that direction, around the corner of the building and peeked down the alley.

Four large youths stood around some empty crates and ale barrels. As she watched, a muscular boy lifted up a smaller, struggling figure against the wall.

"Give it up," the large boy hissed.

"Give up what?" asked Megan in an innocent voice. "Are you tax collectors?"

The thugs whirled and gaped. The leader loosened his grip on a slender boy of about ten, giving his prize the opportunity to wiggle free and dart to Megan's side.

The leader, a dark-skinned fellow with a scar over one eye, glared at Megan and pointed a finger at her. "This is none of your affair, wench. Back off!"

Megan focused her magic power. While a sorcerous display would certainly draw the guards in the square, she had more unobtrusive spells in her arsenal.

"I think not," she replied calmly as the smaller boy hid behind her.

Her demeanor gave the thugs pause because the other three looked at each other with uncertain eyes. They fingered clubs and knives.

Without turning his head, the leader addressed his gang. "It's only one little skirt. We can take both her and the runt. Bonus on her 'cause the Vipers might be interested."

He charged, with his fellows right behind. Megan whispered a word and a trio of lights sprang up in front of the youths. The thugs came to a skidding halt in the pebbly alleyway.

She smiled at them, making her lights dance around. "Care to rephrase that?"

The thugs stared at her wide-eyed. "She's a witch! Or a mage!"

Apparently, the leader had seen magic before, because his eyes narrowed. "Well, making pretty lights isn't the same as fighting. She can't use any big magic because we'll call the guards. Take them!"

Megan prepared a more forceful reply but stopped when she heard Brandi's voice behind her.

"Not recommended."

The thugs froze. Even the leader's eyes widened in fright.

Megan kept smiling.

"We didn't mean —" the leader stammered. "We were just —"

"You can go now," Brandi hissed in a voice full of menace.

The four thugs raced down the alleyway, casting terrified looks over their shoulders. Megan looked down at the boy, who stared at Brandi in terror.

"Don't worry," Megan said. "She doesn't bite if she's fed regularly."

Brandi nodded and headed back towards Daphne and Stephen.

The boy looked up at Megan with uncertain brown eyes.

"What's your name?"

"Henry," he replied, shooting a nervous glance at Brandi's retreating form. "Is that really a Red Veil?"

"It sure looks like it, doesn't it?"

Henry bit his lip, watching Brandi return to the wagon. "You're merchants?"

"Yes, just arrived a week ago." Megan paused, then, on a hunch, continued. "We had a business contact here in Haleville but we can't seem to find him, a Mister Davis. You wouldn't know where to find him, would you?"

The boy kept his eyes down but shook his head.

"Know anyone who might?"

He shrugged. "Mister Dorson in the Razor's Edge, maybe. He knows a lot of people."

"Dorson?"

"The big man with the beard. The owner."

Megan nodded, then appraised Henry. A slender, almost thin child, he wore a patched tunic and short pants and his sandals had seen better days.

She put a hand on his shoulder. "If you find out anything about Mister Davis, let me know please. My bosses are waiting for his share of the venture."

She took his hand and pressed some silver coins into it. He nodded and shoved his hands in his pockets.

"I will. Sure."

Without another word, Megan walked back to her relatives. She took Stephen aside at the first opportunity and described the incident.

"Well," he remarked, not looking up from the page of figures on the table before him, "you could have picked a less flashy way to find a contact, but at this point, I'll take it. See if you get a reaction out of Dorson when you get lunch."

Megan bided her time waiting on a few more customers, then headed over to the Inn to pick up their order. To her surprise, Dorson himself, not the barmaid, gave her the hot, paper-wrapped packages. He nodded to her and touched his forelock.

As she left, Megan saw Henry's slim shape on a stool behind the bar, spooning up a hot stew from a wooden trencher. He looked up, gave her quick wink, then resumed his meal.

"I think we have something," Megan said as she distributed the hot beef and cheese sandwiches back at the wagon.

"And so do I," Stephen said slowly, pulling a small paper out of his package as he sat on the wagon steps. Without missing a beat, he took a bite of his sandwich and leaned back against the side of the wagon, looking at the cloud-scattered sky. With his free hand, he laid the paper on his knees for a few moments as Daphne leaned next to him for a bottle of beer. She nodded and he crumpled it up and slipped it into his pocket.

Megan and Brandi finished their lunch in silence, then continued on to their duties. Megan noted an uptick in traffic to their wagon after the meal, including a military officer and his wife who purchased some of the more expensive fabrics.

The day wore on into afternoon, but when she took a break and sat with a bottle of water and a peach on the steps of the wagon, Brandi stood by her, hands on her sword hilts.

"Good work," she murmured.

"You mean I got a nibble?"

"More like a twelve-pound bass. The note says to meet Henry at sundown out by the abandoned brewery down the street from the Inn. He'll take us to meet Mister Davis."

Megan felt a deep relief and satisfaction, accompanied by apprehension. This could mean that their lead might pay off, or that they had taken the bait in an elaborate sting operation by the local intelligence service.

"Do you think it's legitimate?" she asked.

"If it isn't, we know how to leave town fast," Brandi replied.

Apprehension and hope warred in Megan's mind, making it hard for her to attend to her customers. She managed to keep her focus enough to serve everyone accurately before the approach of sundown. On the far end of the square, a large clock on the front of the Economics Ministry building rang five times, signaling the end of the day. She helped break down their shop site and joined her relatives on the wagon. She settled into her seat next to Daphne as Stephen clucked to the draught horses and turned them down the road past the Razor's Edge.

"Don't worry," said Daphne. "We know how to handle this."

Stephen took his time, careful to act just like all the other merchants heading off to the camping square in the fading evening light. Instead of turning off towards the main road, he continued on to a shuttered building with a faded sign swinging in the breeze. Megan squinted at the sign and was able to make out some faint lettering and the picture of an owl on a cliff.

Owl Rock Brewery, she read. *Too bad it's closed.*

Megan climbed down from the wagon and approached the door, looking for any sign of Dorson or Henry. She tried to peer in the windows using her heat-sensitive vision, but only made out the thermal signatures of rats, spiders and small insects among the shadows.

"Hi."

She jumped, then gave Henry a look of reprimand.

"Don't do that! You scared me half to death."

He grinned. "Dorson says he doubts you're scared of anything if you're looking for Mister Davis."

"Is this your friend, Megan?" asked Daphne as she climbed down as well.

"Yes, this is Henry."

The boy sized up Stephen and Daphne and Brandi and chewed his lip.

"I'm only supposed to bring you and the Red Veil," he said finally.

Megan exchanged a glance with her aunt and uncle. "They're okay, really."

Henry shook his head. "I have orders, miss. No offense."

"Is it far?" she asked, going back to the wagon for her shoulder bag.

Again he shook his head. "Not even a single ping of the town clock."

Ten minutes.

"We'll be all right," she told her relatives. With a glance at each other, they nodded.

Brandi followed Henry and Megan silently as they walked down quiet streets, some dark, and others lit by oil lamps or magical torches. For a ten-year-old boy, he certainly set a brisk pace. Megan had to take long strides to keep up.

He turned down a side street, heading for a barn on the other side of a stable yard. Without a word, he led them to it and gripped the handle of a side door.

"You won't tell anyone?" he asked.

"No one who doesn't have to know. I'll have to tell my bosses sooner or later."

She thought she saw a twinkle in Henry's eye but decided it was just the flicker of distant torchlight.

"Yeah, your bosses. Well, follow me."

Megan and Brandi stood in the large, empty barn, taking in the vacant stalls, smelling the faded odors of horses, manure and hay.

"Well, nobody's used this for a while, Henry," she said, turning around.

She froze. Henry had disappeared.

"Henry?" she asked, hand going to her shoulder bag. "Where are you?"

"I wouldn't move if I were you," said an unfamiliar man's voice. Megan's heart clenched and her breath stopped in her throat.

Lights flared around her and she now saw more than twenty people, all wearing masks or veils and dark clothing. Several had spears and she felt certain that other weapons lurked under their cloaks. Others carried crystals with magical lights glowing white.

"What have you done with Henry?" she demanded, feeling a sudden fear.

A tall and hooded figure gave a short chuckle. "Why do you care? He's just a street urchin. Hundreds like him everywhere."

"He's just a child!" she retorted, feeling her temper flare. Despite the casual demeanor of the people surrounding them, she felt certain they could get into action very fast.

"Interesting words for someone who hires out Red Veils."

She paused, mind racing. "Sometimes one has to keep up appearances," she said, emphasizing the last word.

That made the leader pause. A few of his fellows whispered among themselves.

"Then let us see her face."

Brandi stepped up next to Megan and lowered her veil. "Here. Satisfied?"

The man put a booted foot up on an old crate and leaned on one knee. "Red Veils never lower their veils unless they are in a sister house, so we know you're not really one of them. Who are you?"

Brandi hesitated. Megan looked all around the barn, feeling the tension, not knowing what to do or say.

Okay, God. Taking a big chance here. Help me out, please.

"We're not really merchants and we don't need Mister Davis for his investment," she said boldly. Brandi took her arm but she shook her off.

"We're from the Northern Alliance," Megan continued, "and we're here to protect a certain family and offer them a way out of Torosc."

The leader straightened, hooking his thumbs in his belt and regarding her, palms on the hilts of two daggers. The others behind him became more alert and drew weapons.

"You don't say. Which family?"

Brandi's mouth tightened and she shot a glance at Megan. "Rhivan," she said, putting her hands on her own sword hilts.

The leader shrugged. "Well then. Lots of people, including Torosc agents, would like to know if anyone linked to that family still lives. What can you show us to prove you're not government agents?"

"Would spies reveal their true identities without some glib cover story?" Megan shot back. "We know how spies work."

"Spoken like a spy," remarked a woman from the crowd. "Are you spies then?"

The big barn doors opened behind them and Megan whirled, hearing Brandi's swords hiss out of their scabbards. The people surrounding the sisters spread out and stood en garde.

Megan's eyes widened in surprise. Stephen and Daphne entered, followed by the giant owl Paractus.

"No," Stephen said, "But we've spent a lot of time fighting them."

The leader considered this. "And we're just supposed to believe you."

Stephen held up a silver disk in one hand. "I would hardly expect that, but how about the seal of the Papal Nuncio?"

Megan looked back at the leader, who dropped his hands from his weapons and stepped forward.

"If it was legitimate."

Stephen tossed it to him. "Then see for yourself."

The man held a hand over the disk and his palm glowed. Megan blinked. A wizard?

No wonder they surrounded us without us knowing it. Probably cloaked them with magic.

The hood swept back and now Megan looked upon a middle-aged man with a greying dark beard and blue eyes. He tossed the disk back to Stephen, who caught it and bowed.

"I am Stephen Alenar. This is my sister Daphne and our nieces Megan and Brandawyn."

"Alec Rhivan."

Stephen bowed lower. "Your Highness. I believe we can help you and your family leave this place forever and travel on to safety."

Alec looked amused. "Maybe you can, if you're very, very good. But then, you'd have to be pretty good to get this far, now wouldn't you?"

To Megan's relief, Henry slipped up next to Alec and gave her a smile. Megan felt the tension leave her.

"Give us a chance to show you, Your Highness," said Daphne.

Chapter Fifteen - Dark Upon Dark

Beol Torander stumped into the Lervion House library—correction: his library — and slammed a fist down on the carved oak desk.

"And how exactly did he get into the grounds in the first place?" he thundered.

The pale morning sunlight broke through the windows, casting shafts of brightness into the room, making crystal glint, brass shine and wood glow. It could have been a pile of smoking dung for all he cared. He glared at the trio of dwarves arrayed before him.

They remained silent, casting nervous glances at each other without turning their heads.

"Well? What about you, Thonvar? You're captain."

A grey-bearded dwarf scratched a scar that ran from his forehead down to this jaw. "None of the magic alarms went off, Master Beol, so I can only assume he had help from the inside. I'm not an expert on magic, sir, just a soldier. Could Miss Hannah have done something?"

Beol pressed his lips together and gave him a pitying look. "Are you serious? Hannah has no magical skills other than simple tricks to light a candle and clean her privy! She couldn't have possibly managed to get him inside."

Beol tapped his knuckles on the desktop as his underlings squirmed. "How could he have deactivated the alarms and then reset them so fast? We know from the after-action reports that he had magical ability, but that level of skill — " His voice trailed off and the guards looked at each other and shrugged.

"That level of skill," intoned a deep voice from the other side of the room, "does not necessarily have to reside in a person, Master Torander."

The dwarves, including Beol, gave a collective start of surprise as a blond human male in a robe of riotous colors of pink, red and purple swept in. Imperious blue eyes surveyed the four of them from a narrow face adorned with a neatly trimmed goatee and mustache. Earrings with purple gems flashed as he turned his head to look at the others in the room. He held a staff of spiraling black wood in his hand.

Beol recovered first and cleared his throat. "Er, yes, Master Lorferis. That was my next question."

"Indeed." Lorferis slipped over to a comfortable easy chair and sat, resting his staff against one of the arms. "So tell me your theory."

Beol's mind spun wildly, formulating and rejecting a number of possibilities.

Lorferis favored him with a thin smile. "Let me give you a hint. Might he have had something that he used to infiltrate the manor grounds? A magic item perhaps?"

Beol nodded slowly, then felt confused. "We didn't find anything special on him, though. Well, he had that sword, which I admit is mighty fine, and he had his ring and armor and a magic bag, but nothing spectacular."

Lorferis crossed his legs, showing impeccable black boots with gold spurs. "Correct. But what is to say that he kept the item on his person? After all, such magic would be valuable, so maybe he hid it to avoid the risk of capture."

"That doesn't make sense," Captain Thonvar growled with an acid look at the wizard. "Why didn't he just use it to escape again?"

"Kindly allow your betters to discuss subjects within their areas of expertise, Captain," Lorferis remarked breezily. "I recommend you occupy your mind with other things, like wenching."

Thonvar gritted his teeth, but a look from Beol silenced him.

Lorferis turned his attention back to Beol. "Of course I have already considered that, which naturally leads to the conclusion that the item was limited in power, perhaps only permitting one use within a time period, or perhaps it needed to be recharged with a special material that he knew how to find here in the manor."

Beol bit his lip, pretending to consider this, but eyed Lorferis furtively all the while.

The wizard raised an eyebrow at him. "I would recommend that you undertake a search of the grounds and see if you can find anything out of place."

Beol set his mouth in a thin line, seeing where this line of inquiry led. "He grew up here. He knew every nook and crevice of this property. It could take weeks to find anything. We don't even know what we're looking for. What about the project, and our regular duties?"

Lorferis shrugged. "I suppose I could let you have the services of a couple of my mages, though they were a bit chewed up in the fighting. Speaking of battle damage, how is Miss Hannah? It would be most unfortunate if she died, especially considering what information may be released once her demise is known."

"Yes," Beol growled. "Most unfortunate. I am glad that one of your own priests is tending to her injuries. It is strange, though, how with all the resources of the mighty Ja'al, you cannot seem to find out where she sent a packet of information not two years ago."

"I am sorry," Lorferis replied with a smile that indicated he was anything but. "You must understand that our project is very draining on intellect, resources and attention. Rest assured we are taking steps to discover the location of her letter and deliver it to you. Of course, if you would rather terminate our arrangement, then it will stay wherever it is and we will find a new patron. We can part ways amicably."

In a rat's ass, thought Beol as he fumed and turned away to look out the window. *You just want leverage so you can use me to deliver the parts for that whatever-it-is you're building.*

Something in Beol's stomach tightened. The wizard knew that Hannah and Handor, the true heirs of the Lervion fortune, had sent evidence of Beol's treachery to an unnamed destination to the north. Hannah, the little minx, even had the audacity to announce it to his face after Handor left. She told him that certain persons in far-off lands would find out if she perished and that would be their signal to make public the evidence in the packet.

Could he just kill her out of hand? Certainly. That would be the more satisfying response. But now, with all that had happened, Beol knew he would be ruined if word ever got out about his treachery— and the hangman's noose awaited as well. Even though he might be able to keep any "accidents" from being known outside of Gorostol should Hannah join her parents in the hereafter, he knew Lorferis wouldn't stay silent. Seeing Beol as a liability in that case, there was nothing to stop the wizard from simply publicizing her death far and wide and watching the results with secret glee.

How Lorferis had found out about Hannah's little package of evidence, Beol didn't know, but he felt sure the Shrike assassins had a hand in it.

As his mind whirled and his fury seethed, he tried to figure out a way to double-cross the Ja'al wizard and his masters, but nothing came to him. With a sinking feeling, he realized that this entire enterprise was probably a Ja'al plot from the start. The subtle hints from shadowy agents to murder the Lervion parents, the lucrative contracts smuggling for the Manipulator Church, the oppression Hannah, the exiling of Handor, the hidden evidence, the bribing of magistrates and constables, intimidation of witnesses: all of it, orchestrated by the Ja'al. They wanted access to Lervion House's unparalleled shipment network for their ridiculous secret scheme.

Well, he thought with bitter hatred, *two can play at that game, "Master Lorferis". At some point, you will slip up and leave me an opening, and then Beol Torander will be the one with the upper hand.*

He mastered his emotions and turned back to the others.

"Well?" he said with a look at his guards. "You three had better coordinate with Master Lorferis and start searching. Triple bounty for the person who finds whatever Handor used to get into this place."

Their eyes lit up with greed and he nodded grimly. Regarding Lorferis, he bowed.

"The House of Lervion is at your service, as always, Great One."

"And I am glad of it," replied the wizard. He departed with a swish of colored robes.

You won't be when I get through with you, Beol Torander retorted in his mind. He glared at the door as his subordinates headed that way.

"Thonvar, you stay for a moment."

His captain returned as the other two guards departed, the door closing after them. Thonvar waited silently as Beol stared at the costly Gorostoli carpet, then turned to look out one of the windows, hands clenched behind his back.

He gazed at the street outside. Prancing ponies pulled a red-painted carriage down the street at a brisk trot, tossing their heads. A halfling outrider kept pace on his own pony, a blue and black pennon snapping in the morning air.

"When will Hannah be able to continue her duties?" he asked.

Thonvar took a moment before answering. "Probably not for a week at least. She is still recovering, sir. And I can't speak for her frame of mind when she comes around, either."

Beol's eyes narrowed. "She needs to be seen in her role as company officer. There are approvals that only she can sign, per the laws of the company charter."

"She may be… disinclined, sir."

"Disinclined?" Beol felt a rage boiling but forced himself to answer in a milder tone, though clipped. "She is my ward and has duties. She cannot be disinclined."

"I am referring to her worry over her brother, sir."

Beol now gripped the windowsill with both hands so tightly that he felt surprised he didn't snap it in two. "Her brother," he spat, "is not her concern."

"I'm sure she will see it in a different light, sir."

"Well, then," said Beol. "We will have to change her viewpoint. Perhaps by suggesting that Handor's continued presence here depends on her level of cooperation. She doesn't need to know the truth, just be in a state of uncertainty about it."

"Yes, sir."

Beol continued fuming, formulating all manner of ways of making his niece come to heel, then turned abruptly.

"Have we settled with the magistrate and the constable?"

"Yes, sir. The official report will state that bandits sought to break into the manor, at which point Miss Hannah and the other guards took steps to repel them, resulting in more deaths and injuries. We can use the bodies of some of the dead to pose as burglars."

"Good. Make sure the guards have the same story," Beol waved a hand in dismissal.

"Sir?"

Beol gave his captain a sharp look.

Thonvar inclined his head respectfully. "At some point, Miss Hannah will have to go out into the public eye and her tongue may be loosened to give a different account of the occurrences than the official report. As a matter of fact, from what I have observed of her, it is almost guaranteed."

"I am aware of that," Beol snapped, feeling a headache starting. He pinched the bridge of his nose. "I will have to come up with a bit of persuasion to ensure she doesn't draw attention to herself. Perhaps we can make it clear that her brother's fate is linked to her behavior."

Thonvar shrugged. "That may work for a while, sir, but it will not work forever."

Now Beol did have a headache. He let out a sigh. As if it wasn't hard enough dealing with the infernal Ja'al and their convoluted plots and blasted two-headed hounds, now he had to keep yesterday's incident under wraps. Worse yet, he felt the added pressure from two fronts: Lorferis' veiled hints that Beol could be handed over to uncorrupted authorities, as well as the threat of Hannah simply becoming desperate and bolting at an inopportune time.

This whole accursed thing is unravelling. I should have been made the heir in the first place. But no, the inheritance had to go to my younger half-brother. All this should have been mine by right!

He looked back at Thonvar. "I am aware. Be alert for her to try something, but be discreet in heading her off. I will be close by."

Thonvar bowed. "Yes, sir."

"You can go."

As the door closed behind his dwarven captain, Beol turned back to the window again.

Should have bribed the magistrates when I got here. Even as he thought it, he knew it was nonsense. He only had money to distribute bribes after taking over the shipping line, not before.

Taking a quick look around, he locked the doors to the study, then returned to a drawer of his desk and tapped on the lock with a key he drew from a pocket. The drawer slid open soundlessly and he reached far into it, removing something attached to the inside surface of the top of the desk.

He stared at a vial of swirling black liquid, fascinated by the tiny sparkles of red that looked like microscopic stars suspended in ink.

Back in his days in the bustling city of Bildur, in Merdail, before his mother had married Hannah's grandfather, Beol Torander had delved in a few shadowy areas of city life. Reveling in the freedom given him by forbidden, raging parties of debauchery in old underground ruins, he had made many advantageous contacts. These contacts had been only too ready to give him secret knowledge and effective little tools to make sure his rivals perished discreetly, in exchange for his services in the world of legitimate finance and business.

They showed him tools like subtle poisons to bring on heart failure, tools to produce magically augmented diseases that faded and then resurged and killed within days.

He turned the little vial in his hand. *Tools like this red-starred potion.*

Shadow for shadow, the Vardu priest had told him at a particularly wild bacchanal—a potion to bring the power of the god of Death to reside in Beol himself, a potion that would give him might and deadly abilities and invulnerability to weapons of all kinds.

Beol knew it worked. He had seen it work for others and, indeed, had made it work once by using it himself.

Very expensive bit of dark magic, but extremely useful while the effects last.

The heady euphoria of being beyond life and death beckoned to him and he caressed the vial.

My ace in the hole. If Lorferis makes his move, I will make mine. And he has no defense against this. I think I'll keep it with me from now on.

Beol grinned wickedly, his headache forgotten. Yes, he had the ultimate backup weapon, and by judicious use of it, he would emerge from this ridiculous, muddled mess as the victor.

Let them try their worst. Hannah and Handor's little failsafe plot, Lorferis' meddling, the threat of legitimate authorities finding out about his corruption of local officials - none of it would matter if Beol played his cards right.

He slipped the vial into a hidden pocket in his undershirt and sat back in his chair, eyes closed, formulating a scheme that would accomplish just that.

Chapter Sixteen – Peril of Many Kinds

Great. We run into fog now, of all times.

Brandawyn Alenar slowed her pace, reining in Amicus alongside the huddled group of people picking their way through the forest. She kept her bow across her knees, an arrow nocked, and scanned the misty trees and shrubs. She met Megan's worried gaze.

Traveling this far without any incident defied belief. She knew that some in the Gorostol border patrol received clandestine payments from Torosc agents. In addition, certain commercial interests were only too willing to assist in occasional racketeering if it helped their profits. Someone should have noticed something.

This part of southern Gorostol should have been a sanctuary for the last remnants of the royal House of Rhivan and their loyal retainers. Instead, Brandi felt even more anxious than when they slipped over the border under the cover of darkness.

Oh yes, the Torosci know something is afoot by now. But where are they?

With an effort, she quelled her nervousness. Up ahead, Daphne and Stephen led the twenty or so family members and retainers, spears and shields at the ready. Prince Alec strode by their side, occasionally nodding at something Stephen said.

"Miss Brandi?" asked a boy next to her. She looked down at Henry and smiled. Clad now in a tough leather halfling cuirass and bearing a small crossbow and dagger, he looked more like Prince Emerich of Turis Rhi than Henry the Urchin — which was just as well.

"Yes, Your Highness," she replied.

He waved a hand at her. "Aw, none of that stuff. I'm just Henry."

"Then I'm just Brandi. Unless you want to call me Queen Brandawyn."

He caught he twinkle in her eye and grinned. "No. Let's stick with Henry and Brandi."

"What is it, Henry?"

"Why aren't you and Megan flying?"

She gazed at the surrounding forest to check for enemies, then back to him.

"With all the trees and mist, we wouldn't be able to see you, or any foes, for that matter. And anyone who looked up through a gap in the trees and clouds would see us for sure. No, we'll have to stay grounded for a while."

He looked disheartened. "Okay. But I really wanted to see Amicus fly."

"Let's make a deal. When you're safely in the fortress at Sentinel, I'll fly him around a bit and then let you ride with me on the ground. Your father wouldn't approve of you flying on a pegasus."

He looked torn between elation and disappointment, then decided on resignation. "Deal," he said.

Daphne nodded at Brandi and raised a hand.

"We're stopping for a bit, it seems," Brandi said to Henry.

He made a face, hefting his crossbow. "I really wanted to plug a goblin or something."

She shook her head. "Don't wish for battle. You'll probably see more than you'll ever want when you get older. Pray we make it to Sentinel without incident."

He looked down at his shoes. "Everybody else is so brave and important. I want to help."

She resisted the urge to reach down and ruffle his hair. "Don't worry. Your time will come, Henry."

He shrugged and hopped up on a large rock, crossbow cradled in his arms.

Brandi joined her relatives with Prince Alec. The travelers formed a protective ring, bows and spears pointed outward, watching the forest. They looked exhausted, but determined. Two of their number, grizzled veterans from Alec's personal guard, crept out into the forest.

"There really isn't much difference between northern Torosc and southern Gorostol," Alec said as she approached. "There are agents aplenty here. We won't be safe until we get to Sentinel."

"More accurately," Stephen replied, "Until we can get close enough to signal the garrison. The local bishop knows we're coming. He has a full company of support standing on alert, ready to help us. The Verian church and Kurental high priest have also pledged assistance, so we have friends. We just have to get to them."

"What's the hold up?" asked Megan.

"I want to scout up ahead," Daphne said. "The bishop probably has scouts out here. Alec sent Rupert and George ahead to see if we can make contact."

Elizabeth, Alec's wife, looked up at her husband. "You're sure Torosc knows we're here?"

He nodded. "It was unfortunate we had to draw the border guards attention away with Stephen's fire and smoke display, but it was also necessary."

Elizabeth turned her round, pleasant face northwards, frowning. "How far to Sentinel?"

"Only about two miles," said Daphne. "If it weren't for the fog and the thickness of the forest, we could see it — and they us. But don't worry. It won't be long now."

"We're so close," said Elizabeth. She fell silent for a while, then set her mouth in a firm line. "We will get there if I have to crawl the last few feet."

Alec smiled and put an arm around her. "I wouldn't bet against you, my dear."

"Well, I'm ready to move on," said Megan.

Stephen appraised her. "Just anxious to get to a hot bath?" he teased.

Megan sniffed in disdain but her eyes twinkled. "From the air around here, we all need one."

Daphne smiled and nodded. "I'm with Megan. And I want to be in Sentinel for lunch."

"Where's Henry?" asked Elizabeth.

"Sitting on the big rock," Brandi replied, then froze.

The stone held only lichens and dead leaves.

"Where is he?" his mother asked, a sudden note of worry in her voice.

"He was just there," Brandi said, riding Amicus over to the rock. She peered out into the forest, straining to pick out his slender form.

Daphne loped over to the rock and knelt on the side nearest the forest. "Did anyone see him get down? Hear any sound?" she asked the nearby refugees, eyes scanning the nearby forest floor. They shook their heads, looking suddenly worried. Daphne's hands gently turned leaves and touched the barest hint of a boot print in the soft earth

Brandi felt a shiver of fear.

"This way," said Daphne, fitting an arrow to her bow. "I have a trail."

"Stay here," Alec said as Brandi started to follow. "Two people will attract less attention. A mounted rider is easily spotted."

He and Daphne ghosted out into the misty gaps between the rows of grey trees and tangle of undergrowth. Brandi kept her bow at the ready and exchanged a nervous glance with Megan.

Birds chirped and a fly buzzed past her. Still the refugees waited, silent, frozen like mere sculptures or carvings laid out in the woods by some forgetful artist. Narrow shafts of filtered sunlight illuminated a bearded face here, a burnished shield there, a comforting arm holding a frightened child close.

Then Brandi heard a distinct zip of a projectile and a short cry. The entire group readied their weapons.

"Be on your guard," Brandi said. "It might be a diversion so we can be taken from behind."

She sighted on a pair of figures running towards them through the misty woods, then relaxed as she recognized a third, and shorter figure with them.

"Goblins in the forest!" Henry hissed as he burst into the clearing ahead of Daphne and Alec.

Elizabeth enveloped him in a tight hug. "Then why didn't you tell us, foolish boy! You could have been killed!"

"I didn't know what they were, Mother," he said with an annoyed look at her. "I saw something moving and went to see what it was."

"And bagged one of them," said Daphne, backing into the defensive ring. "They saw Prince Alec and me. One of them was aiming a javelin to throw when Henry shot him."

Henry smiled shyly up at Brandi, who raised an eyebrow. "Nicely done, but not very prudent. You should have alerted us."

"How many?" asked Stephen.

"About twenty that we could see," Alec said. "They'll find out about their missing scout soon enough. There may be more and, knowing goblins, they're setting up an ambush from multiple directions. We have to move, and quickly."

"My lord!"

Alec's two sergeants ran towards them out of the nearby undergrowth, one looking over his shoulder.

"What is it, Rupert?"

Rupert paused to catch his breath, panting, then continued. "We found the scouts — dead. Someone ambushed all four of them to the north east, towards the city road. We can't go that way."

"Straight north then," Daphne said instantly. "There's a big clearing. Not as fast as the road but we can't risk anything else."

"Everyone up," Alec hissed. "Quickly now!"

Brandi moved to the side of their group as they arranged themselves in skirmish formation and headed through the woods at a trot. She peered out at the woods, looking for any sign of imminent attack.

The forest suddenly fell silent. Daphne snapped an order to be on guard. Then, a squad of goblin spearmen boiled up out of a thicket, hooting and screeching. Stephen met them with a stream of firedarts that blew three of them off their feet. Another squad followed the first and soon the forest rang with the ring of steel and goblin war cries. Alec and his band fought silently, hewing down the first attack and then a second that charged in from the opposite side. Brandi used her two cavalry swords and mounted height advantage to maximum effect. She charged into massed formations of goblin warriors, scattering them so the refugees could hack or stab them to death. Megan, Stephen and Alec proved to be a potent combination. They used magic spells of colored lights to confuse the enemy or sent thin beams of white-hot energy to burn through goblin jerkins and leave smoking corpses on the leafy ground.

The surviving attackers withdrew, hurling javelins to discourage pursuit. Brandi took a quick look around as silence fell once again. Almost a score of goblins lay still along with three of their party. Two of the refugees struggled to rise and Elizabeth tended them with the help of one of the other women.

She waved off Brandi when she approached.

"I'm a healer too, Brandawyn. You're more valuable as cavalry," she said, pulling a healing kit from a shoulder bag.

Brandi sheathed her swords and switched back to her bow. "Anything to identify them?" she asked Daphne, kneeling by one corpse.

"Black Knife tribe," said Daphne, tossing down a pewter medallion she had ripped off one of the corpses. "but they're too far north. I doubt if they're here of their own accord, especially this close to Sentinel."

"That means there is more mischief to follow," announced Alec.

Elizabeth helped the wounded to their feet and they continued on at a half-run, spurred by anxiety as well as the beckoning safety of Sentinel. Brandi peered into the forest, on her guard. An ill-aimed arrow sang past overhead and she returned fire, plugging a goblin sniper in the neck. A second loosed two arrows at her and she ducked in the saddle. The goblin raced off into the forest, screeching. She let fly again and let out an oath when her shaft hit a tree trunk instead.

Then she saw something beyond the goblin that made her heart go cold.

Huge, hulking figures tramped through the trees behind the goblin skirmishers, pale sunlight glinting on armor and steel weapons. A few had four arms.

"Prince Alec!" she called out, all pretense of stealth lost. "We have to run for it! Now!"

"Run!" The prince shouted, then waited for her as the refugees hustled past him. "What is it?"

"Ogres and trolls!"

He set his jaw and joined the rush of people. "Run! Everyone! Run for Sentinel! There are more than goblins in pursuit!"

Now the hustle became a mad dash. People tripped and stumbled, but Alec and Elizabeth seemed everywhere, lifting them up, determined not to lose a single member of their party.

The ogres began a low-voiced, staccato chant. Their voices mingled with the thud of their heavy boots through the underbrush. The trolls let out an ululating howl.

A chill of fear raced up Brandi's spine as they headed towards the fortress city.

The forest suddenly thinned to an open expanse of misty grassland. The towers of Sentinel's walls beckoning from about a half mile away. A bridge spanned a stream near the city, teasingly close.

"Hurry!" called out Alec. "Get into the open!"

Then a column of horsemen burst from the woods, spears and shields at the ready, angling to cut them off. Alec turned his refugees to the side. The column split in two, making him turn again. The enemy cavalry wore black brigandines with no insignia and the visors of their helmets were down.

Behind them, a full twenty ogres and five trolls lumbered out of the forest, assembling behind the horsemen. The ogres' red eyes gleamed from under beetling brows. They wore scale mail and metal skull caps on their heads. They carried metal-capped clubs, maces and axes and stumped forward in hobnailed boots.

The ogres, seven feet tall, looked short next to the towering forms of the trolls behind them. The trolls wore leather shirts with metal rings and carried an axe in each upper hand and a short spear in each lower hand. Clawed feet dug into the earth at the edge of the meadow. They snarled, revealing wicked fangs. Their purple, glowing eyes, deep-set in stubby, flat faces, seemed to rake them all with hatred. They were close enough for Brandi to smell their distinct, flat odors, something that reeked of mold and stale sweat.

We're not going to make it. If only I had a horn or something to alert the fortress!

"Ogres and trolls!" cried one of the refugees next to Brandi. "Where did they come from?"

Brandi swallowed her fear and looked them over, trying to keep her tone even and professional. "I don't see a tribal insignia so they're probably bandits, maybe from Torosc. They'll work for whoever pays them."

Pinned by the enemy, the refugees formed a ring. Alec and Stephen and Daphne stepped forward as two riders broke from the enemy ranks.

Neither of the riders wore a helmet and at first Brandi thought that one of them had no clothes either. One was a slim human man with blond hair and the other a beautiful brunette in a revealing chainmail outfit. A two-headed dog loped at her side. Neither they nor any of the rest of the enemy force spared Brandi or Megan more than a contemptuous glance.

The man held up a hand and inclined his head at Alec. "Your Highness. I am honored."

"The feeling is not mutual," Alec snapped, one hand extended and the other on his dagger.

The woman in the skimpy armor looked hurt. "Now, now, that's not very hospitable. Whatever happened to the gentility of royal manners?"

"Gentility is very far from servants of Torosc," spat Elizabeth. Henry hid behind her, his bow pointed in shaky hands.

"Is that the way to refer to your homeland?" asked the man. "I would very much like to get to know you and your charming family, especially your most brave son."

"Enough with the false pleasantries," retorted Alec. "Who are you?"

The man inclined his head again. "Forgive me, I am Berek. This is Adina, of the Gudarti sect of the Ja'al."

Gudarta, goddess of pain and suffering. Brandi's eyes narrowed.

"You will, of course, accompany us back to Torosc," Berek said. "The leaders of the Republic will be very interested in speaking to you. And don't try breaking through our lines. The ogres and trolls are not too smart and might not be able to avoid killing you. I assure you that you won't be harmed."

Right. Not until you can get us to the torture chambers.

Alec raised his hand and Berek clucked his tongue.

"Now, now. None of that. Adina and I know the counterspells to any flashy display you could make to alert the city and there's no way you'd get it off before our men skewered you. Please, try to make this as bloodless as possible."

Brandi racked her brain, trying to think of a way out. She looked across at Megan. To her surprise, her sister had a sly smile on her face.

With a tiny nod, Megan turned Larinor away, then spurred him to full speed. His wings snapped out. The astonished enemy riders struggled to control their mounts as the appearance of the pegasus threw them into turmoil. With a tremendous leap, Megan lifted off between two small trees and soared out over the enemy.

They think these are just regular horses! Their attention is fixed on Prince Alec!

With cries of alarm, some of the enemy horsemen headed off in pursuit, flinging spears ineffectually at Megan as she raced up into the air.

"A pegasus!" shouted Berek, his face a mixture of shock and anger.

"Where in the Nine Hells…"

"Sorry to part ways like this, but you'll understand," Brandi murmured to nearby refugees as she turned Amicus away and headed for open ground.

"There's two of them!" screamed Adina. "You idiots! You didn't say they had pegasi! Get the crossbows!"

Two riders charged to cut Brandi off, but she induced Amicus to leap lightly over a boulder, wings fanned out. Brandi and Amicus floated over the rock, forcing the enemy to turn aside. Amicus landed and Brandi spurred him on between two more trees. She charged straight at a pair of ogres, who grunted and hefted their axes.

"Now, Amicus!"

The pegasus gave a mighty jump and beat his wings. Brandi ducked under a thick tree branch as an axe blade swished through the air two feet under the pegasus' hooves. Brandi turned right, then left, using evasive action as she tried to gain altitude. Crossbow bolts sang past. She hoped that the appearance of the pegasi could cause enough confusion for Alec and the others to get away.

Then a fantastic burst of colored lights exploded high in the air over the scene. She turned in a wide arc, watching in amazement as Megan released another, similar spell. A bell rang in Sentinel. Brandi's eyes shot to the gates. Guards in plate armor shouted and hauled on the massive doors, pulling them open.

A body of cavalry on armored mounts pounded out, the pennants of Verian and Kurental and the Diocese of Sentinel streaming behind them. She saw elven soldiers lower their lances into position next to leaf-shaped shields of steel, their coursers racing at full speed. Dwarven warriors roared challenges and hefted two-handed battle axes as they rode on shaggy ponies armored in scale mail. Christian knights thundered at their sides wearing white plate mail and bearing greatswords. Brandi saw the insignia of a sword-and-angel-wings on their hauberks.

Knights of Saint Michael…

Brandi curved around again, guiding Amicus with her knees as she sighted on a particularly ugly-looking troll at the rear of the enemy force. She levered two arrows into it, eliciting a bellow of rage.

The ogres roared a challenge at the the approaching cavalry. The elves banged their lances on their shields. The dwarves shouted a martial chant in unison, pointing at the enemy. The ogres howled in response and charged, the trolls at their heels.

"No, you fools!" shrieked Adina. "Not them! The royals!"

The refugees sprang into action and attacked the Torosci force. Daphne, Stephen and Alec worked in deadly unison, emptying four saddles in a matter of seconds. Brandi swooped in and shot two of the enemy off their horses as she zipped past. Several of the Ja'al managed to get their crossbows into action but their plunging mounts ensured that their bolts shot out into the meadow.

Brandi turned again to regain altitude, seeing Megan diving at full speed, a swarm of firedarts lancing out from her fingers. Torosc horsemen cried out and reeled in their saddles as the magic darts exploded into them. The refugees stabbed with spear and sword, unhorsing several of the enemy, but several of their number went down. Berek shouted a word and a red explosion of fire burst out at Megan, but she turned just in time and soared away, trailing smoke. Brandi heard Larinor scream in pain from the flames.

Brandi turned again and fired twice at Berek, hitting him once in the leg. He turned his mount, grimacing in pain. Adina thrust both hands up at Brandi with a shouted obscenity.

Brandi spun her mount in a corkscrew as two beams of deadly blackness sizzled past into the sky. Then she pulled Amicus into a climb and turned to survey the battlefield.

Christian, Verian and Kurental knights slammed into the charging ogres and trolls with a tremendous clash of metal and horrid ripping sounds that she could hear even at her altitude. Some dwarves, elves or humans flew off their mounts and troll axes decapitated a couple of horses, but half of the enemy went down in seconds, run through the chest, throat or eye by lance and spear or beheaded by dwarven war axes or greatswords. The remainder tried to regroup but a second wave of horsemen swept past, riddling the enemy with arrows and magic spells.

The first group of cavalry charged on to where the refugees battled against the disoriented Torosc force. They rammed into the enemy, scattering them. Berek and Adina sped away from the fight, a few of their troops accompanying them, Adina's dog racing ahead. Berek turned in the saddle and unleashed a wide fan of flames from his hands, lighting trees and bushes on fire and covering their retreat. The pursuing knights reined in, unwilling to charge through the inferno. In seconds, mages arrived and used magic to snuff the flames but only smoke remained. Berek and Adina were gone.

Megan flew near Brandi and gave her a wide grin. Brandi waved and grinned back.

Down below, two ogres shrieked and fell, pierced by dozens of arrows. A single troll waded in, trying to get at the archers, but two mages fired lighting bolts at it. Its head exploded in a shower of black blood and bone fragments and it keeled over.

The sisters swooped down to land. By the time they landed, the battle was done. No enemy remained on the field and healers moved among the wounded, applying magic potions and spells to try to save as many as possible. Some of them merely covered the fallen with their cloaks, white or blue or red. Brandi and Megan trotted up to Stephen and Daphne.

Daphne shook her head. "You two never cease to amaze me."

"They didn't pay attention to us," said Megan, patting Larinor as a healer tended to his burns. "I realized they didn't know that Larinor and Amicus were pegasi. It doesn't surprise me though. We haven't taken to the air since leaving Torosc so no one even had a clue."

George, Alec's other bodyguard, limped over, waving away a healer who attempted to follow him.

"Victory," Stephen sighed with a sad look at the battlefield.

George nodded, face grim. "Aye, but not without cost. We started with twenty-four, plus the royal family. Very few were soldiers, and the common folk acquitted themselves well, though they were mostly artisans and craftsmen. But now we have only seventeen, and almost all of them, even the children, are injured."

Brandi felt a pang of sorrow, watching the refugees and healers solemnly wrapping the dead in cloaks for transport. A young girl screamed as one of the healers set her broken arm, then fainted in her mother's arms. The healer's hands glowed with warm orange light and he nodded to the mother, then moved on to the next patient.

Seven dead and seventeen wounded… all within a mile of safety. Why couldn't we have been faster or smarter?

196

They stood in weary silence, watching Alec, Elizabeth and Henry moving among their people. With a surge of affection, she saw Henry kneel down in front of a small boy and start helping a healer wind a bandage on his head. The young prince smiled and talked to the younger lad as he worked, the healer giving him instructions as he did so.

"Our guardian angels were busy, for sure," Daphne remarked.

"That and the Torosci obviously didn't have a lot of control over their heavy infantry," Stephen noted, sheathing his sword. "I'm willing to bet they just hired whatever bandits they could find in the wilds and charged off after us. The pegasi made all the difference."

"Sometimes a little confusion is all it takes," Brandi agreed.

"Granted," said Stephen. "But I'd prefer it if you'd let us know."

Brandi was about to protest that they didn't have time when Prince Alec strode over to them.

"How are your folk?" Daphne asked.

"Mending, the ones that can be mended," the prince replied, a bandage over his upper arm and another showing through a rip in his leather cuirass. "The ones that can't..." his voice trailed off.

Brandi blinked back tears. "Prince Alec, I —"

He interrupted her briskly. "But there are still seventeen besides Elizabeth and Henry and I who will live free. Those who died are doubtless celebrating that in the Halls of Heaven."

"Now as for you young ladies," he continued, smiling at the Alenar sisters. "That was amazing! Well, we would all be dead if you hadn't taken such decisive action."

Megan brushed at her eyes and gave him an answering smile. "So would we, Prince Alec. We are all in this together."

A group of officers and accompanying dignitaries headed their way, armor and insignia glittering. Brandi saw the mitered helm of the Bishop of Sentinel.

The prince sighed at the sight of the officials. "We certainly are. But I think the next part is for me and Elizabeth to handle. There is going to be a bit of pomp and ceremony for a while, I'm afraid."

His wife and son joined them. Elizabeth looked worn to the bone, but she smiled at them as they approached.

"Well done, Henry," Brandi said. "I saw you with the wounded. It takes a special person to both fight and heal."

Henry gazed up at Brandi with adoring eyes.

Elizabeth looked down at him, hugged him tightly and kissed him. "I think we will be involved in ceremonial nonsense for a while and it will just bore you, Henry. Weren't you telling me that Brandawyn owes you a ride on the pegasus? It seems like this is the right time, isn't it, Miss Alenar?"

"It certainly is, Your Highness," she replied. With a whoop of glee, Henry looped his bow over his back and charged up to Brandi. She smiled down at him and helped him vault into the saddle in front of her, handing him the reins. His crossbow nearly clocked her in the chin but she shifted out of the way just in time, grinning.

She urged Amicus into a canter. "You earned this, didn't you, Prince Henry?" she continued as they rode off into the grassy field.

"Yes I did," he said, then looked up over his shoulder at her and winked. "Queen Brandi."

Brandi laughed.

Chapter Seventeen – New Life

"It's so good to have you home." Kiranda Eleandir smiled as she laid her arm over the shoulder of her youngest child.

Mother and daughter stood on the balcony of the Eleandir manor, looking out over the vast lawn. Leafless trees towered overhead and many of the shrubs and bushes below them were devoid of flowers. Beyond the lawn, a grove of trees curved to their right. A path led from the front court of the manor to their left, where it joined the main road to Eleth-Anor.

Andyn smiled up at her mother. "It is good to be home," she replied.

Kiranda watched her daughter closely, noting the way her eyes drifted out towards the hills and forests, then to the glittering city some five miles away. Both women wore high-collared jackets over their dresses to keep out the chill in the winter wind.

Kiranda wondered at Andyn's introspection. *What have you seen, dearest? What horrors haunt you at night?*

"But you won't be able to stay," Kiranda finished.

Andyn sighed. "No, I won't. We're just stopping on our way to Gorostol."

She didn't offer anything further and Kiranda left it at that. Familiar with the ways of the government and the military after nearly a century of marriage to Doric, she knew when to ask and when to stay silent.

Five pegasi bearing riders soared in the air towards the home and Andyn's eyes followed them. One of the riders waved down at her and she waved back, shielding her eyes against the glare from the cloudy afternoon sky.

The pegasi rushed past and swooped around in a broad arc, heading back towards the city.

"It was nice of Khyron to take the men on a tour," Andyn said, watching the Grey Riders recede into the distance.

"Yes." Kiranda nodded. "He knows Eleth-Anor almost as well as you. Almost."

Andyn looked up and gave a small laugh. "You remember."

Kiranda withdrew her arm from her daughter's shoulders. Andyn turned away and headed back to the sitting room. Her mother followed her inside.

"I remember a lot," Kiranda noted, still watching Andyn as she closed the glass double doors behind her.

"So do I," Andyn said in a quiet voice. She stepped to a side table, touching a portrait of her sister, Sedryn. Her fingers wandered to a statue of an elk and then her face turned up to regard a painting of the family from their early years: Doric and Kiranda with Richard, Kyle, Sedryn, and Andyn. Her eyes drifted to another painting on the same wall: one with her mother, her prior husband, now deceased, and Andyn's half-siblings.

Kiranda changed the subject. "Your friends seem very nice. Of course, we've heard all about them in news reports, but meeting them all at once is much better. It was a treat to meet Connor. We don't see too many halflings in this part of Terenai."

Andyn continued gazing at the portrait. "He's a very fine man, mother. All of them are, really. Dar can be sarcastic, Buck coarse and Eric enigmatic, but they are loyal, kind and brave. They have saved me many times over."

"And now Khyron joins you."

Andyn sighed and turned to her mother. "Yes. And that is the difficult part."

Kiranda nodded, seating herself on a couch with leaf-shaped arms and scarlet and silver upholstery. She patted a spot next to her.

"Come. Tell me. Your letters were very informative, but there was much you didn't write."

Andyn hesitated and then joined her. She gave a shy smile.

"It's not Khyron himself, Mother," she began. "Seeing him has brought back all the old feelings from so long ago, the good and the painful. He is much as he was when the military sent him off on those secret missions —

the same wry sense of humor, the same thoughtfulness, the same kindness, the same laughter in his eyes…" Her voice trailed off.

"Of course," Kiranda said, taking her daughter's hands. "You were very close to him. Your father and I were preparing for him to make a proposal before he was called away. We did feel some confusion when you accepted Larad, but you were happy and we were content with that."

Andyn looked down. "There is that too. Mother, I never really stopped loving him, even as I made my life with Larad. Don't mistake me: I loved Larad dearly. He was a good husband and I could have remained happy for the rest of my life. I sometimes feel very conflicted that I could love two men so much."

Kiranda felt an old, deep pain and her eyes wandered to gaze at one of the portraits on the wall, then to the land beyond her home. "I understand, dear one."

Andyn reached out and touched her mother's arm. "I am sorry, mother. I forget about Aidan sometimes."

Kiranda took her hand and squeezed it. "It was long ago, Andyn, and he is at peace. Thank Verian that I found your father. He is my steady refuge."

Andyn nodded. "As was Larad to me. And then…" her voice trailed off.

"Yes?"

Now the words came out in a rush. "And then my world came crashing down, and then I went to the Academy. Then I set off for the north lands, seeking a new life and some sense of closure for Larad. Then I met the Riders, and now?"

Kiranda waited.

Andyn shrugged, then looked up at her. Kiranda felt surprise at her daughter's expression, seeing regret, sorrow, pain, confusion and a wistful longing. This she had not anticipated. Certainly, considering Andyn's profession and all she had seen and experienced, Kiranda expected a measure of traumatic stress, but not this.

"Andyn, my heart. Please. What's wrong?"

"Mother, what if I made a mistake?"

"What mistake?"

Andyn held up her hands and let them drop to her sides in a helpless gesture. "All of this: the Grey Riders, free-lance mercenary, the quests and missions, all my training. Being home with Khyron makes me realize again how happy I was with Larad and how I would have been content to be a wife and mother, not a crusading warrior. I have literally seen Hades."

Kiranda's eyes narrowed. "Is this something to do with what happened at the Battle of Hillton? The Christian relic I mean — the crown of the saint."

Andyn considered this. "Well, yes and no. Yes, using it made me understand things about myself: my own limitations and inadequacies. But it isn't just that. Mother, I'm weary. The last year of my life has been spent in facing down creatures from people's worst nightmares, conquering horrible evils, and trying to save the innocent. I know we've done great good, mother, but the people we couldn't save — how many more will die because I couldn't save them? Maybe it's time I stopped. I still think of them."

Kiranda smiled. "I would be alarmed if you didn't. But you know as well as I do that you can't save everyone. And the good went on to a blissful reward."

Andyn said nothing.

Kiranda smoothed her dress. "Maybe some time here at home will help you recuperate."

Andyn stood, looking agitated, then turned away. "I am not sure I'm cut out for this any more. Light of Justice and Lichslayer, Knight of the Empire, all the politics and deep plots of evil and constant threat of danger; my soul feels tired."

"This seems like something you should discuss with High Priestess Taryn."

"I've already talked to her."

"Ah." Kiranda sat with her hands in her lap, waiting.

Andyn turned around again, looking wilted. "She said to listen to Verian's voice, that Verian speaks to the heart. She reminded me of all the good we've done and how much we can do in the future to make life better for others. But what if I'm not meant to follow this path any more?"

"Then you return here, take up the life of heal-craft like you were doing prior to marriage to Larad and life goes on."

Andyn's eyes turned to the open glass doors leading to the balcony, looking towards the distant city. "And yet, they need me."

Kiranda stood and joined her. "Andyn, even I know that the life of a free-lance is changeable and uncertain. Mercenaries retire from that life all the time, for a variety of reasons. It is not uncommon."

"I can't just leave them now."

"That is a different matter," she replied, putting her arm around Andyn again. "Certainly, I wouldn't expect you to abandon your current mission, whatever that is. But after you are done? That seems like a logical breaking point."

"What about Khyron?"

Now it was Kiranda's turn to sigh. "If you really care for Khyron and want to marry him and are willing to follow him wherever he goes, I know he will accept whatever you give him. Indeed, based on his visits here after you left to go up north, I am sure that he still adores you. Dar and the others will understand."

Andyn wrapped her arms around her mother. "Will they?"

"Oh, Andyn," Kiranda said, hugging her tightly. "They *love* you! I can see that already. They want what's best for you, and if being Khyron's wife will make you happy, I can't imagine any of them holding it against you. You are truly blessed to have wonderful friends. Many people go through life without encountering half as many like them."

She held Andyn at arm's length and was surprised to see tears in her eyes. "Andyn…"

"I'm sorry, Mother," she said, wiping at her eyes. "It's just that seeing Khyron again, and all the turmoil of the last few months, and now coming home to visit — I'm a mess."

Kiranda laughed and hugged her again. "That's my Andyn! Always making my life interesting! But I wouldn't have it any other way."

Andyn gave a small laugh of her own.

Kiranda held her daughter's face in her hands. "No matter what you choose, Andyn, I know it will be a good, honest decision without selfishness or an ulterior motive. Those things do not live in you."

Andyn smiled and kissed her. "Thank you, Mother. For everything."

"Always, my heart."

***

"The hardest part is telling her apart from her mother," Buck said, patting Shadowbane on the neck as he held out a handful of oats for the pegasus to munch. Glad for a chance to rest from their travels and labors, he felt himself relaxing.

Dar nodded at Buck's comment. "Tell me about it. And they have the same hair color."

Khyron grinned at them over the withers of Zasural, running a comb through his mount's mane. "If you stay in Terenai long enough, you'll be able to tell. Judging the age of elves is hard, but after a while, there are subtle little hints that will help."

"Such as?" Connor asked from his perch atop one of the stable walls.

"Well," said Khyron, putting away the comb and joining the other Riders on a bench. "First, there are mannerisms. Younger elven women tend to make their motions quicker and with a little more nervous energy. Older women are more serene and composed. Also, older elven women tend to have eyes that aren't quite as brilliant as the younger ones: kind of the difference between highly polished silver and worn silver. Still bright, but different."

"That won't help at a distance," noted Eric, brushing hay off his tunic.

"Well, then there are the fashions. Younger elven women tend to be a bit more on the daring side, especially if they're single."

"What exactly do you mean by 'daring'?" Eric asked with a smirk at Dar.

Khyron raised his eyebrows. "You mean you've been in Terenai for several days and you haven't noticed?"

Dar shrugged and looked innocent.

Khyron nodded gravely, eyes twinkling. "Well, this is winter, so it isn't as obvious, though the necklines on their dresses are a bit lower than the ones the married ladies wear. And the clothes are a little more, shall we say, form-fitting."

Buck certainly had noticed and now that Khyron explained why, he put two and two together. "And in spring and summer?" he asked.

Khyron tried to hide a smile and failed. "Terenai can get quite warm, you know. Let's say that the ladies don't like to be bound up in anything that makes them hot, so they wear less and less as the season goes on. They are quite fond of being noticed by the menfolk for their feminine assets."

Buck imagined some of the elven girls he had seen in the towns and cities wearing less and less and his interest increased.

Connor inspected his fingernails minutely. "How much less are we talking?"

Khyron laughed. "Stick around long enough and you'll find out. Especially at the beach on a sunny day."

"That will be very entertaining," Dar said, turning to Eric with a satisfied look. "Hopefully, Brandi and Megan can join us. Maybe they can show us the summer fashions down by the ocean?"

They all laughed at Eric's expression of mock surprise. Eric bumped Dar with his shoulder, then shoved him, grinning. Dar waggled his eyebrows.

Buck considering the women he had seen in the towns and cities, then Andyn's figure — and Megan's, and Brandi's. He briefly wondered if Carine would ever come this far south.

"That sounds like a great idea. I hear Terenai's coastlines are quite lovely in summer," he opined.

Connor chuckled. "I think we're going to pay a visit to Eleth-Anor in about another seven months. For purely aesthetic reasons, of course."

Khyron slapped his knee. "And I will be glad to show you around. If Andyn's brothers are here you can meet them too."

"Great," said Eric. "Then we'll have to try to tell her brothers apart from her father."

"Yes," replied Khyron. "Same problem, and same characteristics with the eyes. Older elven men tend to be more reserved, like Colonel Eleandir, and think before acting. Again, once you've been around for a while, you'll figure it out."

Buck made a face. "Sounds confusing."

Connor hopped down. "But Andyn's father is half-human."

Khyron nodded. "Yes. And she has two half-siblings from her mother's first husband, the one who died. He was a full elf, as are Andyn's half-brother Telric and half-sister Beldryn."

They thought this over in silence. Finally, Buck stood, brushing his hands on his trousers. "Genetics are *not* my area of expertise," he said firmly.

"I'm with you there," Connor affirmed.

"I'm sure Melinor would bend our ears for two hours explaining it, but I think we should go get some of that wine that Doric offered us when we got here," said Eric, joining them.

"You read my mind," said Buck, feeling his stomach grumble.

"My vote too," said Dar with enthusiasm. "That was a great tour, Khyron, but I'm ready for lunch and something good to drink."

Khyron bowed. "Then I'm sure if we go up to the manor looking famished and tired, the ladies will shoo us right into the dining room. The Eleandir women are known for their hospitality."

Buck wondered at how much "hospitality" Khyron got from Andyn every night, but decided not to pursue it. He had tried to figure out the Eric-Andyn story earlier, only to find that he was wrong about that one. It didn't give him a lot of confidence in trying to unravel the Khyron-Andyn romance.

He shook his head as they trooped out to the manor. Andyn certainly had a string of admirers.

True to Khyron's prediction, Kiranda and Andyn greeted them and ushered them into the dining room, where goblets of pale wine awaited them. Buck took his seat next to Connor.

The halfling looked up at him and grinned. "Let's see what the elves can conjure up."

As it was, they conjured up quite a bit: platters with sliced pears, apples and oranges, bowls of steaming vegetable stew rich with potatoes, carrots, leeks, broccoli, cauliflower and celery, plates of spicy and mild sausage, tiny rounds of creamy cheese and fluffy rolls with a buttery crust. Two maidservants in dark grey dresses kept the meal going with a deft touch, refilling containers almost before anyone noticed that the food or wine was depleted.

As good as Connor's parents, thought Buck as he downed the last bit of a roll. *Lighter, but plenty of it.*

He listened to the conversation around the table. Naturally, Andyn and Khyron sat next to each other, as did Kiranda and Doric. Buck watched the parents especially. As he had noted, Kiranda looked like an older copy of Andyn, but Doric contrasted his wife with dark brown hair, amber eyes, and more rounded features. Still, he could see he was Andyn's father. Doric listened more than he spoke.

The meal completed, they moved into a large parlor, where the servants brought tea.

"So you are from Astarel, Sir Buckminster," Doric said, lowering himself into a seat and looking at Buck over the rim of his teacup.

"From Tyler," Buck replied, accepting a cup himself. "My father owns a store there."

Doric nodded, setting his cup down on a side table. "And how does he fare these days?"

"He is well, sir."

"A bit of nasty business, that was," Doric said. Kiranda shot him a look.

He knows everything by now, Buck realized. *Probably knows all about Derek and the trial and the Eye of Truth and Liander Tolin.*

"Father has recovered well enough," he said. "My brother stops by when his ship is in port, but Da' doesn't want any of us to make a big deal about anything."

"And you, Mister Lomin? How are your parents?" Kiranda asked.

"Keeping up with the grandkids makes busy days even if they didn't have temple duties," Connor replied with a smile, helping himself to a tiny tea cake on a platter.

Buck watched Khyron in particular as Eric and Dar talked about their families with Doric and Kiranda. The Riders had welcomed their newest member openly enough, mostly because of their regard for Andyn and trust in her, but Khyron still didn't know much about their history together.

Unbidden, Buck's conversation with Druidess Carine came to mind. He wondered if Khyron was one of those allies she had mentioned, or whether he might end up being a liability. Considering the fact that Melinor recommended him, it didn't seem likely that he was a servant of the Dark in hiding.

If he's fooled Melinor, we're doomed anyway.

"You just have the one sibling?" Kiranda asked Buck, breaking his musing.

"No, I have a sister, Summer, who lives with her family in Eldir. She was a bit alarmed when she found out about the business with Liander Tolin, but they attended Wintertide Festival with Da' in Tyler, so I know that settled her a bit."

Khyron turned to Andyn. "Liander Tolin. Wasn't he the councilman in Eleth-Anor?"

Andyn smiled sadly, placing a hand on his arm. "Yes, Khy. He was the one who hired the Crossed Swords to kill Larad. We caught up with him near Darlon."

He put his hand over hers. "I'm sorry, Andyn. I trust you brought him to justice."

"We did," added Eric, "But it was just another step on the way to bringing down my parents, and the Crossed Swords Guild."

"Liander had the medallion that helped us find the relic that Andyn used to defeat Zhinia Margoth," Dar pointed out.

"Interesting." Khyron looked thoughtful. "All very fortuitous."

"More than that," said Buck with a sour look at Andyn. "It was predicted. By prophecy."

Khyron's eyebrows rose and Connor filled him in on the Song of the Grey Riders, the Irial prophecy that predicted the rise of the Grey Riders and the fall of the lich princess.

Buck figured his expression probably gave him away because Khyron laughed. "I think the Song is probably Buck's least favorite thing in the world."

Among other things.

"I guess I just don't like being pulled around by something out of my control," Buck said.

"But it did turn out well at the end," Eric said with a grin at Buck. "Even Buck would have to admit that. He got the Eye of Truth out of it."

"Andyn mentioned that before," Doric said. "May we see it?"

Buck removed the Eye from his belt pouch and handed it to Andyn, who gave it to her father. He peered through it and handed it to Khyron, looking impressed.

"Amazing. That must have been some powerful magic."

"Family heirloom," said Buck.

Kiranda also inspected the Eye and then handed it back.

"And your father and mother are no less the worse for wear since the battle at Hillton, I trust," Doric said with a look at Dar.

Dar shrugged, taking a couple of little tea cakes himself. "They were never close to the fighting, and as soon as I was, er, restored, they settled in to the new reality."

They all lapsed into silence as Dar's words about the Battle of Hillton lingered. Buck thought back to that day on the hill, when a dark, horrible fire flashed from the hands of the lich princess and everything went black.

"Forgive me," Khyron finally ventured. "But I have to ask this. What exactly happened? I've seen the military briefings about the battle, just like Colonel Eleandir, but they didn't give a lot of details about you Grey Riders. Apparently, we didn't have the 'need to know'."

"Well," began Andyn, "The Helm of Shadows, which was created by Zhinia Margoth and which Liander Tolin coveted, teleported us to Hillton where the lich's army was besieging the city. She was there, of course, and at first all I felt was this paralyzing terror, like a fog, actually. I became aware of the Crown of Saint Alyssa in my hand and placed it on my head, and then…" her voice trailed off.

"We died," Buck interjected, meeting the eyes of Khyron and the Eleandirs. They stared at him.

"We died," he repeated with a shrug. "Let's face it, Margoth turned into a lich centuries ago and had access to magic we don't even understand. I don't know what she used to do it, but Margoth killed us with dark sorcery. We died, all of us except Andyn. The Crown protected her."

Doric's composure failed him and he gaped at them. "I… you… I mean, the reports said you fell but were restored. They didn't mention that you died."

"We did," Dar added. "But the Crown brought us back to life."

"How is that possible?" breathed Kiranda.

"The Crown enabled me to slow time," said Andyn. "Alyssa, the saint and queen, came to me. She gave me instructions on how to preserve Buck, Connor, Hlerv, Dar and Eric essentially a second after their deaths, so that time would not pass for them while I fought Margoth."

She smiled at Buck and the other Riders in turn. "Then Alyssa guided me in the fight, instructing me on how to use magic it would take me decades to learn. After that was over, she showed me how to bring my friends back."

"Alyssa?" asked Kiranda. She stared at her daughter, then gave a little laugh. "So you are on a first-name basis with a Christian saint, now?"

Andyn blushed and gave a sheepish grin. "Well, that's what she told me to call her. If she were here now and I tried to address her as Holy One or Your Majesty, I think she would forcefully remind me *not* to call her that."

Kiranda sat back in her chair, shaking her head. "I know that high priests of the good religions can sometimes revive someone from death if they are there when the event occurs, but you fought a battle and then restored five people much later. Unbelievable!"

She then chuckled. "Your training as a priestess does you credit, Andyn, if this is the result."

Andyn looked down at her hands, clasping Khyron's. "I am convinced that it was not personal merit on my account, Mother."

Khyron looked at Buck. "So, again, forgive me, but what was it like?"

Buck met Connor's gaze and the halfling shrugged.

"We all saw something different," Buck replied. "Of course, no one knows what Hlerv saw, since he stole the Helm and teleported away after the battle, but Dar and Eric saw things differently than Connor and I. I found myself in a gray, twilight place, with light on one side and darkness behind me. I wasn't alone, but the light came with a sort of comforting presence. Then I heard Andyn's voice calling me back and I returned to the hill by the lake, and a tough battle after that. I didn't even have time to process every-thing until after the awards ceremony."

"And you?" Kiranda asked Dar and Eric.

"I was aware of the darkness and grayness, but they seemed far off, in the background. I was surrounded by warmth and light and happiness. The Light said that He was well-pleased with us," Dar said. "I knew Who it was in-stantly, and I felt the same peace and comfort as Connor and Buck. I remem-ber trying to go with God, away from all the trouble and pain, but He told me I wasn't done yet and that I still had tasks to do. Then, the same as Buck: Andyn's voice and a return to this world."

Silence reigned. Buck spun his wine goblet between his fingers, remem-bering.

"I will never fear death again," Eric said in a quiet voice. "No temptation or threat of the Ja'al or the Vardish or Satan or anyone else will mean anything to me. The grave has lost its terror. I was actually angry at God afterwards for not taking me with Him."

Khyron looked thoughtful, then shot a glance at him. "Is that how you've been able to keep up this madcap pace up until now?"

Eric gave a wry smile. "When you're not afraid of death, you tend to get more focused on the present. Personal danger is not as much of a factor."

"Well," Doric said with an explosive sigh, "My information tells me that your frenetic pace helped keep the Crossed Swords very busy and left them vulnerable to your final attack on their main base. So, then, Verian was with you."

"He certainly was," Andyn finished.

I can't handle all this spiritual seriousness, Buck decided.

"So," he said, sitting back in his chair, "since we're all raised from the dead, we can get on with life. You said earlier that we have dinner with one of the councilmen of Eleth-Anor?"

Doric laughed. "Right back to practical things, Sir Buckminster! Excellent! Yes, we do have a dinner engagement, but it is at the Duke's residence with the full council. There are many people eager to meet you, so I'm afraid you'll have to bring your finery to appear as the crusading heroes and smiters of evil. Only after performing your celebrity duties will you be able to continue on to Meridian."

Buck nodded. "Fair enough. And Colonel? You don't have to call me Sir Buck any more. It's just Buck. Andyn is like family to us."

Andyn's eyes shone with unshed tears at his words and the Colonel gave him a grave nod in return.

"Then you shall call me Doric."

Chapter Eighteen – The World Is A Stage

"Khyron's almost as good as she is," Dar commented, adjusting his closed helm. The headgear muffled his voice and kept his identity secret but he really preferred his more open field helmet. He felt like he was inside a milk can. He held the reins for Zasural and Medianox and tried to appear aloof and disinterested as the crowds in the main market square of Meridian swirled around them.

"If they do get back together, their kids are going to be a handful. I can see that already," Buck answered from inside his own helm.

Like Dar, he wore a plain brown surcoat over dull, ordinary scale mail. To all the world, they looked like a nondescript pair of guards. Their pegasi, wings carefully hidden under black caparisons and saddle bags, helped the appearance — the Riders took the time to trim their manes and tails to make them look worn and unremarkable.

Dar spared a glance at their "patrons". Andyn and Khyron pretended to be a married merchant couple, currently speaking with an elven man and his wife near the entrance of a dress shop. Late afternoon sunshine broke through the clouds over the lake named Kaljirre, or "sky mirror" in the Dwarven tongue. Dar's stomach rumbled a bit. It had been a longer than usual trip into the city. To avoid attracting attention, they had to land under the cover of darkness in the hills outside of Alvindor. Then they rode the highway into Meridian like normal horsemen. They only stopped for a light snack on the way before entering the city.

He wondered about the effectiveness of their disguises. Khyron's associates in the Elven special forces assured them that they looked nothing like the Heroes of Deran. The alterations included extra padding to make Buck look burlier and heavier (which he bore with ill humor since it also made him hot, even in winter) and special boots to make Dar look an inch taller. They even dyed their hair: black for Buck and blond for Dar. After all that, Dar had a lot of sympathy for the careful preparations Andyn made when they were hunting the Serpent in Harlinsville.

To Dar's eyes, they looked like the Grey Riders starring in a particularly tawdry romantic play. However, Andyn's mother pointed out the Ja'al were looking for three warriors in shining armor, a woman priestess and a nimble halfling in black leather, not two nondescript guards and a foppish pair of merchants.

Dar watched as Andyn smiled and simpered, talking in excited tones about the fashions in the shop window. She occasionally stopped to adjust the red velvet cap on her head, an amethyst winking in the winter sunlight. She wore a pink and grey riding outfit, complete with silver spurs on grey doeskin boots. Khyron looked quite the dandy with green velvet doublet and trousers, shiny black boots of his own, a wide-brimmed, feathered black hat and a completely useless decorative short sword at his belt.

"Here they come," Buck said.

Andyn and Khyron swept towards them, arm in arm and chatting gaily.

"We're to meet Mister Highwater at the Red Swallow Inn," Khyron said with an imperious glance at Buck as he accepted Zasural's reins and swung into the saddle. Dar held out a hand and helped Andyn, then mounted up himself. She pulled a tiny mirror out of her belt purse and looked at her reflection critically, touching her hair.

"They had better have an excellent tavern at this Red Swallow Inn," she said to Khyron in a bored voice. "The place in Alvindor was simply ghastly. I certainly expect better for Meridian. It *is* the capital city."

"I am assured by the gentleman and his wife that it is quite comfortable, my love," Khyron said with a particularly vapid smile. "Lake views, hot baths and a comfortable bed. If it is not, they will hear of it and we will find other lodgings. I have a list!"

"I certainly hope so," Andyn sniffed, shoving the mirror back into her purse. "Well, let's get on with it. Mister Highwater is doubtless waiting for us and the sooner we conclude our business the sooner I can enjoy the casino by the lakeside."

Without another look, Dar and Buck led them into the streets, clearing the way with a snarled command at those who didn't move with sufficient alacrity. Dar felt guilty about appearing callous and uncouth. He knew most of the people in the city were just like his own family, simple folk trying to make their way in life and not needing the curt attention of rough guards. Yet he had to keep up the charade.

Dar ran through the map of Meridian in his mind, plotting the easiest course from the Grand Market to Kenwall, the suburb where they would find the Red Swallow Inn. He purposefully took a route that went near shops with window displays to attract Andyn's attention and let her play the role of a hare-brained socialite to the hilt. Khyron followed her lead, adding a stream of *Yes dear*'s and *Of course, darling*'s at random intervals.

Finally, they reined in at a sprawling, two-story complex, set back from the main street on a hillside. Dar stopped at an ornate iron gate with two guard shacks and presented a reservation slip to the slender young guard. The guard nodded and retrieved a red leather book from the shack while four other warriors watched Dar's party with relaxed alertness, crossbows held at port arms.

Dar gave them a careful once-over. Security, he expected. Security this watchful, even at a posh resort, surprised him. The head guard nodded and smiled at Dar, returning the reservation slip and motioning to the gates. Two of the guards opened it and the four Riders passed beyond.

A well-manicured lawn, flowerbeds, a fountain and a driveway for carriages sat before an impressive edifice of grey stone and red wood. A set of double glass doors beckoned, illuminated by magical lamps on either side. A sign hung over the door, made of a silvery metal with three red swallows painted on it.

Dar smiled under his helm as he watched the images of the swallows flit from one edge of the sign to the other. They vanished as they reached the limit, then reappeared, pausing in the middle of the sign before continuing.

"Well, this is certainly looking better," Khyron sniffed as he dismounted.

He held out his hand to Andyn after Dar helped her down. The pair flounced towards the lobby.

Dar and Buck led the pegasi toward the stables, eyes open for a particular stablehand. It didn't take long for them to find Eric Indidarc by the stable doors in the company of two elves. He looked nothing like his usual self, wearing an eyepatch and sporting a thin beard, though his dark red uniform was impeccable.

"See that they get extra oats," Dar barked, tossing a few gold coins to Eric, who nodded meekly and accepted the reins for all four mounts. Buck and Dar hefted the saddlebags and turned on their heels, heading back towards the lobby.

To anyone else, it looked like an everyday exchange, but no one would see that Eric and the two elves, spies from Terenai, would take the pegasi out by a back gate to a loading area. After leading the mounts away from the property, they would take them to an empty barn and remove their disguises to let them open their wings, joining Phantom and Niveral already hidden away. There they would remain under the watchful eye of six more agents until the Riders came to get them.

Dar took off his helm as he entered the lobby. He took in the polished tables, glass figurines, pots with colorful plants, flowers in vases, carpets from Evendale, and tapestries from Eldir. They arrived just in time to see Andyn and Khyron laughing with the hotel clerk at some inside joke.

"Well?" asked Andyn, turning to him.

Dar bowed. "The horses are in the stable, Ma'am, and with instructions for extra care."

"Good," she said with an airy smile. "Follow us to our suite with the bags. Your room is down the hall from us."

"Of course, ma'am," responded Buck. Dar followed him to a set of stairs and they slouched after Khyron and Andyn, setting down the heavy luggage in the suite before bowing and leaving. They stowed their own bags in their room after checking the garderobe and the small balcony as a precaution.

Dar gave Buck a look. "Meeting time?"

Buck shrugged. "Let our masters call us like they're supposed to. We're the hired help." He sat back in a chair, putting his boots up on a wooden table.

Dar smacked his legs. "Didn't your mother teach you any manners?"

Buck closed his eyes. "She never had much luck with me on that score. I don't take well to most lessons."

"Tell that to Jocko Roundtree. He obviously taught you to fight."

"And he was lucky to get that."

When their summons came, Andyn somehow managed to make the ringing of a small bell sound imperious. Buck and Dar trooped over to Khyron and Andyn's room. Much to their surprise, Eric already occupied a seat on a couch.

"Nice work so far," he said.

Buck looked around the room. "How did you get in?"

Eric jerked a thumb at the closed glass doors leading to the balcony. "A little rope ladder that Andyn took from her bag and lowered for me."

"Do you think anyone suspects?" Dar asked.

Khyron reached into a mapcase and drew out a sheaf of papers fastened by a leather band with a silver buckle. He shrugged. "Andyn and I made sure to draw as much attention to ourselves as possible. That and the disguises should keep any observers in the dark a while longer. If we've somehow tipped our hand, we will have to do our best to think on our feet." He unclasped the buckle and flipped it over, removing a tiny piece of paper.

Andyn flopped into a nearby chair, removing her flashy cap and fluffing her hair out. Khyron whispered a phrase and touched the paper, which then expanded into a much larger map. This he laid down on the table.

Next, Khyron detached the buckle from the strap on the papers and set it on the map. He waved a hand over it, closed his eyes and murmured a quiet phrase. The buckle flashed white, then settled into a mild glow somewhat like fog. The misty light soon filled the room.

The Riders waited silently as Khyron sat motionless for several heartbeats. Then, with a smile, he opened his eyes.

"There," he said, smoothing the map. "Anyone spying on us will see a halfling accountant discussing business with a lord and lady while two guards watch from corners of the room. Dar, either you or Buck are going to have to play guard at the door. Connor should be here any minute."

"I'll do it," Dar volunteered, exiting the suite and standing at the door, one hand on the hilt of the short sword at his belt.

He did not have long to wait. Soon, clumping up the stairs with a black walking stick, looking elderly and daft, a disguised Connor Lomin approached. He peered at Dar with a sour expression from behind round spectacles askew on his nose. He scratched his grey hair and leaned on his walking stick, adjusting a valise and quill kit under one arm.

"Guard," he huffed, "Tell Sir Geffand and his lady wife that Mister Highwater awaits their pleasure."

"Yes sir," Dar replied, opening the door and poking his head in. "Mister Highwater is here."

"Bring him in," Andyn ordered and soon, the Grey Riders sat around the table.

"Is this really necessary?" asked Buck, settling onto the couch. "We're doing a lot of play-acting but I haven't seen anyone suspicious yet."

"It is," replied Khyron.

Connor shot a look at him. "I think this isn't his first time doing this, Buck."

The officer nodded. "I can't tell you any more, but I suspect that spies for at least four different factions have already sized us up. They will likely watch us for a couple of days at least before moving on to other observations. Should we act suspicious, they will increase surveillance."

"Who?" asked Andyn, brow furrowed.

Khyron gave her a half-smile. "Most likely Gorostoli Federal Service, Irial Church Intelligence, the local Druid Council, and Torosci Interior Ministry, for starters."

Damn, that's a lot of attention already. Dar shook his head. "Is that normal?"

"Yes," said Khyron, taking out a charcoal pencil. "Gorostol is a border land, wedged between the Northern Alliance on one side and Torosc and its allies on the other. Spies aplenty. You can be sure that the Christians, Ja'al, Vardish, Verian and Cla'Agik all have agents in major cities. One giant board game."

Before Dar could comment further, Khyron pointed at the outlines on the paper.

"This estate here is the Lervion family manor and grounds. Note the large main building, the outbuildings, main gate, delivery gate, servants' quarters, barracks and the underground ramp leading to storage areas."

Dar followed Khyron's finger, memorizing the locations of the barracks and servants' quarters.

"It is well-guarded," Khyron continued, "but agents have noted delivery wagons moving with increasing frequency in the last few months. That in itself isn't out of the ordinary, because the Manor was the site of the original Lervion shipping house and facilities are still on the grounds. Locals say that the Lervions personally process special shipments at the manor for wealthy clients. However, the uptick in frequency is unusual."

"Probably related to the Ja'al project," Connor said with a nod.

Khyron looked at the other Riders. "More importantly, there was a major scuffle at the manor a few nights ago. Apparently, burglars tried to gain entrance and were killed by House guards. At least, that's the official explanation."

"So that's the reason for the heightened security," mused Dar. "Other people of influence are wondering if they're next."

Khyron nodded. "Additionally, there is news of a skirmish down south by the city of Sentinel, something involving Ja'al mercenaries from Torosc. I don't have any more details, but my usual channels are very quiet about it, so it must be a top-secret operation, whatever it was."

"Where is our regular gear?" asked Buck.

"In the stables, in a secret compartment in the floor," Eric replied. "The agents from Terenai brought it down from Alvindor, hidden in a shipment of hay bales, while we were getting our disguises."

"What's our next move?" asked Connor, leaning back and crossing his arms.

"We try to get some local intelligence," Khyron said, folding up the map again and miniaturizing it. He stuffed it inside the cuff of his shirtsleeve. "Andyn and I will be at the casino while you two go to the Witches Brew Tavern. It's about a mile back towards the Grand Market and right on Warehouse Way. Lots of locals stop by there, working folks like guards and merchants and laborers. It's a favorite with halflings and dwarves and gnomes. See what you can find out."

"Won't we stand out?" asked Buck.

"Not if Connor goes with you."

"Just like old times," Connor said with a grin. "Hope the ale is as good as

The Pit in Forester."

"I'll let you know," said Buck, rising.

Connor left with the two humans as Khyron and Andyn instructed their "guards" to make sure Mister Highwater was escorted home safely.

Connor hailed a carriage and the trio climbed in.

"Witches Brew Tavern," Connor barked at the driver, settling his spectacles on his nose.

The carriage rumbled away. Dar looked at his halfling friend.

"I think you're enjoying this," he said in a low voice.

"Eh? What was that? Speak up boy!" Connor responded with a scowl and a wink.

They rode the rest of the way in silence and Buck helped Connor down at the entrance to the tavern. As Khyron had said, many of the customers were indeed dwarves and halflings, but Dar saw a few humans as well.

Slipping inside the tavern, he noted the size of the tables and chairs, mostly fitted for the smaller races. However, a couple of booths near the back looked the right size for elves or humans. To his right, an impressive array of kegs, bottles and barrels crowded behind the huge, darkwood bar. Artwork large and small and of varying degrees of skill and subject matter covered the walls.

Dwarven serving girls bustled in from a pair of swinging kitchen doors that never seemed to stay closed. They swirled around the tables, smiling, collecting coins that winked in the lamp light and bringing steaming platters or frothy mugs in exchange.

Dar's stomach again reminded him how long it had been since his last real meal.

Connor led the way, limping through a crowd. He eased himself into a chair at a gaming table, nodding to the dark-haired young dwarven woman shuffling a pack of cards. A pair of dwarves and a gnome joined him and he turned to Dar.

"Come back in an hour," he ordered amid the murmur of voices and clinking of glass and metal. Dar inclined his head.

Buck smacked Dar in the shoulder and led him to one of the larger booths. A red-haired dwarven lass in a blue dress materialized in seconds.

"What'll you have, lads?" she asked in a cheery soprano.

"What's the special of the house?" Dar asked before Buck could say anything.

"Hmm…" she replied, pursing her lip. "If you've the coin for it, the beef stew with cheese bread and berry tart is the best around. It's a dozen silver disks though."

Dar nodded. He handed her two gold pieces. "And one of your best dark ales, too."

She raised an eyebrow as Buck also paid her. "Well, yes sir! I'll bring back your change."

Dar waved a hand. "Keep it."

She smiled brightly and bobbed her head, then left. Dar and Buck waited silently, watching the patrons. Most of them gave the humans a good long look, then turned away when they didn't do anything untoward. Dar saw one of the other waitresses talking to the barkeep, indicating Connor with a toss of her head and jerking a thumb in Dar's direction. The halfling barkeep, a grey-haired fellow with bright blue eyes, looked at Dar and Buck, then nodded.

Connor soon had an animated conversation going with the gnome woman at his left, saying something that made her giggle as the cards flew around the table. The hum of conversation in the tavern increased in volume as more people entered. Soon even the stools at the bar were filled.

Their serving girl returned with two platters, assisted by another girl with two mugs. Dar breathed in the tantalizing aroma of the stew and smiled at her.

"By the smell of it, you don't lie."

"I would never lie, sir," she said with a pert look. "Unless it's on my back for the right fellow." With that, she spun off into the crowd.

Buck raised an eyebrow as he reached for the cheese bread.

"Gorostol," Dar said with a shrug.

The food disappeared faster than he thought possible, even for him. Soon, he sat back, contentedly sipping the remnants of his ale. The serving girl's assessment had been correct, and the meal was worth every penny.

More patrons entered and exited and Connor continued his charade at the gaming table, sipping from a wine glass and nibbling on slim sandwiches of black bread. Nothing else seemed out of the ordinary.

Let him do his work…

"So many gnomes," Buck said as a young halfling man stumbled past their alcove.

"Some look like Hlerv," Dar mused, remembering.

"Hlerv?"

Dar started and found the halfling staring at him.

"Did you say Hlerv?"

The world froze. Dar could only nod.

"Well, that's the second time I've heard that name in a fortnight, and it's not a usual one," the halfling said with a hiccup.

Buck nodded slowly. "Yes, it's unusual. Do you know someone of that name?"

"Oh yes," said the halfling, stifling a burp with his hand. "Interesting fellow."

Scarcely able to believe his ears, Dar regained his composure and slid over in the booth to make room. "Well, then, friend, come sit here and tell us the tale. What is your name?"

"Thank you kindly," the halfling replied, clambering up into the seat and giving both Riders a broad smile. "The name's Jervan."

Buck motioned the serving maid. "Nice to meet you, Jervan. I'm Horatio and this is Richard. What are you drinking? Our treat."

"Well, that's mighty fine of you, Horatio," Jervan said, nodding to himself. "A pale ale, if you don't mind. Winter Witch Brew."

Buck paid the waitress, who soon returned with a mug for Jervan. The halfling tasted it and sighed. "Now that's the good stuff."

"It is," said Dar. He had a hard time keeping himself from peppering Jervan with questions. He sipped his own ale.

"So this Hlerv is a friend of yours?" Buck asked.

Jervan took a pull from his tankard, waving a hand for Buck to wait, then wiped his mouth and belched again. "No, not a friend. A fellow who came into town recently, or so he said. Gnome. Dark hair and beard. Eyes that don't smile. Looking for information on the wealthy parts of town."

"I see," said Dar, shooting a glance at Buck. "I wonder why?"

"Ha," Jervan replied with a conspiratorial glance at them. He leaned forward. "A thief, or I'm a dragon. He had some fine cloth, but I could see he had a sword under his cloak, so probably an upper-story man, if you take my meaning."

"What happened to him?" asked Buck.

Jervan shrugged. "Who knows? I gave him a tour of Silvervale, then we parted ways. I figure he probably got involved with that crowd that tried to rob the Lervion manor and got his ass chopped up. Not a safe place for thieving, that."

"Good security, I guess," Dar said.

Jervan actually shuddered. He turned wary eyes to the Riders. "Word on the street is that they have a few wizards with bad attitudes. And…"

His voice trailed off.

"And what?" Buck prompted.

Jervan shook himself. "Some say they have Cerberus hounds. That's a load of ogre shit, of course. Nobody but the Dark Faiths can handle them things, and the Ja'al and Vardish aren't tolerated in Meridian, nor Gorostol for that matter."

Dar thought this over, mind spinning.

"Lervion House," Jervan repeated after another pull. "House of death that is."

"How so?" Dar asked with a sense of dread.

"The father died of a heart attack years ago," replied Jervan, staring into his mug. "Then the mother from a wasting disease no healer could treat. Then the older son disappeared. Now the sister, a halfling, hurt in the attack. A cursed house, I say."

Dar's mind whirred. "The mother was a halfling, I assume?"

"Yep. Father a gnome. Son a gnome. Seemed like a good family until all the troubles."

Dar and Buck sat in shock, digesting this.

Jervan drained his mug and gave a loud belch. "Strange name, Hlerv," he said in a voice rapidly becoming slurred. "Secretive sort of guy, but paid well. Found me a lass with perky tits for the money he gave me."

Dar left a gold piece by Jervan's mug. "Well, we have to be off, Jervan. It's been nice passing the time with you."

Jervan nodded, unseeing, lost in his own thoughts.

"This can't be right," Buck hissed as he and Dar slid out of the booth.

Dar shook his head. "We have to get to the others. I can't believe it's even a possibility, but it's too much to be a coincidence."

Dar stopped by the gaming table. "Mister Highwater," he said, tapping Connor on the shoulder.

"Eh? What? Don't bother me, boy," Connor snapped. "Can't you see I'm entertaining my new friends here?"

"Her ladyship calls," Dar said, using their prearranged code word.

"Damn and ashes!" Connor spat. He glared at the gaming table. "And I was on a good run, too. Filthy nobles keep you hopping at all hours."

He smiled up at the others at the table. "My apologies, friends. We will have to continue this another night. Dealer, cash me out."

The dealer handed Connor a small stack of gold and silver coins, which he pocketed. Standing with difficulty, he took up his walking stick and smacked Dar in the hip.

"Well, lead on, you big oaf. To her ladyship then."

Dar resisted the urge to wince. Despite his small stature, Connor was extremely strong.

"Of course, sir."

Outside, they hailed another carriage, clattering off into the night towards the inn. Dar had to admire Connor's restraint. He knew his friend was probably bursting with questions, but he played the part of the grumpy old man all the way into the Red Swallow, into Dar and Buck's room.

"What did you find out?" he asked in a normal voice as soon as the door closed.

"Shh." Dar checked the garderobe and balcony, then motioned to him. Buck lit some of the lamps and candles in the room.

Dar took out a piece of paper and wrote on it.

Hlerv is here. In Meridian. And he's involved.

Connor's eyes grew wide as he read the note.

"You're certain?"

Buck nodded.

Connor took the paper and slipped it inside one of the lamps, watching as it burned into ashes.

"We have to talk to the lord and lady, then," he said in his alter-ego's voice. "Go down to the stables, Horatio, and send a message to the Diamond

Star Casino. See that they are alerted so that we may consult with them."

Buck left.

The next half hour seemed to last forever as Connor and Dar sat in the room, anxiously awaiting the return of the other Riders.

Buck returned. "Ready."

Dar and Connor, still in character, slipped over to Andyn and Khyron's room, where they found the others gathered around the table, veiled in the misty light of Khyron's magic jamming device.

"Hlerv is here?" Andyn demanded. "Where? How long ago?"

Dar held up a hand. "Just let us tell you." Together, he and Buck related the news from Jervan the halfling. The others sat dumbfounded, speechless.

"I know it sounds incredible," Dar concluded, "but Buck and I think that Handor Lervion and Hlerv are one and the same. The description and time-table make perfect sense. If he really is the son of the Lervion House, he may have returned for some reason. Knowing Hlerv, he's probably found a way into the manor grounds, and I wouldn't be surprised if he was the one masterminding the break-in by the burglars."

"But the rumors say the thieves were all killed," said Andyn, brow furrowed with worry. "Do you think…?"

Dar shook his head. "Not if he had the Helm of Shadows. His fellow burglars, yes. Not Hlerv. He'd just teleport out to hatch another plot. I'm just not sure what."

Khyron let out a deep breath. "I wonder if this isn't all connected some-how. Maybe your friend found out about the wizards and Cerberus hounds and decided to do something about it, to try to strike out at evil influences."

Eric shrugged. "While he was with us, Hlerv wasn't that altruistic, but maybe he's changed, especially if his own sister is involved."

Connor smacked his hand on his thigh and stood. "We have to do some-thing now. If the Ja'al have taken over Lervion House and are masterminding the Skull Gate project from there, Hlerv may make another attempt soon and we have to get ahead of him. He has the Helm of Shadows and won't hesitate to use it, but if we strike first, we might be able to talk to his sister. She may at least make him stop and listen."

Andyn sat back in her seat, a forlorn expression on her face. She nodded slowly. "If he has been using the Helm, we have to get to him and quickly. It may already be too late. Zhinia Margoth's magic was ancient and powerful."

She looked up at them. Dar felt a wave of anxiety and frustration.

No! By God, no! I won't lose someone else to her! I won't let him down. I owe him that much.

He stood and put both hands on the table, looking at the Riders, his jaw set in a firm line. "I know we're tired from the trip, but we can't delay. Hlerv is in danger. We can't leave him."

Khyron nodded. "Then let's start planning now. I have an idea on how to make this work."

Chapter Nineteen – Night Hawks

Eric coasted through the night sky on Niveral, curving in a wide circle. He kept his eyes on Connor and Phantom drifting slowly next to Khyron on Zasural. Medianox floated next to him with Andyn in the saddle. Down below, he saw the lights of the Lervion manor complex through the thin clouds. Still Eric guided his pegasus with gentle knee pressure, waiting for Khyron to make the signal.

To execute the plan quickly and quietly, the stealthiest of their number led the attack.

Eric spared a glance at the sky. This was their best chance. The tiny white crescent of Kaliri, the farther moon, and the thin sliver of Diometrius cast only a pale, wan light. This was as close to near darkness as they were going to get for weeks. As it was, they had to wait impatiently for three days for a fortuitous combination of clouds and mild moonlight to give them as much stealth as possible.

He looked at Buck riding Shadowbane near him and shook out one hand to relieve the jitters.

Steady, he thought to himself, adjusting his helmet. *No nerves. Just get this done.*

Khyron's hand shot up. He and Connor turned their mounts and peeled off, heading down towards the manor house in a spiral, followed closely by Andyn. Eric followed, knowing that Buck and Dar soared in right behind.

Khyron and Connor banked and Eric saw his targets: six stocky figures with metal armor and weapons. Eric put forth his hand and called a stunning spell. He saw a matching flash of light from Andyn's outstretched hand. A ghostly-white explosion of faint light struck the rooftop in two places, briefly illuminating the six guards. They collapsed on the roof. Connor and Khyron landed and Andyn and Eric followed.

He alighted Niveral on the rooftop, the cloth-wrapped hooves of his pegasus making little sound. He slid out of the saddle, drawing Fidelis but not activating it. With a whispered word and motion, he sent his pegasus away to wing off into the dark, star-spangled sky.

A mild breeze blew over the rooftop as he raced to one of the nearest figures, a male dwarf in scale mail. He checked his pulse, then quickly drew out rope, tied him securely and gagged him with a cloth.

Dar and Buck finished with another pair of dwarves and soon the Grey Riders stood alone on the rooftop among the sleeping guards.

"Nice work," Connor whispered to Eric.

He nodded in response. "So far so good."

"Here," came Dar's whisper and they joined him at a large trap door in the floor. Dar and Buck made ready, arming themselves for close combat. Eric drew his sword and waited, hefting Fidelis in his other hand.

He peeked over the rooftop wall, looking down on the manor grounds. More guards patrolled in groups of three, their weapons and armor gleaming in the light of lanterns and magical orbs.

Khyron hissed to him and beckoned him over.

A pair of ladders led down into a well-lit room. Andyn repeated her silencing trick with a small piece of leather, dropping it into the room. The area lapsed into utter quiet.

Khyron nodded to Buck and Dar, holding his sword and dagger ready. The warriors swarmed down the ladders, followed closely by Khyron and Connor, then Andyn and Eric.

Eric dropped into the room, already filled with the sight of surprised dwarven guards shouting soundlessly as they attacked Buck, Khyron, Connor and Dar. A guard leaped at Eric, lashing out with a halberd. Eric sidestepped easily, activating Fidelis. The guard's eyes grew wide and he unleashed a wild, almost panicked swing. Eric parried, kicked the guard in the leg, and finished him with a thrust in the side. Fidelis flashed golden as it pierced chainmail and the flesh beneath.

He stepped back into a ready crouch, but all the guards lay dead. Khyron led the Riders to a table, spread out a map, then traced a path with his finger.

Now it gets tricky…

They reformed their group, with Connor and Khyron in the lead, carrying the swatch of leather with the silence spell. Dar and Buck followed and Andyn and Eric took up the rear, watching their back trail for ambush.

They slipped down a corridor, heading towards a staircase. After checking to make sure there were no guards, they descended. As Connor and Khyron reached a landing, Eric saw a flickering spark on the balustrade and cursed his inattentiveness. Sound returned as a mild blue light dissipated around them and Khyron looked at him with grim eyes.

"Damn it! Dispelling symbol in the balustrade," he whispered. "That kills the advantage of silence. You can be sure there are more if Ja'al wizards are involved."

He motioned to Buck, who stepped forward and flipped down the Eye of Truth. He nodded, pointing at hallway below them. "Two symbols," he said.

Buck and Andyn changed places and she disarmed the traps with a magic spell. They reached the end of the stairs and Buck hissed a warning. Andyn had to dispel another magic symbol near the roof.

Too slow, thought Eric, his nervousness increasing. They were already behind schedule with having to dispel the magical sentries. Every extra second meant someone could discover them and raise the alarm.

Khyron led them down another corridor and they flitted past a couple of doors. Looking in quickly, Eric saw only empty guardrooms.

Empty? Why? Where are the guards?

They approached a set of double doors and peeked inside. Khyron's face took on a grim look.

"Four more guards," Connor whispered. "It looks like a library."

"Nothing for it," breathed Khyron. He eased the door open and immediately slipped to the side, hiding behind a desk, then vanished behind some curtains. He peeked through the gap in the fabric as the other Riders entered. Connor flitted away and disappeared next to a bookcase.

The guards, all gnomes, stood talking next to a massive desk. As the other four Riders entered, they looked up. One of them, a black-haired, dark fellow with a mustache, scowled and stalked towards them.

"Here now!" he barked, drawing a mace and sword. "Who are you? No one is allowed here by orders of Beol Torander. Or didn't you and your Ja'al masters understand the first time?"

"We are here under authority of the Northern Alliance and the government of Gorostol," replied Eric. "We are investigating Ja'al activities in the area. Surrender now and you will not be harmed."

"Sound the alarm!" the gnome shouted, hurling himself at Eric, lashing out and dodging. The other gnomes scattered, one of them racing for another set of double doors. Connor darted after him.

Eric parried a mace blow and dodged a sword thrust, took a cut at the gnome's head and missed as the smaller man ducked and rolled out of the way. The gnome attacked again, moving with fluid grace and aiming a flurry of blows at Eric. He had to give ground and the gnome leaped towards the doors, jerking them open.

"Intru — "

Khyron appeared out of the shadows next to the gnome and ran him through with both blades. He dropped.

Eric turned to see two other guards dead but one held in a headlock by Dar.

"Where's your boss?" asked Buck, hefting Khelios.

"Go to the Nine Hells and screw your whore mother," the guard spat and Dar tightened his grip. The gnome choked and gagged, eyes bulging.

"I'll send you there first," Buck shot back, raising Khelios, but Andyn stopped him.

"There are easier ways," she said, replacing her mace. She took a deep breath, then concentrated and pointed a finger at the guard. A pink light flared from her fingertip. She tapped the guard in the forehead. He struggled in Dar's grip and he tried to look away, but eventually his eyes glazed over. Dar released him.

"Where is Beol Torander?"

"Down in the garden, meeting with the wizard, Lorferis," the guard said in a relaxed voice, as if discussing the results of a horse race.

"Where is Hannah Lervion?"

"In her room."

"Show me on the map."

Khyron held out the map and the guard lazily pointed at a chamber on the opposite wing of the manor.

"Is she guarded?" Andyn continued.

"Yes."

"What about guards along the way? Are there any?"

"Most are in the cellars or patrolling the grounds, looking for a hidden entrance."

"Hidden entrance?"

"The assassin got in through a hidden entrance."

"What assassin?" Andyn asked, shooting a glance at her friends.

"The gnome who almost killed Beol."

Andyn nodded to Buck. "Bind and gag him. We'll need him later. Put him behind the drapes."

"We have to fight our way across to the other wing?" asked Eric, frowning.

"It might not be as bad as we think," Khyron said, replacing his sword and dagger and drawing his short bow. "They're all out looking for this secret entrance. We should probably scout ahead and try to snipe any guards. The rest of you be ready to charge if we end up in trouble."

"This was not the plan," Eric said, placing Fidelis in its sheath and drawing his own bow. "We have to avoid contact."

"Plans change," Khyron said. "We have to adjust. Come on."

Gritting his teeth, Eric set an arrow to his bow and stole along down the hallway behind Khyron and Connor. They made it to the center of the Manor, emerging in an open hall with a double-wing staircase and balustrade that looked down on a grand entryway. A set of huge double doors with large panes of glass looked out onto the gardens. Two gnome guards on the ground floor scrambled from chairs as they entered, eyes widening in alarm. They scrambled for nearby crossbows. Connor levered two arrows into one of them and Khyron dropped the other.

They sure made a racket on the marble floor with their armor and weapons.

Eric watched for any other guards approaching but saw nothing.

Khyron motioned to the other Riders and they now moved with haste, certain that they would be detected any minute. They continued along the corridor on the second floor. A door beckoned at the end of the hallway. Connor eased it open. He looked back at Khyron and nodded. Khyron held up three fingers, then two, then one.

They surged through the portal. Two dwarven guards stood next to a door on the right side of the hall and aimed crossbows at them, letting fly.

Khyron, Connor and Eric loosed. A bolt struck Khyron in the side and he buckled, grimacing, as his brigandine flared white. The dwarves dropped, clutching arrows in their chests. Andyn knelt by Khyron, whispering a healing spell as Dar, Buck and Connor raced forwards, securing the area in front of the door, arrows pointed down the hall. Eric eased the bolt out of Khyron's side as Andyn's magic took effect.

Khyron's pale face warmed with color. Finally, he let out a deep breath, then nodded and smiled, patting Eric on the shoulder.

"I'm okay," he told Andyn, and they joined the others.

Eric looked at Buck. The tall warrior gazed at the portal with the Eye of Truth and shook his head.

Eric eased it open. Amid the dark interior, his vision picked up the glowing embers on a pair of candlesticks and the ghostly outline of a small figure near a bed.

"Hannah Lervion?" he whispered.

The figure leaped forward and a light flared over his head. In the pale yellow glow, he saw a brown-haired young halfling woman in a nightgown with a short sword and dagger ready to attack.

"Tell Beol I said he can go to the… Oh! You're not a guard."

Eric motioned to the other Riders as he took a slow step inside. "No, I'm not. My name is Eric Indidarc and I'm from the Northern Alliance."

To his surprise, her face broke out in a joyful, amazed smile. "Eric Indidarc ! You're one of the Grey Riders! Quick! Come in before the other guards see you!"

She waved a hand and the candles flared to brightness again.

"Come on," Eric said to the others and they entered, dragging the dead guards in and closing the door.

Hannah's eyes widened at the sight of all of them as she laid her weapons down on the bed.

"Are you all right?" Connor asked, sheathing Tiuz.

"Yes, I'm fine. You're Connor Lomin," Hannah said in a wondering voice. "You're Andyn Eleandir, Buck Bydecy, Dar Cabot and… I'm not sure who you are," she concluded with a sharp look at Khyron.

He bowed. "Major Khyron Demaris of the Imperial Army of Terenai, at your service."

"How do you know our names?" Andyn asked.

"Handor told me," she said, her green eyes bright with excitement. "He told me all about you."

"Handor!" Andyn exclaimed. "He's here? Where?"

Now Hannah's expression turned to one of worry. "I don't know. He tried to get me out of the complex but we didn't make it. I was injured and I don't know what happened to him. Beol said he's being kept in a secure place. Knowing Beol, I fear for Handor's safety."

"We have to find him," Connor said, meeting her gaze. "He has something very dangerous."

Hannah nodded. "I know. The Helm of the Lich. He's hidden it in a secret location."

"Let's go," said Buck. "If we can find him and the Helm, we can make it out of here."

Connor agreed, turning to Eric. "She should stay here where it's safe."

Hannah reached out and took him by the arm. "Please take me with you. I can get dressed quickly enough. I just need a minute."

He hesitated. Hannah shook her head, looking at him with pleading eyes. "Please. He's my only family. I can't wait here not knowing. Besides, I know how to find the Helm."

Eric watched the interplay between Hannah and Connor and tried to hide a smile. Hannah Lervion was one very pretty halfling girl, and it was clear from Connor's reaction that he was acutely aware of it.

"It will be better to keep us all together," Eric said, looking to Khyron as he returned Fidelis to dagger form.

Khyron pursed his mouth, sizing up Hannah. "Can you fight?"

"Meridian Officer's Academy, third year, First Regiment," she said with a proud toss of her head. "I've completed the squad infantry tactics course, won the intramural fencing competition, and have a rating of eight in seven

232

different weapons, plus unarmed combat."

A ghost of a smile curved Khyron's lips. "Good enough."

Andyn made the men turn around. True to her word, Hannah changed quickly. Eric had only counted to sixty-three when Hannah stepped next to him, attired in breeches, leather jerkin over a white long-sleeved blouse, and black boots, her brown hair tied up in a braid.

She nodded, buckling on a sword belt. "Ready."

Buck took a look at her, shot an amused glance at Dar, and shrugged. "She's his sister all right."

They kept Hannah in the center of their formation, but with her whispering directions, they moved down back staircases, avoiding guards, until she led them into the kitchens.

"Now where did I put it?" she mused, sheathing her weapons and striding around the area.

"Put what?" Connor asked, casting his eyes all around the kitchen. Well lit by lanterns and magical lamps, he saw only pots, pans, skillets, jars, glass cabinets with dishes and silverware, and closets for linens.

"Look for a blue mug with the symbol of a star on it."

"Like this?" asked Andyn, picking up a blue mug from a shelf. As she did so, a paper fluttered to the floor at her feet from the bottom of the mug.

"Ah!" Hannah pounced on the paper. She unfolded it, reading carefully.

"I need some cookies…" she said, tapping her chin.

Eric chuckled and Connor blinked in confusion. "Now?"

She touched his shoulder, a little smile on her face. "No, not me. It's what the paper says… Aha! This is where Handor and I used to hide cookies so we could filch them later."

Hannah led them to a pantry door and the two halflings walked inside, accompanied by Andyn. The other Riders waited in the kitchen proper since the pantry was only large enough for two or three. Hannah knelt on the floor and moved aside a large barrel, then pried up a loose floor tile. A dark, glittering object sat in the dirt under the floor in a square pit.

Andyn's gloved hands clamped onto Hannah and Connor immediately and she pulled them backwards.

"It is there," Andyn said, her face set hard as flint and eyes glittering. "That foul thing is there, in the pit. I can feel it. Hannah, replace everything as we found it."

Eric looked at her, then the other Riders. "Shouldn't we take it with us?"

She shook her head. "I know Margoth. No one should even so much as touch it. No one but us knows it's here. We'll return with others powerful enough to protect themselves."

"You're sure? We couldn't see it very clearly." Khyron asked Andyn, taking her hand gently. Even from here, Eric could see she trembled. He felt a little alarmed at Andyn's expression, so full of both revulsion and righteous anger.

Andyn nodded. "Trust me, Khy. I can feel Margoth's magic even now. It's in there."

Khyron smiled and put his arm around her. "It's okay, Andyn. We're here. We'll keep it hidden."

As if noticing him for the first time, her eyes darted to his face and she nodded, blinking and still looking shaken. "Yes, of course. Let's find the Ja'al and break up this horrid enterprise."

"Beol first," Hannah said.

Connor held up a hand. "Now, wait. I think we should get you out of here."

She shook her head and stood her ground. "No. If we delay, the dead guards will be found and he'll escape. And the Ja'al will also escape. We have this chance to catch him while he's not expecting it. We may not get another."

She led the way to a window. "See there? That's his outdoor meeting area, under the big gazebo. I can see Lorferis, two under-mages and some guards. We should strike now."

The Riders looked to Khyron, their professional tactician.

He gave them a grim smile. "Plans change. Let's take them."

"Wait," said Andyn. She put her hands on Hannah's shoulders and pronounced several short, firm syllables. Her hands glowed and golden light sparked over Hannah's body, then silver and blue.

"It's as good as banded mail," she said to Hlerv's sister with a smile. "It won't last too long, but it's all I have for now."

Hannah gave Andyn a grateful smile and directed them out of the kitchen through the laundry room, then out through a side door that opened not fifty feet from the well-lit gazebo. Eric made out the forms of three humans and five dwarves, one of the latter wearing a rich purple mantle and pointing at something on the top of a table.

Khyron nodded to Connor and they stole ahead, concealing themselves in bushes on opposite sides of the gazebo as the other Riders came forward more slowly.

The dwarf in the purple mantle lifted his head and started, spying Hannah Lervion striding forward with the Grey Riders.

"What is the meaning of this?" he snarled. A tall, elegantly attired human with a neat beard and mustache and staff of intertwining dark wood turned to look. An eyebrow arched as he regarded them.

"It's over," Hannah declared. "These are agents of the government and the Northern Alliance. Your plans are destroyed, Beol. Surrender now."

Eric drew Fidelis but again did not activate it.

Beol hooked his thumbs in his belt and laughed. "So says the little girl who likes to play soldier! What, you and four others? I'm actually insulted. I expected at least a platoon."

"I don't need a platoon," Hannah said, eyes narrowing. "I have the Grey Riders."

Beol's face contorted in a snarl. "Grey Riders, is it? Well, then, Lorferis, earn your pay."

The tall wizard at his side smiled. "For a chance to smear the Grey Riders all over the landscape? I'll do it for free."

He tapped the staff on the wood of the gazebo and a red light flared. Black, glittering tendrils the size of four-foot tree branches erupted from the ground around the Riders to grapple their legs. Eric felt pinned in place as the slithering tentacles wrapped around his legs and hips. Without even looking at Andyn, he started a counter-spell, knowing that she did the same, uniting her magic power with his. A blue light shot from their hands at the tendrils and they dissipated into a steaming mist.

Connor ignited Tiuz and leaped at Lorferis. The wizard turned and slapped at him with the staff. Khyron and Dar leaped to attack the other two wizards as the dwarven guards drew swords and charged.

Lorferis spat a word and firedarts hummed in from the top of his staff, lancing out at all of them. Three of them burst on Eric's armor and he rocked back from the force of the explosions. He gritted his teeth and called Fidelis.

The spear sprang to full size immediately, making the two guards before him stop their charge, eyes wide as they drew back.

Eric jabbed and swung, darting in and out. He blocked sword blades with the haft of the spear, using the butt to slam helmets. Fidelis rang like a bell with every hit. A guard managed to hit him in the leg but the chainmail sparked blue and held. Eric feinted to one side, then stabbed one of them through the heart. He withdrew Fidelis as the dwarf crumpled. The other guard uncorked a wild swing at Eric's head that he easily dodged.

Behind the dwarves, Eric saw Connor battling Lorferis, ducking, rolling and slashing. Khyron and Dar stood over the bodies of the fallen mages, their armor smoking. They leaped to the attack from the other side but Lorferis stepped out of the way, blocking their swings calmly and retaliating with a blow that exploded with magical force. Both men hurtled into the railing and shattered it with a crash, tumbling into the bushes. Connor lunged in, cutting the wizard in the arm and side, but had to dodge as the staff swung down again, sparkling with electricity and smashing a part of the railing with a loud boom.

Lorferis stumbled and cursed in pain, then slammed the butt of his staff on the wooden floor. A sheet of ice spread out on it. Eric's feet nearly slipped out from under him and the dwarven guard lurched, catching himself on the railing. Eric's opponent saw him struggling and leaped forward, sword raised. Eric let himself fall, turning Fidelis to impale the guard.

Eric gripped the railing and stood, jerking his spear out, the tip glowing bright as a bonfire. He tried to help Connor but slipped on the ice again.

Lorferis hissed another arcane syllable and the staff grew blood-red spikes at its tip. Connor parried, stabbed at Lorferis' eyes, then slipped on the ice and went down. Lorferis sneered and stepped in for a killing blow but suddenly flew to the side as a dark maelstrom of female halfling slammed into him, burying her blades to the hilt in his chest and back. He slammed into a support post, cracking it, then whacked her with his staff and Hannah flew to the side, sliding on the icy floor and hitting another railing with a thump.

Blood pooled at the wizard's feet and his eyes grew glassy. "Well-struck, little whore. You have more ability than I thought."

Connor slid to her side in an instant. He helped her rise, holding her up.

"This is MY house!" Hannah screamed at the wizard, pointing her sword at him. "Defiler of Gorostol!"

Lorferis raised his staff and a nimbus of fiery light grew over him.

Eric loosed Fidelis. The spear flew true and thumped into the wizard's chest. Without a sound, he keeled over and the staff exploded with a thunderous crack. The magical force threw Hannah into Connor's arms and they tumbled off the gazebo platform to land on the lawn. Eric flew backwards. He turned his fall into a roll, then popped up on one knee, calling for his spear.

Fidelis teleported back to his hand, vibrating with magical energy. The sound of a thousand bells in exquisite harmony rang in his head as he raised the weapon, sun-bright now.

The Grey Riders faced only Beol, who backed away from them, a wicked leer on his face. The guards and other wizards lay dead all around. Buck limped a little and Khyron leaned on Andyn, his face pale. Dar stalked forward. Blood dripped down one arm.

"It won't help you, you know," said Beol. His eyes looked wild and he actually cackled.

"It's over," said Andyn as the golden glow of healing light washed over Dar's injury.

"For you." Beol said in a soft voice. He reached into a pocket, unstoppered a vial, and swallowed the contents. "It is most certainly over for you."

The air temperature in the garden dropped forty degrees. Eric could see his breath fog in the frosty air. Beol's form became misty, insubstantial, ethereal, almost as if he were made of smoke. His mantle dropped down around him and he appeared like a dwarf-sized piece of the night sky, deepest black and glittering with a thousand red stars.

"Holy Verian!" Andyn said.

"What's going on?" Buck asked, lifting his shield.

"He's become a Shadow Specter!" she said, dragging Connor and Hannah next to her.

"What does that mean?" asked Khyron.

"It means death!" howled Beol in his spectral form, his voice echoing. "I am become Death to you all. Weapons cannot harm me, but I will suck the life out of you like a tap pulling ale out of a keg! You cannot stop me! There is nothing in this world that can stop me!"

"He can't be right," Connor croaked as he held forth blazing Tiuz.

Andyn grimly held up her holy symbol of Verian. "*Verian, Ald-adani!*" she cried. The symbol flared silver and Beol's form hissed and smoked in the light as he drew back with a cry of pain.

Beol screeched in anger and pointed a fist at her. A black ball with glittering red stars shot out. Buck stepped in front, shield up, but the ball passed through him as if he wasn't even there. It hit Andyn's symbol and exploded.

Cold as he had never thought possible slashed through Eric as he reeled against the remnants of the gazebo. He saw Andyn hurled backwards into a bush and Buck sagged, falling to his knees. Connor and Hannah collapsed onto the grass, which shattered into icy particles.

Khyron darted in, lashing out with his blades, but though they glittered with magical light, they passed through Beol's form as if he wasn't even there. Khyron's eyes widened and he stepped back.

Beol gave a triumphant laugh. "You see? Your feeble defenses are no match for the power of the Dark!" He took a backhanded swipe at Khyron but the soldier rolled backwards, holding his blades out in front of him. He licked his lips.

Enough...

"Dar?" Eric said, hefting Fidelis. Eric held the spear before him. Dar's sword, Rhindara, had changed from night black spangled with stars to a blade of pure light.

"Dark flees from the True Light!" Dar said, leaping forward with Eric at his side.

Beol screamed in rage and flew at them. Dar slashed and Eric stabbed, eliciting unearthly shrieks from Beol with every hit. The holy spear and celestial blade cut bright rents of light in Beol's form. He withdrew, then raved and gibbered in some unknown tongue. His injuries shrank.

The spectral dwarf flailed at them with ghostly fists. Eric tried to parry but Beol was too fast and one of his strikes hit him in the side.

He went down on one knee, feeling his left side go numb, unable to stand. Beol screamed in triumph and Eric weaved to the side, then brought up Fidelis and impaled him in his ghostly head. Beol let out a piercing shriek that made Eric's head ring and his eyes hurt. Dar lunged forward, swinging the white-hot blade of Rhindara, decapitating Beol. With a final echoing wail,

Beol disintegrated into a pile of black ash.

Eric felt Khyron lifting him up and leaned on him, still holding his bright spear. The intense cold started to dissipate.

They heard shouts and the sound of running feet. Connor and Hannah helped Andyn to stand and they readied weapons as dwarven and gnome guards came running. Hannah stood proudly at the front of their little group as the guards skidded to a halt in the gravel walkway, eyes wide.

"You have seen what has happened to Beol Torander," she announced in the bright light of Rhindara and Fidelis. "The same fate is before you. Surrender now and receive mercy."

The guards looked at each other. One of them, a dwarf with a scar from his hairline to his jaw, stepped forward.

He sized up the Riders with a practiced eye. "Or you could surrender to us. We outnumber you and you are injured."

"To what end, Captain Thonvar?" Hannah asked, her voice firm. "The Ja'al are dead, Beol is destroyed and this entire area will soon be swarming with constables and military. Which side do you want to be on?"

Eric shook his head, staring at Hannah. Easily the smallest person in the garden, she held their attention like a field marshal reviewing her troops and he saw Beol's guards exchange nervous glances.

Thonvar's face broke into a sardonic smile. "Then please forgive us, Miss Hannah, if we are not here to greet them. We take our leave of you."

He backed away from them, still smiling, eyes glittering, his war axe held across his chest. At the limit of the light from Fidelis and Rhindara, he spun on his heel and led the remnants of the guards away, into the night.

Chapter Twenty – Wildflowers on the Hillside

Connor watched Beol's guards leave.

Hannah stood at his side, eyes hard. "I know their names. We'll find them. I guarantee it."

Connor put a hand on her shoulder. "We should get ourselves together."

She smiled at him, green eyes grateful. "I guess we're a little torn up."

He limped with her to the lawn. Andyn worked on Eric, prone on the grass, as Dar applied healing to Buck and Khyron. Buck leaned back into one of the remaining parts of the gazebo and closed his eyes as Dar laid a hand on his chest. He looked pale. A warm glow spread from Dar's palm, covering Buck from waist to forehead. After a few heartbeats, Buck opened his eyes, his skin regaining its color. He nodded to Dar and sat up straighter. Dar moved to work on Khyron's arm and hand.

"Is Dar a cleric too?" Hannah wondered.

"No, he's actually a scout," Connor said. "They learn some healing magic with practice — it comes from having to survive in the wild on their own. Eric can heal too. Speaking of which…"

The pair watched Andyn lay her hands on Eric's side and leg. The sheen of frost melted away under the pale blue light of her healing magic. Soon, she helped him stand up and put her arm around him, speaking to him as he nodded and shook out his leg. With a quick hug for her, he strode over to Connor and Hannah.

Eric gave them a tired smile as he sat down next to them. "Now that I can feel my left side again, I can help you." He placed hands on Connor's side and head.

Connor relaxed on the grass, feeling warm magic surge through his injuries. He then watched as Eric gently tended to Hannah.

Finally, Eric hung his head and blinked a few times. "It's still a strain, though I'm getting better at this," he said with a grin, running a hand through his short blond hair.

Hannah smiled at him and gave his hand a squeeze. "Thank you, Eric. I feel much better. But we should get going. Handor is held somewhere around here and we have to find him."

"Fair enough," said Eric.

Connor stood, offering his hand to Hannah. While he didn't feel like taking on any more opponents, at least he didn't feel like he was at Death's door.

"Where do we start?" Andyn asked as they regrouped.

"Well, first of all," said Khyron, "One of us needs to alert the authorities. Since Handor is familiar to all of you, I volunteer. I'll catch up with you when I return."

He took up his bow, selected an arrow with a red metal head, and fired it straight up. It disappeared into the blackness, then detonated with a pop and a flash of flickering red lights.

Zasural arrived soon after and Khyron swung into the saddle. "I'll be back in a little while. I have contacts at the constabulary and the Federal Service." He urged Zasural to a canter, then the pegasus lifted off and soared into the night sky.

"The cellars first," Hannah said firmly. "From what I've learned, there are a lot more storage spaces and it wouldn't be above Beol to shove him into a closet."

She led the way and they soon entered a large, open space underneath the manor. The area had all the signs of hasty departure, with books, scattered papers and open crates on the floor.

Connor looked into a crate and his stomach tightened, seeing the many bleached bones therein. "It looks like Khyron's suspicions were correct," he called to the others, reaching into the crate, looking for a list of contents. "This is an assembly area."

"For what?" asked Hannah with raised eyebrows.

"Er, classified. Sorry," Connor said with an apologetic shrug. "Just know that your Ja'al 'guests' were up to no good."

"That's an understatement," replied Hannah, hands on her hips. "Come on. There are a few closets over here."

She led the Riders all over the underground work room at a brisk pace, helping them break locks on closets and rooms, but Handor was nowhere to be found. They did find books and scrolls which Dar and Andyn packed away into their backpacks for further study.

"Where next?" asked Connor.

She made a face. "I don't think they'd put him into his old room, but it's worth a look. There's always the library and my parents' bedchamber. Beol took it for himself when he moved in."

Eric shook his head. "We've already been in the library. Is there a secret closet or something?"

"Yes, behind the bookcases," she said, biting her lip. "It was a storage area with a safe for sensitive records." Hannah tapped her fingers rapidly on a tabletop, frowning.

Connor sensed her unease and smiled at her. "Don't fret. It will be all right. Show us the way to his room."

"I just want to find him and get away from this place for a while," she said, her frown remaining. "I know we'll have to come back and take charge at some point, but I just want some space, for both of us."

Her eyes darted around the cellar, looking distant and worried. "Come on. Let's hurry this up. He's got to be around here somewhere."

She set a brisk pace and the Riders followed her upstairs to a room down the hall from her bedchamber. It was not locked, but their quick search came up empty. They even tapped on walls and floors, Hannah calling her brother's name.

"What have they done with him?" Hannah cried, looking more agitated. "Think, Hannah! Where else would Beol try to hide him? The outer buildings?"

Connor sensed her worry starting to turn to panic and put a hand on her shoulder. "Maybe we can do this faster if we split up. We can cover multiple areas at the same time."

"That's a good idea," Eric suggested, shooting a look at Connor. "We'll go to your parents' old room while you open the records area in the library."

Hannah nodded in a distracted fashion but led them to the other wing of the manor. She told them how to find her parents' room. Andyn, Dar and Eric went on while Connor and Buck helped her search the library.

"Handor!" she called after their investigation showed nothing. "Where are you?"

They heard only silence.

"Where is he?" she whispered, her frightened voice wavering. She clenched her fists. "Could they have moved him to some location in town?"

Andyn appeared in the doorway and Connor started in shock. She looked devastated, face pale and haunted. Unshed tears shone in her eyes.

"Hannah," she started, then stopped. She cleared her throat. "Hannah…"

"What is it? Is it Handor?" Hannah interrupted, striding over to her. "Where is he? Has something happened to him?"

Without waiting for an answer, she darted towards the doorway.

"No, Hannah!" Andyn protested, trying to stop her. "Don't go in there before I can tell you—"

"Handor?" Hannah called in panic as she burst past Andyn. "Where are you?"

"Hannah, wait!" called Andyn, chasing after her.

Connor followed on her heels as she turned the corner into her parents' room. The first thing he saw was Dar and Eric, their faces pale, staring in shock, dismay and horror at something on the top of a dresser.

"What?" Connor said, then froze, his heart stopping when he saw what they saw. His stomach clenched and it was all he could do to keep from retching.

"Nooooo!" Hannah screamed in agony. It sounded like something had ripped the very soul out of her. She dropped to her knees and clenched her fists in front of her face, eyes staring at the object on the dresser.

A glass case sat on top of the dresser: a glass case that held a head, the decapitated head of Handor Lervion. Eyes closed in death, he looked almost as if he were sleeping. A mage-fire light glowed in mid-air above the dresser.

To one side of the case, a card held the words "Beol Torander is my master now."

The pink glow of the mage-fire made the whole scene appear to be some horrid painting.

It can't be, Connor thought. *It's just a wax model or something. Maybe it's a carving, like the artwork we've seen in Ja'al temples. That can't be Hlerv.*

"Nooooo!" Hannah wailed even louder. Connor had never heard anyone give voice to such a scream of anguish and despair. "Handor! No, no, no, no, no, no!"

Connor slid to her side in an instant and threw his arms around her. She continued screaming, then began to tremble with each shriek.

"Andyn!" he shouted, only to find her right next to them.

"I'm here," Andyn wept. "Verian's mercy, Hannah! I'm here! Oh sweetheart! We're here."

Hannah began to sob violently, collapsing towards the thick rug. Connor clutched her to his chest, tears streaming down his face as he shook his head, unable to speak.

Andyn bent down low to her, speaking quiet words, her hands glowing white.

Connor heard someone speaking behind him, uttering the longest string of vile, vulgar and profane curses he had ever heard, ending with Beol Torander's name at the end.

He looked up. Buck Bydecy stood next to him, hands hanging slack at his sides, a mixture of rage and abject sadness on his face. Slowly he repeated every profanity and curse.

"Connor!" Andyn called. "Help me with her! She's going into shock! Dar, Eric, I need your help."

Connor lifted Hannah into his lap. She was completely limp now. He put a hand to her forehead. It was cold to the touch. He felt for a pulse and his alarm grew as he found it erratic and weak.

Andyn, Eric and Dar bent to their work, magical light glowing from their joined hands. Andyn reached out and placed one hand on Hannah's forehead. A soft golden glow covered the halfling girl's entire body. Connor bent his head next to hers.

"Hannah," he whispered, "We're here. Your brother is at peace now. No one can hurt him any more. Live for him. Please, Hannah, come back."

He felt her stir and her skin warmed under the effect of the healing spells. Finally, her eyes fluttered open and she looked up into his eyes.

"Connor?" she asked.

"I'm here."

"Handor… oh Handor…" The tears came again and she pulled him close, weeping into his shoulder.

Connor held her in his arms as Andyn continued her ministrations and Dar and Eric sat back on their heels, panting with exhaustion.

The sound of other boots tramping in the hallway made him look up. Khyron loomed in the open doorway, a quartet of dwarven city guards at his heels.

"Hey!" said Khyron with a smile. "I found you. Wait. What?"

His smile faded at their expressions. One of the guards uttered a harsh phrase in Dwarven.

"Oh no," Khyron said, his smile fading to disbelief. "Oh no. That's not — " He stopped, seeing Connor's expression.

"Oh Mindra's Heart," he said with a deep sigh. "I…I'm so sorry."

Connor turned away to stare at nothing out the nearby window.

"I'm so sorry," Khyron repeated. He stood next to Buck, looking helpless.

In the background, Connor dimly heard the sounds of other officers entering the house, shouting to each other, giving orders. It seemed like a faint wind. He heard only Hannah's voice, crying for a brother she would never see again.

***

"I'm not leaving her," Connor said, eyes locked on the figure of Hannah Lervion lying under the covers in her bed. The pale afternoon light streamed in through the windows. He felt only cold.

"Connor," Andyn said gently, taking a seat across from him. "You can't do any more. The doctors have sedated her and she'll sleep for quite a while. You need to get some rest too."

He shook his head wearily. "I can't, Andyn, not now. I know what this pain feels like. So do you."

She gave him a sad smile, bending her head down to meet his eyes. "Yes, but harming your health isn't going to bring him back, nor ease her pain. She will need us fully recovered and strong when she awakens. Especially you."

He stared past her to the sleeping girl in the bed. "I can't sleep. I see him when I close my eyes."

He still couldn't believe Hlerv was dead. Actually, he figured he should probably call him Handor, now that they knew his true identity. He always felt that the sly, cunning, capable Handor, would defeat just about anyone with his determination and resourcefulness. Now he was dead. All their plans to rescue him from Beol, from the Ja'al, from his own weakness concerning the Helm of Shadows—everything evaporated in the cold light of late winter.

Andyn sighed. "So do I. But I see him as I did at Shadow Lake, on Twinspire Peak, when I received the Crown of Saint Alyssa. That's the Hlerv I see, and will always see, not what we discovered last night. That's the man who walks among the holy trees in Verian's Kingdom now."

Connor felt only an emptiness. "I can't shake the feeling that we were so close and blew our chance to save him."

"I'll shake it for you," said Khyron as he entered the room.

"What?" snapped Connor. "What do you mean?" He tried and failed to keep the irritation and shortness out of his voice.

Khyron gave him a look of sympathy. "I just finished interrogating one of the prisoners we captured. One of the guards on the roof."

He pulled an easy chair next to the bed and sat.

Connor and Andyn looked at him. He pressed his fingertips together.

"Hannah and Handor tried to escape four days ago," he said. "That was the genesis of the story about the burglary attempt. Apparently, a magical trap knocked Hannah senseless and Handor deposited her outside the servants' gate, then tried to draw Beol's forces away. He succeeded admirably. By all accounts, he killed seven guards, two Ja'al wizards, and four Cerberus hounds as Beol emptied his barracks trying to bring him down. He held them off until he was wounded multiple times. Finally, one of the remaining wizards hit him with a Lightning Spear spell and he died. Beol flew into a rage, had him decapitated, put his head in the glass case, and threw his body to the remaining hounds, of which there are only two. We found some bones in the holding pit."

Connor sighed, feeling his sorrow and dejection escape him like a dry, hot wind. "So what you're saying is that we were too late no matter what."

"Yes," Khyron said, nodding. "We would have had to attack immediately upon entering Meridian to have a chance of rescuing him and Hannah, and we didn't even know they were here until the night after their escape attempt. We had no chance, Connor, not a one."

"And Hannah?" asked Andyn.

"Well," Khyron continued, "Beol's forces scoured the grounds and found her outside the gate just as she revived. They tried to take her but she fought like a tigress, killing another three guards before she was laid out by repeated blows and spells. Beol insisted that she be kept alive and hired a crony doctor to nurse her back to health, all the while spreading a tale of burglars attempting to infiltrate the complex. Apparently, Beol was on his way to using her as a figurehead for the company, at least until he could figure out what to do about Handor. He told her that her brother was in a secure location, which wasn't technically a lie; he just didn't tell her he wasn't alive any more."

"Poor Hannah," said Andyn, looking at the sleeping girl. "They tried so hard to escape and it came to this."

Khyron smiled gently and took her hand and Connor's, giving them a squeeze. "Handor Lervion was a blessed man, indeed, to have friends who loved him so much as to mourn his passing like this. I am truly sorry not to have met him."

He stood. "Andyn is right, though, Connor. Hannah appears to have latched onto you. She will need you to be strong for her in the coming days as we piece everything together. You won't do her any good by being so fatigued and weak that you can't help her."

He's right. She's right. They're both right. I just can't get rid of the feeling that we failed him.

"Agreed," he said finally. "But I'll sleep here, on that couch, in case she wakes up."

He stood, kissed Andyn, exchanged a handclasp with Khyron, and wandered over to the couch. He arranged pillows and a blanket as he heard them leave together.

"He hasn't slept," Andyn said, her voice fading as she and Khyron departed. "And he's not eating either. For a halfling, that worries me. We might have to have the doctor have a look at him…" The door closed.

Connor pulled the couch close to Hannah's bed so that he could face her, then climbed in, pulled the covers up and kept his eyes on her.

To his great surprise, he fell asleep and dreamed of Janey and Rose, his dead wife and daughter. They greeted a smiling Handor Lervion in the sunshine on a green field, surrounded by butterflies and wildflowers.

***

Connor awoke to the sound of someone calling his name. He opened his eyes to find it was the next morning, he was ravenous, and a dwarven doctor stood by Hannah's bedside, smiling at him.

"Mister Lomin," the doctor said. "Good to see you up."

The doctor looked down at Hannah. "There, you see? Connor is awake now."

Hannah turned her head slowly to him and gazed at him with sad green eyes. He rolled off the couch and rubbed his face, taking her hand as he stood next to the bed.

"How long have you been there?" she asked in a drowsy voice.

"A while."

"Pish-posh," the doctor clucked, closing his medical kit bag and slinging it over his shoulder. "I understand Mister Lomin hasn't left your side since we brought you here. You have a good protector, Miss Lervion."

Connor looked at him. "Will she be all right?"

The doctor nodded, smiling at Hannah and moving her hair off her forehead. "Yes. She is nearly mended, physically. With the help of her friends, she will mend in spirit as well."

He left them. Connor stayed where he was.

Hannah squeezed his hand. "I can't begin to thank you, all of you. Here you are, the famous Grey Riders, and yet you take such good care of someone you only just met."

He patted her hand awkwardly. "It's the least we could do. We couldn't stand by and do nothing during such sorrow. Handor was a Grey Rider too. We don't desert our own."

She stared into his eyes for a while. "You and Handor must have been close."

He gave a half-shrug. "As close as any. Your brother didn't divulge much of himself or his real life, but we were good comrades, and I believe good friends too. He had a wry sense of humor, saved our lives more than once, never complained, and helped as best he could. We wouldn't have succeeded without him."

"But he left you."

"Yes."

"To find me. With that vile helmet."

"Yes. We didn't know about you or that part of his life and I guess he took the opportunity when he saw it. I can't help feeling that we failed him."

She squeezed his hand again. "You didn't fail him. He made some bad choices and should have trusted you. Just before we tried to escape, he rejected the Helm of Shadows and regretted his mistakes. He was going to go seek your forgiveness and ask for your help. The Helm changed him and he saw that it was taking his life, changing him to a creature of evil, so he renounced it."

Connor smiled at her. "And he had someone to live for, I think."

She smiled back, sadly, a tear running down her cheek. "And now he's gone."

"For what it's worth, I know what it feels like."

Hannah regarded him, eyes intent. "You have had a severe loss, too, then."

He nodded. "But I'm not here to talk about me."

"No, I want to hear it."

He almost refused, but then thought again. Maybe his own story would help her know that there was recovery and healing.

"All right then." He perched on the edge of the bed and told her about his courtship with Janey, their marriage, the birth of his daughter Rose, then the onslaught of the Whispering Death — the vile disease that ravaged Evendale and northern Terenai, resulting in the deaths of so many, including his little family. He told of the Grey Riders' suspicion that Zhinia Margoth, the lich princess, had released the plague in order to clear the area so her agents could find a magical toy that was the key to the prophecy of the Song of the Grey Riders. He related how they had found the toy in the keeping of his niece and nephew and used it to find the location of the holy Crown of Saint Alyssa, then how the Crown helped Andyn destroy Margoth and fulfill the prophecy.

She lay there silently, listening. When he finished, she didn't speak for a long time.

"Do you miss them?" she asked, her voice breaking.

He swallowed the lump in his throat. "Every day. But the pain is less with every season. I know they are at peace."

Tears leaked out of the corners of her eyes and he wiped them away with an edge of the blanket.

"I'm sorry. Your loss is worse than mine," she said miserably.

"It is not. We both lost our families."

"I can't imagine what it's like to be married, have children, then lose my love and child all at once."

He smoothed her hair from her forehead. "The pain of loss is still pain, Hannah."

She remained quiet, turning her head to look out the window. Her eyelids drooped. He released her hand but she took his again.

"Connor," she murmured. "If you want to eat something, ring the little bell and a servant will come. Just don't leave me."

His heart turned over and he felt a sudden war break out within him— fear of connection and intimacy with another woman against an intense desire to protect and help Hannah Lervion.

"I won't," he said. She closed her eyes.

He gently rang the bell and she sighed, falling asleep instantly.

***

Agents of the Alliance arrived two days later to whisk away the Helm of Shadows in Handor's magic bag. The Grey Riders held meetings with analysts to decipher the papers left behind. The Meridian City Guard managed to capture of many of Beol's underlings, including Thonvar, and Hannah recovered enough to take over management of her new commercial empire.

They held a memorial service for Handor a week after Hannah's rescue. Connor stood at her side in the sunshine on a hilltop overlooking the Kaljirre, next to the graves of her parents. The other Riders gathered nearby, but aside from them, an Irial priest intoning blessings over the casket of Handor, and the priest's two attendants, only the wind accompanied them. Hannah and the Riders wore Irial mourning garb of deep grey with a single yellow band from shoulder to hip. It symbolized both the sorrow of loss and the bright hope of the afterlife for faithful servants of good.

The sunlight cast a bright shimmering patch on the water below them and birds soared above. Clouds ambled across the blue sky.

"All paths lead to the Master of All," said the priest, a grey-haired halfling in a brown and tan mantle. "Those who follow light and truth and struggle against the Dark have a ready ally in the Worldmaker, and he brings home all who serve him."

For some reason, Connor's eyes locked onto the small square plate on the front of the priest's copper headband. The plate depicted one of the symbols of Irial, a wheat sheaf.

His thoughts strayed to his mother, high priestess of Irial in her own right, back in their family home. She had the same headband, except it was gold and held the other symbol of Irial: a spinning wheel.

How far afield have I come, Mother?

His eyes flitted to the wildflowers growing on the lawn. In Evendale or Deran, still under the white blanket of winter, no flowers would grow for months at least, but here in warmer climes, they made a splash of color.

"Now we bow our heads and give a final farewell to our brother, Handor Samar Lervion, a valiant warrior against evil," the priest finished, closing his book and looking up to the sky. "May the Worldmaker welcome him into the Blessed Lands and reward him for his courage and steadfast love of family."

Connor bowed his head with the others. Hannah's hand found his own. He held it firmly, trying to transfer some of his strength to her.

"Praise the One! Praise Irial! Praise the Maker!" the priest concluded.

"Praise the One," Hannah said at his side.

The priest approached. "Again, my sincerest condolences on the loss of your brother, Miss Hannah."

She looked up at him with dead eyes and tried to smile. "Thank you, Master Hollins. I appreciate all that you and the temple community have done for me. You are most kind."

He embraced her. "We are here for you. All you have to do is ask. I will be by to visit in a couple of days, if that is all right with you."

She nodded and he stepped to the side. Hannah walked forward, hand still clasping Connor's. She laid a bundle of flowers and herbs on the casket. Connor recognized lavender and forget-me-not's and a single yellow rose.

Hannah kissed her brother's coffin and nodded to the attendants, who slowly lowered it into the ground.

Goodbye, Hlerv. I hope you have peace at last, Connor thought.

The Riders gathered around.

"Farewell, Lone Brave Rider of Grey," murmured Buck.

Hannah's composure finally broke and she put a hand to her eyes and broke into tears as the attendants gently covered the casket with earth. Connor pulled her close again and she clung to him, crying.

Why is she drawn to me? I don't need this. I can't do this again. I don't have much of a heart left after Janey and Rose.

Andyn enveloped both halflings in a hug. "Sorrow fades, pain recedes, and regrets vanish, giving way to fond memory," she said, "I know this and Connor knows this. It will be so for you, Hannah."

Hannah nodded into his chest and Connor blinked away tears.

The taller Riders all knelt around Hannah and she nodded again. "I am so blessed to have such friends as you," she managed, wiping her eyes with a handkerchief, "I have no words to express what this means to me."

"Think nothing of it," replied Buck with his homespun smile. "Once a Rider, always a Rider. You are family now."

She laid a hand on his face, then kissed him on the forehead, lips and cheeks. "Thank you then, brother Buckminster."

He blinked, wiped his eyes and ducked his head. Hannah looked at each of the Riders in turn. "You are welcome to stay as long as you can."

Connor looked at her beautiful, sad face and felt a pang of regret. "Unfortunately, Hannah, it cannot be for long. We have to get back up North to meet with agents of the Alliance related to the objects we found in your home."

She nodded, looking resigned. "I understand. Any time I can have with you is a gift. And if you are going north, I need you to speak to someone concerning a packet that we sent there."

"Of course," said Eric. "What is the packet? Whom do you want us to contact?"

"Handor and I collected evidence of Beol's dealings with the Cla'Agik and the Ja'al but he watched our every move, so we sent it to a friend of our uncle Reginald, up in Deran, near Oakmoor. She is a druidess named Carine."

"What?" exclaimed Buck.

The Riders exchanged shocked looks and Hannah's eyes flickered back and forth from one of them to another. "Is something wrong?"

"How do you know the Druidess?" Buck asked.

"Well, my uncle Reggie has worked with the druids in that part of the world for a long time," she began, "He supplies them with certain herbs they need for medicines and potions that they use to treat injured animals. He's a veterinary apothecary. When Handor and I figured that Beol would intercept anything we sent in the mail, we decided to put the packet into a shipment going to Druidess Carine in Oakmoor. Beol didn't know the connection so he didn't even bother to check. We left instructions with her that if anything happened to us, she was to go to the authorities, then we told Beol that we had evidence against him. He didn't like that one bit, but it stopped him from doing anything to us. How do you know Carine?"

"She is a mentor to Buck," Andyn said, shooting a glance at him.

"Why not just try to smuggle the information to the authorities here in Meridian?" asked Connor.

She shook her head. "Beol had paid off some magistrates and constables, but we didn't know which ones. We felt it was safest to send the evidence away to a secret ally instead, then try to get it to the right people in Gorostol after we had time to figure out whom to trust. As it was, we never really did get much of a chance, because Handor fled when Beol tried to frame him for Mother's death, and then he held me prisoner and used me to run the company."

"So that's why you didn't try to escape on your own," Dar said.

She shrugged, looking frustrated. "Beol's network was everywhere. I didn't know who was on his payroll. I had no one to escape to, and without some serious supplies and assistance, I couldn't have done it on my own. Handor's arrival was the catalyst that threw all Beol's plans into disarray."

"The one thing he didn't count on," Eric mused.

They stood in silence for a while, then Connor turned to Hannah. "We would like to escort you home."

"Please," she said, with a genuine smile this time.

They accompanied Hannah to her curricle. Mounting up on their pegasi in full view of curious onlookers outside the graveyard they rode alongside all the way back to the manor. Pedestrians stopped and stared at the sight of the winged steeds in grey caparisons with golden gilt script at the edges. When they recognized Hannah in the curricle, they nodded their heads in respect.

Then, with new servants and the fortune of the shipping line at her disposal, Hannah made sure they had every comfort she could think of. For the next few days, Connor found himself relaxing. He tried to give Hannah plenty of space, but Andyn took him aside on the first day and told him that he needed to be available.

"She feels a kinship with you, Connor," she told him. "You're both halflings and are united by family loss. Help her out."

In his company, Hannah seemed to recover some of her spirit. By the time they had to leave a week later, she told them that her two cousins, Marigold and Lana, were on their way from Deran to help her and would arrive within a few days. Though Connor could see that she did not want to be left alone, she told him she realized that he had to depart and that she understood.

He found everything about her to be immensely attractive.

He wrestled with his feelings, fighting an attachment growing between them. He remembered the pain of losing his wife and daughter, but Hannah's beauty, vulnerability, purity of spirit and friendly demeanor broke apart every wall before he could even build it up. They spent much time together and he grew to appreciate her sense of honor, kindness, and honesty. She promised to write to him, care of Melinor Indidarc, and asked him to write back. She even took charge of Shriek, Handor's sword, and his other effects, vowing to renew her training as a warrior.

Three weeks after arriving in Meridian, they departed. Connor lifted off on Phantom and waved to her tiny figure, receding into the distance at her manor gates, surrounded by her servants and guards.

He felt a that piece of his heart remained behind.

Why? Why now? I can't let this happen again.

The Grey Riders winged off towards Deran, away from the Kaljirre and

Meridian and all its sorrows and intrigues. The wind whipped around him and the sun split the clouds as always. Connor Lomin tried to put her out of his mind, but his thoughts kept straying to a pair of bright green eyes framed by nut-brown hair.

And he knew he was lost.

Chapter Twenty-One – Spider Web

"Well?" Brandawyn Alenar asked.

Daphne slipped through the undergrowth towards them. She kept a hand to her bow, watching the meadow and the encircling woods. Daphne stepped next to Stephen and shot a look at her brother.

"Your suspicions were right."

Brandi let out a breath, looking at Megan, who raised an eyebrow.

"How many?" asked Stephen.

"At least eight that I could count," Daphne said. "Hidden in the under-brush, camouflaged with cloaks colored like the forest, holding crossbows and watching the cottage. This was a trap."

Brandi bit her lip. Their latest source had told them that someone with a lead on another royal family lived in the hut. Supposedly an old woman used to be a nursemaid to a family of scholars by the name of Goldar and lived here in southern Gorostol. According to Stephen's information, that meant some of the descendants of the kingdom of Golad, far to the south of Merdail, could be alive.

However, Stephen felt they found out this information with more ease than he expected. This made him suspicious and they decided to lie in wait near the location and send Daphne in to scout.

"What now?" asked Megan.

Her aunt shrugged. "We steer clear of this place, go back to Starpoint, and make our plans to return to Meridian. We will talk to our contacts and decide our next move."

Daphne took the medallion of Paractus out from under her armor and brought the magical construct to its full size. The giant owl blinked its golden eyes at Brandi.

Brandi wondered if it recognized her.

Silly. It's a construct, not a creature.

Daphne and Stephen climbed into the saddle.

"Northwest, I think," said Stephen. Daphne nodded and turned Paractus in that direction.

Brandi and Megan mounted Larinor and Amicus as the owl hopped into the meadow, then took wing. All four Alenars soared up into the air. Puffy clouds sailed serenely through the vast blue expanse and Brandi began her quadrant search, remembering her failure with the dragons.

The owl flew up and up, heading towards the blue glittering sea to the west. At a high enough altitude, Brandi saw the outlines of the Gorostoli city of Starpoint, a grey blotch near a natural harbor. She cast her gaze up, down and all around.

I wonder if we'll go back to Deran.

The thought of maybe tracking down Eric and the other Riders up north filled her with a thrill of hope.

Please God.

Her eyes narrowed as she spied something against the clouds to the north. It looked like a shimmer in the air where none should be.

Brandi pointed a hand in that direction, then cast a spell of discernment.

Her heart skipped a beat. She saw the outlines of winged creatures, hidden behind a wall of air. She counted six, not a half mile away and approaching fast.

Brandi cast a light spell in front of Paractus. Stephen looked up at her and she pointed in the direction of the creatures.

He turned in the saddle and put forth his hands. A faint blue star of light shot out and hit the air wall. With a shimmering sparkle, the windy barrier dissipated, revealing six creatures.

They had the forequarters of eagles and the hindquarters of horses, great tan wings spread out as they flew on the rising wind. Larger than a pegasus, they each held two riders, one in black chainmail and the other in dark robes.

Studded leather barding covered the mounts. The creatures screeched as their pilots urged them on.

Hippogriffs...

Daphne turned Paractus away and down. Brandi followed, reaching for her bow.

The magical construct could keep its distance from the hippogriffs and the pegasi could easily outrun them, but the presence of the hippogriffs prickled a chill of fear down her spine. Someone knew to fight airborne agents with airborne troops and that meant that Berek and Adina were involved.

A couple of firedarts hummed past harmlessly and Brandi shot a look over her shoulder. At that range, their pursuers weren't likely to hit anything and she would reach the cover of the forest before them. Then, the Alenars held the advantage, as hippogriffs did not do well in the woods while pegasi could be ridden like normal horses.

Brandi kept pace with Paractus. Just by chance, she happened to look down and gasped.

On a nearby knoll, a trio of warriors turned a ballista in their direction. Brandi waved frantically to Daphne, who quickly pulled the owl into a loop.

The ballista let fly, but they were already turning away.

Missed, Brandi thought with elation.

The ballista bolt glittered, then broke apart into a veritable hailstorm of normal-sized crossbow bolts.

Damn it!

She hauled on the reins and Amicus whinnied in protest. Two bolts hit the pegasus in the shoulder, but only one got through his leather barding. Brandi rolled her mount and wheeled back towards her relatives.

With dismay, she saw that the majority of the bolts had hit Paractus. Several rents in its feathered body leaked out a dark blue gas and it slowed noticeably. Stephen pointed downwards and Daphne turned the giant owl down towards the sheltering forest and hills. Brandi made note of their path, spying a clump of grey rocks that she could recognize.

Then, Brandi saw another ballista on a nearby hillock. It fired, but the bolt didn't come anywhere near Paractus, breaking into a cloud of smaller bolts that fell harmlessly into the verdant trees below.

Brandi looked back at the pursuing hippogriffs, then caught Megan's eye.

Her sister nodded and they both turned to charge at the enemy.

It looked like Larinor had escaped unscathed. Megan stood in her stirrups and unleashed a lightning spear at the lead hippogriff. A pink globe of color flickered around the enemy when the lightning hit, dissipating it into a cloud of sparks.

Brandi drew back her bow and let fly, then fired another. Both arrows missed as the hippogriff dodged, but it turned towards one of its fellows and they had to momentarily veer off course. Megan continued without stopping, firing off a sheet of flame that enveloped the protective sphere on the hippogriffs. With a flash of pink light, the globe disappeared. Megan rolled Larinor and dove.

Brandi went in the other direction, loosing two more arrows. One glanced off barding. The other thumped into the shoulder of the robed figure, who cried out as his spell went awry, lancing a green beam of light into the empty sky. The hippogriff turned towards her, but Brandi looped still higher, then curved Amicus into a dive of her own.

The two sisters raced among the enemy formation like darting hawks against eagles, scoring hits with spells and arrows, dodging acid globs, ice grenades and beams of searing light. Larinor got scorched by an energy beam and Brandi took an arrow in the upper arm that she pulled out and hurled away with a muttered curse. One of the enemy mages used a wind wall to try to slow Brandi down and she barely managed to avoid it at the last second.

Her heart pounded in her chest. If she had hit the wall at full speed...

The enemy force's larger mounts, though better armored and able to withstand more punishment, couldn't match the pegasi for speed and maneuverability. Eventually, Megan caught two of them in a fireball. One reeled and fluttered towards the ground, barding and riders aflame and followed by a black trail of smoke. Brandi got a lucky break when a hippogriff came too near and she slashed through the barding with her swords as she shot past. The wounded mount did a slow roll and fell, trying to regain its bearings and trailing a stream of blood. It barely attained control before crashing into a large clump of bushes, its two riders sailing off to sprawl in a meadow.

The other four hippogriffs tried in vain to hit them, but the Alenar sisters' time in the air under the tutelage of their aunt and uncle made the difference. Soon, one of the other enemy mounts sported three arrows in its hide and the mage in the saddle lolled against the pilot, the victim of Megan's firedarts.

Brandi signaled to Megan and they broke contact, streaking away through nearby clouds, heading back towards where Paractus had landed among the trees. She cast a look over her shoulder, but the hippogriffs didn't pursue. Knowing that Megan followed, she sped towards the grey rocks.

Amicus landed in a clear space near the rocks, trotting slowly as he blew air from his nostrils. Brandi patted him on the neck.

"Good job, boy," she said, then saw the blood on her glove.

Megan landed next to her.

"Are you hurt?" Brandi asked her, dismounting.

"A little. How's Amicus?"

"I have to heal him. See if you can find Daphne and Stephen."

Brandi found three other wounds and felt a pang of guilt. She and Megan had been so intent on attacking that they didn't realize their pegasi were heroically carrying them into war while taking hits the sisters didn't even notice.

"I'm sorry, fellow," she murmured to Amicus as she applied healing ointments to his injuries. "I didn't see. Will you forgive me?"

Amicus tossed his head as if nodding and Brandi grinned, kissing him on the nose.

"That's my boy."

Megan arrived with Daphne and Stephen soon after.

Brandi turned her attention to Larinor, but Stephen pointed at her arm. "You first, young lady."

The stinging pain of her injury hit and Brandi winced, then nodded and downed a potion from a belt loop. She waited for the pain to recede, then turned back to Larinor, glad to find her sister's mount wasn't hurt as badly as Amicus.

"How's Paractus?" Brandi asked as she finished, looking at her relatives sitting on the grass, taking drinks from their water skins.

Daphne shook her head, looking grim. "Badly damaged. The bolts were magical and his faculties are greatly reduced. I need to get him repaired. As long as we can get to Meridian it's not a problem. Corbin's Mechanical Infirmary in Meridian does good work."

Brandi led Amicus over to them. "We'll have to ride double then."

"Yes," said Stephen, "and we can't continue the way we've been going. I used a far-seeing spell and there are skirmishers in the woods out there."

Brandi took the time to catch her breath, take a drink and eat a quick snack before setting off again, riding in front of Daphne. Megan sat behind Stephen.

"Which way?" she asked her aunt over her shoulder.

Daphne waited a long time before answering. "Starpoint is closer, so they will expect us to go there. We can strike out north, heading for Ryker's Shoal, but riding double means we can't fly for long distances and it will take several days. That's not a good option. Turning south heads to Torosc, so that's out. Sentinel is our best bet, I think. We should head north, as if heading for Ryker's Shoal, then turn east when we get a chance."

Daphne didn't say it, but Brandi felt it, and her stomach clenched. They were in the middle of a dragnet. Someone wanted them very badly. Guessing from the amount of effort, their liberation of the royal family of Turis Rhi probably caused quite a stir among the leadership in Torosc.

Without another word, she turned Amicus northwards. They rode carefully, Daphne directing their path. When night fell, they found a copse of trees near a jumble of large boulders and made their camp.

The Alenars ate a sparse meal and set up a schedule of watches. Daphne established a perimeter with her Guardian Rod. Brandi watched as her aunt planted the shaft of crystal and metal into the earth and tiny red lights skittered along in a circular pattern away from them. At a distance of thirty feet, the lights sank into the ground. There, they would remain dormant until an enemy or wild creature would make them burst into brilliant light. Usually, knowing the Guardian Rod kept watch for them made for a restful sleep, but Brandi spent a fitful night in the shelter of the trees and stones.

Morning came sooner than she would have liked, but she didn't complain as they readied themselves and again set to riding double, heading north.

Daphne made them stop to rest, both to give the pegasi a break and to prevent the constant vigilance from fatiguing them into inattentiveness. In late afternoon, she broke away from their group to scout, carrying one of her Sending Mirrors for communications.

Stephen sat against a tree with the other mirror in his hands, eyes closed, resting. Megan and Brandi stood watch, looking through the trees and undergrowth for some sign of movement. The air itself seemed tense, watchful, almost as if the forest knew about the potential for violence.

Stephen sat up and raised the mirror. Brandi stepped next to him. The mirror frame looked like twisted vines and the symbol of an eye looked at her from the top center of the frame.

Daphne's face showed in the glass. "I've seen two groups of twenty skirmishers, one to the west and one to the north. It looks like they have figured out our path, but the way to the east looks clear. I checked my map and there is a break in the woods approaching Sentinel near some cliffs. If we can get past that, we have a place where we can take off flying and hopefully get close to Sentinel."

Stephen nodded. "Can you tell who the skirmishers are?"

Daphne shook her head. "Dark cloaks and armor, closed helms. They look like humans or elves though, from their size. I did see a pair of ogres with each group and they wore scale mail and had battle axes. I don't think they're mercenaries like the ones we fought near Sentinel. My guess is Torosci auxiliaries."

"Have you seen any Gorostoli patrols?" Stephen asked. "Maybe we can signal one of them."

"Yes. A trio of hippogriff riders with Gorostol livery flew overhead to the north and the skirmishers hid in the bushes. If I had a way to contact the patrol without giving away my position, I would have done it. But know this: I also saw other hippogriffs just like the ones that tried to ambush us. They didn't appear until after the patrol moved on."

"Do you think we can risk flying double?" Stephen continued.

Daphne bit her lip. "Based on what we've already seen, I'm not willing to try it. The skirmishers have heavy crossbows and those have greater range and accuracy. Plus with the hippogriff riders lurking around, we won't be able to outrun them."

Stephen nodded. "The mirror is almost out of energy. Come back to us and we'll find another campsite."

The image in the glass flickered. The tiny eye on the mirror frame closed.

"How long until we can use that again?" Megan asked.

Stephen wrapped the mirror in a large rectangle of cloth and leather and put it into his backpack. "About a day. These are not very powerful, but they don't leave a magical signature to trace, so they're the best for our uses."

Daphne arrived soon afterwards and they climbed back into the saddle, following her directions. Once again, they found a reasonably well-hidden refuge near a rivulet on a hill, hidden on three sides by brush and trees.

Daphne planted the Guardian Rod after darkness fell and they spent another night without a fire.

Brandi awoke for the last watch, kneeling in the morning mist with Eric's cross in her hands. She prayed for their safe return to Sentinel, for Eric's well-being, for their efforts to rescue people from Torosc, but mostly she prayed for guidance and protection. She gazed at the tiny ruby heart at the center of the cross and kissed it.

Soon, I hope, my love. Maybe we will find our way north and I can see you again.

When light tinged the sky with pink and crimson, she awoke her relatives and they mounted up. No one spoke much and Brandi felt the fatigue and tension of being hunted for the last couple of days wearing on her nerves. She kept an arrow alongside her bow as she rode Amicus through the forest, skirting piles of rocks and ducking under boughs heavy with curtains of moss. The air felt like winter in the southlands: crisp, with a hint of chill and a touch of damp.

They halted briefly for a rest but started again soon after. Brandi could tell something bothered Daphne.

"What's wrong?"

Daphne shook her head, lips tight. "I don't know. It's almost like I can sense things that I can't see. I know there are Ja'al in the forest because I can feel them. It makes me nervous, yet I don't feel jittery — it's kind of a relaxed alertness. I don't know what to make of it and I'm not sure I'm comfortable with it."

Brandi looked at Stephen, who nodded. "Me too."

"Why don't I feel it?" Brandi wondered.

Stephen smiled at her. "You're still a young pup, of course! Such marvelous and otherworldly gifts only settle on those with sufficient maturity and discernment to use them properly. I thought you knew that!"

She tried not to smile and failed. "Uncle Stephen, you are nutty as dwarven pastry."

Megan sighed. "Dwarven pastry! What I wouldn't give for some right now... and a cup of jekka."

"Stop torturing us," said Daphne with a smile of her own. Suddenly, she put her hand up, head cocked and listening.

"They're close!"

Brandi held still, bow up and ready. Then she noticed the woodland sounds had ceased.

"Down! Off the pegasi now!" Daphne hissed and Brandi dismounted without question just as a pair of crossbow bolts sang past overhead. The missiles hit nearby trees and exploded in small blooms of fire.

Brandi sighted along her arrow, looking for a target, finally seeing a dark form in a tree, astride a thick branch. She loosed a pair of arrows in quick succession, satisfied to see them strike the figure in the chest. It lurched and plunged down into the underbrush.

Then, she fell into the familiar discipline of combat — dodging, firing arrows and seeking cover. Megan, Stephen and Daphne did the same. Soon the forest came alive with flickering fire darts, spears of lightning, globes of light, cubes of fog and whirling pinwheels of rainbow colors. Arrows sang past, glittering with magic. She heard cries of pain and then a sound that made her heart cringe — the whinny of an injured pegasus.

She saw two humans charge at Amicus. She dropped her bow and drew her blades, racing forward. The pegasus screamed and reared, striking out with his hooves. She saw two bolts lodged in his barding and blood running down his flanks.

Sudden anger seized her and Brandi slammed into the figures, slaying one with a thrust in the heart and slashing the chainmail of the other. A human male with a brown beard and black eyes whirled on her, thrusting with a short spear. She dodged and attacked, but he sidestepped into the bushes and drew back. His eyes flickered to something behind her and she rolled to her left, away from him and her mount. A heavy axe-head slammed into the ground where she had just been. She spun. An ogre jerked his axe out of the ground, red eyes glaring.

She lashed out at him. Green sparks leaped from the ogre's scale mail as her swords struck home. She darted in and back, dodging another swing and hitting it in the arm and chest, but the ogre's armor sparked and held.

Ogres with magic armor? What the hell?

The ogre lifted its weapon for another strike, then lurched and cried out as Amicus slammed it in the back with two hooves. The human spearman lunged forward to impale Brandi, but she slapped the weapon aside with her left-hand blade, spinning with her other sword and planting it in his back as he went past. She continued the motion, using momentum to jerk her blade free.

The ogre looped its axe around for a swipe at Amicus, who backed up. Brandi raced at the ogre's back, tucking into a slide as she shot between its legs and hacked its hamstrings. She popped up and turned to face her enemy. The ogre gave out a bellow of rage and fell to its knees, dropping the axe. It drew two short swords of its own and swung at her, but she methodically parried and countered, hitting it in the arm and shoulder. It feinted, hit her in the left thigh with a bruising blow that caused a burst of blue light from her chainmail, then narrowly missed hitting her in the eye with its other sword.

Brandi countered, going for the thing's head, but it ducked and tried to trap her blade with its own swords. Brandi just barely withdrew her sword in time and had to dodge a double thrust.

Damn it! It's on its knees and I still can't kill it!

The ogre swung overhand. Brandi sidestepped. Amicus reared and lashed out with both hooves, hitting the ogre in the helmet. The ogre reeled, shaking its head.

Brandi swung upward with both blades, severing an arm at the elbow. Before the ogre had a chance to shriek, she spun and shoved both swords up under its jaw through to the top of its skull. The ogre managed a gurgle before collapsing.

Brandi staggered back, swords up, but the forest was silent.

"Megan?"

"Here!" Brandi felt weak with relief as her sister, aunt and uncle stumbled through the underbrush, leading a clearly-limping Larinor.

"I'm here, Amicus. *Calsha, Enyem,*" she said, taking her mount's reins. The pegasus rolled his eyes and snorted, then calmed as he recognized his mistress.

"Who's hurt?" she asked, inspecting Amicus. Two bolts had struck through his barding and worse, both had also caused acid burns. She saw three lacerations in his hide.

"All of us," said Stephen with a grimace, holding a bloodied hand to one shoulder. Brandi felt a twist in her gut. Daphne and Megan also looked injured.

Magical weapons, if they caused all this damage.

"Larinor got a mace to the leg while defending me," Megan said in a guilty voice. "Can you help him?"

Brandi nodded. "Uncle Stephen? Aunt Daphne?"

"Take care of Larinor," Daphne replied, reaching into her backpack. She and Stephen sat under a tree, tossing back potion vials.

Brandi cleaned her weapons, sheathed them, then dropped into a healing trance. She repaired Amicus's wounds soon enough, but Larinor's leg had broken and it took a lot of her energy to bind it back together and seal it. She turned her efforts to several cuts on Larinor's neck and head, then left him to find that her relatives sported bruises and lacerations aplenty. It took quite a while to fix everyone up, including herself. Her tasks completed, she found she had only one small pot of healing medications left.

Panting and dizzy from the effort of healing, she finally dropped to the mossy carpet under a huge willow tree. Megan bent over her and laid a hand to her forehead.

"Are you okay?"

Brandi nodded, closing her eyes. "Just need a minute. That's a lot of healing in a short time. How are we on medical potions?"

"I think we have three left for each of us."

Brandi nodded again, feeling her dizziness start to fade as she rested. "Let's just get to Sentinel."

Daphne and Stephen joined them. Brandi's aunt clenched her fists and muttered under her breath.

"It's not your fault," Stephen said. "They had silencing spells laid on them, so we never heard them sneak within range."

"Yes," Brandi added, closing her eyes. "And it tipped us off when everything went quiet around us."

"I still should have trusted my instincts, and whatever this new sensitivity is," Daphne fumed.

"Aunt Daphne, you're not perfect," said Megan, sitting next to her and taking her hand. "We're all right now. I think we got them all, so none will report back to their masters."

"For now, we're okay," Daphne agreed in a grudging tone. Her eyes looked haunted as she raised her head. "I just don't want anything to happen to any of you."

Megan gave her a hug and Daphne smiled.

Stephen set his jaw. "And there's something else. They had mages with them. Every one of those scouts had magical ammunition and I checked their other equipment. They carried magic weapons and I found empty potion bottles, which meant they augmented themselves before attacking."

Brandi nodded. "I can attest to that. The ogre was not a rookie and he wore magic armor. He had quite a bit of skill and it took a lot to bring him down. This is no ordinary strike force."

They all took drinks and gave the pegasi water by pouring some into their helmets.

Stephen stood off to himself as they did so and Brandi wondered. After Amicus had finished, she picked her way across the jumble of roots, branches and dead enemies to him.

"What is it?"

He stared off into the forest, his eyes glowing silver. "Far-seeing shows me more of them, in the woods. We'll have to go northwest to get between them."

The silver glow faded and he shook his head. "There's no way we can get the pegasi through that area. The underbrush is thick and will slow us down. The trees are shorter so there are less places to hide. They'll be seen for sure."

Stephen stood for a while, lost in thought, then sat on a nearby rock, removing his backpack.

"This will not be easy, so I think I should show this to you in case this does not go well. Megan, you need to see this too."

Brandi, curious now and more than a little alarmed, sat on another rock as Megan and Daphne joined them.

"This is something my grandfather gave me. Daphne has already seen it." Stephen said, holding a little black box. He whispered soft words and the box fell apart into six metal plates. In the center of the bottom plate lay a ring of gold with a symbol etched in the bezel. He held the ring up.

Brandi peered at the etched symbol: the figure of a tower with a cross above and three stars below. Her eyes flickered to her uncle.

"What does it mean?"

He put the box plates aside and tossed the ring in his hand. "It is an heir-loom of the kingdom we came from. You can see it has the heraldry of our homeland. The band even has the ancient spelling of our family name etched inside: Aldenar. This could prove valuable if we find anyone from the royal house. They would recognize it and know that we are originally from that land, before the rule of Torosc. I was counting on using it to convince them of our good intentions if we found any of them. I think one of you should have it, in case — "

"No," Brandi interrupted, shaking her head. "No! Don't talk like that. We're going to make it out of here."

She had never seen her happy-go-lucky, teasing uncle Stephen look so serious. "We are in a tight spot, Brandi. If we're captured, the enemy could use it to lure them out instead."

Brandi stood her ground. "Then why not send it away, to the Nuncio, if it's that important? We should report to him about the attack on us and the troop movements in Southern Gorostol anyway. And we definitely need to advise him about the attempt to ambush us."

"She has a point," Daphne offered.

Stephen sighed. "All right. That makes sense. I'll write a short report, put it and the ring into the last sending bag, and off it goes."

He did so. Megan stepped close to Brandi.

"I've never seen him like this," Megan whispered.

"Me neither."

Daphne added a map to the bag with the letter and ring and Stephen used the seal. The bag dissolved into a cloud of sparkles and vanished. Stephen took the seal and laid it on a nearby rock, then struck it with his sword, shat-tering it.

"What are you doing?" asked Megan, sounding alarmed. "Now we can't get any more bags or communicate with headquarters. They won't know where we are."

Daphne put a hand on her shoulder. "Neither can the enemy. If we're captured, they can't use the seal either."

"We're cut off," Brandi said, a sinking feeling in her heart.

"Yes. It's regrettable, but yes. For now, at any rate. When we get free of this place, we can head back up to Deran and start over." Daphne sounded resolute, calm—calmer than Brandi felt.

Stephen stood, brushing his hands on his armor. "I admit that your solution is probably best, Brandi," he noted. "Now, let's get moving. We have to figure out how to get away from this area."

"Maybe now is the time to fly double," Megan suggested. "If the woods are so thick, the enemy can't see us well enough to shoot us down."

He held up a hand. "There are four hippogriffs up above. I saw them. They're just waiting for us to show up. We won't be able to outrun or out-maneuver them with two on each pegasus."

Brandi's stomach tightened. "There must be some other way."

Daphne sighed and nodded, putting an arm around her. "There is. You can send the pegasi away. The two of them can easily outrun the hippogriffs, and we're near enough to Sentinel that they can see a signal if we send it up from one of the city towers."

Brandi licked dry lips. "I can't abandon Amicus."

Stephen smiled. "You're not. You're protecting him. Amicus is so loyal, he'll kill himself defending you, and you don't want that. He's safer on his own until we can slip the trap."

"That's what I don't understand," Megan said. "Why spend this many resources trying to catch us?"

Daphne made a wry face. "We've stung them and shown that we can whisk members of the ancient families out from under their noses. They have to eliminate us, if only to prevent rumors of their vulnerability from spreading in Torosc. The all-powerful Republic cannot be seen to be threatened by anyone."

Brandi considered that. "But why here?"

No one had an answer.

She exchanged a look with Megan.

Her sister nodded. "The sooner the better, Brandi. The pegasi will distract them for a while and we might slip through while they're trying to figure out what's going on."

Stephen nodded. "I can help a bit. If I take our cloaks, I can craft small air golems that will hold them up and make it look like we're riding the pegasi.

Under scrutiny, they won't fool anyone, but from a distance they will make them believe it for a little while."

Daphne nodded. "Let's do it, and quickly. They certainly have mages by now with all that magic going on and they would expect us to try to escape soon."

Brandi took what she would need from her saddlebags and handed her cloak to Stephen. A sudden feeling of dread took her then, looking at her beloved Amicus. The pegasus seemed to feel her unease and nickered softly, nipping her armor with his incisors as if to goad her into telling him her troubles.

She shook her head, blinking away tears. "Soon, Amicus, soon. Fly free and safe. We will send for you."

It took only a minute or two for Stephen to call forth the air golems and drape the hooded cloaks over them. Then, taking the pegasi to a clear spot, Megan and Brandi made circular motions with their hands and pointed up. The pegasi balked, but they repeated the command and finally both mounts soared up into the air, the decoys' cloaks flapping in the breeze.

Almost as soon as the pegasi cleared the tree line, a piercing whistle sounded and Brandi saw four hippogriffs wheel through the sky to the west and head towards them. Amicus and Larinor hit full speed and shot away from them. Four more riders swooped in from the east in pursuit.

"Be safe," Brandi prayed.

"Now, ladies and dear brother," Daphne said, clapping them on the shoulders. "Let's make the most of the diversion we just created."

Brandi nodded, her heart in her shoes.

"Hey."

She looked up to see Daphne smiling at her, eyes gentle. "You'll see them again, and soon. Don't worry."

Brandi hefted her pack, took up her bow and arrows. She followed her relatives into the woods with a final glance at two fast-receding winged specks in the blue sky, rapidly outdistancing their eight dark pursuers.

Chapter Twenty-Two – Checkmate?

"Now what have we here?" asked Stephen, stroking his beard as he crouched behind shrubs and boulders.

Megan stared down at the scene, a knot of fear forming in her stomach as unfamiliar emotions swirled within her. At the base of the cliff about two hundred feet away, a stone altar squatted in the dirt. Two giant black ceramic pots containing blazing fires flanked it on either side. Carved stone benches sat in six neat rows before the altar. Behind the altar, a massive structure of bones arced upwards, reaching towards the sky like an ivory hand against the dark grey rock of the cliff. The structure looked exactly like the drawings in the blueprints the Alenars had captured from the Ja'al many weeks ago.

"So they built one," mused Daphne.

"Yes, but what does it do?" Megan asked.

"Something vile, I assure you," hissed Brandi. Her sister set her jaw, eyes glaring at the structure.

Another swirl of emotions tore at Megan — revulsion, certainly, but also a strange fascination and desire. She felt a need to go to the structure and claim it, make it perform its dark purpose.

She closed her eyes. "God, why do I feel this way?"

"You feel it too?"

She opened her eyes to see her relatives staring at her. "Yes."

For the first time she could remember in a while, Daphne looked uncertain. "I have felt dark emotions lately, and my dreams have been troubled.

271

However, if I pray, everything becomes calm and clear, and I am unafraid."

Stephen nodded. "Take a deep breath and center yourself, girls. It helps, no matter what is causing it."

Brandi raised fearful eyes to hers, then nodded and took in a slow breath and exhaled. Megan copied her sister.

Lord, whatever these feelings, please show me how to banish them.

As Daphne had said, the dark desires faded, replaced by a calm confidence and a sort of righteous determination. In her eyes, the structure of bones looked weak and feeble, a symbol of Evil's futile attempts to extinguish the Light.

"Wow," she breathed. Stephen nodded at her with a little smile.

Brandi looked as surprised as Megan felt. "What is going on, Uncle?"

Stephen's smile faded. "I don't know, Brandi. I'm as confused as you are. It could be that the proximity of this evil thing is affecting us, or it could be some kind of magical effect designed to confuse anyone who gets near it."

Motion in the trees near the cliff face drew their attention. A bearded old man in dark green robes strode out of the woods, flanked by four warriors in plate armor bearing halberds. A few seconds later, the now-familiar figure of Adina stalked after them, clad this time in skin-tight leather armor. She and the old man approached the bone structure as the guards took up positions nearby.

Megan couldn't hear their discussion, but saw the old man nodding as Adina explained something. Adina handed over a shiny object and gestured at the bone structure, then left, heading back into the trees where other troops awaited. She waved a hand at them and stalked back into the woods.

Daphne nodded. "I think I know why there are so many in the woods now. We were wrong. It's not us. It's that thing. They're guarding it and we penetrated their perimeter, so we have to be eliminated. What do you think?" She looked at Stephen.

Her brother stroked his beard again, shaking his head. "There are only five of them but the older man bothers me. Do you and Brandi think you can take the guards?"

Daphne and Brandi nodded.

"You're suggesting we attack?" Megan asked. "What if they alert the skirmishers in the forest?"

Stephen smiled. "Adina has gone for now. As long as we don't take too long, we can slip away. But we have to take that thing down, or at least capture the old man so he can tell us its purpose."

Megan considered this, watching the old man as he sat on one of the benches. He examined the shiny object he had received from Adina. He opened a shoulder bag and placed the item inside, then went to inspect part of the bone structure.

Another, intense feeling of need rose within her, but this time it urged her to destroy the structure.

She nodded. "Then let's do it."

Megan, Stephen and Brandi cast protective spells on all of them. As the last magical light faded, Stephen picked up a small pebble and closed his eyes.

"Brandi, set up a wind wall in front of us so we'll be unnoticed until we get close."

As Brandi cast her concealing spell, Stephen murmured a word. The pebble flashed with light and the area fell into dead silence. He handed the pebble to Daphne.

The four Alenars slipped out of their hiding place and headed towards the structure and the guards. Megan prepared a set of spells in her mind, ready to cast whichever might be the most advantageous. Despite the tension and danger, her mind remained crystal clear.

Why am I so calm?

They reached the farthest of the stone benches when lights flared around them. Brandi's wind wall vanished. The old man and the guards turned in their direction.

Daphne tossed the pebble. It bounced off the ground near the altar, then off the cliff face and came to rest at the old man's feet. Three guards charged while the fourth reached for a horn at his belt. He blew on it but no sound came out.

Brandi made a beeline for him and his fellow as Daphne headed for the man in the green robes. The other two warriors intercepted her and the old man reached into a pocket and put on a silver ring. He then back-pedaled at tremendous speed and turned to run past Brandi.

Once outside the effect of the silencing spell, he stopped and replaced the ring, visibly winded. Megan hit him with a lightning spear spell. He flinched and recoiled as the fork of electricity hit a shield around him and dissipated into a cloud of sparks.

She sensed Stephen next to her. He fired off his own spell, a bright beam of light. The wizard in green waved his hands in a counter-spell and the beam faded as it hit his shields.

Then came the most amazing duel Megan had ever seen. The enemy mage countered their spells and released his own, including an acidic cloud that depleted her shields rapidly until her uncle dispelled it. Firedarts, acid balls, arrows of frost and beams of darkness flew from the old man's hands effortlessly, his eyes intent and eager. The ground rocked under her feet, clouds of earth and stone battered her magical shields, and shimmers of light distracted her from seeing her enemy. She spent much of her time dodging and defending.

She hadn't seen a practitioner this good since her academy days.

All the time, the bone structure drew her eyes and she had to force down the urge to claim and control it, trying to focus on the righteous confidence she had felt earlier.

Finally, Stephen just charged the old man, sword out. The Ja'al wizard thrust both hands forward, palms glowing. Megan leaped forward as well, daggers drawn.

A sphere of darkness shot out at Stephen, shoving him backwards as his shields wavered.

Megan reached the wizard's side in a few steps. He raised his hands to cast a spell, but she slashed and stabbed. He deflected her attacks with bronze bracers on his wrists, but she managed to cut him three times and make him retreat. He gave a little smile and an impressed nod, then sidestepped and pointed at the ground.

The earth under Megan's feet exploded upward, hurling her backwards. Rolling to her feet, she deflected a beam of green light from the wizard's hand, countered with whirling pinwheels of rainbow colors, and then dodged to the side as a ball of flame hurtled past her, exploding in a bloom of fire, blasting one of the stone benches into fragments.

Megan prepared fire-darts, but the wizard raised his hands overhead, then cast them down. A thick fog boiled up around her. She rolled to the side, anticipating a killing spell, but the fog swept away as Stephen uttered the counter.

She stood. The wizard had a shiny bag of metal in his hands and removed a dark object. With a clench of her stomach, Megan realized it was a heart.

The wizard made a thrusting motion with his hand and the heart flew from his palm, soaring up to the skull at the apex of the bone structure. There, it lodged in the mouth of the skull and began to glow with purple light.

"I must compliment you," the wizard said, wiping his bloody hand on the edge of his robes. "You are both very skilled. Particularly you, young lady, for one so young."

"Charming," said Stephen with a smile. "But you have us at a disadvantage."

The wizard smirked and bowed, still keeping both hands up. Megan sensed Daphne and Brandi joining them.

How do I know they are behind me without seeing them? she wondered.

"My name is George Oxbridge," he said. "But that won't matter very much in a little while."

Oxbridge! Why does that sound familiar?

The skull at the apex of the structure snapped shut and the interior of the frame flashed with pink and yellow light. Megan started as the ceramic pots blazed with roaring flames. The air inside the structure seemed to warp and twist, then, it resolved into a swirling purple void.

Megan felt her senses intensify and sharpen, almost as if she could feel every molecule in the air, forest, earth and trees. The skeletal structure seemed to beckon to her.

To her horror, some dark part of her recognized the void and exulted. Another part of her felt anger and determination to defeat whatever evil lurked therein. She shuddered, fighting the urge, willing her earlier quiet confidence to return.

Oxbridge stepped backwards, eyes mocking. Megan got a good look at him. He appeared to be over seventy years old by his white hair and beard but moved more like a man of fifty.

"What are you talking about?" asked Daphne.

Oxbridge's smile now matched his eyes. "Wait and see."

The swirling void convulsed and bulged, then parted. A creature from a nightmare emerged.

It stood as tall as a troll, with deep red bat wings growing from its shoulders. A bestial visage with four eyes glared out at them, horns and fangs gleaming black. Shoulders rippling with muscle connected to four arms that ended in claws. Massive legs thudded into the ground, grinding small stones under taloned feet. It — or rather, he — carried a dagger in each hand, the blades lit with red fire. His hide looked rather like a tiger's that Megan had seen in a picture book as a child, except that it was red and black.

Part of Megan's mind gibbered in terror as she realized what approached them: daemon. Just as quickly, she felt a sudden surge of triumph and a desire to command and control the creature. With this being at her beck and call, she could conquer as she pleased. Visions of power danced before her eyes.

Oh my God! What's happening? Jesus help me!

Shaking her head, she tried to connect to the earlier feeling of righteous confidence and courage and gratefully found it returning. As she focused, her fear receded and now she felt at ease, buoyed by some unknown hope.

"Ah, Lord of the Fallen Ones!" Oxbridge said, moving towards the trees, away from Megan. "You will rid me of these nuisances and fulfill the Oath."

The daemon turned towards her. Four eyes filled with hatred locked on the Alenars. It peered at them as if assessing them, then, to Megan's astonishment, the daemon stepped back.

Without turning its head, he spoke to Oxbridge in a deep, rumbling tone.

"There is something amiss, wizard," he said. "What manner of creatures are these?"

Oxbridge started and stared at the daemon. "What do you mean, Battle Lord? These are merely humans and half-breed elves. They are nothing to you."

The daemon's eyes narrowed. "They are surrounded by a cloud of light and their scent is redolent of the Enemies."

"Nonsense," Oxbridge said, fists clenching. "They are no more remarkable than any others of this world."

"Not so, wizard of Gudarta," the daemon replied. "I know not this strange, hybrid aura."

"What are you blathering about, you idiot?" Oxbridge snapped. "They are nothing to your might and power. Destroy them!"

The daemon shook his head. "I must needs allies in this battle."

Oxbridge frowned and he pulled out a dark purple medallion from his belt. He held it forward and muttered harsh syllables under his breath. The daemon flinched and a flash of green light surrounded his skull. The light appeared to constrict around him and he squeezed his eyes shut with a howl of pain.

"By the might of Gudarta, I command you to attack, Lord of the Fallen! You are compelled!"

With an inarticulate snarl, the daemon surged forward. Megan tried to intercept Oxbridge as he darted into the forest, but the daemon stamped down a massive leg and swung a dagger at her and she dodged.

"So this is what the structure does," Brandi said in a calm voice.

The daemon leered at her. "Aye, indeed, the Gate of Skulls is most useful, little harlot. It shall be the ending of thy world."

"Nay. We shall be thy ending," said Daphne with a crisp sword salute.

The world dissolved into a swirl of combat. The daemon attacked with blasts of fire, beams of green light, clouds of acid and dagger slashes. He buffeted the Alenars with its wings and cast up dust and pebbles to obscure their vision. Despite her initial terror, Megan felt almost serene. Spells flew from her fingertips with remarkable, unfamiliar potency and she fairly danced through the battle with inhuman agility. Somewhere in the depths of her soul, she felt calm despite knowing she faced her death.

What is happening to me?

The daemon took a phenomenal amount of damage. Daphne, Brandi and Stephen cut, stabbed and hacked at it, causing many wounds that dripped dark blue ichor, but it just kept going. Their spells bounced off the daemon's shields for the most part, with only a few getting through. Megan's breath soon came in gasps from magical exertion and her head pounded. The fiery daggers began to find gaps in their defenses and soon all of them bled from at least a half-dozen wounds. Finally, Stephen drove his blade between two massive ribs and Daphne slashed the daemon in the right thigh, opening a gaping wound.

The combatants broke apart, panting. The daemon stepped back and went to one knee.

"Why dost thou not die?" he growled. "What manner of enchantment sustains thee? Verily, I vow thou hast some spells of the Enemies upon thee."

"Any —" Daphne began, then winced in pain and supported herself on a bench. "Any enemy of thine is a friend of ours. Your attack is in vain, Dark One. Return now to Hades."

The daemon smirked. "I have not been given leave, slutling, ere I have secured thy demise. But never fear. Thou shalt feel Hell's dark embrace yet."

Despite the ichor flowing down his side and his injured leg, he hurled himself forward, slashing with fiery blades. A ring of flame leapt up around him, swirling around in a blazing disk.

He swung two blades at Daphne, but she leapt over the attack. She planted a foot on his elbow and leaped up into the air, her blade shining bright as she stabbed it into his collarbone. He roared and whipped two daggers at her, cutting her twice. She twisted out of the way, withdrawing her blade. With his other two arms, he parried a flurry of attacks from Brandi and aimed a kick at her head that she ducked.

Megan and Stephen hurled ice grenades at him. They detonated into deadly frozen shards. The daemon lurched from the impact and his injured leg buckled. Daphne and Brandi stabbed for his heart with weapons glowing white and the daemon howled in pain and rage. Bright light filled the glade. With a violent spasm, he exploded in a fiery maelstrom of bones and chunks of flaming meat.

Megan felt stinging pains all over her body and saw only darkness. She heard a loud ringing in her ears. Everything hurt. She rolled to her side, looking for her aunt, uncle and sister. Seeing some human-like shapes moving nearby, she crawled towards them.

She heard Brandi's exhausted voice whispering a prayer and her eyes cleared, then some of the sting of her injuries abated. She reached for healing potions in her belt loop to find that only one remained intact. This she downed, basking in the soothing, cooling sensation of healing. She still felt battered and exhausted.

Brandi sat on a bench next to her. "Good," she rasped in a dry voice. "Be right back."

Megan numbly watched her sister drag Daphne and Stephen over to them. Her aunt and uncle looked horrible, covered in blood, their skin red from burns. Brandi bent over them as they downed the last of their healing potions and a warm glow removed the burns and some of the other wounds.

"So that's a daemon," said Megan, sitting on a bench with a groan.

Stephen nodded wearily. "A major one too. Wizard called it a Battle Lord."

"Where are the Elohir?" Megan asked, her fear growing. "Aren't they supposed to show up if a daemon arrives on Damora?"

"I don't know," Stephen said, breathing hard. "Maybe since we stopped it at the point of entry, they didn't get enough of a signature to track it."

"We have to get away from here," Daphne said, heaving herself up to stand shakily. "That Oxbridge fellow will be back."

"We have to destroy that thing first," Brandi said, resettling her helmet on her head. "We can't let them port in another daemon."

She led them to the skeletal gate and looked at it.

"We don't have much time," said Daphne.

Megan exchanged a weary look with her uncle. "Where do you think it's vulnerable?"

Stephen picked up a discarded halberd from one of the fallen guards, eyes narrowed. "If we can expose the metal, you and I can hit it with successive blasts of fire and cold to weaken it. Then Brandi and Daphne can strike it low near the base. We might be able to topple it over."

He tossed the halberd to Brandi and another one to Daphne. "Knock some of the bones apart."

The pair did as he instructed, bashing the lower right side of one of the supports until only bare metal showed.

"Stand back," he said, then nodded to Megan. "You use fire first."

Megan took a deep breath, then released a Fire Fan spell, concentrating on roasting one section of it. The metal glowed red.

Stephen released a stream of ice at it, frosting it over. Megan heard a distinct groaning sound.

"Now!"

Daphne and Brandi slammed the halberd blades into the weakened metal. Just as Stephen had guessed, the metal gave after a few stout blows and that side of the structure sagged, then leaned over. While the skeletal gate didn't collapse, it did bend and bow to the side, looking warped. Bones creaked and cracked under the stress and two horizontal beams ripped loose from their connections.

"That's the best we can do for now." Daphne said, taking up her bow.

Megan joined her relatives, head throbbing. She almost didn't notice a hissing sound from her right. Four arrows thumped into the grass near her.

Stephen straightened, then looked at the nearby forest in alarm. He raised his hand to cast a spell. "Archers!"

Megan whirled. She watched in horror as two glittering shafts struck her uncle in the chest, flashing with blue fire as they blew through the feeble remnants of his shields. He reeled backwards and fell.

Brandi raced to his side. "Take out the archers!"

With a scream of rage, Megan unleashed a fire ball at a trio of figures in the woods. The blazing comet shot out and hit the tree line, detonating with a thunderous boom and blossom of flame. The three figures flew through the air and hit nearby trees to fall into unmoving, burning corpses.

Brandi knelt by Stephen, frantically trying to help him. Daphne took up her bow and loosed two arrows at some other figures. Megan's head began to throb again from all the fatigue of magical combat. She saw George Oxbridge as well as the figures of Adina and Berek, accompanied by a phalanx of troops.

More arrows rained around them. Daphne nailed two archers in the chest but three arrows hit her, flashing red fire as they penetrated her armor. She went down, one shaft in a leg, another under her collarbone, and one in the ribs.

"No!" Megan cried hoarsely, diving to her aunt's side. More arrows rained down around her. Daphne returned fire, dropping two more, then sagged to her knees and keeled over.

Two arrows blew through the last of Megan's shields, one of them hitting her in the hip. Gritting her teeth against the pain, she cradled her aunt in her arms.

"Daphne!"

Her aunt gripped her arms, smiling up at her. Her eyes looked misty, distant.

"You're a good girl, Megan. Stay that way."

"No, Aunt Daphne! Hold on! Brandi is coming."

Daphne's eyes clouded over. "Live, Megan. Live for me. Never forget.

Live."

She stared off at nothing, then closed her eyes, still smiling.

"No. No, no, no, no, no…" Megan wept, uncaring of her injuries, her fatigue. She shook Daphne by the shoulders.

God, PLEASE! Don't take her from me!

"No!" she wailed, feeling her soul rip in two. "Wake up! Don't leave me!"

A glittering object landed a couple of feet away and flashed bright white. Megan felt herself fly through the air backwards.

She stared up at the blue sky, wondering how she had gotten there. Sound returned to her, then feeling as four hands roughly jerked her to her feet. She heard voices, dim as if from a far distance.

"Are you brain-dead? I said I wanted them all alive!" That sounded like Adina.

"How were we to know? They were half-dead already." A male spoke this time.

"What about that other one?" Adina sighed in exasperation.

"Alive. The male is dead, though."

"No," Megan tried to shout, but it came out as a whisper. A hand slapped her face.

They can't be dead…

"Strip them," Adina ordered. "I want to see what they're hiding."

Megan could barely stand as hands ripped her blouse, trousers, boots, socks, and underclothes off. Soon, she hung between two guards and raised her head to see Brandi across from her, as naked as she.

"Good weapons, excellent armor, a couple of Sending Mirrors…" this voice sounded like Berek. "What else? Looks like some of those worthless Christian prayer books, some food, about two hundred gold coins in total. They have some jewelry that's probably enchanted and two religious symbols. We'll just bury those stupid things."

Adina stood before Megan, scowling. She gripped Megan's jaw so hard that tears sprang to her eyes. "What else do you have, slut? Hmm? Orders from your masters?"

"Some letters," Berek added. "Want me to read them?"

"Are they from their commanders?"

Berek read silently, skimming over one of the letters. "Letters from some-one named Dar and another from some Eric fellow. Lovers, apparently. Nothing of military value from what I can tell."

"Anything else?"

"No, just letters. Should we keep them?"

Adina released Megan. "No. Keep what we can sell and burn the rest. Burn the bodies too. Don't want any sort of Christian mischief after the fact."

Megan's mind reeled in shock. She expected Daphne and Stephen to rise up behind their enemies and use their formidable skills to rescue her.

Can't be dead... she thought, mind refusing to face what her eyes told her.

"They can't travel like this," Berek declared. "Heal them so we can transport them to headquarters."

Adina turned on Berek. "Waste healing magic on them?"

Now that Megan could see better, she watched Berek shrug. "Unless you want to deal with the high priestess when she asks why they're dead."

Adina growled, then nodded. One of the guards forced Megan's mouth open and a peppery, lemony potion hit her mouth. She swallowed and blessed healing coursed through her. After two more of the same, her head-ache faded and her injuries stopped throbbing. Her vision cleared.

Two guards held her upright next to Brandi. Berek looked them over, nodding.

"Very impressive, actually. They're in great shape. Could be used in a harem, or at least sold as pleasure slaves. I want to try the younger one out first though."

Now she heard George Oxbridge's voice. "I claim the younger one. She's a wizard and she's mine."

"You?" Berek protested. "Why do you need her? You said you were — how did you put it? 'Beyond the baser instincts'."

"Just so," Oxbridge replied. "I don't want her for that. I need her for my part in the project. She has a phenomenal amount of power for one so young, and I sense it in the older one too. You would be well-advised to make use of her yourself."

"You are in no position to give advice or make demands," Adina snapped.

"I beg to differ," Oxbridge said. "The High Command has given me au-thority."

Adina whirled on him but he produced the black medallion from his belt pouch. This time, it flashed with red fire and a twisted symbol hung in the air. Adina hissed and turned away, throwing her hands up.

Berek looked disappointed. "Shit. Well, I guess I can get a whore from somewhere else." He motioned to one of the guards.

"Bind her up."

While two guards held Megan upright, another one clamped manacles and chains on her wrists and ankles. Numb with sorrow, shock and despair, she didn't react.

"Megan," said Brandi. "Don't give up."

Megan met her sister's eyes, filled with unshed tears and a fiery determination.

"Silence, strumpet!" snapped Adina. "I have another use for you."

She stalked to a place behind the troops, where a horse and cart awaited. After rummaging around in a backpack, she returned with a triumphant look, carrying the backpack and something shiny.

She dangled a thin gold chain in front of Brandi. From it hung a circular gold setting with a clear, black gemstone. Megan saw tiny glittering symbols writhe on the surface of the jewel.

"Do you know what this is, my dear? No? Well, it will help you avoid destruction from the sunlight. Yes, sunlight will be a problem for you unless you have this."

She looped the chain over Brandi's head, the dark gem resting between her breasts.

"Now," Adina said with a smile. "You will receive a great privilege."

She reached into the backpack and drew forth an obsidian chalice in the shape of a skeletal hand holding a bowl. Setting it down on the ground, she removed a vial of dark purple liquid and poured some into the cup.

"Hold her," she barked to the guards.

"Are these theatrics really necessary?" Berek asked, sounding bored.

"Shut up, Berek. You chose the wrong harlot and lost out to the wizard," she retorted. "This one is mine."

Brandi struggled and the guards had difficulty holding her but Adina waved a hand to the troops holding Megan. Instantly, one of them laid a dagger at her throat, pressing into her jugular.

"She is your sister, yes?" Adina smirked. "You had better be a good girl, unless you want to lose a relative."

Brandi met Megan's eyes again. Megan felt a lump in her throat. She felt as if something had burned through her soul.

"No, Brandi," she whispered.

"It's okay," her sister said, "I can't lose you too."

Adina nodded and the knife moved away from Megan's throat. The Ja'al priestess bent low over the chalice, muttering harsh words, then took out a tiny stone from her belt purse that seemed to glow with darkness. This she dropped into the cup. The liquid within took on a misty quality, as if it were suddenly made of black fog.

Brandi didn't resist as two guards forced her mouth open and Adina poured the fog into her.

At first, nothing happened. Then, Brandi doubled over in pain, crying out. A spasm of agony hit her and she arched her back, falling to her knees. In horror, Megan watched as her sister's eyes clouded over with darkness, then turned blood red. A flash of dark purple fire burst out from her body. Brandi dropped on hands and knees, the sound of her harsh breathing loud in the stillness of the glade. She managed a pitiful moan.

"NO!" Megan screamed. "Brandi! No!"

A guard kicked her in the calf and she fell to her knees.

"There now," Adina purred. "You have achieved your destiny. Arise, Servant of Gudarta, Mistress of Pain."

She lifted Brandi up. Megan stared in disbelief at her sister's red eyes and white fangs.

George Oxbridge grunted. "I should think that your coreligionists who follow Torvu might be insulted that you changed her into a vampire without their permission."

"Idiot," Adina didn't even bother to look at him, keeping her smile. "A high priest of Torvu gave me the coffin-gem I used in the potion. I had to pull a few favors in order to get it, so shut your trap."

"Brandi?" Megan asked. Her sister fixed her with an imperious look and her lip curled in a sneer. She ran her tongue over one of her fangs.

"Who is this, Mistress?" she asked Adina. "Is she one of your servants?"

Megan shook her head in helpless denial. She felt numb all over and no words came out as tears rolled down her cheeks.

Berek waved a hand at Oxbridge. "Take your little girl-toy and begone, wizard. You have work to do and so do we."

Guards jerked Megan to her feet and lifted her into the wagon, chaining her firmly.

Oxbridge clambered aboard and nodded to a guard next to him. The wagon started to roll away. Now Megan noticed the flames and smoke of the funeral pyre of her aunt and uncle. A dark cloud billowed up into the sky.

Her entire world collapsed.

"No," she whispered, blinking the tears away and brushing at her eyes. "Please, God, no."

She stared numbly at the battlefield and her eyes alighted on the ruined Skull Gate. For some reason it held her gaze as she rattled away slowly in the cart. The might of the daemon-summoning structure now seemed feeble, ineffectual; she and her relatives, just four people, had nearly destroyed it and defeated a daemon Lord.

They can be beaten. She realized. *We slew a daemon, just the four of us, and if these others hadn't come along at the wrong time, we would have escaped. The Skull Gates can be destroyed.*

Her aunt's face hovered in her mind's eye. "Live, Megan. Never forget. Live." Megan's hands clenched into fists.

They can be beaten…No matter what plots they hatch, the Light has shown that Death is defeated forever.

Then something in her turned — that vibrant, almost holy feeling of surety and righteousness she had felt before when fighting the daemon. She saw a vision of the future suddenly, as clear as day. All of this sorrow was merely a passage in time, a bump in the road, a temporary trial on the road. Her aunt and uncle were at peace, in Heaven with her parents.

All would be set right in the end. She knew it as surely as the sun shone in the sky.

"Brandi!" she called out. "Don't give in! Remember who you are! You are Brandawyn Veronica Therese Alenar, a child of God! I will be back for you!"

Oxbridge laughed.

Something changed in Brandi's expression. The red glow faded and Megan saw her sister's eyes return to their natural color. A tear leaked out of the corner of her eye and she gave a tiny smile and a nod.

Dear Jesus, please save her...

She watched as Brandi's form receded, watched as the last of her family faded into the distance. She closed her eyes, clinging to the image of her sister's last expression.

She's still in there. Somewhere in there, Brandi is resisting. I've got to hold onto that...

"You will like the tasks I have for you, my dear," Oxbridge said, sounding very satisfied. "Cutting-edge magic, and well-suited to someone with your talents. You and I will make history, I know it! Just remember that I am your master and all will be well."

Megan barely heard him as the figure of her sister faded into a tiny speck in the glade and black smoke trailed into the sky.

Chapter Twenty-Three – A New Mission

She seemed close enough to touch, her chainmail armor gleaming with some kind of inner light as she walked through utter blackness. She turned, drawing her swords. Both flared white and he saw a flash of deep purple light surround her. Then a misty silver fog surrounded her beautiful form. Her red-gold hair seemed to glow.

He reached out to her and called her name, running towards her. She didn't seem to hear him. He tried to go to her, to stand by her side in the darkness, but no matter how hard he tried, he could not close the gap.

He saw red eyes glowing in the shadows and screamed a warning, but she saw the danger. Her jaw set in determination. She lashed out as dark, spectral shapes swarmed around her, hooked claws reaching.

Sun-bright blades flashed and ebon specters shrieked as the swords ripped them apart, but some slashed her with their talons, cutting dark gashes in her armor. She called out soundlessly, and white light burst from her breast, disintegrating the nearby wraiths and giving her a momentary respite. She turned to run, but the darkness closed in again and more shadowy, red-eyed forms surged forth in a wave. She fought on, her armor and swords like bright stars. Just before the wave overcame her, the deep purple light flashed again and her eyes turned as red as the specters'. She stopped fighting, her face taking on a sly, evil aspect.

"Brandi!"

Eric Indidarc blinked in the dim light, unsure of his surroundings. He lay still and his memories returned: the long journey north from Gorostol, through Terenai, stopping at the Eleandir home once again. He remembered the kind sympathy of Andyn's parents upon hearing of Handor's demise, then an all-too-soon departure, passing through the northern counties of the Elven Empire, through the southern territories of Deran, and finally ending up in Saint Martin's. The Papal Nuncio provided rooms for them at the chancery. A journey that should have taken at least two weeks, even by a fast courier ship, they covered in slightly more than a week, with two rest stops.

He sat up in his bed, now aware of the early morning hour. He let his eyes drift around the room, a small, sparsely-furnished yet comfortable place with a window looking out on the courtyard. Two wooden chairs, a small table, bed with a firm mattress, curtains, and a large woven rug made it less like a monk's cell and more like a chamber suited for an assistant of a visiting dignitary. He tried to relax and let the memory of the dream fade. It stayed vivid in his mind's eye.

She's in trouble.

Part of him fought against that conclusion. He told himself it was nothing, just the fragments of worry and tension from the sadness and strife of the past few weeks, all combining to play on his worst fears. Dreams were the mind's way of clearing itself out for the more urgent task of daily living— or at least, so the doctors said.

Another part of him felt an icy dread, like a cold, clammy hand squeezing his chest. With Brandi's secret mission, whatever it was, peril lurked behind every shadow. She and Daphne and Stephen and Megan travelled in secret, dark paths, no doubt.

He shook himself. This fretting was pointless. He'd had uneasy, indeterminate dreams off and on in the past. The older Alenars were veteran freelancers, schooled in the ways of the forces of Evil and possessing formidable skills and keen minds.

He remembered the Nuncio's words to them upon their arrival and felt calmer.

"Prayers are the most potent weapon in the universe. That's why they're the secret advantage for all who serve God —other people think they're useless when in fact they are mightier than anything."

Despite his worry, he took a deep breath and let it out, then rose to wash and get dressed. He had just slipped into his trousers and put on his shirt when he heard a knock at the door.

"Come in."

Dar Cabot poked his head in. "Hey. Ready?"

"In a little bit. Have a seat."

Eric put on his doublet and buttoned it as Dar sat in a carved wooden chair near the bureau. Dar bounced his leg up and down, eyes unfocused and staring at the painting of a castle in a rainstorm over Eric's bed.

Eric plopped down on the mattress, pulling his boots on and eyeing his friend. "Okay, what's wrong?"

Dar looked up at him, startled. "What?"

"You're fidgeting."

Dar sighed. "I had a rough night."

Eric slowly buckled a bootstrap. "You did?"

Dar nodded. He wore the green tunic of his Order, Saint Kira's, over grey pants, with black boots. The ever-present Rindara Starblade was missing— the Chancery was probably one of the few places he felt safe without it.

Will we ever truly feel safe? Eric wondered. He watched Dar, aware of his unease.

"Dreams of Megan?" he asked.

Dar looked at him sharply. "How did you know?"

"Dreams of Brandi." The clammy hand took hold of Eric's chest again and he tried to remain calm.

"Tell me."

Eric did, in as few, objective words as possible. Dar listened, chin on his fists, then nodded and wiped his face with both hands.

"A lot like mine."

"Really?"

"Megan was in a dark forest, pursued by flitting shadows with yellow eyes. She fought them with spells and daggers until a dark net dropped on her. The next thing I saw she was in chains in a dark room, pushing what looked like a mill wheel. She kept turning to me, trying to say something, but I couldn't hear her voice."

This is too much of a coincidence.

"Let's see Father Edward. Maybe he can tell us something."

"He's a busy man, Eric."

"And we're his guests and he told us to tell him if we needed anything. Well, we need. Get your backside out of the chair and let's go."

The pair headed out into the hallway, dotted with doors of other guest rooms, striding towards the entrance hall. Eric thought of checking on Khyron, Buck and Connor but decided against it. Uninterrupted rest was a luxury in their profession. He knew Andyn, ensconced in the women's wing, probably still slept.

The early spring sun had broken through the clouds by the time they reached the entrance hall, bathing the tiled floor with multicolored patterns from the stained-glass windows. Eric located one of the Nuncio's servants at the far end of the hall. As he and Dar approached, he heard a familiar voice behind him.

"So Grey Riders awake early? No secret mission, great heroes? Then must sleep and rest while chances remain!"

Eric grinned. Gorlak the goblin strode towards them, a spring in his step. He wore the house livery of the Nuncio: white hauberk with a dark blue cross over dark blue trousers and black boots. He grinned back and bowed.

"Sir Indidarc. Sir Cabot."

"Gorlak the Mighty," Dar said with a smirk. "I'm surprised you're up. It's Saturday."

Gorlak shrugged. "No rest for servants of the Dark, so servants of the Light must be alert and ready. But you, Grey Riders, have earned rest, so Father Edward says."

"Where is he, by the way?" Eric asked.

"Study. I take you to him."

"We don't want to disturb him," Dar interjected.

Gorlak shook his head. "You? You not disturb him. He wants to see you, I think."

He beckoned to them, then led Dar and Eric through a set of double doors, up a flight of stairs, then to another set of double doors carved with the motif of the Resurrection. He knocked and then pushed them open upon hearing Father Edward's voice within.

The Nuncio looked up from his huge dark wooden desk covered with neat stacks of paper. He smiled, rising to greet them as they bowed. Eric kissed the Nuncio's ring and straightened.

He saw Father Edward's face and schooled his features to avoid showing the shock he felt. The Nuncio looked old now, weathered and tired. Eric always had the impression of the Nuncio as being ageless and vigorous despite his years. Now, Eric wondered at his health and considered asking about it. He decided not to. Father Edward would just brush off any inquiries.

"Your Eminence."

"Sir Indidarc. Sir Cabot. I see you are up early."

Dar shot a glance at Eric before answering. "Yes, we were heading this way when Gorlak found us in the hall and brought us."

The Nuncio's eyes flitted to Gorlak. "And that was well done. Thank you, Gorlak."

With a grin, the goblin bowed and slipped out, closing the doors behind him.

"So, what awakens you this early?"

"A need for your counsel, Eminence," Eric said. "We both had disturbing dreams. We understand if you are busy."

Father Edward's eyebrows rose. "Not at all, Eric, not at all." He indicated four chairs and a table off to the side, near tall windows overlooking the yards and streets outside.

The Nuncio rang a small bell and a young blond man appeared at a side door with a bow.

"Detlef, please bring tea for us."

Detlef bowed again and left, returning with a tray and tea service. He served them all with a deft hand and departed.

"Now," Father Edward said, laying his hands in his lap. "Tell me what's troubling you."

Dar spoke first. Eric was surprised to find that Dar had been experiencing other foreboding dreams for the last few days, ones that he couldn't remember but which a vague unease in their wake.

"Just like me," he breathed. Dar looked at him in surprise.

"You too?"

Eric nodded. He related his dream in much the same manner as Dar. Father Edward listened, not speaking, his face still in concentration. Finally, he sat back, sipping from a steaming teacup, eyes focused on something faraway.

Eric thought he looked strangely sad.

Eric waited, sipping from his cup, his senses becoming more clear as the tea perked him up.

"Father Edward?" Dar finally asked.

The Nuncio blinked as if noticing them for the first time. "Forgive me. I have had much on my mind and this latest information from you has given me more to consider."

He looked at each of them in turn and set his cup and saucer down. "I think that I will call all the Grey Riders together. Let's have breakfast in the solarium. Come. I will ask Gorlak to bring them."

He rose, rang the bell again and told Detlef to ask Gorlak to awaken the Grey Riders, with His Eminence's apologies. Dar and Eric followed him out of the study to a circular, domed room with one wall composed entirely of tall panes of glass that curved up overhead to meet with the wooden ceiling, giving Eric the impression of a bird cage. Beyond the windows, Eric saw a lawn and trees leading out to a tall iron fence next to a boulevard outside the Chancery. Lush green plants grew in pots and containers near the windows and a large round table with wicker chairs sat in the exact center.

"This green at the end of winter," Dar said with a grin at Father Edward. "Magic?"

The Nuncio winked. "Science. It's amazing what a good architect and a competent botanist can do."

Dar and Eric didn't have long to wait for their friends. Soon, Buck, Connor, Khyron and Andyn joined them, the latter still yawning, though she looked impeccable in a tan and brown dress with a gold and white scarf.

"Sorry," she said as she sat in one of the chairs when Edward swept his hand towards the table. "I'm not used to sleeping in."

"I understand."

Detlef led a pair of servants in. Soon they had plates of pancakes studded with nuts and covered with honey, crisp bacon and plump sausages, soft-boiled eggs, slices of oranges and apples, mugs of jekka, and a particularly odd-looking fruit that resembled a small, green cone object with mild white stripes.

Eric selected one. No bigger than the end of his thumb, they felt firm but not hard.

"Witchberries!" said Andyn with delight.

"What-berries?" asked Buck.

"Witchberries," she repeated, slicing the pointed end off the berry. She popped the larger piece it into her mouth. She consumed it before continuing, a happy smile on her face. "They don't grow here. You have to send away to Derelia to get them. How did you manage it, Father Edward?"

He inclined his head. "Sometimes, this job has a few advantages, shall we say."

Eric followed Andyn's lead and tried one. To his surprise, he found it had a mildly tart flavor with a creamy sweetness and a hint of salt.

He looked at Andyn. "How do you know about these?"

She shrugged as she snipped the end off another berry. "My half-brother Telric owns a pair of merchant ships and they brought in a shipment of them once, for the Duke of Eleth-Anor, when I was young. He was able to buy a few for himself and brought them over to the house."

"Why are they called witchberries?" asked Connor.

"In the old days, people thought that they got their unique shape from witchcraft, since they are unlike any other berry," Father Edward said. "I also think there was bit of folklore based on the fact that they are triangular and witches abhor anything that smacks of the Holy Trinity."

He winked at Andyn. "Pure superstition, of course."

She nodded back. "But very tasty."

They spoke among themselves of their trip up from Gorostol. Father Edward extended his condolences over the loss of Hlerv, whom he had never met.

The meal completed, the servants arrived to the clear the table and, after they left, the Nuncio stood and closed the door, locking it.

"Now this part *is* magic," he said to Eric.

He held up his palm towards the ceiling. A light flashed in his hand and an identical light answered from the apex of the arc of the glass windows. A glittering golden radiance shimmered down the wrought iron frames of the windows, then flowed across the floor to the back wall, where it ran up to the ceiling again. In a matter of seconds, a golden light filled the solarium. It faded in the space of a few heartbeats. Now, instead of looking out at a green lawn and trees and a street, Eric saw a wide green field of waving grass, rocky hills and towering pine trees.

Eric realized his mouth was open and closed it.

Father Edward resumed his seat. "Now we are hidden from prying eyes and listening ears."

"Did— " Dar started, then tried again. "Did we just travel somewhere?"

"Did I mention that the architect was aided by the Order of the Three Magi? No? That was remiss of me. And yes, we are now somewhere else."

From the twinkle in Father Edward's eye, Eric felt for sure that the cleric enjoyed teasing the Grey Riders.

Khyron shook his head. "Even *I've* never seen anything like it. And I've been a few places."

"Now, to more sober matters," Edward said, interlacing his fingers and laying his hands on the table. "Eric, Dar, would you please tell them what you told me about your dreams?"

They did so. The other Riders stared at them.

"No wonder the two of you have been so distant lately," Andyn finally said. "I thought it was because of Hlerv. Why didn't you tell us sooner?"

Dar held up his hands. "Well, yes, part of it was because of Handor. But there was nothing to tell until today, honest. This is the first dream I could remember enough to tell anyone."

Father Edward looked even more somber and he sighed. That clammy hand of fear gripped Eric's heart again as he saw the Cardinal's expression.

"I have some rather disturbing news to give you all," he began, staring at his folded hands. "It concerns the Alenars."

They sat in dead silence.

"We received a teleported bag from them about four days ago. In it were a ring, a map and a letter. Nothing more. The letter said that they had found one of the Ja'al Skull Gates in the uninhabited forests of southern Gorostol. It was apparently fully constructed and there was an altar near it."

"No," Andyn breathed. "They finished one! That means…"

The Nuncio held up a hand. "We are not sure exactly what it means. The area was heavily guarded. From the description, it appears that there were Ja'al legionnaires on hand, and a magic-user or Ja'al priest. The Alenars did not report any daemons, but they stated they were going to try to destroy the Gate."

Eric tried to say something, anything, but his mind kept reeling back to an image of his beloved Brandawyn fighting alone against red-eyed wraiths in the dark. He found himself gripping the edge of the table so hard his knuckles were white.

Connor cleared his throat. "Did they succeed?"

Father Edward actually looked deflated. "We don't know. After that first letter, only silence. It was then that we did an inventory and realized that they had used their last Sending Bag. They didn't ask for any more to be sent, which can usually be done if they still have the seal."

"What does that mean?" asked Andyn, gripping Khyron's hand.

Khyron squeezed her hand in return. "It means," he said in a clipped voice, lips tight, "that Colonel Alenar didn't want to risk the enemy capturing the seal. If they do that, they could try to impersonate the Alenars and possibly glean information before we realized the seal was stolen."

"Do we know where they were?" Dar asked, his voice sounding frustrated, tense.

Father Edward sighed. "We have an approximate location, but apparently they were in some haste. It appears that the Ja'al were actively hunting them. No doubt Daphne thought they could slip out and return to us for a more thorough briefing."

Eric's mind reeled. Brandi and Megan in peril — he battled a sudden urge to charge out, saddle Niveral and fly day and night to Gorostol, to search every copse of trees, every thicket, every hollow to find them. The images in his dream haunted him and he felt his throat tighten.

He caught Dar's eyes and saw the same fear and anxiety.

I'm not the only one. Dear God, don't let them take Brandi from me...

A hand clamped on Eric's shoulder.

"Don't worry," Buck said, giving him one of his trademark homespun smiles. "They're tough, they're smart, and they have two professionals with them. And if I know them they've learned a thing or two since we saw them last."

Eric felt some of his anxiety diminish and looped his arm over Buck's shoulders. "Thanks. It means a lot."

"We're with you, Eric and Dar," said Khyron, standing. "Just say the word and we'll do whatever it takes."

"Unfortunately," the Nuncio said, rising, "your own mission has now changed. We in the Alliance need your unique skills in another matter."

ric looked at him in shock and all the tension and fear boiled over. "We can't just leave them there!"

"Eric," Dar said, holding his hand up. "I don't think that's what he meant."

Instead of a well-deserved reprimand, Father Edward stood, came over to him and put his hands on his shoulders, looking into his eyes. Eric saw a vast well of compassion and empathy and regret and realized that this was probably one of the hardest things the Nuncio had to ask.

"I do not ask this lightly. But Buck is right. They are capable and we have to trust to God's grace to see them through."

"But why?" Eric tried not to sound plaintive and failed.

"Come, look at what they sent." The Nuncio sat again and reached inside his cassock. He drew out a gold signet ring. He handed it to Eric, who examined it and before handing it on to the others.

"What does the heraldry mean? The tower with a cross above and three stars below?"

"According to the letter," Father Edward said, "It is an heirloom, a signet ring that Brandi and Megan's ancestors hid away when Alenar fell so many years ago. It has the ancient spelling of their last name etched in the band just there, see? Stephen's letter said they were going to use it as proof that they weren't Torosc agents. He claimed it would be a symbol that any heir of the kingdom might recognize. Then they could whisk any remnants of the Alenar Royal House away to safety."

"Whisk them away?" Connor asked, looking confused.

"Ah. Forgive me. I never told you their mission. The Alenars were charged with infiltrating the southern regions in order to track down and find any remaining descendants of the original kingdoms so that we could spirit them to safety, if there were any still alive. Having scions of those ancient houses here in the north could be the beginning of the undoing of Torosc, if they could establish realms-in-exile and attract followers for an eventual coup."

"Could they do that?" Andyn asked in wonder. "Sneak refugees out from under the very noses of Torosc and its spies, that far south? It seems impossible."

Khyron smirked. "From what I've heard of Daphne and Stephen Alenar, they certainly could."

"Well, they did."

Eric stared at the Nuncio. "What?"

Father Edward smiled. "They did. They found descendants of the Royal House of Rhivan, heirs to one of the northernmost kingdoms in present-day Torosc, Turis Rhi. Not only did they find them, but they brought them over the border to the Gorostoli city of Sentinel, though they had to fight a pitched battle at the end."

Something clicked in Eric's brain. "That's why there was such high security in Meridian! We heard rumors of some kind of skirmish to the south."

"Indeed," Father Edward said with a nod. "Much of the security was to prevent Torosc from infiltrating to try to steal them back. Fortunately, they were long gone by the time you arrived in the capital."

"So that was their secret mission," Dar mused.

Edward nodded again.

They sat in silence.

"But now, on to *your* new mission, Grey Riders," Edward said, taking an envelope out another pocket in his cassock.

"To find the descendants, just like Megan and Brandi?" Buck interjected.

"Well, no." Edward unfolded a paper on the table. "We dare not risk any further incursions at this time. The Torosci are on high alert. Certainly, if you find any such descendants, by all means, bring them to safety. But your mission will be related to the Skull Gates."

Eric looked at the paper. It was a map of Terenai, Gorostol and Merdail. Edward removed a small black feather from the envelope and waved it over the map.

Eric gasped. Letters and symbols glittered to life.

"These are the locations of agents of the Northern Alliance," Edward continued as they crowded around. "They have all reported activities near their duty stations that might be the Ja'al trying to set up another Skull Gate. From the lack of daemonic mayhem in Gorostol, at least, we can surmise that the Alenars prevented it from being used. Your mission is to find any and all

Skull Gates or construction sites and destroy them. We have other free-lance teams in action to the north and across the sea in Derelia and the kingdoms on the western seaboard, such as Targanon. You will be our agents in the Terenai and Gorostol region."

He looked at Connor with a twinkle in his eye. "It may interest you to know that a young halfling woman who recently inherited a certain shipping line is one of our agents."

Connor's cheeks colored slightly but he nodded. "That doesn't surprise me. She is a very honorable person. And she has a score to settle with the Ja'al."

The Nuncio looked at all of them in turn. "I know your obvious affection for the Alenar sisters. I also know their aunt and uncle quite well. The sisters are in the best possible hands. If there is a way out of the predicament they described, Stephen and Daphne will find it. In the meantime, you can help them most by finding the Skull Gates and destroying them. It will take the pressure off them and direct the Ja'al's attention to you."

Eric's feeling of desperation diminished and he tried to remain optimistic.

He felt the Nuncio's eyes on him and let out a deep breath. "I understand, Eminence. You can count on me."

"Thank you," the old man replied. "I can only imagine what this is costing you and Dar to focus on your mission, but truly, we have other agents on hand who can look for the Alenars. Your talents are better used in what I asked of you."

Eric's mind whirled, trying to hold down his apprehension for Brandi and think clearly enough to focus on the assignment.

Father Edward sized all of them up before continuing. "To make this easier, I will place at your disposal a Sending Bag with four tokens. It functions much like the Express Tele-Post except that the volume that is teleported is much less. Small items like letters can be placed in it; this is the way that we sent your letters to the sisters and acquired materials and reports from Colonel Alenar in return. Just remember to ask for additional seals once you get down to one or two. Otherwise, the bag is useless until you get another seal."

"Thank you, Eminence," said Dar. He faced the Nuncio with his chin up and eyes steady. "We won't let you down."

Edward Simpson smiled. "I know you will not. God is with you. Remember the words of the angel at the Nativity: Fear not."

He replaced the map and feather. "I will have Gorlak and Detlef supply you with an identical map and a list of contacts. Your first contact is in northern Terenai, a married couple named Rhonin and Belinda Handor, code-named 'The Blue Mark'. They run a horse property and are well-connected to many of the noble houses and military due to their supply of high-quality steeds."

Eric nodded as Father Edward raised his palm upward at the ceiling and the golden light suffused the room again. When it faded, he again saw the lawn and boulevard beyond the glass windows.

He bent to kiss the Nuncio's ring and felt his hand on his head in benediction. He straightened as Edward blessed Dar as well and bowed to Buck, Connor and Andyn, who bowed low in return.

"Go with my prayers and best wishes. Know that the might of the Northern Alliance stands ready to assist you."

The Grey Riders left the area in silence and returned to their quarters. Eric went through the motions of packing, still trying to come to grips with the implications of his dream and the Nuncio's information. Once finished, armored and packed, he sat on the edge of his bed and tried to pray.

The only phrase on which he could focus was "Please God. Don't take her from me."

It seemed like hours later when he heard a knock on the door and Dar entered.

His friend let out a deep breath. "So, what did you need?"

Eric looked at him in confusion. "I didn't call you."

"No," said a melodious alto that sounded like a mix of speech and song. "I did."

They whirled towards the far corner of the room. A shimmering screen of air slid aside to reveal an incredibly gorgeous woman, winged and over six feet tall. Her tanned, flawless skin seemed to glow. Soft golden hair cascaded down onto her shoulders, framing a heart-shaped face with jewel-like, sapphire-colored eyes. She wore a short, sleeveless tunic that reached to mid-thigh. A silver belt encircled her waist and held a short sword in a scabbard at her side. Her wings, white tinged with tan, lay furled against her back. She was barefoot.

"Melissa!" Eric gasped, falling to one knee.

"Ah, Eric Daniel," she said, clucking her tongue as Dar knelt as well. "And Darius Richard. Did I not tell you at our first meeting that we kneel only before God?"

"Forgive me, lady," Eric said, rising. "It is a natural reaction of respect."

Her eyes twinkled. "I understand and am flattered by the honor you pay me. But please, we are comrades of old, are we not?"

She looked much the same as she had all those months ago, when she appeared to the Riders at Twinspire Peak and bestowed the Crown of Saint Alyssa to Andyn. Fidelis and Rindara Starblade had come to Eric and Dar, respectively, that same day.

Eric nodded, still dazzled. In his mind, Brandawyn Alenar surpassed all other women in beauty and virtue, but Melissa the Elohir literally took his breath away.

Her jovial expression faded. "Unfortunately, this is not a social call, as pleasant as that would be."

"I'll go get the others," Dar offered, but she stopped him with an upraised hand.

"Not yet," she said. "My words now are only for you, since your beloved ones are involved in what I am about to relate to you."

She moved to the bed and sat on it, gesturing to them to do likewise. Dar took one of the chairs while Eric sat near her, but not too close. Her proximity still unnerved him and he noticed a subtle perfume of lavender and vanilla in the air.

Melissa paused before continuing. "Something strange has occurred in Gorostol, near where the Alenars are assigned."

They both nodded. She paused as if weighing her words.

"The Elohir are aware that a rip in the fabric of space and time has occurred near that area, a rip that is much more substantial than the small, temporary ones that come about because of the teleportation devices on Damora. We think that it was a planetary gate."

Eric's heart stopped. "Does the Nuncio know?"

Melissa shook her head. "Not yet. I will speak to him after I leave you. However, in a strange twist that we have as yet been unable to analyze, the signature of the space-time anomaly suddenly cut off not more than a half-hour after it occurred. We are still unsure as to what happened."

Dar stared at her, then at Eric. "The Skull Gate. The Ja'al opened it and somehow Megan and her family closed it again."

Melissa looked at him curiously and he explained what the Nuncio had just told them. She nodded, her brow furrowed and sapphire eyes becoming stormy. She raised her gaze to his and he suddenly had a vision of what an angry Melissa of Celestia would look like. He gave a start.

Melissa didn't appear to notice. "If what you say is true and the Ja'al have somehow opened a gate, this has implications for the terms of The Ban. I will need to report to King Kelson after I speak to Father Edward. Thank you for your information."

She rose and reached behind her back, pulling out a small black leather bag. "If you are indeed looking for planetary gates, then you will need this."

She handed it to Dar and he opened it, drawing forth a silver chain with a milky white gemstone that seemed to have a tiny star imprisoned in its depths. Eric stared at it, fascinated.

"It is a special item," Melissa said. "You would not understand the concepts behind it, but know that it is called a Relativity Stone and will alert you if such a gate is anywhere close by, within two hundred yards."

Dar carefully replaced it in the bag and put it into his belt purse. "Thank you. Should we tell the others?"

"Certainly, after I have left. I felt I needed to talk to you first because of your love for the Alenar sisters. Unfortunately, I must speak with the Nuncio right away and then return to Celestia with all due haste. Otherwise, I would visit the other Riders. Please give them my fondest wishes and my apologies for leaving so soon."

"Of course," Eric said. "Is there anything else?"

Melissa's stern look faded and she smiled sadly. To Eric's astonishment, she pulled him close in a hug and kissed his forehead. Eric's entire body tingled. She repeated the same to Dar.

"Do not fear," Melissa said, giving them a look full of gentleness and compassion. "All will be well. The Most High watches over you. I will contact you again when there is a need."

She strode to the door and opened it. "Now, if I am not mistaken, the

Nuncio's office is that way, is it not?"

Eric saw the familiar twinkle of amusement in her eyes and he shook himself. "Yes, of course, lady. We will accompany you."

He and Dar followed Melissa the Elohir out into the hallway, minds whirling. To their amazement, the halls were clear of people. It was as if the servants and priests and nuns decided that they had things to worry about in other parts of the Chancery.

At the door to the study, Melissa stopped, gazing at the carving of the Resurrection scene. She reached up and touched the feet of the Christ-figure. She let one of her fingers rest on the nail-wound for a moment.

"They thought they had defeated Him, you know," she said to no one in particular. "Silenced Him and tortured Him to death. Scattered His followers, put the whole bothersome business to an end, secured their power. They were wrong. Death does not have the final word. Life does. He does. This is the ultimate message of hope. Remember that, Grey Riders."

Without another word or backward glance, she pushed the doors open and entered, leaving Dar and Eric speechless and wondering in the hallway.

Epilogue

It must be morning, she thought, looking up at the narrow window slit in the grey stone wall. She recoiled from the sunlight but then remembered her medallion. Sunlight wouldn't harm her as long as she wore that, even in her current state.

She counted it her third morning in this cell, but couldn't estimate how long she had spent in other, darker places. She didn't know why they had moved her here.

Brandawyn Alenar pulled her legs up close to her chest and hugged her knees. The weariness still made her dizzy, but one item helped her focus. She fixed her eyes on a symbol she had carved into the rock wall with bits of stone.

They took everything, but I can still remember. And I remember what he gave me.

She stared at the rough pattern of a cross with a ruby heart at the center, a copy of her own cross, a gift from Eric that the Ja'al had buried in the glade.

I have no more tears, Eric. Stephen and Daphne are dead now. The Ja'al saw to that. Four of us against a deamon, a true daemon of the Dark from Hades, and we won, but then we had nothing left for the others just waiting in the forest to finish us off. At least Stephen and Daphne died cleanly.

A wave of hellish rage swept over her and her vision swam red.

Kill them! I will kill them all for what they did!

The memory of the two people in the world who loved her like parents made tears spring to her eyes and her vision cleared.

No, God, I won't give in, she prayed wearily. *I will live for Megan, and for the memory of Stephen and Daphne.*

She sat still for a while, feeling more and more weary. A seductive whisper started in her mind.

You don't need them any more! You don't need Eric any more. You hold true power now, a generous gift of Gudarta, goddess of pain: a gift of immortality. What need have you of family or lovers? Gudarta will give you might and power aplenty and you can choose what lovers you will.

Part of Brandi thrilled at that gift and the power it promised. She felt a surge of intoxicating energies flow over her. She closed her eyes and exulted in the heady swirl of lust and greed.

Anything I want, I can have! No one can tell me "No"! All those who have harmed me or laughed at me or persecuted me will suffer.

She breathed deep of the dungeon air, feeling the power rising, held rapt by its intensity.

Yet somewhere inside her, a tiny light sparked to life. It reminded her of sunlight and spring days and the scent of flowers and the sound of church bells, and it brought to mind a tiny whispering sound.

With a start, Brandi shook her head and rose, fists balled at her side as she fought against the vampiric curse. She locked her eyes on the cross etched into the wall. Her hands trembled as she forced the seductive darkness to the side of her consciousness.

Her head swam from the effort and she leaned on the nearby wall, sliding down it in exhaustion, feeling the gritty stone against her naked hips and legs and loose dirt under her bare feet. Breathing heavily, she kept her eyes on the cross etched into the wall. Slowly, the evil urges diminished and she felt a great peace and calmness, along with a certainty of hope.

She pulled up a knee and laid her head down on it, rocking a little back and forth, feeling the stone floor against her skin and hearing only the occasional scrabble of a rat.

For the thousandth time, she prayed the Our Father.

Dungeon cells were supposed to be cold. In Torosc in winter, they were bearable.

She considered her captors, agents of the "Republic" of Torosc. Their viciousness and malice knew no bounds. However, she knew that they grasped the concept that true torture happened in the mind – physical torments had their limits. Besides, they had plans for Brandawyn Alenar.

Brandi had no idea what had been done to her. All the events of the past weeks melded together. She could remember nothing concrete after her capture except images of wild orgies and bloody, horrible tortures interspersed with a swirl of dark clouds and violently clashing colors. It was as if she screamed in agony for centuries, then had periods of complete loss of memory.

Somewhere in the fog of it all, she also recalled moments of soaring sexual ecstasy. They made her feel ashamed and guilty. She wondered what they had forced her to do and was glad she couldn't remember.

Of course, there was always that insidious voice, telling her to abandon her faith, her family, her friends, her love.

She curled her fingers into her palm, hoping that the pain would break through the seductive lure of vampirism.

They compel me because of the curse, but they are the ones who hold the burden of guilt, she reminded herself firmly. *I do not consent to their evil demands.*

A hollow feeling started in her middle and she curled up tighter. Her heart, already torn in two by the death of Stephen and Daphne, would simply stop beating if her only sister died. She knew it.

Megan, where are you?

She had given up the idea of ever seeing her love, either.

"Oh Eric," she whispered. "I so wanted to see you again…"

She heard footsteps outside her cell door and the rattle of a key in the lock. A red magical spark flared on the door and raced around the edges. Adina's voice floated in to her.

"Brandawyn, my dear, I have a nice surprise for you. You have been approved to begin your first task for the Ja'al. We have some pretty clothes for you and an exciting assignment, to the North."

Brandi shook her head, glaring defiantly up at Adina. The priestess stood in the light of the doorway, resplendent in a dark red dress, a golden belt around her waist, flanked by two guards in splint mail. They held staves that sparkled with purple light.

"Never!" Brandi spat. "I will never obey you."

Adina smirked. "Ah, but you will. I command you. Gudarta commands you."

She held up a hand and a ring on her pinky finger flashed crimson.

A wave of dark power swept over Brandi and she rose against her will, heedless of her nudity. Her vision turned red as another priestess entered holding a black dress and slippers.

"Yes, my mistress," Brandi answered in an echoing voice not her own.

Adina smiled. "Good girl."

The euphoria of limitless power and wild, uninhibited license surged within Brandi. Nothing in the universe mattered more than doing Adina's bidding. The woman who was Brandawyn Alenar receded into the background.

Yet that same defiant, vibrant spark remained, hidden within her.

They may think I am their slave, but my soul is still my own. I will watch and wait for my time. I will be free, with God as my witness.

Someday. Soon.

Appendix - Glossary

<u>Adalbert (Davis)</u> – The butler to Saren and Terenil DeMey (q.v.).

<u>Agent</u> - A spy, bounty hunter or thief, depending on context and the particular agent's morals and ethics. Connor Lomin, an agent, tended more towards the "spy" variety. Most agents provide a stealthy component to the groups they support. In military terms an agent would be part of a reconnaissance unit.

<u>Alenar, Brandawyn (Brandi)</u> - One of the original Grey Riders, a half-elven female, trained as a soldier and combat medic/corpsman. The older sister of Megan (q.v.), she and her family were persecuted for their Christian faith and eventually fled their homeland of Torosc under tragic circumstances. During her time with Dar Cabot and his friends, she fell in love with Eric Indidarc. Reserved but kind and devoutly religious, Brandi is quite pretty, with red-gold hair and violet eyes, but doesn't see herself as attractive. Brandawyn is also ambidextrous. Her pegasus is named Amicus.

<u>Alenar, Daphne</u> - Ranger knight and agent of the forces of good in the Realms. The only sister of Megan and Brandi's human mother, she spirited her nieces northward away from Torosc to safety. Sometimes thought of as overly serious (like her niece, Brandawyn), she served as a devoted mother-figure to the sisters after the death of their parents. Her brother is Stephen, a scholar and wizard.

<u>Alenar, Megan</u> - Another of the original Grey Riders and sister of Brandawyn Alenar, she attended college in Terenai and graduated as a wizard and scholar. Possessing red-gold hair like her sibling, Megan is friendly and outgoing, somewhat vain and impetuous, yet fiercely loyal and brave. She is also very attractive, with strawberry blonde hair and amber eyes, and is fond of baubles and fancy clothes. With her sister, she fled persecution in Torosc to arrive in Deran. She loves Dar Cabot (q.v.) and rides a pegasus named Larinor (q.v.).

<u>Alenar, Stephen</u> - Uncle of Brandawyn and Megan Alenar, he is the younger brother of Daphne Alenar. Despite being a scholar, Stephen is also a skilled warrior and wields potent magic in battle. He likes to tease both his sister and his nieces but regards them with deep and abiding affection.

<u>Alrihan</u> (Elv. "*light - seven*") – Coastal metropolis in western Deran (q.v.).

A very large city with more than 200,000 inhabitants, Alrihan is a major import/export hub and sports seven fortresses, each with its own distinctive tower lit by magical light. It is ruled by a Duke.

<u>Alyssa of Tor Haldin, Saint</u> – Powerful and holy queen of a petty kingdom during the late Paragon Age (q.v.), Alyssa ruled over a domain located in present-day Torosc (q.v.). Her battles against Zhinia Margoth (q.v.) near the ending of the age were legendary and all the more remarkable since Margoth was Alyssa's first cousin. After Margoth was finally defeated at the Battle of Three-Nation Lake and disappeared, Alyssa returned to her kingdom. She and her husband and family died ten years later when a combination of wild tribes and opportunistic foreign powers overran her war-depleted nation. Her crown is a relic of jaw-dropping power, bestowing impressive magical abilities, healing capabilities and protections to someone of sufficiently pure heart, though such a benefit it comes with a price.

<u>Amicus</u> (Lat. *"friend"*) Brandawyn Alenar's pegasus.

<u>Astarel</u> - Kingdom to the north of Deran, along the coast. The homeland of Buck Bydecy, it is a seafaring nation with a robust navy and an eclectic society comprised equally of elves, humans, dwarves and halflings.

<u>Benitez ORD, Gerardo, Colonel</u> – Military commander of espionage units for the Duke of Alrihan, Benitez is a member of the Royal Order of Deran (Orden Regis Deranensis) and titular Baron of Halfdan. Wry, perceptive and fatherly, Lord Benitez is a veteran of decades of service as spymaster.

<u>Bydecy ROA, Buckminster (Buck), Sir</u> - Another of the original Grey Riders, Buck is a tall, rangy, sandy-haired human male warrior and free-lance. He is a native of Tyler, Astarel and was made a Knight of the Royal Order of Astarel (ROA, a hereditary knighthood) after the Battle of Hillton (q.v.). His easygoing nature is often mistaken for boredom. His father is named Alfred and his brother is Jack and he has a sister named Summer. His pegasus is named Shadowbane (q.v.).

<u>Cabot OSK, Darius (Dar), Sir</u> - One original Grey Rider and native of the town of Forester on the northern border of the kingdom of Deran, Dar ran afoul of Ja'al goblin troops in the wilds and headed back to town for help, setting the events of *Whitehorse Peak* in motion. A young, dark-haired human male, he is a ranger/scout and adept in the woods. He grew to love Megan Alenar (q.v.) during their time together fighting the Ja'al near Forester. He

rides a pegasus named Virasi (Elv. *"white star"*). After the defeat of Zhinia Margoth (q.v.) he was knighted into the Order of Saint Kira (Orden Sancta Kiraensis).

Calsha, Eynem – (Elv. *"be calm, favorite of mine"*)

Carine – Druid leader of one of the many druidical groves near Oakmoor, Deran, she is a mentor and confidant of Buck Bydecy (q.v.) though she is only two years older. Dark-haired and green-eyed, she is a competent care-taker of the open lands near the city and can shape-change to the form of a black doe.

Cerberus Hound – An evil mutation of a normal hound, it is larger than a normal dog and boasts two or more heads. They have extraordinary senses and can detect invisible or hidden creatures. It is rumored that they were warped by evil magic by unscrupulous wizards or even daemons (q.v.).

Chamber of Decision – A mysterious place that the Riders (minus the Alenar sisters) encountered on the way to find the Helm of Shadows. Each Rider was separated from the others and shown two paths they could take in their lives— for good or ill. According to the Song of the Grey Riders, they had to choose.

Coastwatch - Seaside town in Torosc where the Alenar sisters were born and raised.

Crossed Swords - Guild of assassins based in Deran and Terenai. Founded and ruled by the Hylar family, the Crossed Swords are often used by evil forces to eliminate opposition. Eric Indidarc's real family name is Hylar and he is a son of the guild master; he escaped his former life and was adopted by Melinor Indidarc (q.v.)

Culver, Arlene, Countess – Lady and ruler of Harlnisville (q.v.). She is middle-aged, with brown hair and green eyes and is significantly younger than her husband. Her eyes indicate she thinks much but says little.

Culver, Dunston, Count – Lord and ruler of Harlinsville (q.v.). He is over seventy but spry and shrewd. He hires the Grey Riders to investigate a series of mysterious murders in his city.

Daemon - Evil to the core, the otherworldly race of daemons spend most of their time trying to overthrow the Elohir (q.v.) or conquer various regions of Damora. They are known as the Fallen because legend has it that they were originally Elohir who turned to the side of evil and worship of themselves (and the Dark One). While many Daemons look like nightmarish beasts, some are very attractive and almost human-like or elven in appearance. The overriding philosophy of the Daemons is that Damora is a free zone, ripe for the picking.

<u>Damora</u> - Imaginary world setting for the Grey Riders novels. The fourth planet orbiting the star 82 Eridani, it is roughly 1.15 times the size of Earth and possesses climate regions and flora/fauna similar to Earth. The parent star is a G5V spectral class, main-sequence yellow star approximately 20 light years from Earth. It has two moons, Kaliri and Diometrius, which provide both tidal forces and substantial moonlight for the planet's surface. The technology level of Damora approximates the High Middle Ages of real life, with significant differences due to the use of magic and scientific advancement.

<u>Darlon</u> - Major city in Northern Deran, pop ~ 70,000. Home to people of many races, creeds and professions, it is a trading center and university town. Ruled by a duke, it controls trade, borders and access between Deran and the northernmost nations of Astarel, Elder and Rokon.

<u>DeMey, Saren</u> - The half-sister of Eric Indidarc by adoption, Saren DeMey was found by Melinor Indidarc as an infant and raised by him and his wife, Anne. A devout Christian, Saren appears to be a complete contradiction in terms as she is half-daemon but fights for the forces of good. Dark-haired and dark-eyed, she transforms to a bat-winged, horned half-daemon at will. Saren continually guards against her daemonic background, as it is a permanent temptation to lust and savagery; however, to the common folk of Deran, she is known to be unfailingly kind, warm, generous, wise and gentle. As the wife of Terenil, the Earl of the Oakmoor (q.v.) suburb of Tallemar, she is a Countess of Deran.

<u>DeMey, Terenil</u> - The half-elven husband of Saren, he is an earl and the ruler of Tallemar, a suburb of Oakmoor, Deran. A skilled wizard and soldier in his own right, he is adaptable, thoughtful and unfailingly kind. His devotion to Saren is unquestioned. He has a personal guard of a platoon of magic-wielding armored knights. As part of the Foreign Ministry of Deran, he is privy to information about other nations and is rumored to have an extensive spy network.

<u>Deran</u> - Constitutional monarchy in the northern lands of the Western

continent of Damora (q.v.). A nation built from the remnants of the Esten Empire, Deran is also a meritocracy, where nobles are elected by their peers and the legislature based on merit and ability more than noble connections. Deran has an advanced network of roads, potent military, and several universities. The seat of the Christian Church, Saint Martin's Town (St. Martin's) is in Deran.

Detlef - The young half-elven clerk and assistant to Edward Cardinal Simpson (q.v.), Papal Nuncio (q.v.) to Damora.

Devrin, Rongit – Dwarven scholar and expert in ancient histories and archeology. He is somewhat down on his luck due to losing out on a power struggle in the court of the Duke of Bildur, Merdail.

Diometrius – The larger of Damora's two moons.

Dwarf - One of the major races of Damora. The term "Dwarf" comes from the ancient elvish word, *duarfaen* (Elv. *duar* = 'stone' + *fae/ fey/ fej* = 'magic', literally "those of stone-magic"). A typical dwarf male is about four feet six inches tall. Dwarves tend to be burly, sturdy or muscular for their size and can live for almost two hundred years. Males are often bearded (though not all are). They are generally honorable and appreciate strength and resolve in others. Their main talent, as indicated by the name bestowed on them by the Elves, is in stonework and metallurgy.

Dwarfshire - A town in Evendale with almost equal numbers of dwarves and halflings. One of the few areas with accessible minerals in the halfling nation, it has a peculiar character to it because of the dominant races. Many of the gnomes (a mix of dwarf and halfling) in Evendale come from the region.

East River – One of the large rivers that flows through the Deranese capital of Oakmoor (q.v.)

Earth Mother – Nature-concept deification of the world of Damora as expounded by the Druids. Roughly equivalent to the concept of Gaia in the real world.

Eleandir SMT, IO, Andyn, Lady – One of the Grey Riders, Andyn is a priestess of the Elven god Verian and a wizard. She has honey-blonde hair and amber eyes, a trim figure and a marvelous singing voice. Rather impatient and quick-tempered, she nonetheless displays unwavering faith, mercy, warmth and a nimble mind. She is a widow whose husband was killed by Crossed Swords (q.v.) assassins. At the Battle of Hillton (q.v.), she used a holy relic (the Crown of Saint Alyssa (q.v.)) to destroy Zhinia Margoth (q.v.). For her exploits, she was knighted by the Elven Empire of Terenai (q.v.) and given the title of Light of Justice and Lichslayer. She is styled as Lady Andyn Eleandir, Servant of Mindra of Terenai, Imperial Order, Light of Justice. Her pegasus is named Medianox (Lat. *"midnight"*).

Eldir – A nation of the Northern Alliance, Eldir is a patriarchate and the seat of the faith of Verian. Possessing a climate similar to Germany in the real world, it used to be at odds with Rokon (q.v.), a breakaway duchy, until the need for collaboration against the forces of evil caused them to bury the hatchet. It is ruled by the Patriarch of Verian.

Eleison (Gr. *"have mercy"*) – A powerful magic horseman's mace found by the Grey Riders near Twinspire Mountain during the search for the Helm of Shadows (q.v.). It strikes against evil with holy power and amplifies healing magic. Andyn Eleandir carries it and another, lesser magic mace; the smaller size of a horseman's mace (as opposed to the more massive footman's mace) allows her two wield them ambidextrously.

Elf - One of the major races of Damora. The term "Elf" comes from the ancient word for their race, *Ellfaen* (Elv. *ell* = 'life' + *fae/ fey/ fej* -= 'magic', literally "those of life-magic"). Elves are more slender than humans and possess intriguing eye colors, such as aqua, amber or violet; they also have a slight point to top of the ear, though this is not usually pronounced or even noted if the ears are concealed under hair, hat or helm. Elves tend to be a bit more reserved than the other races and have more of an affinity for magic of all kinds. They possess skills for getting along well with animals and have a remarkable talent for healing trees and plants.

Elohir - Denizen of the planet of Celestia (the 5th planet of the 61 Virginis star, a single G6 spectral class, main-sequence yellow star approximately 28 light years from Earth). Sometimes called "Celestials", they appear to be winged humans. Skin color covers the range of typical shades seen in humans (porcelain, tanned, brown, yellow, dark brown) and their eyes are the color of jewels. Their beauty is often described as 'unearthly'. All possess potent magical and martial skills but are usually reluctant to meddle in the affairs of Damorans. They are uniformly kind, wise, honest and just. Elohir live extremely long lives (~ 1000 years) if not killed in warfare with their evil kindred.

Erleth - In the middle of the Greatsea is the tropical island group known as the Erlethi Empire, or simply Erleth. Blessed with a Hawaii-like climate and an energetic people, it is the predominant naval and economic power in the south. There are a total of twenty-one islands, ranging in size from over 200 square miles to barely over 10. The Empire trades freely with all the nations along the Western seaboard, but keeps a wary eye on Torosc. It is a favorite resort vacation spot for travelers from all nations who have the money to get there.

Esten Empire - An empire formed of various kingdoms controlling much of the known world during the second age of Damora (known as the Imperial Age and denoted in calendars by the letters IY (for Imperial Year)). It fell after over a thousand years of rule due to infighting, a breakdown in the social fabric and the influence of evil.

Evendale - Small halfling nation south east of Deran and northeast of Terenai (q.v.). A republic, Evendale consists of seven districts or counties, each of which have a prescribed number of representatives (aldermen) and senators who draft laws that are approved by the High Minister, another elected position. A land with mild climate and productive farmland, Evendale nonetheless has a border with the Wilderness, which means the halflings are always on vigilant watch, having been invaded by evil tribes from the wild lands multiple times. Its capital city is Lakeview.

Eye of Truth - A magical diamond, the Eye of Truth is actually a sort of lens that allows the owner to see the true nature of things and people. It can detect evil or good auras, see through illusion and discern truth from lies. It was crafted by an ancestor of Buck Bydecy (q.v.) and is owned by him.

Falcon, Order of – Christian order of free-lance sell-swords spanning the gamut of occupations and professions, from warriors to wizards. The most numerous of all the Christian Orders on Damora, the Falcons have an elite special operations group called the Kestrel Knights, Servants of Mary (KKOSM) whose colors are black, gold and white. The Kestrels are known for lightning raids, bravery and the ability to adapt to any required role, from heavy infantry to reconnaissance. Some are trained in airborne riding.

Faldanor ORD, Andareth, Lord - Half-elf healer and wizard, retired. He and his free-lance group, the Four Silvers, defeated the evil wizard Galchimor in the wilderness near Evendale, mapping the route to Twinspire Mountain which was eventually used by the Grey Riders to find the Crown of Saint Alyssa (q.v.). He and his wife, Sidara, are Count and Countess of Deorfast, a mountain city in Deran. Though not a member of the Order of the Three Magi (q.v.) he often assists them on behalf of his wife. He and Sidara are both Christian.

Faldanor OTM, ORD, Sidara, Lady – The wife of Lord Andareth Faldanor, Count of Deorfast, Sidara is an elven wizard, a member of the Order of the Three Magi (q.v.) and the Royal Order of Deran. She met Andareth when part of his free-lance adventuring group, the Four Silvers. They fell in love, married and were elected Baron/Baroness, then Count/Countess after their retirement from free-lancing. She is very conservative, extremely pretty, and has a rascally sense of humor. She and Andareth have two children.

Fallbrook, Larad - The deceased husband of Andyn Eleandir (q.v.), Larad was assassinated by agents of the Crossed Swords Guild (q.v.). He was a carpenter by trade and childhood friend of the Eleandir family.

Fidelis – A magic spear that can contract to the size of a dagger or telescope to the length of a medium infantry spear, it was awarded to Eric Indidarc by Melissa of Celestia (q.v.). It strikes with great power against evil things and, if thrown, returns unerringly to its wielder's hand via teleport when called. Though Melissa did not say it, there is some speculation that it is from the Paragon Age (q.v.).

Firedart - A magical attack spell used by wizards and sorcerers. It is essentially a small projectile of flame with a detonable core that looks rather like a tiny comet and a limited range (about 100 feet or so). It produces the effect equivalent to a 9 mm pistol bullet and rarely misses.

Firefall (Conspiracy of the)– A conspiracy from the time of Melinor's mother and father (Telric and Cara Indidarc(q.v.)). Its details are considered top-secret. The Council of the Order of the Three Magi does not discuss it openly, but it is obvious that a disaster of Biblical proportions was averted when the conspiracy was defeated.

Forester - Large town along the northern border highway of Deran. Forester is ruled by a baron and controls trade along the borderlands. Its defining feature is the central town proper, which is surrounded by a tall, well-built palisade with giant, living trees as its guard towers. It is the hometown of Dar Cabot (q.v.)

Fortuna, Elisa – Fictional aunt of Connor Lomin's alias, Neville Pennyhand.

Gnome - Half-breed race resulting from the marriage of halfling and dwarf, gnomes possess features from each parent: natural affinity for stone and the underground from the dwarves and a cheerful disposition and natural talent with all things organic. Somewhat taller than halflings but shorter than dwarves, gnomes are industrious and found in all the known lands. They usually have dark hair, tan-to-dark complexions, and brown, amber or grey eyes. A typical gnome lives about 180 years or so.

Goblin - Short, half-simian creatures who often serve as foot-soldiers for the forces of evil, looking somewhat like horned chimpanzees. Extremely agile and able to use any available weapon that is sized for them, they are also good at hiding in shadows. They dislike sunlight. Their social structure is usually in a hierarchical monarchy, with the chieftain or king of a particular tribe wielding absolute authority. Goblins particularly hate dwarves since the two races compete for underground areas and resources. They are capable miners and are about the size of a gnome or tall halfling (a few inches short of four feet tall).

Gonosz, Professor – An underhanded, duplicitous and sly dwarven scholar who framed Rongit Devrin (q.v.) for plaigiarism.

Gorlak - A goblin formerly in the employ of the Ja'al, he switched sides after the Battle of Hillton (q.v.) when his life was spared by the Riders. Captured after the battle, he was asked to join the household of the Papal Nuncio (q.v.). Under the Nuncio's tutelage and care, he flourished and often serves as a spy, with devastating success since no one would ever consider a Christian goblin. He admires the Grey Riders, adores Andyn and Saren, and soaks up new learning like a sponge.

Gorostol (Dw. *'friend alliance'*) – A large and somewhat eclectic nation south of Terenai (q.v.) and north of Torosc (q.v.). Originally founded by dwarves, over the years it attracted folk of all races. It is now a buffer state between the oppressive Republic to the south and the Elven Empire to the north.

Grey Riders – The formerly free-lance mercenary group famous for defeating Zhinia Margoth (q.v.) at the Battle of Hillton. The original members were Buck Bydecy (q.v.), Dar Cabot (q.v.), Eric Indidiarc (q.v.), Connor Lomin (q.v.), Andyn Eleandir (q.v.) and the Alenar sisters, Brandawyn and Megan (q.v.). After the departure of the Alenars, they added Hlerv (Handor Lervion) (q.v.) to their numbers.

Grey Riders, Song Of – An ancient prophetic poem from the Church of Irial (q.v.) it foretold the coming of riders on winged horses who would save a kingdom from a horrible evil. It came true when the real Grey Riders (q.v.) destroyed Zhinia Margoth (q.v.), a lich princess, at the Battle of Hillton.

Gudarta - The evil goddess of torture and suffering, the seductive and sadistic Gudarta is a member of the Ja'al pantheon.

Guide, The – A mysterious figure from Handor Lervion's (q.v.) past who gave him the set of equations and algorithms necessary for controlling the Helm of Shadows (q.v.). His motivations are unknown.

Half-Elf - The offspring of a union between an elf (q.v.) and human, half-elves are a mix of their parents' heritage: magically talented, strong, adaptable and capable of learning new skills quickly. If it were not for the fact that they are noticeably larger than elves by a couple of inches in height, they would be indistinguishable from elves due to their predilection to inherit their elven parent's eye color, hair color and ear shape. Half-elves live to between 100 and 150 years.

Halfling - The smallest of the races, halflings (from the elven for "those of hearth magic" - *haliv-fae*) prefer pastoral villages and countrysides to large cities, though they are at home in any setting. As adaptable as humans, halflings have a talent for craftsmanship (with things other than stone) and farming. They are known for their skill in the kitchen and the durability of their finished goods. Their hair color (blonde, brown or black), skin color (porcelain to dark brown) and eye color (blue, green, black or grey) remind the other races of miniature humans. They live about 100 years or so.

Harlinsville – A mid-sized suburb of the Deranese capital of Oakmoor (q.v.), Harlinsville has about 35,000 inhabitants. It is ruled by Lord Dunston and Lady Arlene, Count and Countess.

Helm of Shadows – A magical helmet manufactured by Zhinia Margoth (q.v.), it allows its wielder to teleport great distances if the keywords are known. Since Margoth's destruction, it has been claimed by Handor Lervion (q.v.). Ineffably and wholly evil, it is a perilous item that seeks to pervert its bearer.

Heritage Stone - A magical item, a Heritage Stone is used to prove paternity and lineage. It uses magical analysis of DNA from a blood sample to ascertain the relationship of the subject to a predetermined DNA pattern associated with a target family or person.

Hillton - Fortified city (pop ~ 27,000) positioned on the shores of Sun Lake, a very large body of fresh water on the plains near the center of the country. It is ruled by a Count. Due to its position on the plains, it is a major trading center and hub for agricultural areas nearby. It was the site of a siege and battle when Zhinia Margoth (q.v.) invaded Deran from the Wilderness. The battle ended when Andyn Eleandir (q.v.) used the Crown of Saint Alyssa (q.v.) to destroy Margoth. Her army disintegrated without her iron will to keep them from attacking one another.

Hippogriff – Creatures that are half-eagle and half-horse, they are used as military steeds and transports. They can wear barding (armor specifically designed for mounts) and carry two riders.

Hlerv (Handor Lervion) - A gnome wizard and spy, he joined the Grey Riders in *Eye of Truth* and helped them clear Buck Bydecy's name and avenge the murder of Andyn Eleandir's husband. Secretive and somewhat aloof, he is nevertheless loyal, resourceful and intelligent, possessing a sometimes wry and sardonic sense of humor. Despite the openness of the other Riders, he is not comfortable sharing any information about his past and makes up a pseudonym that is an amalgamation of his real name. He has a penchant for chemistry. Connor Lomin (q.v.) lets him ride on his pegasus, Phantom. He is the heir of the fortune of the Lervion family, owners of a trans-national shipping line based in Gorostol.

Human - Humans on Damora (q.v) are much like real-life people of the planet Earth, with the exception that they can use magic in the same manner as elves, dwarves, halflings and other denizens of the fourth planet of 82 Eridani. Humans are energetic, adaptable, learn quickly and are endlessly curious about Damora and its people, flora and fauna. They live in all climates and places that will welcome them. The origin of the word "human" has no

Damoran equivalent as it does not translate from any Elven or Dwarven syntax.

Humana - Language of the human race on Damora (q.v.).

Hylar, Harkin – The leader of the Guild of Crossed Swords (q.v.), he is the father of Eric Indidarc, who ran away from the Guild at an early age because he was sickened by the ways of the assassins. A crude yet calculating man, Harkin tends to think before acting and carefully plans for contingency scenarios. He tends to view people as objects to be used rather than individuals. His official wife is Taramis (q.v.), an elven priestess of Neralia (q.v), though marital fidelity is only a marginal concept at best for followers of the Ja'al (q.v.).

Hylar, Taramis – The nominal wife of Harkin Hylar of the Guild of Crossed Swords (q.v.), she provides magical and spiritual resources for the guild. She is Eric Indidarc's birth mother, though she views him more as an annoyance and a failure than anything else. Vulgar, profane and savage, Taramis is nonetheless stunningly beautiful and haughty and possesses impressive magical abilities. She views all other females as competition to be eliminated or manipulated.

Hylar, Terrell – Eric Indidarc's older brother, he serves his father as a front man for interfacing with the world of legitimate business while also performing as a broker for the Guild.

Indidarc OST, Cara, Baroness – The mother of Melinor and Kalinor Indidarc, she was shipwrecked without identification on the coast of Targanon (q.v.) at the age of four and lost her entire family. Taken in by the royal family of Targanon as a slave, she was immediately noticed for her superior intelligence and made a personal attendant of one of the queens of that land. She accompanied Telric Indidarc (q.v.) on a secret mission and helped him defeat a great evil in Deran. They married and became Baron and Baroness of Kiarre, Deran. Cara was known for her intellect, sense of justice and discernment. A human, she died at age 92.

Indidarc SSM, Eric, Sir - One of the original Grey Riders, Eric is the adopted son of Melinor Indidarc (q.v.) a famous wizard. Able to use magic and martial weapons with equal proficiency, Eric is cheerful, optimistic and friendly. He treats everyone he meets with the same courtesy and kindness, whether a beggar or noble. Eric has violet eyes and blond hair and is a half-elf (q.v.). His pegasus is named Niveral (Elv. "*snow bright*"). For his role in the defeat of Zhinia Margoth (q.v.), he was made a Knight of the Order of Saint Michael (*Servus Sancta Michael*). He seeks redemption by means of bringing down the Crossed Swords guild (q.v.), run by his birth parents.

Indidarc OTM, Melinor, Lord - High Wizard of the northern kingdom of Deran, nobleman and confidante of royalty in the Kingdoms of the Northern Alliance (q.v.). He adopted both Eric and Saren (q.v) after his own children were grown. A formidable ally and genius with knowledge of magic, science, medicine, literature and history, Melinor is fluent in several languages. A kind but somewhat absent-minded man, he is singularly focused on thwarting evil plots in the known lands.

Indidarc OF, Telric, Baron – The husband of Cara and father of Kalinor and Melinor, he was a military officer who was sent across the sea to Targanon on a secret mission. There, he met the slave Cara, who helped him defeat a menace to the land of Deran. A half-elf, he was already in his 60's when he met his future wife. He died at the age of 148. He was a warrior, a knight of the Order of the Falcon, and a mage, though not of the same ability as Cara. After his marriage, he was made Baron of Kiarre, Deran.

Irial - The halfling god of harvests, craftsmen and home, Irial is a benevolent deity who sometimes counts elves and humans among his adherents. The precepts of Irial are hospitality, kindness, courtesy, respect for people, animals and nature, and steadfastness in the face of hardship, whether caused by nature or evil designs.

Ja'al - Also known as the Manipulator Church (for their penchant for twisting words, lying and otherwise using others callously for their own ends) the Ja'al are one of the evil religions on Damora. The cult is a polytheistic religion worshiping a number of harsh and cruel deities. The precepts of the Ja'al are world domination, rule of the strong over the weak, eugenics, personal gain at the cost of others, and treachery.

Jandren, Tahni – Andyn Eleandir's (q.v.) alias when she tries to draw out the Crossed Swords (q.v.) in Harlinsville.

Jered – A large nation south of Torosc (q.v.), it is a confederacy of kingdoms originally established by pirates. Possessing miles of coastline, a multitude of islands, and a tropical climate, Jered is wealthy, powerful, and an ally of Torosc in opposing the Northern Alliance (q.v.).

Jervan – A halfling day laborer and sometime spy/thief in the capital city of Meridian, Gorostol.

Jolek OTM, GA, Konadar, Lord – Dwarven Christian member of the Order of the Three Magi. Konadar hails from Merdail (q.v.) where, prior to joining the Order, he distinguished himself as a free-lance wizard. He was given the title of "*Gorost Algrodin*", meaning "*Royal Friend*" for his efforts on behalf of the dwarven kingdom. He is irascible, crusty, perceptive and brilliant and counts both Melinor Indidarc (q.v.) and Sidara Faldanor (q.v.) as close personal friends.

Kaliri – The smaller of the two moons of Damora.

Karandi OTM, Simrit, Lord – Another of the members of the Order of the Three Magi (q.v), Simrit is dark-skinned, dark-eyed, reserved and calm. Along with his impressive arsenal of magic skills, he is an expert in ancient history, including geography and anthropology. He originally hails from Targanon (q.v.) but lives in Northern Terenai (q.v.) among elves, though he is human. His wife is an elf and they have six children.

Kaljirre (Dw. "*sky mirror*") - Beautiful lake near the Gorostolian capital city of Meridian.

Kenwall - A suburb of Meridian, Gorostol.

Kortos – An alliance of duchies on the great island of Derelia, northwest from Deran across the GreatSea.

Larinor – (Elv. "*ranger*" or "*faithful guide*") Megan Alenar's pegasus.

Lervion, Hannah – The sister of Handor (q.v.), Hannah was studying at a military academy at the time of the death of both her parents. A fierce defender of her family with a high sense of justice, she is forthright, honest, friendly and open. She worries constantly about her absent brother, who is the only family she has left in the world. A brown-eyed brunette, she is fit and very attractive but acts like the girl next door.

Lich - An undead wizard. Liches are created when a wizard or sorcerer makes a pact with Dark Powers in order to forestall his/her own death, gaining immense magical power and undead status in the bargain. They perpetually exude an aura of terror but are greatly harmed by holy spells and items.

Lomin, Connor - Another of the original Grey Riders, Connor is a halfling who hails from Evendale (q.v.). Serious, but with a somewhat ribald sense of humor, Connor appears stoic and sober most of the time. He is knowledge-able about traps, curious about ancient ruins and secrets, and wields a broad-sword, a rather heavy weapon for a halfling. Dark-eyed and dark-haired, he has a muscular build but has an almost uncanny skill for moving unseen. His pegasus is named Phantom.

Lomin, Janey - Deceased wife of Connor Lomin. She and her mother-in-law were at odds before her wedding to Connor due to several differences, not least of which were her friends of somewhat unsavory reputation and the fact that she was pregnant at the time of her wedding. They eventually rec-onciled not long before Janey perished in a plague from the Wilderness known as the Whispering Death (q.v.).

Lomin, Rose - Deceased daughter of Connor Lomin, aged just less than a year. Only a few hours after the passing of her mother from the Whispering Death, Rose died. Connor Lomin sometimes dreams of her.

Lonmar – Major river that flows through the Deranese capital of Oak-moor (q.v.).

Margoth, Zhinia - A former Paragon Queen (q.v.) who used fell and evil magics to transform herself into an undead sorceress (a lich) to avoid death near the end of the Paragon Age. Margoth is vicious, conniving, and cruel. She appeared as a skeleton with pinpoint eyes of purple light, clothed in rot-ting royal robes and wielding a skull-headed staff. Her standard was a fanged skull with a crown of flame. Andyn Eleandir (q.v.) destroyed her at the Battle of Hillton, Deran (q.v.) using a powerful holy relic. She created a cursed magic helmet of teleportation named the Helm of Shadows (q.v.).

Medianox (Lat. "*midnight*") – The name of Andyn Eleandir's pegasus.

Melen – Large seafaring nation on the great island of Derelia, across the sea from Deran.

Melissa - An Elohir (q.v.) knight tasked with watching for the Grey Riders to arrive at Twinspire Mountain. She gave the Crown of Saint Alyssa (q.v.) to Andyn Eleandir to use in bringing down Zhinia Margoth. She also provided the angelic sword Rhindara Starblade (q.v.) to Dar Cabot, the elven fire-blade Tiuz (q.v.) to Connor Lomin, and the magic spear Fidelis (q.v.) to Eric In-didarc. She is wise, kind, fierce in defending against evil and seems to be perpetually amused by the Grey Riders, whom she regards with great affection. She is stunningly gorgeous but acts like she doesn't know it.

Mense Motus (Lat. "*mind move*") - A spell of telekinesis.

Meridian – The capital city of Gorostol (q.v.), it is a large metropolis in the foothills overlooking a beautiful lake known as the Kaljirre (Dw. "*sky mirror*"). It has over 200,000 inhabitants.

Mikman, Kili – A halfling spy in the service of the Ja'al High Command, Kili has a long history with the Grey Riders. Along with his companion, James LeFond, he initially tried to recruit Megan and Brandawyn Alenar to the service of the Ja'al, but that failed when Brandi refused. He and James were routed by Dar and his friends in the ensuing brawl. Later, he schemed against the Riders when they attempted to find the person responsible for the death of Andyn's husband and kidnapped Buck's father, but this also failed. He has an intense hatred for Connor Lomin. Kili has an assortment of clever devices for spying and following targets.

Mindra – A Verian hero from the Paragon Age (q.v.). A soldier in the service of her king, she followed his orders without question until, in a vision from Verian, she realized that he was being manipulated by his councilors into oppressing those who disagreed with him. Taking up arms against the councilors, she was pursued but prevailed with the aid of the Church of Verian. She ultimately defeated her enemies, converting two of them and returning the king to the ways of justice. She is the epitome of the concepts of mercy, bravery, wisdom and discernment and is often invoked by those seeking to cut through the lies of the forces of evil.

Minnie (Walters) – Maidservant to Terenil and Saren DeMey (q.v.).

Neralia - Evil goddess of child sacrifice, murder and domination, Neralia is one of the members of the Ja'al pantheon. Similarities between her church and the defunct worship of Garon-Zith (q.v.) have led many to speculate that the two goddesses are one and the same.

New Faith – Term sometimes used by non-Christians on Damora (q.v.) to describe Christianity.

Northern Alliance - A multinational alliance similar to NATO in the real world, the Alliance is composed of Deran, Astarel, Rokon, Eldir, Evendale and Terenai.

Oakmoor - The capital city of Deran, home to over a quarter of a million people. Oakmoor is based on three large hills at the confluence of the East River and Lonmar Rivers. It has several suburbs in addition to the main city proper.

Ogre - Large, human-like creatures with fangs and odd-colored hair, ogres are brutish, violent, and not particularly bright. Their leaders are usually the more intelligent members of a particular tribe. Some of their number are smart enough to use magic. They are usually over seven feet tall and three hundred and fifty pounds. Used as shock troops by the forces of evil, Ogres are also greedy and fearless.

Paladin's Rest Inn – The finest, most expensive inn and tavern in Oakmoor, Deran, it sports a rooftop atrium that doubles as a reception area and feasting hall. Its most notable feature is the glass dome that is placed over the atrium in winter and removed in summer, a feat of engineering that draws onlookers from all over (considering that the atrium is 100 feet in diameter).

Paractus - A magical medallion like Stealth (q.v.), Paractus is much more powerful. Its owner, Daphne Alenar, can summon a magical construct in the shape of a massive giant owl, nine feet tall at the head and sporting a saddle capable of bearing two riders.

Paragon Age – One of the major epochs of the history of Damora, it was ushered in by the event known as the Skyfire, when humans first appeared and brought Christianity with them. Records prior to this time are sketchy and incomplete. It is so named because of the rise of rulers of petty kingdoms who were all superior practitioners of a particular branch of a free-lance career (i.e. warrior, healer, mage, etc.). It ended when some of the Paragon rulers succumbed to evil influences and tried to expand their nations at the expense of their neighbors. Alyssa of Tor Aldin (q.v.) and Zhinia Margoth (q.v.) were two Paragon rulers.

Patian, Richard – An agent of the Crossed Swords Assassins Guild (q.v.), he leads a team of thugs and murderers in the Deranese city of Alrihan (q.v.).

Pegasus – A winged horse. In the Grey Riders novels, they are omnivores due to their part-raptor heritage and can be domesticated. They are wildly expensive to acquire and maintain and are the fastest flying mounts alive.

Pennyhand, Neville – Alias that Connor Lomin (q.v.) uses during the hunt of the Grey Riders (q.v.) for the leaders of the Guild of Crossed Swords.

Phantom – The name of Connor Lomin's pegasus.

Puup - Buck Bydecy's pet pigeon who somehow manages to avoid getting killed despite being in or near several battles.

Red Griffon Inn – Tavern and Inn in Oakmoor city (proper). Known for the two red-tipped griffon feathers in a trophy case; there is dispute as to their true origin.

Reilly OTM, Finbar, Lord - A secret member of the Order of the Three Magi, he is blond, blue-eyed and sports a scar along his jaw line, making him look rakish. Despite this, his background is in logistics and supply and he owns a set of warehouses in Seacrest (q.v.), Alrihan (q.v.) and Fenbluff (q.v.), Deran. Like all the members of the order, he is a formidable wizard. He also has advanced knowledge of healing magic.

Rhivan, Alec – Heir to the ancient southern kingdom of Turis Rhi, he is the husband of Elizabeth and father of Henry (Emeric). He is tall, dark-haired and blue-eyed and about forty-two years old. A skilled wizard, he is also very cagey and has a sophisticated network of spies in Northern Torosc for the sole purpose of maintaining his family secret.

Rhivan, Elizabeth – The wife of Alec, Crown Prince of Turis Rhi, she is pleasant-looking in a plain sort of way with brown hair and eyes. Her rather average appearance masks a fierce determination and formidable healing skills. She worries constantly about her eleven-year-old son, Henry, having lost his older brother and sister already.

Rhivan, Emeric (Henry) – The son of Elizabeth and Alec, Prince Henry of Turis Rhi is eleven but looks younger due to the hardships of life in Torosc. He is precocious, fearless and a little foolhardy, but very sly and intelligent. He idolizes Brandawyn Alenar.

Rokon – A member of the Northern Alliance, Rokon is one of the smaller nations. Originally a duchy of the Patriarchate of Eldir (q.v.), Rokon broke away prior to the forming of the alliance. The two countries have since resolved their differences, attributable to the need for teamwork as required by the Alliance charter. Rokon has a climate much like Norway in the real world.

Saint Benjamin – A city in the nation of Gorostol. Named for one of the first dwarven saints, it is a seat of learning and has institutions of all the major world religions.

Saint Kira, Order of – Christian order of military scouts, guides, mages and agents operating worldwide. They are often members of elite strike teams.

Saint Martin's (Town) - Major port city in Deran (pop ~ 80,000). It is the seat of the Christian church and the base of the Curia, the ruling council of Christianity on Damora. The Papal Nuncio (q.v.) makes his residence there.

Saint Thomas, Order of - Christian order of musicians, artists and writers who try to counter propaganda that is subtly introduced into society by the forces of evil.

Saint Michael, Order of - Christian military order of knights and warriors dedicated to protecting the innocent against evil. They are often used as heavy assault infantry or cavalry but include mages and clerics among their numbers.

Sarkany – The smallest and swiftest of the dragon sub-races, Sarkany about twenty feet long and weigh upwards of eight hundred pounds. They can breathe a stinging acid at their targets. Like all dragon-kind, they can choose between Light and Darkness and some can become wizards.

Seacrest – As its name implies, a large coastal city in Deran (q.v.), with a population over 50,000.

Shadow Sculpt – A magic spell that renders the caster blurry to the naked eye and confuses exact location. Someone under a Shadow Sculpt spell could move twenty feet from their original location and go unnoticed.

Shadow Lake - Medium sized freshwater lake in the wilderness east of Evendale. It lies in the shadow of the local mountains, one of which is Twinspire (q.v.). It is near the location of a ruined fortress where the Grey Riders found the Helm of Shadows (q.v.) and were given powerful magic items, such as Tiuz (q.v.).

Shriek - A magical infantry sword found by the Grey Riders near Twinspire Mountain. It makes its wielder stealthier and does great harm to undead. It is owned by Handor Lervion (q.v.), otherwise known as Hlerv, one of the Grey Riders.

Shrikes – Another assassins guild on Damora (q.v.), it often competes with the Crossed Swords (q.v.) and the Whiteclaw (q.v.) for business. Its emblem is a small black bird sitting atop a white skull.

Silvervale – A wealthy suburb of Meridian (q.v.) where Handor Lervion's (q.v.) ancestral home is located.

Simpson OTM, O.Praem, Edward Cardinal – The official representative of Christianity to Damora, the Papal Nuncio. Edward Simpson is a spare human man who appears to be about seventy years old but is rumored to be much older. His nation of origin is unknown. Though he has great knowledge and is alleged to have awesome, otherworldly powers, he rarely takes part in any action and is content to lead the Order of the Three Magi and Christendom on Damora. His demeanor is humble, thoughtful, and kind, yet demanding. He is known for asking probing questions. To those he knows well, he insists they call him "Father Edward".

Skyfire - A mysterious event from antiquity that changed the face of Damora (q.v.) Legends say that visitors from another place arrived on disks or globes of fire and brought with them the Christian faith. The location of the actual arrival and the details of the event are lost in history. As a point of reference, it is rumored to have taken place more than 5000 years before the events of *Whitehorse Peak* (the first of the Grey Riders novels).

Skullhead Legion - Paramilitary guard force in the service of the Ja'al cult leadership. Known for their brutality, greed and utter disregard for life, they are often used as shock troops. They are fanatical and fight to the death.

Spectral Sword / Sword of the Devoted Defender – A magical blade, it is actually contained in a small silver brooch. It is individually keyed to one person only. At the command word, a misty, ethereal sword leaps into being in front of the owner of the brooch. The spectral blade defends its owner and attacks any other opponents on command. It can harm apparitions such as ghosts, specters and wraiths. Connor Lomin (q.v.) owns one as a reward for his part in the victory over Zhinia Margoth (q.v.).

Starsilver - A light and strong metal similar to titanium alloy (Ti-6Al-4V) but stronger and with a greater amount of flexibility. It is very expensive and is often used in the fashioning of armor.

Stealth - Eric Indidarc's enchanted familiar. Summoned from a magic item called a Companion Pin, it transforms to a realistic hawk upon command. When active, he gives Eric the ability to see through his eyes as he flies high above.

Sun Lake - Body of fresh water near the Deranese city of Hillton.

<u>Tahni</u> – Crossed Swords assassin. A pert and attractive halfling lass, she is nonetheless deadly and immoral.

<u>Tallemar</u> – A major suburb of Oakmoor (q.v.), Deran, it is home to more than 30,000 souls. It is ruled by the DeMeys, Earl Terenil and Countess Saren.

<u>Tennyson, Juliette</u> – A stout woman with a penchant for flashy clothes, she is one of Harkin Hylar's chief agents and has the authority to approve assassination contracts. She has a talent for sniffing out spies.

<u>Terenai</u> (Elv. *"Realm of the Elves"*) - The hereditary homeland of the Elven people, Terenai lies due south of Deran and also shares borders with Evendale (q.v.), Gorostol and Merdail. A verdant and fruitful land, it is heavily forested in places. It is ruled by an Emperor (or Empress) and is the oldest of the nations on Deran. Its capital city is Mil-Tereth (Elv. *"King's Palace"*).

<u>Three Magi, Order of the</u> - Secretive order of Christian mages and scholars in service of the Papal Nuncio (q.v.). Composed of extremely skilled practitioners, it counts Melinor Indidarc as one of its number (and he is one of the few publicly acknowledged members).

<u>Tielo </u>– Petty kingdom south of Gorostol (q.v.) and one of the original nations that make up what is now Torosc (q.v.). It was overthrown and absorbed into the Republic. Its ruling family is rumored to be extinct.

<u>Tiuz</u> – (Elv. *"fire/ flame"*) An infantry sword resembling a gladius, it is a magic blade of ancient origin wielded by Connor Lomin (q.v.). At a command word, it blazes to life with a fiery edge.

<u>Torander, Beol</u> – Uncle to Handor and Hannah Lervion. The half-brother of Handor and Hannah's father, he took over management of the Lervion Shipping Line, Ltd, after the untimely death of the Lervion parents. Handor and Hannah are convinced he has nefarious motives.

<u>Torvu</u> - Another of the Ja'al pantheon, Torvu is the evil god of corruption and the undead. He is sometimes at odds with the religion of Vardu (q.v.).

<u>Troll</u> - Large, brutish bipedal creatures similar to ogres but taller and heavier. Trolls are hairless and can have four arms rather than two. Somewhat related to giants, they are considerably less sophisticated. They prefer mountains and forests and will kill and eat anything edible. Cruel, greedy and selfish, they can nonetheless be outwitted by smarter creatures. Some more intelligent of their species can learn to use rudimentary magic. Trolls have the

unnerving talent of being able to blend in with trees and rocks by merely holding still and use this ability to ambush the unwary.

Turis Rhi – (Elv. *"coast march"*) Similar to Tielo (q.v.), it was a former Paragon (q.v) kingdom that was overthrown by usurpers who subsumed the kingdom into what would become the evil Republic of Torosc (q.v.).

Twinspire Peak - A mountain in the wilderness east of Evendale (q.v.) near Shadow Lake (q.v.), it held secrets related to the Helm of Shadows (q.v.).

Tyler - A major city of Astarel (q.v.) located on the coast just north of the border with Deran (q.v.) It is known for its large harbor, excellent fishing fleet and naval base. It is the hometown of Buck Bydecy (q.v.).

Vardu – The evil god of death. A close second to the Ja'al as the most feared of the evil religions on Damara is the Church of Vardu. Adherents are known as the Vardish. The religious symbol is a skull and crossed sword. Priestly vestments are usually dead black, a deathly grey or bone-white. Due to their connection to the undead, they are in competition with the Cla'Agik (q.v.)(who claim the sphere of corruption and rot). They also compete with Arachnia of the Ja'al (q.v.) for rule of the sphere of assassination and Torvu (q.v) for rule over the undead. The church is highly organized.

Verian - Elven god of forests and nature (from the Elven "Veri" meaning "Lord" and Verian meaning "Highest Lord".) Followers of Verian worship in open structures usually in groves or copses of trees. The organizational structure is somewhat loose, with a council of high priests and priestesses making decisions of doctrine and teachings every year. Andyn Eleandir (q.v.) is a priestess of Verian.

Vipers (slavers) - An organized criminal group hailing from Jered (q.v.) specializing in human trafficking and drugs.

Vunethir – (Dw. *"lake manor"*) A large city in the nation of Gorostol.

Wilkins OTM, Jordan, Lady – A motherly woman with blonde hair and mischievous eyes, she is nonetheless a clandestine member of the Order of the Three Magi and a fearsome spellcaster. She owns a tea shop in Alrihan, Deran.

Whispering Death - A magically-induced plague infestation originating in the wilderness near Evendale (q.v.) and Terenai (q.v.). It killed many thousands before a cure was found by the Church of Irial. Survivors have damaged vocal cords and cannot raise their voices above a whisper. Rumor has it that Zhinia Margoth (q.v.) was its inventor and perpetrated it to thwart the Song of the Grey Riders (q.v.)

Whiteclaw – An assassins guild on Damora (q.v.) that often competes with the Crossed Swords (q.v.) and the Shrikes (q.v.) for customers. Their emblem is a white, clawed hand. They have, in the past, targeted the Grey Riders (q.v.).

Whitehorse Peak - A large mountain north of Forester, Deran, so named because its geology and snow-fall pattern reminded the people nearby of a white-maned horse. It is the site of the recovery of the pegasi (as described in *Whitehorse Peak*) that the Grey Riders own at the time of the novels *Eye of Truth* and *Helm of Shadows*. Its dwarven name is Kelematris (Dw. *"Mountain - Horse"*).

Whitepine - Small town (pop ~ 700) near Deorfast, Deran. It is the home of Melinor Indidarc.

Wit's End - Small (pop ~ 800) village along the northern border of Deran.

Witches Brew Tavern – A popular tavern and inn located in a working-class neighborhood in Meridian, Gorostol. (q.v.)

ABOUT THE AUTHOR

A route to fantasy fiction through the aerospace industry may seem an odd one to take, but PG Badzey has been writing stories since grammar school and has never stopped even though his path took an unconventional turn for someone interesting in writing. A trained systems engineer, he kept up with creative writing and coursework throughout a career working on the C-17 airlifter, the International Space Station, the Delta IV Rocket and the James Webb Space Telescope. He has enjoyed and been influenced by JRR Tolkien, C.S. Lewis, Katherine Kurtz, Christopher Stasheff, Terry Brooks and C. Dale Brittain, to name a few. Previous publications include short stories published in *Dragonlaugh*, an online fantasy humor magazine, and the publication of the first three novels in the *Grey Riders* series, *Whitehorse Peak, Eye of Truth* and *Helm of Shadows*. PG Badzey has studied martial arts for many years, helps mentor a world-class high school robotics team, and is active in his parish community. He lives in California, is a member of the Orange County Writers Guild and has taught seminars on fantasy writing in Orange County Libraries.

Find out more about the World of the Grey Riders at
https://pgbadzey.wordpress.com!

www.ingramcontent.com/pod-product-compliance
Lightning Source LLC
Chambersburg PA
CBHW072203130726
47910CB00011B/1798